CARNAL
INNOCENCE

Bantam Books by Nora Roberts

Brazen Virtue

Carnal Innocence

Divine Evil

Genuine Lies

Hot Ice

Public Secrets

Sacred Sins

Sweet Revenge

Nora Roberts

····

Carnal Innocence

BANTAM BOOKS TRADE PAPERBACKS
New York

2010 Bantam Books Trade Paperback Edition

Published in the United States by Bantam Books, an imprint of
The Random House Publishing Group, a division of
Random House, Inc., New York.

BANTAM BOOKS and the rooster colophon are registered trademarks
of Random House, Inc.

Originally published in the United States by Bantam Books,
an imprint of The Random House Publishing Group,
a division of Random House, Inc., in 1992.

ISBN 978-0-553-38643-1

Printed in the United States of America

www.bantamdell.com

2 4 6 8 9 7 5 3 1

CARNAL
INNOCENCE

Prologue

THE AIR WAS RAW with February the morning Bobby Lee Fuller found the first body. They would say he found it, when in truth what he'd done was trip over what was left of Arnette Gantrey. Either way, the end was the same, and Bobby Lee would live with that wide white face floating into his dreams for a long time to come.

If he hadn't broken up with Marvella Truesdale—again—the night before, he'd have been hunkered over his desk in English lit, trying to twist his brain into coping with Shakespeare's *Macbeth,* instead of dropping his line into Gooseneck Creek. But this last fight in his rocky eighteen-month romance with Marvella had worn him down. Bobby Lee'd decided to take himself a day off, to rest and reflect. And to teach that sharp-tongued Marvella that he wasn't no pussy-whipped wimp, but a man.

The men in Bobby Lee's family had always ruled the roost—or pretended to. He wasn't about to break the tradition.

At nineteen, Bobby Lee was long past grown. He was six one and gawky with it, the filling-out years still to come. But he had big, working-man's hands, like his father's, on the ends of long skinny arms, and his mother's thick black hair and luxuriant lashes. He liked to wear that hair slicked back in the style of his idol, James Dean.

Bobby Lee considered Dean a man's man, one who wouldn't have tolerated book learning any more than Bobby Lee did. If it had been up to him, he'd have been working full-time in Sonny Talbot's Mobile Service Station and Eatery instead of hacking his way through twelfth grade. But his mama had other notions, and nobody in Innocence, Mississippi, liked to cross Happy Fuller if they could help it.

Happy—whose childhood name was appropriate enough since she could smile beauteously as she sliced you off at the knees—hadn't quite forgiven her eldest boy for being held back twice in school. If Bobby Lee's mood hadn't been so low, he wouldn't have risked hooking a day, not with his grades already teetering. But Marvella was the kind of girl who pushed a man—a man's man—into doing rash and reckless things.

So Bobby Lee dropped his line into the sulky brown waters of Gooseneck Creek and hunched in his faded denim jacket against the raw air. His daddy always said when a man had powerful things on his mind, the best cure was to take himself down to the water and see what was nibbling.

It didn't matter if you caught anything, it was the being there that counted.

"Damn women," Bobby Lee muttered, and peeled his lips back in a sneer he'd practiced long hours in the bathroom mirror. "Damn all women to hell and back again."

He didn't need the grief Marvella handed out with both pretty hands. Ever since they'd done the deed in the back of his Cutlass, she'd been picking him apart and trying to put him back together her way.

It didn't sit right with Bobby Lee Fuller, no indeedy. Not even if she made him dizzy with love when they weren't scrapping. Not even if she had those big blue eyes that seemed to whisper secrets just for him when they passed each other in the crowded hallways of Jefferson Davis High. And not even if, when he got her naked, she near to fucked his brains out.

Maybe he loved her, and maybe she was smarter than he was, but he'd be damned if she was going to tug him along like a pig on a rope.

Bobby Lee settled back among the reeds along the skinny creek fed by the mighty Mississippi. He could hear the lonesome whistle from the train that was heading down to Greenville, and the whisper of the damp winter breeze through the limp reeds. His line hung slack and still.

The only thing nibbling this morning was his temper.

Maybe he'd just take himself down to Jackson, shake the dust of Innocence off his shoes, and strike out for the city. He was a good me-chanic—a damn good one—and figured he could find work with or without a high school diploma. Shitfire. You didn't need to know nothing about some fag named Macbeth, or obtuse triangles and the like, to fix a dinky carburetor. Down to Jackson he could get himself a job in a garage, end up head mechanic. Hell, he could own the whole kit and kaboodle before too long. And while he was at it, Marvella I-told-you-so Truesdale would be back in Innocence, crying her big blue eyes red.

Then he'd come back. Bobby Lee's smile lit his tough, good-looking face and warmed his chocolate eyes in a way that would have made Marvella's heart flutter. Yeah, he'd come back, with twenty-dollar bills bulging in his pockets. He'd cruise on back into town in his classic '62 Caddy—one of his fleet of cars—duded up in an *I*-talian suit, and richer than the Longstreets.

And there would be Marvella, thin and pale from pining away for him. She'd be standing on the corner in front of Larsson's Dry Goods, clutching her hands between her soft, pillowy breasts, and tears would be streaming down her face at the sight of him.

And when she fell at his feet, sobbing and wailing and telling him how sorry she was for being such an awful bitch and driving him away from her, he might—just might—forgive her.

The fantasy lulled him. As the sun brightened to ease the stinging air and danced lightly on the dun-colored water of the creek, he began to contemplate the physical aspects of their reunion.

He'd take her to Sweetwater—having purchased the lovely old plantation from the Longstreets when they'd fallen on hard times. She'd gasp and shiver at his good fortune. Being a gentleman, and a romantic, he'd sweep her up the long, curving stairs.

Since Bobby Lee hadn't been above the first floor in Sweetwater, his imagination shifted into high gear. The bedroom he carried the trembling Marvella into resembled a hotel suite in Vegas, which was Bobby Lee's current idea of class.

Heavy red draperies, a heart-shaped bed as big as a lake, carpet so thick he had to wade through it. Music was playing. Something classic, he thought. Bruce Springsteen or Phil Collins. Yeah, Marvella got all gooey over Phil Collins.

Then he'd lie her down on the bed. Her eyes would be wet as he kissed her. She'd be telling him again and again what a fool she'd been, how much she loved him, how she was going to spend the rest of her life making him happy. Making him her king.

Then he'd run his hands down over those incredible white, pink-tipped breasts, squeezing just a little, the way she liked it.

Her soft thighs would spread apart, her fingers would dig into his shoulders while she made that growly sound in her throat. And then . . .

His line tugged. Blinking, Bobby Lee sat up, wincing a little when his jeans bunched against the bulge at his crotch. Distracted by the hard-on, he flicked the fat fish out of the water, where it wriggled in the silvering sun. With his hands clumsy and slippery with arousal, he thumped his catch into the reeds.

Imagining himself about to pop it to Marvella had him tangling his line in the reeds. He hauled himself up, swearing a little at his carelessness. Since a good fishing line was as valuable as the fish it caught, Bobby Lee waded into the reeds and began to set it to rights.

The perch was still flopping. He could hear its wet struggles. Grinning, he gave the line a quick tug. It resisted, and he muttered a half-hearted oath.

He kicked a rusted Miller can aside, took another step into the high, cool grass. He slipped, his foot sliding on something wet. Bobby Lee Fuller went down on his knees. And found himself face-to-face with Arnette Gantrey.

Her look of surprise mirrored his—wide eyes, gaping mouth, white white cheeks. The perch lay quivering with its last breaths beneath her naked, mutilated breasts.

He saw she was dead—stone dead—and that was bad enough. But it was the blood, frosty pools of it, soaking into the damp ground, turning her limp, peroxided hair into something dark and crusty, drying hideously from where it had spilled out of dozens of jagged holes in her flesh, necklacing her throat where a long, smiling gash spread—it was the blood that forced the harsh, animal sounds out of him and had him scrambling back on his hands and knees. He didn't realize the sounds came from him. But he did realize that he was kneeling in her blood.

Bobby Lee struggled to his feet just in time to lose his breakfast grits all over his new black Converse Chucks.

Leaving his perch, his line, and a good portion of his youth in the bloody reeds, he ran for Innocence.

Chapter 1

SUMMER, THAT VICIOUS GREEN bitch, flexed her sweaty muscles and flattened Innocence, Mississippi. It didn't take much. Even before the War Between the States, Innocence had been nothing but a dusty fly-speck on the map. Though the soil was good for farming—if a man could stand the watery heat, the floods, and the capricious droughts—Innocence wasn't destined to prosper.

When the railroad tracks were laid, they had stretched far enough to the north and west to tease Innocence with those long, echoing whistles of pace and progress without bringing either home. The interstate, dug through the delta nearly a century after the tracks, veered away, linking Memphis to Jackson, and leaving Innocence in the dust.

It had no battlefields, no natural wonders to draw in tourists with cameras and cash. No hotel to pamper them, only a small, painfully neat rooming house run by the Koonses. Sweetwater, its single antebellum plantation, was privately owned by the Longstreets, as it had been for two hundred years. It wasn't open to the public, had the public been interested.

Sweetwater had been written up once in *Southern Homes*. But that had been in the eighties, when Madeline Longstreet was alive. Now that she and her tosspot, skinflint of a husband were both gone, the house was owned and inhabited by their three children. Together, they pretty nearly owned the town, but they didn't do much about it.

It could be said—and was—that the three Longstreet heirs had inherited all of their family's wild good looks and none of their ambition. It was hard to resent them, if the people in that sleepy delta town had churned up the energy for resentment. Along with dark hair, golden eyes, and good bones, the Longstreets could charm a coon out of a tree quicker than you could spit.

Nobody blamed Dwayne overmuch for following in his daddy's alcoholic footsteps. And if he crashed up his car from time to time, or wrecked a few tables in McGreedy's Tavern, he always made smooth amends when he was sober. Though as years went on, he was sober less and less. Everyone said it might have been different if he hadn't flunked out of the fancy prep school he'd been shipped off to. Or if he'd inherited his father's touch with the land, along with the old man's taste for sour mash.

Others, less kind, claimed that money could keep him in his fancy house and in his fancy cars, but it couldn't buy him a backbone.

When Dwayne had gotten Sissy Koons in trouble back in '84, he'd married her without a grumble. And when, two kids and numerous bottles of sour mash later, Sissy had demanded a divorce, he'd ended the marriage just as amiably. No hard feelings—no feelings at all—and Sissy had run off to Nashville with the kids to live with a shoe salesman who wanted to be the next Waylon Jennings.

Josie Longstreet, the only daughter and youngest child, had been married twice in her thirty-one years. Both unions had been short-lived but had provided the people of Innocence with endless grist for the gossip mill. She regretted both experiences in the same way a woman might regret finding her first gray hairs. There was some anger, some bitterness, some fear. Then it was all covered over. Out of sight, out of mind.

A woman didn't intend to go gray any more than a woman intended to divorce once she'd said "till death do us part." But things happened. As Josie was fond of saying philosophically to Crystal, her bosom friend and owner of the Style Rite Beauty Emporium, she liked to make up for these two errors in judgment by testing out all the men from Innocence to the Tennessee border.

Josie knew there were some tight-lipped old biddies who liked to whisper behind their hands that Josie Longstreet was no better than she had to be. But there were men who smiled into the dark and knew she was a hell of a lot better than that.

Tucker Longstreet enjoyed women, perhaps not with the abandon his baby sister enjoyed men, but he'd had his share. He was known to tip back a glass, too—though not with the unquenchable thirst of his older brother.

For Tucker, life was a long, lazy road. He didn't mind walking it as long as he could do so at his own pace. He was affable about detours, providing he could negotiate back to his chosen destination. So far he'd avoided a trip to the altar—his siblings' experiences having given him a mild distaste for it. He much preferred walking his road unencumbered.

He was easygoing and well-liked by most. The fact that he'd been born rich might have stuck in a few craws, but he didn't flaunt it much. And he had a boundless generosity that endeared him to people. A man knew if he needed a loan, he could call on old Tuck. The money would be there, without any of the sticky smugness that made it hard to take. Of course, there would always be some who muttered that it was easy for a man to lend money when he had more than enough. But that didn't change the color of the bills.

Unlike his father, Beau, Tucker didn't compound the interest daily or lock in his desk drawer a little leather book filled with the names of the people who owed him. Who would keep owing him until they plowed themselves under instead of their fields. Tucker kept the interest to a reasonable ten percent. The names and figures were all inside his clever and often underestimated mind.

In any case, he didn't do it for the money. Tucker rarely did anything for money. He did it first because it was effortless, and second because inside his rangy and agreeably lazy body beat a generous and sometimes guilty heart.

He'd done nothing to earn his good fortune, which made it the simplest thing in the world to squander it away. Tucker's feelings on this ranged from yawning acceptance to an occasional tug of social conscience.

Whenever the conscience tugged too hard, he would stretch himself out in the rope hammock in the shade of the spreading live oak, tip a hat down over his eyes, and sip a cold one until the discomfort passed.

Which was exactly what he was doing when Della Duncan, the Longstreet's housekeeper of thirty-some years, stuck her round head out of a second-floor window.

"Tucker Longstreet!"

Hoping for the best, Tucker kept his eyes shut and let the hammock sway. He was balancing a bottle of Dixie beer on his flat, naked belly, one hand linked loosely around the glass.

"Tucker Longstreet!" Della's booming voice sent birds scattering up from the branches of the tree. Tucker considered that a shame, as he'd enjoyed dreaming to their piping song and the droning counterpoint of the bees courting the gardenias. "I'm talking to you, boy."

With a sigh, Tucker opened his eyes. Through the loose weave of his planter's hat, the sun streamed white and hot. It was true that he paid

Della's salary, but when a woman had diapered your bottom as well as walloped it, you were never in authority over her. Reluctantly, Tucker tipped the hat back and squinted in the direction of her voice.

She was leaning out, all right, her flaming red hair peeking out from the kerchief she'd tied around it. Her broad, heavily rouged face was set in the stern, disapproving lines Tucker had learned to respect. Three strings of bright beads slapped against the sill.

He smiled, the innocent, crafty smile of a boy caught with his hand in the cookie jar. "Yes'm?"

"You said you'd drive into town and bring me back a sack of rice and a case of Coca-Cola."

"Well, now . . ." Tucker rubbed the still-cool bottle over his torso before bringing it to his lips for a long swallow. "I guess I did, Della. Figured I'd ride in once it cooled off some."

"Get your lazy ass up and fetch it now. Else there'll be an empty plate on the table at dinner tonight."

"Too damn hot to eat," he mumbled under his breath, but Della had ears like a rabbit.

"What is that, boy?"

"I said I'm going." Graceful as a dancer, he slid out of the hammock, polishing off the Dixie as he went. When he grinned up at her, the hat tipped rakishly on his sweat-curled hair, and the light of the devil in those golden eyes, Della softened. She had to force herself to keep her mouth pursed and stern.

"You're going to root to that hammock one day. See if you don't. A body'd think you were ailing the way you'd rather lie on your back than stand on your feet."

"Lots more a man can do lying down than nap, Della."

She betrayed herself with a loud, lusty laugh. "Just make sure you don't do so much you end up getting hauled to the altar with someone like that slut Sissy, who snagged my Dwayne."

He grinned again. "No, ma'am."

"And bring me back some of my toilet water. It's on sale down at Larsson's."

"Toss me down my wallet and keys, then."

Her head withdrew, then popped out a moment later just before she flung both objects down at him. Tucker snagged them out of the air with a deft flick of the wrist that reminded Della the boy wasn't as slow as he pretended to be.

"Put your shirt on—and tuck it in," Della ordered, as she would have had he been ten.

Tucker lifted it from the hammock, shrugging into it as he walked around the front of the house, where a dozen Doric columns rose from the covered porch to the lacy ironwork of the second-story terrace. His skin was clinging to the cotton before he reached his car.

He folded himself into his Porsche—an impulse buy of six months before that he'd yet to grow tired of. He weighed the comfort of air-conditioning against the excitement of wind slapping his face, and opted to leave the top down.

One of the few things Tucker did fast was drive. Gravel spat under the tires as he slammed into first and streaked down the long, meandering lane. He swung around the circle where his mother had planted a bounty of peonies, hibiscus, and flashy red geraniums. Old magnolia trees flanked the lane, and their scent was heavy and pleasing. He flicked by the bone-white granite marker where his great-great-uncle Tyrone had been thrown from a bad-tempered horse and had broken his sixteen-year-old neck.

The marker had been set by Tyrone's grieving parents to honor his passing. It also served as a reminder that if Tyrone hadn't chosen to test himself on that mean-spirited mare, he wouldn't have broken his stubborn neck, and his younger brother, Tucker's great-great grandfather, wouldn't have inherited Sweetwater and passed it down.

Tucker could have found himself living in a condo in Jackson.

He was never sure whether to be sorry or grateful when he passed that sad old piece of stone.

Out through the high, wide gates and onto the macadam was the scent of tar going soft in the sun, of still water from the bayou behind the screen of trees. And the trees themselves, with their high, green smell that told him, though the calendar claimed summer was still a week away, the delta knew better.

He reached for sunglasses first, sliding them onto his face before he chose a cassette at random and punched it into its slot. Tucker was a great lover of fifties music, so there was nothing in the car recorded after 1962. Jerry Lee Lewis shot out, and the Killer's whiskey-soaked voice and desperate piano celebrated the fact that there was a whole lot of shakin' going on.

As the speedometer swung toward eighty, Tucker added his own excellent tenor. His fingers drummed up and down on the steering wheel, looking like piano keys.

Barreling over a rise, he had to swing wide to the left to avoid ramming into the backside of a natty BMW. He tooted his horn, not in warning but in greeting as he skidded around the elegant maroon fender. He didn't slacken his speed, but a glance in his rearview mirror showed him the Beemer was stopped, half in and half out of the lane leading back to Edith McNair's house.

As Jerry Lee switched into his raw-throated "Breathless," Tucker gave a passing thought to the car and driver. Miss Edith had passed on about two months before—around the same time that a second mutilated body had been discovered floating in the water down at Spook Hollow.

That had been sometime in April, and a search party had been whipped up to look for Francie Alice Logan, who'd been missing for two days. Tucker's jaw clenched when he remembered what it had been like, trudging through the bayou, carrying a Ruger Red Label and hoping to hell he didn't shoot off his own foot, or find anything.

But they'd found her, and he'd had the bad luck to be with Burke Truesdale when they did.

It wasn't easy to think about what the water and the fish had done to sassy old Francie, the pretty little redhead he'd flirted with, dated a time or two, and had debated sleeping with.

His stomach clenched and he bumped up the volume on Jerry Lee. He wasn't thinking about Francie. Couldn't. He'd been thinking about Miss Edith, and that was better. She'd lived to be nearly ninety and had passed on quietly in her sleep.

Tucker recalled that she'd left her house, a tidy two-story built during the Reconstruction, to some Yankee relative.

Since Tucker knew that no one within fifty miles of Innocence owned a BMW, he concluded that the Yankee had decided to come down and take a peek at his inheritance.

He dismissed the northern invasion from his thoughts, took out a cigarette, and after breaking a thumbnail-length piece from the tip, lighted it.

◆ ◆ ◆ ◆

*H*ALF A MILE BACK, Caroline Waverly gripped the wheel of her car and waited for her heart to slide back down her throat.

Idiot! Crazy bastard! Careless jerk!

She forced herself to lift her trembling foot off the brake and tap the gas until the car was all the way into the narrow, overgrown lane.

Inches, she thought. He'd missed hitting her by inches! Then he'd had the gall to blast his horn at her. She wished he'd stopped. Oh, she wished he'd stopped so she could have given that homicidal jackass a piece of her mind.

She'd have felt better then, having vented her temper. She was getting damn good at venting since Dr. Palamo had told her that the ulcer and the headaches were a direct result of repressing her feelings. And of chronically overworking, of course.

Well, she was doing something about both. Caroline unpried her sweaty hands from the wheel and wiped them against her slacks. She was taking a nice, long, peaceful sabbatical here in Nowhere, Mississippi. After a few months—if she didn't die of this vicious heat—she'd be ready to prepare for her spring tour.

As for repressing her feelings, she was done with that. Her final, ugly blowout with Luis had been so liberating, so gloriously uninhibited, she almost wished she could go back to Baltimore and do it again.

Almost.

The past—and Luis with his clever tongue, brilliant talent, and roving eye definitely belonged to the past—was safely behind her. The future, at least until she'd recovered her nerves and her health, wasn't of much interest. For the first time in her life, Caroline Waverly, child prodigy, dedicated musician, and emotional sap, was going to live only for the sweet, sweet present.

And here, at long last, she was going to make a home. Her way. No more backing away from problems. No more cowed agreeing to her mother's demands and expectations. No more struggling to be the reflection of everyone else's desires.

She was moving in, taking hold. And by the end of the summer, she intended to know exactly who Caroline Waverly was.

Feeling better, she replaced her hands on the wheel and eased the car down the lane. She had a vague recollection of skipping down it once, on some long-ago visit to her grandparents. It had been a short visit, of course—Caroline's mother had done everything possible to cut off her own country roots. But Caroline remembered her grandfather, a big, red-faced man who'd taken her fishing one still morning. And her girlish reluctance to bait a hook until her grandfather had told her that old worm was just waiting to catch himself a big fat fish.

Her trembling thrill when her line had jerked, and the sense of awe and accomplishment when they'd carried three husky catfish back home.

Her grandmother, a wiry stick of a woman with steel-gray hair, had fried up the catch in a heavy black skillet. Though Caroline's mother had refused to taste a bite, Caroline herself had eaten hungrily, a frail, tow-headed six-year-old with long, slender fingers and big green eyes.

When the house came into view, she smiled. It hadn't changed much. The paint was flaking off the shutters and the grass was ankle-high, but it was still a trim two-story house with a covered porch made for sitting and a stone chimney that leaned just slightly to the left.

She felt her eyes sting and blinked at the tears. Foolish to feel sad. Her grandparents had lived long, contented lives. Foolish to feel guilty. When her grandfather died two years before, Caroline had been in Madrid, in the middle of a concert tour, and swamped by obligations. It simply hadn't been possible to make the trip back for his funeral.

And she'd tried, really tried, to tempt her grandmother to the city, where Caroline could have flown easily between tour dates for a visit.

But Edith hadn't budged; she'd laughed at the notion of leaving the house where she'd come as a new bride some seventy years before, the house where her children had been born and raised, the house where she'd lived her whole life.

And when she died, Caroline had been in a Toronto hospital, recovering from exhaustion. She hadn't known her grandmother was gone until a week after the funeral.

So it was foolish to feel guilt.

But as she sat in her car, with the air-conditioning blowing gently on her face, she was swamped with the emotion.

"I'm sorry," she said aloud to the ghosts. "I'm so sorry I wasn't here. That I was never here."

On a sigh, she combed a hand through her sleek cap of honey-blond hair. It did no good to sit in the car and brood. She needed to take in her things, go through the house, settle herself. The place was hers now, and she meant to keep it.

When she opened the car door, the heat stole the oxygen from her lungs. Gasping against its force, she lifted her violin case from the backseat. She was already wilting when she carried the instrument and a heavy box of sheet music to the porch.

It took three more trips to the car—lugging suitcases, two bags of groceries which she'd stopped to pick up in a little market thirty miles north, and finally, her reel-to-reel tape recorder—before she was done.

Once she had all her possessions lined up, she took out the keys. Each one was tagged: front door, back door, root cellar, strongbox, Ford pickup. They jangled together like musical notes as Caroline selected the front-door key.

The door squeaked, as old doors should, and opened on the dim dust of disuse.

She took up the violin first. It was certainly more important than any of the groceries.

A little lost, and for the first time lonely, she walked inside.

The hallway led straight back to where she knew the kitchen would be. To the left, stairs climbed, hooking to a right angle after the third tread. The banister was dark, sturdy oak, layered now with a fine cloak of dust.

There was a table just beneath the stairs, where a heavy black dial phone sat beside an empty vase. Caroline laid down her case on it and got busy.

She carried groceries back to the kitchen with its yellow walls and white, glass-fronted cabinets. Because the house was oven-hot, she put them away first, relieved that the refrigerator was sparkling clean.

She'd been told some neighbor women had come in to wash and scrub after the funeral. Caroline could see that this country courtesy was true. Beneath the dust of two months, beyond the lacy webs that industrious spiders had woven in corners, was the faint, lingering smell of Lysol.

She walked slowly back to the front hall, her heels echoing on the hardwood. She peeked into the sitting room with its petit point cushions and big RCA console television that looked like an ancient artifact. Into the living room, where faded cabbage roses climbed the walls and "company" furniture was ghosted under dust covers. Then her grandfather's den with its case of hunting rifles and target pistols, its big easy chair, ragged at the arms.

Hefting her suitcases, she started upstairs to choose her room.

Both sentiment and practicality had her settling on her grandparents' bedroom. The heavy four-poster and wedding-ring quilt seemed to offer comfort. The cedar chest at its foot might hold secrets. The tiny violets and roses twined on the walls would soothe.

Caroline set her valises aside and walked to the narrow glass door that led to the high, open porch. From there, she could see her grandmother's roses and perennials struggling against the weeds. She could hear the lap of water against some rock or downed log behind the tangle of live oaks and Spanish moss. And in the distance, through the haze of heat, she saw the brown ribbon of water that was the powerful Mississippi.

There were birds calling, a symphony of sound through the hot air—jays and sparrows, crows and larks. And perhaps the gargled call of wild turkey.

She dreamed there for a moment, a delicately formed woman, a shade too thin, with exquisite hands and shadowed eyes.

For a moment, the view, the fragrances, the sounds, faded away. She was in her mother's sitting room, with the whispering tick of the ormulu clock, the scent of Chanel. Very soon they would be leaving for her first recital.

"We expect the best from you, Caroline." Her mother's voice was smooth and slow and left no room for comment. "We expect you to *be* the best. Nothing else is worth aiming for. Do you understand?"

Caroline's toes were curled nervously in her glossy Mary Janes. She was only five. "Yes, ma'am."

In the parlor now, her arms aching after two hours of practice. The sun so bright and golden outside. And she could see a robin perched in the tree. He made her giggle and pause.

"Caroline!" Her mother's voice flowed down the stairs. "You still have an hour of practice left. How do you expect to be ready for this tour if you have no discipline? Now start again."

"I'm sorry." With a sigh, Caroline lifted the violin that to her twelve-year-old shoulders was beginning to feel like a lead weight.

Backstage, fighting off the queasy nerves of opening night. And tired, so tired from the endless rehearsals, preparations, traveling. How long had she been on this treadmill now? Was she eighteen, twenty?

"Caroline, for heaven's sake, put on more blusher. You look like death." That impatient, hammering voice, taut fingers taking her chin and lifting it. "Why can't you at least show some enthusiasm? Do you know how hard your father and I have worked to get you where you are? How much we've sacrificed? And here you are, ten minutes before curtain, brooding into the mirror."

"I'm sorry."

She had always been sorry.

Lying in a hospital bed in Toronto, sick, exhausted, ashamed.

"What do you mean you've canceled the rest of the tour?" Her mother's tense, furious face looming over hers.

"I can't finish it. I'm sorry."

"Sorry! What good is sorry? You're making a shambles of your career, you've inconvenienced Luis unpardonably. I wouldn't be surprised if he broke your engagement as well as cutting you off professionally."

"He was with someone else," Caroline said weakly. "Just before curtain I saw him—in the dressing room. He was with someone else."

"That's nonsense. And if it isn't, you have no one but yourself to blame. The way you've been acting lately—walking around like a ghost, canceling interviews, refusing to attend parties. After all I've done for you, this is how you repay the debt. How do you expect me to deal with the press, with the speculation, with the mess you've left me in?"

"I don't know." It helped to close her eyes, to close them and shut it all away. "I'm sorry. I just can't do it anymore."

♦ ♦ ♦ ♦

No, CAROLINE THOUGHT, OPENING her eyes again. She just couldn't do it anymore. She couldn't be what everyone else wanted her to be. Not now. Not ever again. Was she selfish, ungrateful, spoiled—all those hateful words her mother had hurled at her? It didn't seem to matter now. All that mattered was that she was here.

◆ ◆ ◆ ◆

TEN MILES AWAY, TUCKER Longstreet streaked into the heat of Innocence, kicking up dust and scaring the spit out of Jed Larsson's fat beagle Nuisance, who'd been resting his bones on the pad of concrete beneath the striped awning of the dry goods store.

Caroline Waverly would have understood the dog's distress when he opened one eye to see the shiny red car barreling straight for him and skidding to a stop a bare eighteen inches from his resting place.

With a yipe, the dog gained his feet and took himself off to safer ground.

Tucker chuckled and called to Nuisance with a click and a whistle, but the dog kept moving. Nuisance hated that red car with a passion so great he never even ventured near enough to pee on its tires.

Tucker dumped his keys in his pocket. He fully intended to get Della's rice and Cokes and toilet water, then head back to stretch out on the hammock again—where he figured a smart man belonged on a hot, airless afternoon. But he spotted his sister's car, tilted across two parking spaces in front of the Chat 'N Chew.

It occurred to him that the drive had made him thirsty, and he could do with a tall glass of lemonade. And possibly a hunk of chilled huckleberry pie.

Later, he'd spend a lot of time regretting that small detour.

The Longstreets owned the Chat 'N Chew, just as they owned the Wash & Dry Laundromat, the Innocence Boarding House, the Feed and Grain, the Hunters' Friend Gun Shop, and a dozen or so rental properties. The Longstreets were wise enough—or lazy enough—to have managers for their businesses. Dwayne took a mild interest in the rental houses, cruising along to each on the first of the month to collect checks or listen to excuses, and note down a list of needed repairs.

But Tucker kept the books, whether he wanted to or not. Once when he'd bitched about it long enough, Josie had taken them over. She'd screwed them up so royally, it had taken Tucker days to set them to rights again.

He didn't mind so much, really. Bookkeeping was something you could do in the cool of the evening, with a cold drink at your elbow. His head for figures made it an annoying chore rather than a difficult one.

The Chat 'N Chew was one of Tucker's favorite places. The diner had one of those big, wide-pane windows that was forever dotted with posters announcing bake sales, school plays, and auctions.

Inside, the floor was made of linoleum tiles, yellowed with age and dusted with brown flecks that looked like fly spots. The booths were rugged red vinyl, an improvement over the ripped and tattered brown that Tucker had replaced just six months before. The red was already fading to orange.

Over the years, people had carved messages into the laminated table-tops. Sort of a Chat 'N Chew tradition. Initials were a big favorite, along with hearts and stick figures, but occasionally someone was inspired to hack in HEY! or UP YOURS! Or in the case of one grumpy individual, EAT SHIT AND DIE.

Earleen Renfrew, who managed the establishment, had been so put out by that suggestion, Tucker had been forced to borrow an electric buffer from the hardware store and smudge out the offending words.

Each booth had its own individual juke where you could turn the knob and flip over selections—still three for a quarter. Because Earleen favored country tunes, so did the jukes, but Tucker had managed to sneak in a few cuts of rock or R & B from the fifties.

The big counter was lined with a dozen stools, all topped with the same fading red vinyl. A clear three-tiered dome held that day's offering of pies. Tucker's gaze lighted on the huckleberry with pure delight.

Exchanging waves and "heys" with a scattering of customers, he made his way through the grease- and smoke-tinged air to where his sister perched at the counter. Deep in discussion with Earleen, Josie gave her brother an absent pat on the arm and kept talking.

"And so I said to her, Justine, if you're going to marry a man like Will Shiver, all you've got to do to stay happy is buy yourself a padlock for his fly and make sure you're the only one with a key. He may wet himself now and again, but that's all he's going to do."

Earleen gave an appreciative cackle and wiped a few wet rings from the counter. "Why she'd want to marry a no-account like Will's beyond me."

"Honey, he's a regular tiger in bed." Josie winked slyly. "So they say. Hey, Tucker." She turned to give her brother a smacking kiss before wriggling her fingers in front of his face. "I just got my nails done. Hotshot Red. What do you think?"

Dutifully he examined her long scarlet nails. "Looks to me like you've just finished scratching somebody's eyes out. Gimme a lemonade and some of that huckleberry, with French vanilla on top, Earleen."

Rather pleased with Tucker's description of her nails, Josie ran them through her artfully tangled mane of black hair. "Justine would've liked to scratch mine out." Grinning, she picked up her Diet Coke and sipped through the straw. "She was over at the beauty parlor getting her roots done and flapping her hand around to show everybody this eensy speck of glass she called a diamond. Will probably won it knocking down bottles at the fair."

Tucker's golden eyes twinkled. "Jealous, Josie?"

She stiffened up, bottom lip poking out, then her face cleared as she tossed back her head and hooted, "If I'd wanted him, I'd've had him. But outside of bed he just about bored me senseless." She stirred what was left of her soda with the straw and sent a quick flirtatious look over her shoulder at two boys lounging in a booth. They puffed up quickly, sucking in beer guts. "We've got this burden, you and I do, Tuck. About being damn near irresistible to the opposite sex."

After smiling at Earleen, he dug into his pie. "Yeah, it's our cross to bear."

Josie drummed her newly painted nails on the counter for the pleasure of hearing them click. The restlessness that had driven her to marry and divorce twice within five years had been flaring up for weeks. Nearly time to move on, she thought. A few months back in Innocence made her yearn for the excitement of anywhere else. And a few months anywhere else made her yearn for the quiet aimlessness of her hometown.

Someone had popped a quarter in a juke and Randy Travis was crooning about the miseries of love. Josie drummed her fingers in time and scowled at Tucker as he shoveled in huckleberries and ice cream.

"I don't see how you can eat like that in the middle of the day."

Tucker scooped up more pie. "I just open my mouth and swallow."

"And never gain a goddamn ounce. I have to watch every blessed thing I eat or my hips'll be as wide as Mamie Gantrey's." She stuck a finger in Tucker's ice cream and scooped up a lick. "What're you doing in town besides stuffing your face?"

"Errands for Della. Passed a car turning into the McNair place."

"Hmmm." Josie might have given that piece of news more attention, but Burke Truesdale strolled in. She wriggled straighter in her chair, crossing long, smooth legs, and sent him a honey-dripping smile. "Hi there, Burke."

"Josie." He came over to give Tucker a thump on the back. "Tuck. What're you two up to?"

"Just passing the time," Josie said. Burke was six feet of solid muscle with a linebacker's shoulders, and a square-jawed face softened by puppy-dog eyes. Although he was Dwayne's contemporary, he was closer to Tucker in friendship, and he was one of the few men Josie had wanted and done without.

Burke rested one hip on a stool, his heavy ring of keys jangling. His sheriff's badge winked dully in the sunlight. "Too hot to do anything else." He muttered a thanks to Earleen when she set an iced tea in front of him. Burke guzzled it down without taking a breath.

Josie licked her top lip as she watched his Adam's apple bob.

"Miss Edith's kin's moving into the house," Burke announced as he set the glass aside. "Miss Caroline Waverly, some kind of fancy musician from Philadelphia." Earleen had refilled his glass, and this time he sipped slowly. "She called down to have the phone and power hooked up."

"How long's she staying?" Earleen always had her eyes and ears open for news. As proprietress of the Chat 'N Chew, it was her right and her duty.

"Didn't say. Miss Edith wasn't one to talk about her family over-much, but I do remember hearing she had a granddaughter who traveled around with an orchestra or something."

"Must pay well," Tucker mused. "I saw her car turn into the lane fifteen minutes ago. She was driving a brand new BMW."

Burke waited until Earleen had moved away. "Tuck, I need to talk to you about Dwayne."

Though his face remained passive and friendly, Tucker's shield slid into place. "What about?"

"He got juiced up again last night, had a pushy-shovy going over at McGreedy's. I put him in a cell for the night."

Now there was a change, a darkening of the eyes, a grimness around the mouth. "You charge him with anything?"

"Come on, Tuck." More hurt than offended, Burke shifted his feet. "He was raising hell and too drunk to drive. I figured he could use a place to sleep it off. Last time I drove him home in the middle of the night, Miss Della was spitting mad."

"Yeah." Tucker relaxed. There were friends, there was family, and there was Burke, who was a combination of both. "Where's he now?"

"Over at the jail, nursing a hangover. I figured since you're here, you could haul him home. We can get his car back later on."

"Much obliged." His quiet words masked the raw disappointment in his gut. Dwayne had been on the wagon nearly two weeks this time. Once he'd fallen, Tucker knew, it would be a long, slippery climb back on. Tucker stood, pulling out his wallet. When the door slammed open behind him, rattling glasses on the back shelves, he glanced around. He saw Edda Lou Hatinger and knew he was in trouble.

"Belly-crawling bastard," she spat out, and launched herself at him. If Burke hadn't retained the same reflexes that had made him a star receiver in high school, Tucker might have had his face sheared off.

"Hey, hey," Burke said helplessly while Edda Lou fought like a bobcat.

"You think you can toss me off just like that?"

"Edda Lou." From experience, Tucker kept his voice low and calm. "Take a deep breath. You're going to hurt yourself."

Her small teeth bared in a snarl. "I'm going to hurt *you*, you fucking weasel."

With reluctance, Burke slipped into his sheriff's mode. "Girl, you pull yourself together or I'll have to take you over to the jail. Your daddy wouldn't be happy about that either."

She hissed through her teeth. "I won't lay a hand on the sonofabitch." When Burke's grip loosened, she slipped free, dusting herself off.

"If you want to talk about this—" Tucker began.

"We're going to talk about it, all right. Here and now." She swung in a circle while customers either stared or pretended not to. Colorful plastic bracelets clicked on her arms. Perspiration gave a sheen to her face and neck. "Y'all listen up, you hear? I got something to say to Mr. Bigshot Longstreet."

"Edda Lou—" Tucker took a chance and touched her arm. She swung out backhanded and knocked his teeth together.

"No." Wiping his mouth, he waved Burke away. "Let her get it out."

"I'll get it out, all right. You said you loved me."

"I never did that." That Tucker could be sure of. Even in the throes of passion he was careful with words. Especially in the throes of passion.

"You made me think you did," she shouted at him. The powdery spray she was wearing was overwhelmed by the hot sweat of temper and combined in a sickly-sweet aroma that reminded Tucker of something freshly dead. "You wheedled your way into bed with me. You said I was the woman you'd been waiting for. You said . . ." Tears began to mix with the sweat on her face, turning her mascara into wet clumps under her eyes. "You said we were going to get married."

"*Oh* no." Tucker's temper, which he preferred not to have riled, began to stir. "That was your idea, honey. And I told you flat out it wasn't going to happen."

"What's a girl to think when you come whistling up, bringing flowers and buying fancy wine? You said you cared about me more than anybody else."

"I did care." And he had. He always did.

"You don't care about nothing or nobody, only Tucker Longstreet." She pushed her face into his, spit flying. Seeing her like this, all the sweetness and flutters gone, he wondered how he could have cared. And he hated the fact that some of the boys who'd been lounging over their sodas were elbowing each other's ribs and chuckling.

"Then you're better off without me, aren't you?" He dropped two bills on the counter.

"You think you're going to get off that easy?" Her hand clamped like iron on his arm. He could feel her muscles quiver. "You think you can toss me off like you did all the others?" She'd be damned if he would—not when she'd hinted marriage to all her girlfriends. Not when she'd gone all the way into Greenville to moon over the wedding gowns. She knew—she *knew* half the town would already be smirking about it. "You've got an obligation to me. You made promises."

"Name one." His temper building, he pried a clutching hand from his arm.

"I'm pregnant." It burst out of her on a flood of desperation. She had the satisfaction of hearing a mutter pass from booth to booth, and of watching Tucker pale.

"What did you say?"

Her lips curved then, in a hard, merciless smile. "You heard me, Tuck. Now you'd better decide what you're going to do about it."

Tossing up her head, she spun around and stormed out. Tucker waited for his stomach to slide back down from his throat.

"Oops," Josie said, grinning broadly at the goggle-eyed diners. But her hand went down to take her brother's. "Ten bucks says she's lying."

Still reeling, Tucker stared at her. "What?"

"I say she's no more pregnant than you are. Oldest female trick in the book, Tucker. Don't get your dick caught in it."

He needed to think, and he wanted to be alone to do it. "You get Dwayne over at the jail, will you? And pick up Della's stuff."

"Why don't we—"

But he was already walking out. Josie sighed, thinking the shit was going to hit the fan. He hadn't told her what Della wanted.

Chapter 2

DWAYNE LONGSTREET SAT ON the rock-iron bunk in one of the town's two jail cells and moaned like a wounded dog. The three aspirin he'd downed had yet to take effect, and the army of chain saws buzzing inside his head were getting mighty close to the brain.

He took his head out of his hands long enough to slurp down more of the coffee Burke had left him, then clamped it tight again, afraid it would fall off. Half hoping it would.

As always, during the first hour after waking from a toot, Dwayne despised himself. He hated knowing that he'd strolled, smiling, into the same ugly trap again.

Not the drinking. No, Dwayne liked drinking. He liked that first hot taste of whiskey when it hit the tongue, slid down the throat, settled into the belly like a long, slow kiss from a pretty woman. He liked the friendly rush that spread into his head after the second drink.

Hell, he fucking loved it.

He didn't even mind getting drunk. No, there was something to be said about that floating time after you'd knocked back five or six. When everything looked fine and funny. When you forgot your life had turned ugly on you—that you'd lost the wife and kids you'd never wanted much in the first place to some fucking shoe salesman, that you were stuck in a dusty pisshole of a town because there was no place else to go.

Yeah, he liked that floaty, forgetful time just fine.

He didn't particularly care for what happened after that. When your hand kept reaching for the bottle without warning the rest of you what was coming. When you stopped tasting and kept on swallowing just because the whiskey was there and so were you.

He didn't like the fact that sometimes the drink turned him nasty, so he wanted to pick a fight, any fight. God knew he wasn't a mean-tempered man. That was his father. But sometimes, just sometimes, the whiskey turned him into Beau, and he was sorry for it.

What scared him was that there were times when he couldn't quite remember if he'd turned nasty or just passed out quietly. Whenever that happened, he was more than likely to wake up in the cell with a hangover fit to kill.

Gingerly, knowing that the movement could change the busy loggers in his head into a swarm of angry bees, he got to his feet. The sun streaming through the bars at the window all but blinded him. Dwayne shielded his eyes with the flat of his hand as he groped his way out of the cell. Burke never locked him in.

Dwayne fumbled his way into the bathroom and whizzed out what felt like a gallon of the Wild Turkey that had filtered through his kidneys. Wishing miserably for his own bed, he splashed cold water in his face until his eyes stopped burning.

He hissed through his teeth when the door slammed in the outer office, and whimpered just a little when Josie cheerfully called his name.

"Dwayne? Are you in here? It's your own sweet sister come to bust you out."

When he stepped into the doorway to lean weakly on the jamb, Josie raised her carefully plucked brows. "My oh my. You look like something three cats had to drag in." She stepped closer, tapping a bright red nail on her bottom lip. "Honey, how do you see through all that blood in your eyes?"

"Did I . . ." He coughed to clear the rust out of his throat. "Did I wreck a car?"

"Not that I know of. Now, you come on along with Josie." She moved to him to take his arm. When he turned his head, she stepped back fast. "Sweet Jesus. How many men have you killed with that breath?" Clucking her tongue, she dug in her purse and pulled out a box of Tic Tacs. "Here now, honey, you chew on a couple of these." She popped them into his mouth herself. "Otherwise I'm likely to faint if you breathe on me."

"Della's going to be real pissed," he mumbled as he let Josie guide him to the door.

"I expect she will—but when she finds out about Tucker, she'll forget all about you."

"Tucker? Oh, shit." Dwayne staggered back as the sun slammed into his eyes.

Shaking her head, Josie pulled out her sunglasses, the ones with the little rhinestones circling the lenses, and handed them to him. "Tucker's in trouble. Or Edda Lou's claiming he got *her* in trouble. But we'll see about that."

"Christ almighty." For a brief moment his own problems faded away. "Tuck got Edda Lou knocked up?"

Josie opened the passenger door of her car so Dwayne could pour himself in. "She made a big scene over at the Chat 'N Chew, so everybody in town's going to be watching to see if her belly bloats."

"Christ almighty."

"I'll say this." Josie started the car, and was sympathetic enough to flick off the radio. "Whether she's knocked up or not, he'd better think twice before moving that whiny slut into the house."

Dwayne would have agreed wholeheartedly, but he was too busy holding his head.

◆ ◆ ◆ ◆

TUCKER KNEW BETTER THAN to go back to the house. Della would be on him in a New York minute. He needed some time alone, and once he drove through Sweetwater's gates, he wouldn't get any.

On impulse he swerved to the side of the road, leaving a streak of rubber on the sweaty macadam. With home still the best part of a mile away, he left his car on the grassy verge and walked into the trees.

The paralyzing heat lessened by a few stingy degrees once he was under the shelter of green leaves and dripping moss. Still, he wasn't looking to cool his skin, but his mind.

For one moment back at the diner, for one hot, hazy-red moment, he'd wanted to grab Edda Lou by the throat and squeeze every last accusing breath out of her.

He didn't care for the impulse, or for the fact that he'd taken an instant's sheer pleasure from the image. Half of what she'd said had been lies. But that meant half of what she'd said had been the truth.

He shoved a low-hanging branch aside, ducked, and made his way through the heavy summer growth to the water. A heron, startled at the intrusion, folded up her long, graceful legs and glided off deeper into the bayou. Tucker kept an eye out for snakes as he settled down on a log.

Taking his time, he pulled out a cigarette, pinched a miserly bit from the tip, then lighted it.

He'd always liked the water—not so much the pound and thrust of the ocean, but the still darkness of shady ponds, the murmur of streams, the steady pulse of the river. Even as a boy he'd been drawn to it, using the excuse of fishing to sit and think, or sit and doze, listening to the plop of frogs and the monotonous drone of cicadas.

He'd had only childish problems to face then. Whether he was going to get skinned for that D in geography, how to finesse a new bike for Christmas. And later, whether he should ask Arnette or Carolanne to the Valentine's Day dance.

As you got older, problems swelled. He remembered grieving for his father when the old man went and got himself killed in that Cessna traveling down to Jackson. But that had been nothing, nothing at all compared to the sharp, stunning misery he'd felt when he found his mother crumpled in her garden, already too close to death for any doctor to fix her seizured heart.

He'd come here often then, to ease himself past the misery. And eventually, like all things, it had faded. Except at the odd moments when he'd glance out a window, half expecting to see her—face shaded by that big straw hat with the chiffon scarf trailing—clipping overblown roses.

Madeline Longstreet would not have approved of Edda Lou. She would, naturally, have found her coarse, cheap, and cunning. And, Tucker thought as he slowly drew in and expelled smoke, would have expressed her disapproval by that excruciating politeness any true southern lady could hone to a razor-edged weapon.

His mother had been a true southern lady.

Edda Lou, on the other hand, was a fine piece of work. Physically speaking. Big-breasted, wide-hipped, with skin she kept dewy by slathering on Vaseline Intensive Care Lotion every morning and night of her life. She had an eager, hardworking mouth, willing hands, and by God, he'd enjoyed her.

He hadn't loved her, nor had he claimed to. Tucker considered promises of love a cheap tool for persuading a woman into bed. He'd shown her a good time, in bed and out. He wasn't a man to stop the courtship process once a woman had spread her legs.

But the minute she'd started hinting about marriage, he'd taken a long step back. First he'd given her a cooling-off period, taking her out maybe twice in a two-week period and cutting off sex completely. He'd told her flat out that he had no intention of getting married. But he'd seen by the smug look in her eye she hadn't believed him. So he'd broken it off. She'd been tearful but civilized. Tucker saw now that she'd believed she'd be able to reel him back.

Tucker also had no doubt now that she'd heard he'd been seen with someone else.

All of that mattered. And none of it mattered. If Edda Lou was pregnant, he was pretty sure—that despite precautions he was the one who'd made her so. Now he had to figure out what to do about it.

He was surprised Austin Hatinger hadn't already come looking for him with his shotgun loaded. Austin wasn't the most understanding of men, and he'd never been fond of the Longstreets. The fact was, he hated them, and had ever since Madeline LaRue had chosen Beau Longstreet, ending forever Austin's blind dream of marrying her himself.

Since then Austin had turned into one mean, hard-bitten son of a bitch. It was common knowledge that he slapped his wife around when the mood was on him. He used the same thumping discipline with each of his five children—the oldest of which, A.J., was now serving time in Jackson for grand theft auto.

Austin had spent a few nights behind bars himself. Assault, assault and battery, disorderly conduct—usually carried out while spouting scripture or calling on the Lord. Tucker figured it was only a matter of time before Austin came after him with that shotgun or those ham-sized fists.

He'd just have to deal with it.

Just as he'd have to deal with his responsibility to Edda Lou. Responsibility was what it was, and he'd be damned if he'd marry responsibility. She might have been skilled in bed, but she couldn't keep up her end of a conversation with a hydraulic jack. And, he'd discovered, she was as small-brained and cunning as a she-fox. That was one thing he wasn't about to face over breakfast every morning for the rest of his life.

He'd do what he could, and what was right. There was money, and there was his time. That much he could give. And maybe, once the worst of the anger wore off, he'd feel affection for the child, if not for the mother.

He hoped there'd be affection rather than this sick feeling in his gut.

Tucker scrubbed his hands over his face and wished Edda Lou would just disappear. That she would pay for that ugly scene in the diner where she'd made him look worse than he was. If he could just think of a way, he'd . . .

He heard a rustle in the leaves and swung toward it. If Edda Lou had followed him, she was going to find him not only ready to fight, but eager.

♦ ♦ ♦ ♦

WHEN CAROLINE STEPPED INTO the clearing, she muffled a scream. There, in the shady spot where she'd once fished with her grandfather, was a man, golden eyes hard as agate, fists clenched, mouth pulled back dangerously in something between a snarl and a sneer.

She looked around desperately for a weapon, then realized she'd have to depend on herself.

"What are you doing here?"

Tucker shucked off the tough shell as quickly as he might have peeled off his shirt.

"Just watching the water." He flashed her a quick, self-deprecating smile that was supposed to signal he was harmless. "I didn't expect to run across anyone."

The taut and ready stance had relaxed into idleness. But Caroline was not convinced he was harmless. His voice was smooth, with that lazy drawl that could so easily be mocking. Though his eyes were smiling at her, there was such melting sexuality in them that she was ready to run if he so much as leaned toward her.

"Who are you?"

"Tucker Longstreet, ma'am. I live just down the road. I'm trespassing." Again that "don't worry about a thing" smile. "Sorry if I gave you a turn. Miss Edith didn't mind if I wandered in here to sit, so I didn't think to stop by the house and ask. You *are* Caroline Waverly?"

"Yes." She found her own stiff answer rude in the face of his country manners. To soften it, she smiled, but didn't lose that reserved, tensed stance. "You startled me, Mr. Longstreet."

"Oh, just make that Tucker." Smiling, he took her measure. A tad too thin, he thought, but she had a face as pale and elegant as the cameo his mama had worn on a black velvet ribbon. Usually he preferred long hair on a woman, but the short style suited her graceful neck and huge eyes. He tucked his thumbs in his pockets. "We're neighbors, after all. We tend to be friendly 'round Innocence."

This one, she thought, could charm the bark off a tree. She'd known another like him. And whether the words were delivered in a southern drawl or a Spanish lilt, they were deadly.

She nodded—regally, he thought.

"I was just taking a look around the property," she continued. "I didn't expect to come across anyone."

"It's a pretty spot. You settling in all right? If you need anything, all you have to do is holler."

"I appreciate that, but I think I can manage. I've been here only an hour or so."

"I know. I passed you coming in, on my way to town."

She started to come up with another bland response, then her eyes narrowed. "In a red Porsche?"

This time his grin was slow and wide and devastating. "She's a beauty, huh?"

It was Caroline who stepped forward, eyes hot. "You irresponsible idiot, you must have been doing ninety."

She'd gone from being fragile and lovely to downright beautiful with that flush of heat in her cheeks. Tucker kept his thumbs in his pockets. He'd always figured if you couldn't avoid a woman's temper, you might as well enjoy it.

"Nope. As I recollect, I was just coming up on eighty. Now, she'll do a hundred and twenty in a good straightaway, but—"

"You almost hit me."

He seemed to consider the possibility, then shook his head. "No, I had plenty of time to swing around. Probably looked closer from your point of view, though. I sure am sorry for giving you a scare twice in the same day." But the glitter in his eyes had nothing to do with apology. "Mostly I try to have a different effect on a pretty woman."

If there was one thing Caroline's mother had pounded into her head, it was dignity. She caught herself before she could sputter. "You have no business being on the road at all. I should report you to the police."

All that Yankee indignation tickled him. "Well, you can do that all right, ma'am. You call into town and ask for Burke. That's Burke Truesdale. He's the sheriff."

"And your cousin, no doubt," she said between her teeth.

"No, ma'am, though his baby sister did marry a second cousin of mine." If she assumed he was a southern rube, he'd oblige. "They moved across the river into Arkansas. My cousin? That's Billy Earl LaRue. He's on my mama's side. He and Meggie—that's Burke's baby sister—they run one of those storage places. You know, where people store furniture or cars or whatever by the month? Doing right well, too."

"I'm delighted to hear it."

"That's neighborly of you." His smile was as slow and easy as the water beside him. "You be sure to tell Burke I said hey when you talk to him."

Though he was taller by several inches, Caroline managed to look down her nose at him. "I think we both know it would do very little good. Now, I'll thank you to get off my property, Mr. Longstreet. And if you want to sit and watch the water again, find someplace else to do it."

She turned and had taken two steps before Tucker's voice—and dammit, it was mocking—called out to her. "Miz Waverly? Welcome to Innocence. Y'all have a nice day now, you hear?"

She kept walking. And Tucker, being a prudent man, waited until he figured she was out of earshot before he started to laugh.

If he weren't up to his neck in quicksand, he'd enjoy teasing that pretty Yankee on a regular basis. Damn if she hadn't made him feel better.

♦ ♦ ♦ ♦

EDDA LOU WAS PRIMED and ready. She'd been worried that she'd botched things by going on a rampage after she heard Tucker had taken that bitch Chrissy Fuller over to Greenville to dinner and the movies. But for once, it seemed, her temper had worked in her favor. That scene in the diner, and her public humiliation of Tucker, had brought him around as surely as a brass ring through his nose.

Oh, it could be that he'd try to sweet-talk her into letting him off the hook. Tucker Longstreet had the smoothest tongue in Bolivar County. But he wasn't going to waggle himself loose with it this time. She was going to have a ring on her finger and a marriage license in her hand quick as a lick. She'd wipe the smug look off every face in Innocence when she moved into the big house.

And she, Edda Lou Hatinger, who'd grown up on a dirt farm with dusty chickens squawking in the yard and the smell of pork grease forever in the kitchen, would wear fine clothes and sleep in a soft bed and drink French champagne for breakfast.

She had a fondness for Tucker, and that was the truth. But she had more room in her thirsty heart for his house, his name, and his bank account. And when she swept into Innocence, she'd do it in a long pink Caddy. There'd be no more working the register at Larsson's, no more scraping pennies together so she could keep her room at the boarding-house instead of living at home where daddy would as soon smack her as look at her sideways.

She'd be a Longstreet.

Weaving her fantasies, she pulled her rattletrap '75 Impala to the side of the road. She didn't question the fact that Tucker's note had asked her to meet him back at the pond. She found it sweet. Edda Lou had fallen in love—as much as her avaricious heart would allow—because Tucker was so downright romantic. He didn't grab and grope like some of those who sidled up to her at McGreedy's. He didn't always want to get right into her pants either, like most of the men she dated.

No, Tucker liked to talk. And though half the time she didn't know what in the blue blazes he was talking about, still she appreciated the courtesy.

And he was generous with presents. Bottles of perfume, bunches of posies. Once, when they'd had a spat, she'd made herself cry buckets. That had landed her a genuine silk nightie.

Once they were married, she'd have herself a whole drawerful if she wanted. And one of those American Express cards to buy them with.

The moon was full enough, so she didn't bother with a flashlight. She didn't want to spoil the mood. She fluffed her long blond hair, then tugged her skinny tank top down until her ripe breasts all but spilled over the edge. Her hot-pink shorts cut into her crotch a bit, but she figured the effect was worth it.

If she played her cards right, Tucker would have her out of them in no time. Just thinking of it made her damp. Nobody did it like Tucker. Why, sometimes when he was touching her, she forgot all about his money. She wanted him inside her tonight, not only for the thrill of doing it outside, but because the timing was just right. With luck her claim about being pregnant would be fact before morning.

She moved through the thick leaves, the vines, through the heady smells of wet and honeysuckle and her own perfume. Moonlight spilled onto the ground in shifting patterns. Country born and country raised, she didn't shiver at the night sounds. The plop and peep of frogs, the rustle of marsh grasses, the high song of cicadas or rude hoot from owls.

She caught the glint of yellow eyes that might have been a coon or a fox. But they vanished when she stepped closer. Some small victim squealed in the grass. Edda Lou paid no more attention to the sound of the creature's death than a New Yorker would have to the commonplace wail of a siren.

This was the place of the night hunter—the owl and the fox. She was too pragmatic a woman to consider herself as prey.

Her feet were silent on the soft ground and marshy grasses. Moonlight filtered over her, turning the skin she religiously pampered into something almost as elegant as marble. And because she was smiling, certain in her victory, there was a kind of hot beauty to her face.

"Tucker?" She used the little girl voice that was her way of wheedling. "I'm sorry I'm late, honey."

She stopped by the pond, and though her night vision was almost as sharp as a cat's, saw nothing but water and rock and thick vegetation. Her mouth thinned, erasing the beauty. She'd purposely arrived late, wanting to keep him sweating for ten or fifteen minutes.

In a huff, she sat on the log where Tucker had sat only hours before. But she didn't feel his presence. Only annoyance that she had come running when he'd crooked his finger. And he hadn't even crooked it in person, but with a stingy little note.

Meet me at McNair Pond at midnight. We'll fix everything. I only want to be alone with you for a little while.

And wasn't that just like him? Edda Lou thought. Making her go all soft, saying how he wanted to be alone with her, then pissing her off because he was late.

Five minutes, she decided. That was all he was getting. Then she was going to drive on up the road, right through those fancy gates and up to the big house. She'd let Tucker Longstreet know that he couldn't play around with her affections.

At the whisper of sound behind her, she turned her head, prepared to flutter her lashes. The blow to the base of her skull had her tumbling facedown in the earth.

♦ ♦ ♦ ♦

*H*ER MOAN WAS MUFFLED. Edda Lou heard it in her head, and her head felt as though it had been split in two by a dull rock. She tried to lift it. Oh, but it hurt, it hurt! When she started to bring her hands up to hold the ache, she found them stuck tight behind her.

The first quiver of fear pierced through the pain. Opening her eyes wide, she tried to call out. But her mouth was gagged. She could taste the cloth and the cologne that scented it. Her eyes rolled wildly as she fought to work her hands free.

She was naked, and her bare back and buttocks were scraping into bark as she wriggled against the tree. She'd been tied hand and foot to a live oak, her feet expertly cinched so that her legs were spread in a vulnerable V. Visions of rape danced hideously through her mind.

"Edda Lou. Edda Lou." The voice was low and harsh, like the scrape of metal against rock. Edda Lou's terrified eyes wheeled in their sockets as she tried to find the source.

All she saw was the water and the thick black of clustered leaves. She tried to scream and choked on the gag.

"I've had my eye on you. I wondered how soon we'd get together like this. Romantic, isn't it, being naked in the moonlight? And we're all alone, you and me. All alone. Let's have sex."

Paralyzed with terror, she watched the figure slip out of the shadows. Saw the moonlight glint on naked skin. Saw it flash for one hideous instant on the long-bladed knife.

Now it was terror and revulsion she felt as she recognized what was coming toward her. Her stomach clenched and rolled, and she tasted sickness on her tongue. But the figure came closer, gilded by a fine sheen of sweat and smelling of madness.

Her pleas and prayers were smothered by the gag. Thin streams of blood ran down her back and legs as she twisted desperately against the tree. The hands were on her, squeezing, stroking. And the mouth. Hot, frightened tears slid down her cheeks as the mouth closed hungrily over her defenseless breasts.

Slick with sweat, the body rubbed against hers, doing things she didn't want to believe could be done to her. Her weeping was mindless now, her body shuddering at every touch of the wet mouth, the intruding fingers, the smooth flat of the buck knife.

For she had remembered what had happened to Arnette and Francie, and knew they had felt this same numb terror, felt the same sick revulsion in the last moments of their lives.

"You want it. You want it." The breathless chant rolled over the dull buzzing in Edda's brain. "Whore." The knife turned, slicing delicately, almost painlessly, down Edda Lou's arm. As the mouth closed greedily over the wound, Edda Lou slumped into a half faint.

"No, you don't." A hand slapped playfully across her face to revive her. "No sleeping on the job for whores." There was a quick, almost giggly laugh. Blood smeared the smiling lips. Edda Lou's glazed eyes opened and fixed. "Better, that's better. I want you to watch. Ready?"

"Please, please, please," her mind screamed. "Don't kill me. I won't tell, I won't tell, I won't tell."

"No!" The voice was husky with arousal, and Edda Lou smelled her own fear, her own blood, when that face leaned close to hers, with madness shining out of eyes she'd known very well. "You're not worth fucking."

One hand ripped aside the gag. Part of the pleasure, the need, was to hear that one high scream. It was cut off as the knife slashed Edda Lou's throat.

◆ ◆ ◆ ◆

CAROLINE SAT STRAIGHT UP in bed, heart thudding like a Maytag with an unbalanced load. She was clutching both hands to it, nearly ripping her thin sleep shirt in reaction.

A scream, she thought wildly while her ragged breathing echoed in the room. Who was screaming?

She was nearly out of bed and fumbling for the light when she remembered where she was and sagged back against the pillows. Not Philadelphia. Not Baltimore, or New York or Paris. She was in rural Mississippi, sleeping in the bed her grandparents had slept in.

Night sounds seemed to fill the room. Peepers, crickets, cicadas. And owls. She heard another scream, eerily like a woman's. Screech owls, they called them, she remembered now. Her grandmother had soothed her one night during that long-ago visit when the same rusty cry had awakened her.

Just an old screech owl, pumpkin pie. Don't you worry now. You're safe as a bug in a rug.

Closing her eyes, Caroline listened to the long whooo-whooo of another, better-mannered owl. Country sounds, she assured herself, and tried to ignore the creaking and settling of the old house. Soon they would seem as natural to her as the whoosh of traffic or the whine of distant sirens.

It was just as her grandmother had told her. She was safe as a bug in a rug.

Chapter 3

UCKER SAT ON THE side terrace where purple clematis wound up the white wicker trellis. A hummingbird streaked behind him, iridescent wings a flashing blur as it hovered to drink deeply from one of the wide, tender blooms. Inside, Della's Electrolux hummed busily. The sound drifted through the screened windows to mix with the drone of bees.

Underneath the glass table sprawled the aged family hound, Buster, a huddle of loose skin and old bones. Occasionally, he worked up the energy to thump his tail and look hopefully through the glass at Tucker's breakfast.

Tucker wasn't paying conscious attention to any of the morning sounds and scents. He absorbed them in the same absent way he absorbed the chilled juice, black coffee, and toast.

He was performing one of his favorite daily rituals: reading the mail.

As always, there was a stack of fashion catalogues and magazines for Josie. He tossed them one at a time onto the padded seat beside him. Each time a catalogue plopped, Buster would shift his rheumy old eyes hopefully, then mutter in canine disgust.

There was a letter for Dwayne from Nashville, addressed in Sissy's childishly correct handwriting. Tucker frowned at it a minute, held it up to the sunlight, then set it aside. He knew it wasn't a request for child support. As family bookkeeper, he made out the monthly checks himself and had sent one two weeks before.

In keeping with his filing system, he tossed bills on another chair, personal correspondence was shoved over to the other side of the coffee-pot, and those letters obviously from a charitable organization or some other group sneakily begging for money were tossed in a paper sack at his side.

Tucker's way of handling them was to dig into the bag once a month, choosing two envelopes at random. Those would receive generous contri-butions, whether they were for the World Wildlife Fund, the American Red Cross, or the Society for the Prevention of Hangnails. In this way, Tucker felt the Longstreets were fulfilling their charitable obligations. And if certain organizations were confused when they received a check for sev-eral thousand dollars one month, and nothing for several years thereafter, he figured it was their problem.

He had problems of his own.

The simple routine of sorting the mail helped shift those problems to the back of his mind, at least for the moment. The fact was, he didn't know what his next move should be, since Edda Lou wasn't even talking to him. She'd had two days to follow up on her staggering public announce-ment, but was apparently playing possum. Not only hadn't she contacted him, but she wasn't answering her phone.

It was worrying—particularly since he'd had a taste of her temper and knew she could lash out with the stealth and skill of a water moccasin. Waiting for the sting made Tucker jumpy.

He piled up the YOU ARE A WINNER! envelopes Dwayne liked to ship off to his kids, and found the lilac-colored and -scented stationery that could only belong to one person.

"Cousin Lulu." His grin flashed and his worries drained away.

Lulu Longstreet Boyston was from the Georgia Longstreets and a cousin of Tucker's grandfather. Speculation put her age in the mid-seventies, though she had stubbornly clung to sixty-five for many years. She was spit-in-your-face rich, a dainty five foot in her sensible shoes, and crazy as a June bug.

Tucker flat out adored her. Though the letter was addressed TO MY LONGSTREET COUSINS, he ripped it open himself. He wasn't about to wait until Dwayne and Josie wandered back from wherever they'd gone.

He read the first paragraph, written with a hot-pink felt tip, and let out a hoot.

Cousin Lulu was coming to call.

She always phrased it just that way, so you could never tell if she'd stay for dinner or settle in for a month. Tucker sincerely hoped it was the latter. He needed a distraction.

The last time she'd come to call, she'd brought along a whole crate of ice cream cakes packed in dry ice, and had worn a paper party hat with an ostrich feather poking through the pointy top. She'd kept that damn hat on for a full week, waking and sleeping, saying she was celebrating birthdays. Anybody's birthday.

Tucker licked strawberry jam from his fingers, then tossed the rest of his toast to Buster. Leaving the rest of the mail to be picked up later, he started toward the door. He was going to tell Della to have Cousin Lulu's room ready and waiting.

Even as he swung open the door, Tucker heard the dyspeptic rattle of Austin Hatinger's pickup. There was only one vehicle in Innocence that made that particular grunt-rattle-belch sound. After giving one brief thought to going inside and barring the doors, Tucker turned and walked out to the porch, prepared to face the music.

Not only could he hear Austin coming, he could see him, by the stream of black smoke rising up between the magnolias. With a half-hearted sigh, Tucker waited for the truck to come into view, and pulling a cigarette out of his pocket, broke off a fraction of the tip.

He was just enjoying his first drag when the truck pulled up and Austin Hatinger rolled out of it.

He was as grizzled and bulky as the old Ford, but was held together by sinew and muscle rather than baling twine and spit. Beneath his grease-stained planter's hat, his face looked as if it had been carved out of tree bark. Deep lines flared out from his walnut-colored eyes, scored his wind-burned cheeks, and bracketed his hard, unsmiling mouth.

Not a speck of hair showed beneath the hat. Not that Austin was bald. Every month he drove into the barber shop and had his gray-flecked hair buzzed. Perhaps, Tucker sometimes thought, in memory of the four years he'd served in the Corps. *Semper Fi.* That was just one of the sentiments he had tattooed on his cinder-block arms. Along with it, rippling over muscle, was the American flag.

Austin—who would be the first to tell you he was a God-fearing Christian—had never gone in for such frivolities as dancing girls.

He spit a stream of Red Indian into the gravel, leaving a nasty-looking puddle of yellow. Beneath his dusty overalls and sweaty work shirt—which even in the heat Austin wore buttoned clear to the top—his chest was broad as a bull's.

Tucker noted that he hadn't brought out any of the rifles slotted into the rack in the back window of the cab. He hoped he could take that courtesy as a good omen.

"Austin." He came down one step, a sign of marginal friendliness.

"Longstreet." He had a voice like a rusty nail skidding over concrete. "Where the hell is my girl?"

Since it was the last question Tucker expected, he only blinked politely. "Excuse me?"

"You godless, rutting fuck. Where the hell is my Edda Lou?"

The description was a little more along the lines of what Tucker had expected. "I haven't seen Edda Lou since day before yesterday, when she went at me in the diner." He held up a hand before Austin could speak. There was still something to be said for being part of the most powerful family in the county. "You can be as pissed as you want, Austin, and I'd expect that to be mighty damn pissed, but the fact is I slept with your daughter." He took a long, slow drag. "You probably had a pretty good idea what I was doing when I was doing it, and I don't figure you liked it much. And I don't figure I can blame you for it."

Austin's lips peeled back from yellowed, uneven teeth. No one would have mistaken it for a smile. "I shoulda skinned your worthless hide the first time you came sniffing around her."

"Maybe, but seeing as Edda's been over twenty-one for a couple years or more, she does her own choosing." Tucker drew on the cigarette again, considered the tip, then flicked it aside. "The point is, Austin, what's done's done."

"Easy to say when you planted a bastard in my daughter's belly."

"With her full cooperation," Tucker said, slipping his hands into his pockets. "I'm going to see to it that she has everything she needs while she's carrying the baby, and there'll be no pinching on the child support."

"Big talk." Austin spat again. "Smooth talk. You've always been able to get your tongue around words real good, Tucker. Now you listen to a few. I take care of my own, and I want that girl out here, now."

Tucker merely lifted a brow. "You think Edda's here? She's not."

"Liar! Fornicator!" His grating voice rose and fell like an evangelist's with strep throat. "Your soul's black with sin."

"I can't argue about that, " Tucker said as agreeably as he could, "but Edda Lou's not here. I've got no reason to lie about that, and you can take a look for yourself, but I'm telling you I haven't seen or heard from her since she made her grand announcement."

Austin considered barging into the house, and he considered just what kind of fool that would make him. He wasn't about to play the fool for a Longstreet. "She ain't here, she ain't nowhere in town. I tell you what

I think, you sonofabitch, I think you talked her into going to one of those murder clinics to get rid of it."

"Edda Lou and I haven't talked about anything. If that's what she's done, she came up with it all on her own."

He'd forgotten just how fast the big man could move. Before the last word was out of his mouth, Austin had leapt forward, grabbing him by the shirt and lifting him clean off the steps.

"Don't you talk that way about my girl. She was a God-fearing Christian before she got hooked up with you. Look at you, nothing but a lazy, rutting pig living in your big, fine house with your drunk of a brother and whore of a sister." Fine spit sprayed Tucker's face as Austin's skin turned a mottled, angry red. "You'll rot in hell, the lot of you, just like your sin-soaked father."

As a matter of course, Tucker preferred to talk, charm, or run his way out of confrontations. But there was always a point, no matter how he tried to prevent it, when pride and temper kicked in.

He plowed a fist into Austin's midsection, surprising the older man enough to make him loosen his grip. "You listen to me, you sanctimonious bastard, you're dealing with me, not my family. Just me. I told you once I'll do right by Edda Lou, and I'm not telling you again. If you think I was the first one to get her on her back, then you're crazier than I figured." He was getting himself worked up, and knew better. But the embarrassment, the annoyance, and the insult outweighed caution. "And don't think being lazy means stupid. I know damn well what she's trying to do. If the pair of you think that screams and threats are going to have me dancing down the aisle, then think again."

The muscles in Austin's jaw quivered. "So, she's good enough to fuck but not good enough to marry."

"That says it plain enough."

Tucker was quick enough to duck the first swing, but not the second. Austin's ham-sized fist shot into his gut, stealing his breath and doubling him over. He took a rain of blows on the face and neck before he managed to find the wind to defend himself.

He tasted blood, smelled it. The fact that it was his own sent a ripe, dazzling fury pouring through him. He didn't feel the pain when his knuckles rammed into Austin's chin, but the power of the punch sang up his arm.

It felt good. Damn good.

A part of him continued to think with a silver-edged clarity. He had to stay on his feet. He would never match Austin for size or strength, and had to depend on agility and quickness. If he was brought down, and managed to get up again, he'd likely do so with broken bones and a bloody pulp for a face.

He took one just beneath the ear and heard the archangels sing.

Fists thudded against bone. Blood and sweat flew out in a grisly spray. As they grappled, lips peeled back in animal snarls, Tucker realized it wasn't simply his pride he was defending, it was his life. There was a dull gleam of madness in Austin's eyes that spoke more clearly than hard grunts or sneering curses. The sight of it had a snake of panic curling in Tucker's gut.

His worst fears were realized when Austin came at him, head down, bulldozer body behind it. He let out a long triumphant cry as Tucker's feet skidded on the gravel and he went flying backward into the peonies.

His wind was gone. He could hear the pathetic wheeze of air struggling to get down his throat and into his lungs. But he still had his fury, and he had fear. When he started to scrabble up, Austin fell on him, one beefy hand closing over Tucker's throat, the other pummeling his kidneys.

Even as he levered a hand under Austin's chin, frantically struggling to pry the head up and away, his vision dimmed. All he could see were those eyes, bright now with the pleasure of the kill, blank with madness.

"Send you to Satan," Austin chanted. "Send you to Satan. Should've killed you before, Beau. Should've done it."

Feeling his life passing, Tucker went for the eyes.

Austin threw back his head and howled like a wounded cur. When his hand slipped off Tucker's throat, Tucker sucked air in big greedy gulps that burned and revived.

"You crazy sonofabitch, I'm not my father." He choked, gagged, and managed to haul himself to his hands and knees. He was terrified he would toss his breakfast into the crushed peonies. "Get the hell off my land."

He turned his head and felt a moment's thrill of satisfaction at seeing Austin's bloodied face. He'd given as good as he'd got—and a man couldn't ask for more. Unless it was a cool shower, an ice pack, and a bottle of aspirin. He started to sit back on his heels. Quick as a snake, Austin's hand darted out for one of the heavy stones that circled the peonies.

"Good Christ" was all Tucker could manage as Austin levered the stone over his head.

The shotgun blast had them both jolting. Pellets skimmed through the peonies.

"I've got another full barrel, you bastard," Della said from the porch. "And it's aiming right at your useless dick. You put that stone back where you got it, and mighty quick, 'cause my finger's dripping sweat."

The madness was fading. Tucker could actually see it drain out of Austin's eyes, to be replaced by a violent but somehow saner anger.

"It probably won't kill you," Della said conversationally. She was standing on the edge of the porch, the 30-30 resting comfortably on her shoulder, her eye at the sight and a grim smile on her face. "You might have another twenty years to pee in a plastic bag."

Austin dropped the stone. The sickening thud it made when it hit the mulch had Tucker's stomach lurching. " 'For judgment I am come,' " Austin quoted. "He's going to pay for what he did to my girl."

"Paying's just what he'll do," Della said. "If that girl's carrying what's his, Tucker'll see to it. But I ain't as gullible as the boy, Austin, and we're going to see what's what before he signs any papers or writes any checks."

Fists clenched at his side, Austin rose. "You saying my girl's lying?"

Della kept the shotgun sighted mid-body. "I'm saying Edda Lou's never been any better than she had to be, and I ain't saying I blame her for it. Now, you get the hell off this land, and if you're smart, you get that girl to Doc Shays and have him see if she's breeding. We'll talk this through, civilized. Or you can come ahead and I'll blow you apart."

Austin's impotent hands clenched and unclenched. Blood ran unheeded down his cheeks like tears. "I'll be back." He spat again as he turned to Tucker. "And next time there won't be no woman 'round to protect you."

He strode back to his pickup, gunned around the circle of flowers, and rattled down the drive. Black smoke belched in his wake.

Tucker sat in the ruined flower bed and dropped his head on his knees. He wasn't getting up yet—no, not just yet. He'd sit a spell on the mangled blooms.

Letting out a long breath, Della lowered the gun. Carefully, she propped it against the rail, then walked down, stepping over the border stones until she could reach Tucker. He looked up, the beginnings of thanks on his tongue. She smacked the side of his head hard enough to make his ears ring.

"Christ, Della."

"That's for thinking with your glands." She smacked him again. "And that's for bringing that Bible-thumping maniac around my house." And another flat-handed slap on the top of his head. "And that's for ruining your mama's flowers." With a satisfied nod she folded her arms over her chest. "Now, when you get your legs out from under you, you come back into the kitchen and I'll clean you up."

Tucker wiped the back of his hand over his mouth and looked down absently at the smear of blood. "Yes'm."

Because she figured her hands were about steady now, she tipped a finger under his chin. "Going to have a shiner," she predicted. "But it looked to me like he was going to have a pair of 'em. You didn't do too bad."

"Guess not." Gingerly he got to his knees again. Breathing shallowly, he inched his way to his feet. It felt as if he'd been trampled by a herd of runaway horses. "I'll do what I can with the flowers later."

"See that you do." She slipped an arm around his waist, and taking his weight, helped him inside.

♦ ♦ ♦ ♦

THOUGH HE DIDN'T MUCH care to get himself riled up on Edda Lou's behalf, Tucker couldn't quite get past the niggling sense of worry in his gut. He told himself to let crazy Austin worry about his crazy daughter—who'd more than likely gone to ground for a few days to avoid her daddy's wrath and to stir up Tucker's guilt. But he couldn't forget what it had been like to find sweet little Francie floating, those bloodless wounds gaping all over her fish-white skin.

So he stuck on a pair of sunglasses to conceal the worst of the sun-burst bruise on his left eye and, downing two of the painkillers Josie took for menstrual cramps, set out to town.

The sun beat down mercilessly, making him wish he'd just crawled off to bed with an ice pack and a long whiskey. That was what he was going to do once he talked to Burke.

With any luck Edda Lou would be behind the counter at Larsson's selling tobacco and Popsicles and bags of charcoal for barbecues.

But he could see plainly through the wide front window as he drove past, and it was young, gawky Kirk Larsson at the main counter, not Edda Lou.

Tucker pulled up in front of the sheriff's office. If he'd been alone, he would have eased himself out inch by painful inch. Whimpering. But the three old coots who always planted themselves out in front, to chew the fat, curse the weather, and hope for gossip, were in position. Straw hats covered grizzled heads, wind-burned cheeks were puffed out with chaws, and faded cotton shirts had gone limp with sweat.

"Hey there, Tucker."

"Mr. Bonny." He nodded to the first man, as was proper, seeing that Claude Bonny was the eldest of the group. All three had lived off social security for more than a decade and had staked out the awning-shaded sidewalk in front of the rooming house as their retirement heaven. "Mr. Koons. Mr. O'Hara."

Pete Koons, toothless since his forties and no fan of dentures, spat through his gums into the tin bucket his grandniece provided. "Boy, looks like you ran into a mean woman or a jealous husband."

Tucker managed a grin. There were few secrets in town, and a smart man chose his wisely. "Nope. A pissed-off papa."

Charlie O'Hara gave a wheezy chuckle. His emphysema wasn't getting any better, and he figured he'd die of it before another summer came, so he appreciated all of life's little jokes. "That Austin Hatinger?" When Tucker jerked his head to the side in acknowledgment, O'Hara wheezed again. "Bad apple. Once saw him whale into Toby March— 'course Toby was a black boy, so nobody paid much mind. Must've been in sixty-nine. Stove in Toby's ribs and scarred his face."

"Sixty-eight," Bonny corrected his crony, because accuracy was important in such matters. "That was the summer we got the new tractor, so I remember. Austin said Toby'd stole a length of rope outta his shed. But that was nonsense. Toby was a good boy and never took nothing wasn't his. He come to work out on the farm with me after his ribs healed. Never had a bit of trouble outta him."

"Austin's a mean one." Koons spat again, either from need or to emphasize his point. "Went to Korea mean and came back meaner. Never did forgive your mama for marrying up when he was over there fighting slant eyes. Had his mind set on Miss Madeline, though Christ knows she never looked at him twice when he was smack in front of her." He grinned toothlessly. "You taking him on as a daddy-in-law, Tuck?"

"Not in this life. Y'all don't work too hard now."

They chuckled and wheezed appreciatively as he made the turn and pushed open Burke's door.

The sheriff's office was a steamy box of a room holding a metal army surplus desk, two swivel chairs, a scarred wooden rocker, a gun cabinet for which Burke held the keys on the heavy chain at his belt, and a shiny new Mr. Coffee, a gift from Burke's wife at Christmas. The wood floor was scattered with hard little dots of white paint from the last time the walls had been done.

Beyond the office was a closet-sized john and through the john a narrow storage room with metal shelves and just enough room for a fold-up cot. This was used if Burke or his deputy needed to watch a prisoner overnight. More often it was used if either man found himself in the domestic doghouse and needed to give his spouse a night to cool off.

Tucker had always wondered how Burke, the son of a once-prosperous planter, could be happy here, making his living processing traffic tickets, breaking up the occasional brawl, and watching out for drunks.

But Burke seemed content enough, just as he seemed content to be married for nearly seventeen years to the girl he'd gotten pregnant while they were both still in high school. He wore his badge easily and was affable enough to remain popular in Innocence, where people didn't like to be told what they couldn't do.

Tucker found him huddled over his desk, frowning over files while the ceiling fan stirred stale smoke and hot air overhead.

"Burke."

"Hey, Tuck. What're you . . ." He trailed off as he took in Tucker's swollen face. "Holy hell, boy, what did you run into?"

Tucker grimaced, the movement costing him no little discomfort. "Austin's fists."

Burke grinned. "How'd he look?"

"Della says worse. I was too busy holding my insides where they belonged to notice."

"She probably didn't want to hurt your feelings."

Knowing the truth of that, Tuck eased himself down on the frayed seat of the swivel chair. "Probably. Still, I don't think all the blood on my shirt was mine. Hope not."

"Edda Lou?"

"Yeah." Tucker poked gentle fingers under his sunglasses to probe his bruised eye socket. "Way he sees it, I debauched a lily-white virgin who'd never seen a dick before."

"Shit."

"There you go." Tucker caught himself before he made the mistake of shrugging. "Thing is, she's twenty-five, and I slept with her, not her old man."

"Happy to hear that."

Tucker's quick grin pulled at his puffy lip. "Edda Lou's ma must close her eyes and pray to Jesus every time he takes a poke at her." Then he sobered, the image of Austin pounding it to his frail-boned, miserable-eyed wife too disturbing to dwell on. "Thing is, Burke, I want to do what's right." He blew out a breath, realizing there was more than one reason he'd come into town. This was the opening for the first one. "Things worked out for you and Susie."

"Yeah." Burke drew out a pack of Chesterfields, took one, then tossed the pack across the desk for Tucker. "We were too young and stupid to think they wouldn't." He watched as Tucker broke off a fraction of the tip. "And I loved her. Flat out loved her then. Still do." He flipped his matches to Tucker. "It hasn't been easy, with Marvella coming along before graduation, our having to live with my folks for two years before we could afford our own place. Then Susie pregnant again with Tommy." Blowing out smoke, he shook his head. "Three babies in five years."

"You could have kept your fly zipped."

Burke grinned. "So could you."

"Yeah." Tucker blew smoke between his teeth. "Well, it comes to this. I don't love Edda Lou, flat out or any other way, but I've got a responsibility. I can't marry her, Burke. Can't do it."

Burke tapped his ash into a metal ashtray that had once been blue and was now the color of smut. "I gotta say you'd be a fool if you did." He cleared his throat before venturing onto boggy ground. "Susie tells me that Edda's been bragging for weeks about how she's going to be living up in the big house with servants. Susie said she never paid it much mind, but some of the others did. Sounds to me like that girl was set on life at Sweetwater."

It was both a blow to his pride and a great relief. So it had never been him, Tucker realized. It had been the Longstreet name. But she must have figured that would get back to him sooner or later.

"I came in to tell you I haven't been able to get hold of her since that day in the diner. Austin came down on me, figuring I was hiding her there at the house. She been around town?"

Slowly, Burke crushed out his cigarette. "I can't say as I've seen her myself for a day or two."

"Probably with a girlfriend." The idea settled him. "Thing is, Burke, ever since we found Francie . . ."

"Yeah." Burke felt a twang inside his gut.

"You got anything on that—or Arnette?"

"Nothing." The failure had heat rising up his neck. "County sheriff's mostly in charge. I've been working with the medical examiner, and the state boys have helped, but there's nothing solid. Some woman was sliced up in Nashville last month. If they can find a connection, we'll call in the FBI."

"No shit?"

Burke merely nodded. He didn't like the idea of federal officers in his town, taking over his job, looking at him out of the corner of their city eyes and thinking he was a rube who couldn't lock up a passed-out drunk.

"It was remembering Francie that had me worrying," Tucker continued.

"I'll ask around." He rose, wanting to do so quickly. "Like you said, she's probably staying with a girlfriend for a few days, thinking that'll sweat you into a proposal."

"Yeah." Relieved that he'd passed his burden onto Burke, Tucker stood and limped to the door. "You'll let me know."

"First thing." Burke walked out with him, took a long slow look at his town. Where he'd been born and raised, where his children raced the streets and his wife shopped. Where he could raise a finger in salute to anyone and be recognized and acknowledged.

"Look at that." Tucker let out a little sigh as he watched Caroline Waverly climb out of her BMW and stroll toward Larrson's. "That's one long, cool drink of water. Makes a man thirsty just to look."

"Edith McNair's kin?"

"Yep. Ran into her the other day. Talks like a duchess and has the biggest green eyes you've ever seen."

Recognizing the signs, Burke chuckled. "You've got problems enough, son."

"It's a weakness." Tucker limped a little as he walked to his car. Changing his mind, he headed across the street. "I think I'll go buy a pack of smokes."

Burke's grin faded as he turned toward the rooming house. He remembered Francie, too. Surely Edda Lou would have stayed close by to pressure Tucker into marriage. The fact that she hadn't left a sick taste in the back of his throat.

♦ ♦ ♦ ♦

SHE WAS SETTLING IN just fine, Caroline told herself as she walked across the heat-baked lawn toward the trees. The ladies she'd met in Larrson's that afternoon had been more curious than she was used to, but they'd also been friendly and warm. It was nice to know if she got lonely, she could drive into town for company.

She'd particularly liked Susie Truesdale, who'd stopped in to buy a birthday card for her sister in Natchez, and had stayed for twenty minutes.

Of course, that Longstreet man had come in as well, to flirt with the women and dispense southern-fried charm. His dark glasses hadn't disguised the fact that he'd been fighting. When questioned about it, he'd milked sympathy from every female in the store.

His type always did, she thought. If Luis had gotten a hangnail, women were ready to donate blood.

Thank God she was through with him, with men, with everything about them. It had been pathetically easy for her to rebuff Tucker's smooth charm.

"Miz Caroline" he'd called her, she remembered with a thin smile. She was quite sure his eyes had been laughing behind those dark lenses.

A pity about his hands though, she thought as she ducked under hanging moss. They were really quite beautiful, long-fingered, wide-palmed. It had been a shame to see the knuckles skinned and bruised.

Annoyed, she shook off the sympathy. The moment he'd strolled out—limping slightly—the women had begun to buzz about him and someone named Edda Lou. Caroline took a deep breath of the verdant smell of heat and green, and smiled to herself.

It looked like our slippery-smooth Mr. Longstreet had gotten him-self into a nasty little mess. His girlfriend was pregnant and screaming for marriage. And, according to the local gossip, her father was the type who'd be more than willing to load up the shotgun.

Trailing a finger over a branch, she began to scent the water. Lord, she was a long way from Philadelphia. How could she have known it would be so peaceful and so entertaining to listen to the chatter about the town lothario?

She'd enjoyed her half-hour visit to town, the ladies' talk about children, recipes, men. Sex. She laughed a little. Apparently, North or South, when women got together, sex was a favored topic. But down here they were so frank about it. Who was sleeping with whom, and who wasn't.

Must be the heat, she thought, and sat down on the log to watch the water and listen to the music of early evening.

She was glad she'd come to Innocence. Every day she could feel her-self healing. The quiet, the vicious sun that baked all of the energy out of you, the simple beauty of water shaded by moss-hung trees. She was even getting used to the night noises, and that blacker-than-night country darkness.

The previous night she had slept for eight hours straight, the first time in weeks. And she'd awakened without that plaguing headache. It was working, the solitude, the serenity of small-town and rural rituals.

The roots she'd never been allowed to plant, the roots her mother would have furiously denied existed, had begun to take hold. Nothing and no one was going to pull them free again.

She might even try her hand at fishing. The idea made her laugh and wonder if she still had a taste for catfish. She shifted and picked up a peb-ble to toss in the water. It made such a satisfying plop that she picked up another, and another, watching the ripples spread. Spotting a flat-sided stone by the verge of the water, she rose to pry it up. It would be fun to try to skip it. That, too, was an old, almost forgotten image. Her grandfather standing here, just here, and trying to teach her how to skip the rock over the water.

Pleased with the memory, she bent, curled her fingers around it. Odd, she had the most ridiculous sensation of being watched. Stared at. Even as the first shiver worked down her spine, she caught something white out of the corner of her eye.

She turned, looked. And froze. Even the scream turned to ice in her throat.

She was being stared at, though the eyes that watched saw nothing. There was only a face, bobbing above the rippling surface of dark water, with a hideous mop of long blond hair that had tangled and caught in the roots of an old tree.

Her breath hitched, coming through her lips in small, terrified whimpers as she stumbled back. But she couldn't take her eyes off that face, the way the water lapped at the chin, the way a shaft of sunlight beamed off those flat, lifeless eyes.

It wasn't until she managed to throw her hands over her face, blocking the image, that she was able to draw the air to scream. The sound echoed through the bayou, bouncing off the dark water and sending birds streaking from the trees.

Chapter 4

MOST OF THE SICKNESS had passed. Sour waves of nausea still rose in her stomach, but if she forced herself to breathe slowly, Caroline could manage to hold down a little tepid water. She sipped again, breathed deeply, and waited for Burke Truesdale to come back out of the trees.

He hadn't asked her to go in with him. She supposed he'd taken one look at her face and known she wouldn't have made it ten feet. Even now, as she sat on the top step of the porch, her hands almost steady again, she couldn't remember how she'd gotten from the pond back to the house.

She'd lost one of her shoes, she noted absently. One of those pretty navy and white flats she'd bought in Paris a few months before. With glazed eyes she stared down at her bare foot streaked with dirt and grass. Frowning with concentration, she toed the other shoe off. It seemed important somehow that she have both feet bare. After all, someone might think she was crazy, sitting there on the porch with one shoe on. And with a body floating in the pond.

When her stomach pitched, rolled, and threatened to expel even the tap water, she dropped her head between her knees. Oh, she hated to be sick, hated it with a passion only someone who had recently recovered from long illness could feel. The weakness of it, the shaky loss of control.

Clenching her fists, she used all her concentration to pull herself back from the edge. What right did she have to be sick and scared and dizzy? She was alive, wasn't she? Alive and whole and safe. Not like that poor woman.

But she kept her head down until her stomach settled, and the dull buzzing faded from her ears.

She lifted it again when she heard the sound of a car bumping down her lane. Caroline brought a weary hand up to her face as she watched the dusty station wagon squeeze through the overgrowth.

She'd have to cut those vines back, she thought. She could hear them brushing against the already scarred paint of the car. Must be some clippers in the shed. Best do it in the morning, before the day heated up.

Dully, she watched the station wagon stop beside the sheriff's cruiser. A wiry man with a red tie knotted around a turkey neck climbed out. He wore a short-sleeved white shirt, and a white hat atop a full head of hair he'd dyed as densely black as coal and slicked into a modified pompadour. Pouches of loose flesh dipped below his jaw and his eyes, as if the skin had once been full of fat or fluid and had stretched under the weight.

His black slacks were hauled up with sassy red suspenders, and he wore the heavy, shiny black tie shoes Caroline associated with the military. But the cracked leather bag he carried announced his profession.

"You must be Miz Caroline." His high-pitched voice would have made her smile at any other time or place. He sounded eerily like a used-car salesman she'd seen on the old RCA console only the night before. "I'm Doc Shays," he told her as he propped one foot on the bottom step. "I tended to your grandfolks near to twenty-five years."

Caroline gave him a careful nod. "How do you do?"

"Fine and dandy." His sharp physician's eyes scanned her face and recognized shock. "Burke gave me a call. Said he was headed on down here." Shays took out a huge white handkerchief to mop his neck and face. Though he could move fast when he had to, his slow and easy pace was more than bedside manner. It was the way he preferred to do things. "Hell of a hot one, ain't it?"

"Yes."

"Why don't we go on inside, where it's cooler?"

"No, I think . . ." She looked helplessly back toward the shielding trees. "I should wait. He went in there to see . . . I was throwing stones in the water. I could see only her face."

He sat beside her, took her hand in his. Fingers still nimble after forty years of medicine monitored her pulse. "Whose face, darlin'?"

"I don't know." When he reached down to open his bag, she stiffened.

Months of vigilant doctors with their slim, shiny needles had her system jittering. "I don't need anything. I don't want anything." She jolted to her feet, and though she tried, she couldn't keep her voice from shrilling. "I'm all right. You should try to help her. There must be something you could do to help her."

"One thing at a time, darlin'." To show good faith, he shut his bag again. "Why don't you sit on down here and tell me all about it? Nice and slow. Then we can figure out what's what."

She didn't sit, but she did gain enough control to take several long breaths. She didn't want to end up in the hospital again. Couldn't. "I'm sorry. I don't suppose I'm making much sense."

"Well, now, that don't worry me none. Most people I know spend about half their lives making sense and the other half exercising their jaw. You just tell me how it occurs to you."

"I think she must have drowned," Caroline said in a calm and careful voice. "In the pond. I could see only her face . . ." She trailed off, forcing the image before it nudged her toward hysteria again. "I'm afraid she was dead."

Before Shays could question further, Deputy Carl Johnson came out of the trees and started across the sun-bleached lawn. His usually spotless uniform showed traces of dirt and streaks of wet. Still, he walked with military precision, a commanding figure, six foot six of taut muscle. His glossy skin was the color of chestnuts.

He was a man who enjoyed his authority and prized his control. Just now he was fighting to maintain his professional aura when what he wanted to do was find a secluded spot to lose his lunch.

"Doc."

"Carl."

It needed only that for the two men to exchange information. Muttering an oath, Shays mopped his face again.

"Miss Waverly, I'd be obliged to use your phone."

"Of course. Can you tell me what . . ." Again, her gaze was drawn toward the trees, her mind to what was beyond them. "Is she dead?"

Carl hesitated only a moment, pulling off his cap to reveal tight black curls as close and neat as a newly mowed lawn. "Yes, ma'am. The sheriff'll talk to you as soon as he can. Doc?"

With a weary nod, Shays rose.

"There's a phone right here in the hall," Caroline began as she started up the stairs. "Deputy . . ."

"Johnson, ma'am. Carl Johnson."

"Deputy Johnson, did she drown?"

He shot Caroline a quick look as he held open the screen door for her. "No, ma'am. She didn't."

◆ ◆ ◆ ◆

*B*URKE WAS SITTING ON the log, turned away from the body. A Polaroid camera sat beside him. He needed a minute before he slipped back into his law-and-order suit. A minute for his head to clear, for his stomach to settle.

He'd seen death before—had known the look and the smell of it from boyhood, hunting with his father. First they'd gone out for the sheer pleasure of it. Then, when crops and investments had failed, they'd hunted to put meat on the table.

He'd seen the death of his own kind as well. Starting with his father's suicide when the farm had been lost. And wasn't it that death that had led him to this one? Without the farm, with a wife and two young children to support, he'd signed on as town deputy, then as sheriff. The rich man's son who had detested the futility of his father's death, and the cruelty of the land that had caused it, had chosen to channel his talents, such as they were, toward law and order.

But even finding his father hanging in the barn, hearing the quiet creak of the rope rubbing over the thick beam, hadn't prepared him for what he'd found in McNair Pond.

He still had much too clear a picture of what it had been like to wrestle that body from the water, to drag it out onto the ground.

It was funny, he thought, drawing hard on a cigarette, he'd never liked Edda Lou. There had been a coarseness about her, a sly look in her eyes that had milked away any sympathy he might have felt for her being unfortunate enough to be kin to Austin Hatinger.

But just now he was remembering the way she'd looked one long-ago Christmas when he and Susie had come across her in town. She'd have been no more than ten, mousy hair stringing down her back, patched dress hiking up too far at the side hem and drooping at the front. And her nose pressed up to Larsson's window as she stared at a doll with a blue cape and rhinestone tiara.

She'd just been a little girl then, wishing there was a Santa. Already knowing there wasn't.

He turned his head when he heard the rustle of brush. "Doc." He blew out a stream of smoke on the word. "Christ."

Shays laid a heavy hand on his shoulder, squeezed once, then moved to the body. Death wasn't a stranger to him, and he had come to know that death wasn't only for the old, either. He could accept that the young were taken, through illness, through accident. But this mutilation, this wild destruction of a human being was beyond acceptance.

Gently, he picked up one of the limp hands and studied the raw wrist. The same telltale signs braceleted the ankles. It hurt him more somehow, this ring of broken skin and the hopelessness it represented, than the vicious slices on her torso.

"She was one of the first babies I delivered when I came back to Innocence." With a sigh he did what Burke had not been able to do. He reached down and shut Edda Lou's eyes. "It's hard for parents to bury their children. By Jesus, it's hard for doctors, too."

"He messed her up pretty good," Burke managed to say. "Just like the others."

He picked up the camera. They would need more pictures, and God knew he had to do something before the coroner came. He swallowed a hard knot of anger.

"She was tied to that tree there. There's blood dried on it. You can see from the scrapes on her back where she rubbed against it. Used clothesline. Pieces of it are still there." He lowered the camera again, and his eyes were bright with fury. "What the hell was she doing here? Her car's back in town."

"Can't tell you that, Burke. Can't tell you a hell of a lot. She was hit on the back of the head." Shays's hands were as soothing as they would have been had his patient been alive to feel them. "Maybe he hauled her out here. Maybe she came on her own and riled him up."

Struggling to hold on to his nerves, Burke nodded. He knew, just as everyone in town knew, who it was Edda Lou had riled up.

◆ ◆ ◆

CAROLINE PACED THE PORCH. If she could have worked up the courage, she'd have marched into the bayou and demanded information. She wasn't sure how much longer she could stand this waiting. But she knew she'd never make it past the first stand of trees, not when she knew what was beyond them.

She saw the dark sedan creep down the drive, followed by a white van. Coroner, she thought. When the men got out of the van with a stretcher and a thick black bag, she turned away. That bag, that long black bag not so different in shape and size from the kind people used to haul off things they no longer wanted, that bag reminded her much too forcibly that it wasn't a person in the pond, it wasn't a woman, it was only a body that wouldn't suffer from the indignity of being taken away in a big piece of plastic.

It was the living who suffered, and Caroline wondered who the woman had left behind to grieve and mourn and question.

Her heart ached to make music, to make music so passionate it would drive away everything else. She could still do that, thank God she could still do that. Escape there when there was nowhere else to run.

Leaning against the post, she closed her eyes and played it in her head, filled her mind with melody so rich she didn't hear the next car jolt down the lane.

"Hey there." Josie slammed her car door, and finishing off the last of a cherry Popsicle, started toward the porch. "Hey," she said again, and offered a friendly, curious smile when Caroline raised her head. "Y'all got a commotion here." She licked the stick clean with a savoring tongue. "Saw all these cars turn in while I was heading home and thought I'd see what was doing."

Caroline gave her a blank look. It was odd, almost obscene, to see someone so vivid and pulsing with life when death was still hovering. "I beg your pardon?"

"No need for that, honey." Still smiling, Josie walked up the steps. "I'm just nosy, that's all. Can't stand for something to be going on and not know about it. Josie Longstreet." She held out a hand still a bit sticky from the melted ice.

"Caroline. Caroline Waverly." After she'd shaken hands, Caroline thought how innate manners were, how absurdly automatic.

"You got trouble here, Caroline?" Josie set the sticks on the porch rail. "I see Burke's car. Gorgeous, isn't he? Hasn't cheated on his wife, not even once in better than seventeen years. Never seen anyone take marriage so damn serious. But there you go. Doc Shays, too." She glanced back at the crowded lane. "Now, *he's* a character. That shoe-black hair all puffed up and slicked back like a fifties rock and roll singer? Sounds a little like Mickey Mouse, don't you think?"

Caroline nearly smiled. "Yes. I'm sorry, would you like to sit down?"

"Don't worry about me." Josie took a cigarette out of her purse. She lighted it with a gold butane. "You got all these visitors, but I don't see a soul."

"They're . . ." She looked toward the trees. She swallowed hard. "The sheriff's coming now."

Josie shifted her position subtly, turning her body slightly, lifting her shoulders. The sassy smile she offered Burke faded when she saw his eyes. Still, her voice was bright. "Why, Burke, I'm jealous. You hardly ever come to pay calls on us at Sweetwater, and here you are."

"Official business, Josie."

"Well, well."

"Miss Waverly, I need to speak to you. Could we go inside?"

"Of course."

As he started by, Josie took his arm. The teasing had gone out of her face. "Burke?"

"I can't talk to you now." He knew he should tell her to leave, but he thought Caroline might want another female around when he'd finished with her. "Can you wait? Maybe stay with her awhile?"

The hand on his arm trembled. "How bad is it?"

"As bad as it gets. Why don't you go in the kitchen, fix us something cold? I'd be obliged if you'd stay in there until I call you."

Caroline settled him in the front parlor, on the striped divan. The little cuckoo clock that she had wound faithfully since her arrival tick-tocked cheerfully. She could smell the polish she'd used on the coffee table just that morning, and her own sweat.

"Miss Waverly, I'm awful sorry to have to ask you questions now, when you must be upset. But it's best to get to all this quickly."

"I understand." How could she understand, she thought frantically. She'd never found a body before. "Do you know . . . do you know who she is?"

"Yes, ma'am."

"The deputy—Johnson?" Her hand was up at her throat, rubbing up and down as if she could stroke the words free. "He said she didn't drown."

"No, ma'am." Burke took a notebook and pencil from his pocket. "I'm sorry. I have to tell you she was murdered."

She only nodded. She wasn't shocked. A part of her had known it from the moment she had looked into the wide, sightless eyes. "What do you want me to do?"

"I want you to tell me anything you saw, anything you heard in the last forty-eight hours."

"But there's nothing, really. I've only just arrived, and I've been try-ing to—to settle, to put things in order."

"I understand that." He tipped his hat back on his head, used his forearm to dab at sweat on his brow. "Maybe you could think back. You didn't maybe hear a car pull into your lane at night, or anything that didn't sound quite right to you?"

"No . . . that is, I'm used to city noises, so nothing really sounds right to me." She dragged an unsteady hand through her hair. It was going to be all right, she told herself, now that they were down to the questions and answers, the mechanics of law and order.

"The quiet seems so loud, if you know what I mean. And the birds and insects. The owls." She stopped, and what was left of her color drained away. "The other night, the first night I was here . . . oh, God."

"You just take your time, ma'am."

"I thought I heard a woman scream. I'd been asleep, and it woke me. Frightened me. Then I remembered where I was, and about the owls. Those screech owls." She closed her eyes on a flood of guilt. "I went back to sleep. It could have been her, calling for help. I just went back to sleep."

"Or it could have been an owl. Even if it was her, Miss Waverly, you couldn't have helped. Could you tell me what time it woke you up?"

"No, I'm sorry. I have no idea. I didn't look."

"Do you walk back there much?"

"I have a couple of times. My grandfather took me fishing back there once when I visited."

"I've gotten some good cats back there myself," he said conversationally. "Do you smoke?"

"No." Manners rising again, she glanced around for an ashtray. "Please, go ahead."

He pulled one out, but he was thinking about the single cigarette butt he'd found near the log. Edda Lou didn't smoke either. "You haven't noticed anyone poking around here? No one's come by to see you?"

"As I said, I haven't been here long. I did run into someone the first day. He said my grandmother let him come down to watch the water."

Burke kept his face impassive, but his heart began to sink. "Do you know who that was?"

"His name was Longstreet. Tucker Longstreet."

◆ ◆ ◆ ◆

𝒥UCKER WAS BACK IN the hammock holding a cold beer against his swollen eye and sulking. His body no longer felt like it had been tramped by horses. It felt like it had been dragged a few miles first. He was regretting, bitterly, his decision to face Austin. Far better to have slunk off to Greenville or even Vicksburg for a few days. What the hell had made him think that pride and honesty were worth a fist in the eye?

Worse yet was the fact that Edda Lou was probably off somewhere smirking at all the trouble she'd caused. The more he thought about it, the surer he was that Austin had battered him for no good reason. Edda Lou wasn't about to have an abortion. Not that Tucker figured she'd turn from one on moral or maternal grounds. But if she wasn't pregnant, she wouldn't have any hold on him.

A hold, he thought miserably, that would last the rest of his life.

Nothing took hold of you like family, he thought. And his blood would mix with Edda Lou's in the baby she was carrying. All the good and bad there was between them would stir around, leaving it up to God or fate or maybe just timing to determine which traits endured.

He took a long swallow of beer, then rested the bottle against his eye again. It wasn't any use thinking about something that wasn't going to happen for months yet. He was better off worrying about the almighty present.

He hurt, and if he didn't feel so damn stupid about the whole mess, he'd have called Doc Shays.

To lull himself, he let his thoughts drift to more pleasant matters.

Caroline Waverly. She was as pretty as one of those tall, glossy ice-cream parfaits. The kind that cooled you off and made you greedy for more. He grinned to himself as he remembered the snooty look she'd given him in Larsson's that afternoon.

That queen-to-peasant look. Christ, it made him want to just scoop her right up.

Not that he had any plans to. He was swearing off women awhile. Not only did his body hurt, but he figured his luck was a bit shaky. Still, it was pleasant to think about it. He liked the way her voice sounded, all soft and smoky, so different from her cool, hands-off look.

He wondered just what he'd have to do to convince her to let him get his hands on. Tucker fell asleep with a smile on his face.

"Tuck."

He muttered and tried to shrug off the hand shaking his shoulder. The sudden movement brought pain back with a bang. He swore, opened his eyes.

"Jesus, can't a man get any peace around here?" He blinked up at Burke. The shadows were lengthening, and his first thought was Della hadn't called him in for supper. His second, as he swung around to sit, was that his stomach was so sore, it was just as well. "Remember when the Bonny brothers and their crazy cousin jumped us down at Spook Hollow?"

Burke kept his hands jammed in his pockets. "Yeah."

"We were younger then." Tucker flexed his swollen knuckles. "I don't recollect it hurt so damn much taking a licking then. Why don't you go in, get us a couple beers?"

"I'm on duty, Tucker. I gotta talk to you."

"Talk better with a beer." But when he looked up and focused on Burke's face, his quick grin faded. "What is it?"

"It's bad. Real bad."

And he knew, as if it had already been said. "It's Edda Lou, isn't it?" Before Burke could answer, Tucker was up and pacing, his hands dragging through his hair. "Oh, Jesus. Jesus Christ."

"Tuck—"

"Give me a minute. Goddammit." Sick, furious, he pounded a fist against the tree. "You're sure?"

"Yeah. It was like Arnette, and Francie."

"Holy God." He leaned his brow against the rough bark and struggled to keep the image out of his mind. He hadn't loved her, had gotten to the point where he didn't even like her, but he had touched her, tasted her, been inside her. He felt a well of grief rise up that was staggering not only for her, but for the child he hadn't even wanted.

"You ought to come on and sit down."

"No." He turned from the tree. His face had changed. It had taken on that hard, dangerous look so few were allowed to see. "Where did you find her?"

"McNair Pond, just a couple hours ago."

"That's less than a mile from here." He thought first of his sister, of Della, of protection. Then he thought of Caroline. "She—Caroline—she shouldn't be alone there."

"Josie's with her now, and Carl." Burke rubbed a hand over his face. "Josie bullied her into drinking some of Miss Edith's apple brandy. She's—Caroline—she's the one who found the body."

"Fuck." He sat on the hammock again, put his head in his hands. "What the hell are we going to do, Burke? What the hell's going on here?"

"I gotta ask you some questions, Tuck, but before I do I want to tell you I went to see Austin. I had to tell him." He pulled out a cigarette. "You watch your back, son."

Tucker took the cigarette. "He can't believe I'd hurt Edda Lou. For chrissake." He lit a match, then stared as it burned down toward his fingers. "You don't believe . . ." He dropped the match and sprang to his feet. "Goddammit, Burke, you know me."

Burke wished he'd taken the beer—or anything else to wash this nasty taste from his mouth. Tucker was his friend, the closest thing he had to a brother. And his most likely suspect. "Knowing you's got nothing to do with it."

Tucker felt a punch of panic worse than any fist to the gut. "The hell with that."

"It's my job, Tucker. I got a duty." Sick at heart, he took out a notebook. "You and Edda Lou had a public argument only a couple days ago. She's been missing nearly ever since."

Tucker struck another match. This time he lighted the cigarette and drew and expelled smoke. "You going to read me my rights, put the cuffs on me? What?"

Burke's hand fisted at his side. "Goddammit, Tucker, I just spent two hours looking at what someone did to that girl. This ain't the time to push me."

Tucker held out a hand, palm up, but there was too much sarcasm in the gesture for it to be taken as one of peace. "Go on, Burke, do your frigging job."

"I want to know if you saw Edda, or talked to her, after you left the diner."

"Didn't I come in your office this afternoon and tell you I hadn't?"

"Where'd you go after you left the diner?"

"I went to—" He broke off, paling. "Christ, I went to McNair Pond." He started to bring the cigarette to his lips, then stopped. His tawny eyes glittered in the lowering light. "But you already knew that, didn't you?"

"Yeah. But it helps you telling me yourself."

"Fuck you."

Burke grabbed him by the shirtfront. "Listen to me. I don't like what I've got to do. But this is nothing *nothing* compared to what the FBI'll do once they get here. We've got three women dead, sliced up like catfish. Edda Lou threatened you in public, and she's found dead not two days later. I've got a witness who puts you at the scene a day, maybe hours, before the murder."

The first lick of fear joined the tension in Tucker's stomach. "You know I've been over to McNair Pond hundreds of times. So've you." He shoved Burke's hands away. "And being pissed at Edda Lou doesn't make me a killer. What about Arnette, Francie?"

Burke's jaw set. "You dated them, all three of them."

It wasn't temper now, but simple shock. "Jesus, Burke." He had to sit again, and do so slowly, feeling his way. "You can't believe that. You can't."

"What I believe doesn't have a damn to do with the questions I have to ask. I have to know where you were night before last."

"Why, he was losing his shirt to me, playing gin rummy." Josie strolled over to them. Her cheeks were pale, but there was a hard gleam in her eye. "You interrogating my brother, Burke? Why, I'm surprised at you." She walked between them to lay a hand on Tucker's shoulder.

"I've got a job to do, Josie."

"Then you ought to be doing it. Why aren't you out looking for someone who hates women rather than someone who has such a powerful affection for them like Tuck here?"

Tucker put a hand over hers. "I thought you were staying with Caroline."

"Susie and Marvella came down to be with her." She shrugged. "It gets to be too many women in one place, and she's holding up just fine now anyway. You might want to run on home, Burke, make sure those boys of yours aren't tearing up the house."

He ignored the suggestion and the anger in Josie's eyes. "You and Tucker played cards."

"That's not a crime or a sin in this county, is it?" She took Tucker's cigarette from between his fingers and drew on it. "We sat up till two, maybe two-thirty. Tucker got a little bit drunk and I won thirty-eight dollars."

A wave of relief thickened Burke voice. "That's good. I'm sorry I had to ask, but when the federal boys get in, you'll have to talk to them, too. Thought it'd be easier from me the first time."

"It wasn't." Tucker got to his feet again. "What are they going to do with her?"

"Took her down to Palmer's Funeral Parlor. Hold her there, over-night anyway, till the FBI gets here." He stuffed the notebook back in his pocket, shuffled his feet. "Steer clear of Austin, long as you can."

With a sour grin Tucker rubbed an absent hand on his bruised ribs. "You don't have to worry about that."

Awkward, miserable, Burke stared off at a trio of rhododendrons. "I'll be going, then. It might look better if you came on in tomorrow, talked to the feds right off."

"Right." Tucker let out a long breath as Burke walked away. "Hey." When Burke turned around, he offered a half smile. "I still got that beer, if you want."

The tension seeped out of Burke's shoulders. "I appreciate it, but I best go see to my kids. Thanks."

"I'm a sick person, Tucker," Josie said with a sigh. "I'm as pissed off at that man as I can be, and I'd still like to get in his pants."

With a half laugh Tucker laid his cheek on her head. "That's just re-flex, honey. The Longstreet reflex." With an arm draped around her waist, he began to lead her toward the house. "Jose, not that I'm in any position to question your veracity, but we haven't played gin in weeks."

"That so?" She tucked her tongue in her cheek. "Well now, the days just seem to blur together, don't they?" She pulled back to study him. "Seems better that way. Simpler."

"Maybe." Cautious, he took her face in his hands. He had a way of looking into a person when he had to—and he needed to see into Josie now. "You don't think I killed her."

"Sweetie pie, I've lived with you most of my life, and I know you just about choke with guilt if you have to squash a beetle. You've got too much heart, even when your temper's up." She kissed both his cheeks. "I know you didn't kill anybody. And if it makes it all go away quicker, what's the harm in saying we were at cards that night? We were at cards some night or other anyway."

He hesitated. It didn't seem quite right. Then he shrugged. Right or wrong, it was easier than the truth, which was that he'd fallen asleep while reading Keats.

What the hell would the boys down at the Chat 'N Chew say if they found out he read poetry on purpose?

And who'd believe him?

Chapter 5

LIKE FIRE THROUGH DRY brush, news of Edda Lou Hatinger's murder had spread like dust from the bayous to the levees, from town square to farm, all the way from Market Street down to Hog Maw Road, where Happy Fuller discussed the event with her dear friend and bingo partner, Birdie Shays.

"Henry wouldn't talk about it," Birdie said as she cooled her face with a Church of Redemption paper fan. "Burke Truesdale called him on down to the McNair place 'bout two o'clock, and he didn't get back till five." The fierce-eyed Jesus painted on the fan blurred as she waved it. "He came home all pale and sweaty, told me Edda Lou Hatinger was dead and to cancel all the appointments this evening. Said she was murdered just like Arnette and Francie, and wouldn't say another word."

"Lord love us." Happy looked out over her trim backyard, satisfied with the backwash of Birdie's fan. "What's the world coming to? A woman's not safe walking the streets."

"I passed by the diner before I came out." Birdie gave a knowing nod. Her lacquered hair, which Earleen Renfrew colored every six weeks with Bombshell Beige, sat still and stiff as a helmet with its two rigid curls like question marks on either side of her forehead. "Heard that Burke's called for the FBI, and maybe the National Guard."

"Hmph." Happy made a sound between a snort and a grunt. She

was fond of Birdie, mighty fond, but that didn't stop her from seeing faults. Birdie had a tendency to be gullible, which in Happy's opinion fell just behind laziness on the top ten list of sins. "We've got us a homicidal maniac, not a riot, Birdie. I don't think we're going to see soldiers marching down Market Street. Now, the FBI maybe, and I expect they'll call my boy in to talk since he found poor Arnette back in February."

Her handsome face set into thoughtful lines. She'd yet to forgive Bobby Lee fully for hooking school—and damn near flunking out again—but it was hard to resist the prestige of being the mama of the one who'd found the first body.

"Bobby Lee's carried that sadness with him ever since," Birdie put in. "Why, you can see it in his eyes. Just this morning when he filled up my tank down to Sonny's, I thought to myself, that Bobby Lee, he's never going to be the same."

"Had nightmares for weeks," Happy said with only the faintest trace of pride.

"Only natural. I know Henry's heart's about broke. And I'll tell you, Happy, it's worrisome. Why, it could've been my own sweet Carolanne—not that she'd be wandering around somewhere alone when she's got a husband and two children to tend to. But it makes you worry. And there's your own Darleen, and her being best friends with Edda. I tell you, I can barely stand to think on it."

"I expect I'll have to call Darleen, see how she's bearing up." Happy let out a sigh. It had been a great relief to her when Darleen had married Junior Talbot and settled down in town with her husband and brand new baby. But she knew Darleen's wild ways were flaring again. "We're going to have to get some of the ladies together, Birdie, and go pay our respects to Mavis Hatinger."

Birdie started to make an excuse, but the paper Jesus glared at her. "It's the Christian thing to do. Do you think Austin'll be there?"

"Don't you worry about Austin." Happy set her chin. "We'll have the power of motherhood on our side."

That night, doors were locked in Innocence, guns were loaded, and sleep came hard.

◆ ◆ ◆ ◆

COME MORNING, EDDA LOU was the first thought on many minds.

For Darleen Fuller Talbot, Happy's third child and first great disappointment, grief was mixed with lethargy. Throughout her teenage years, Darleen had trailed along behind Edda Lou, thrilled by the risks they took together. Hitching clear to Greenville, swiping cosmetics from the counter at Larsson's, hooking school with the Bonny boys to have sex down at Spook Hollow.

They'd worried together if their periods were late, talked frankly about their own sexual encounters, and double-dated at the Sky View Drive-In Theater more times than she could count. Edda Lou had been her maid of honor when Darleen had married Junior, and Darleen was to have returned the favor when Edda Lou finally snagged Tucker Longstreet.

Now she was dead, and Darleen's eyes were puffy from weeping. She barely had the energy to settle little Scooter in his playpen, wave her husband out the front door, and shuffle into the kitchen to let her lover, Billy T. Bonny, in through the back.

"Oh, now, darlin'." Billy T., already sweaty in his athletic T-shirt and torn jeans, took the red-eyed Darleen into his tattooed arms. "You shouldn't go on like this, sugar plum. I just hate to see you cry."

"I can't believe she's gone." Darleen sniffed against his shoulder and comforted herself by squeezing his butt. "She was my dearest, closest friend, Billy T."

"I know." He moved his full, ready mouth down to hers, sliding his tongue in and around in sympathy. "She was a great girl, and we're all going to miss her."

"She was like my sister." Darleen drew back so he could slip his hands under her nylon nightie and find her breasts. "More a sister than Belle or Starita ever were."

"They're just jealous 'cause you're the prettiest." He pinched her hardened nipples while he backed her up against the counter.

"I'd rather it'd been one of them instead of Edda Lou." Tears sparkling in her eyes, she unzipped his jeans. "I don't care if they are my blood kin, I could always talk to Edda Lou, you know. Just talk about anything. Even us." She sighed as he pulled her nightie down far enough to nip at her breasts. "She was always happy for me. She was a little jealous when I married Junior and had Scooter, but that was only natural, don't you think?"

"Mmmm."

"I was going to be her maid of honor when she married Tucker Longstreet." She tugged his jockeys down. "I can't hardly stand to think about how she was killed."

"Don't think about it, honey." His breath was coming quick and hard. "Let Billy T. help you forget all about it." He brought his hands down to push her thighs apart. "Edda Lou would've wanted it that way."

"Yeah." She sighed and snuggled against his hand. With a shiver she shoved a bowl of Cheerios aside to brace herself on the counter. "She'll al-ways have a place in my heart." When she wrapped her fingers around him, she opened her eyes, love shining. He was already wearing a condom. "You're just so good to me, honey." She guided him in and he began to grind. "So much more fun than Junior. Why, since we got married, we don't do it anywhere but in bed."

Highly flattered, Billy T. hitched up her hips, rapping her head against an open cupboard door. Since she was already coming, Darleen didn't notice.

◆ ◆ ◆ ◆

CAROLINE WAS SURPRISED SHE'D slept so well. Maybe it was her mind's way of escaping, or the security of having Susie Truesdale and her daughter tucked into the next bedroom. Or maybe it was just that she felt safe in her grandparents' bed. Whatever it was, she awakened to sun-light and the smell of coffee and bacon.

Her first reaction was embarrassment, that she should have slept while her guests fixed breakfast. That reaction struck her as so feeble after the horror of the day before, she was tempted to roll over and will herself back to sleep.

Instead, she took a long cool shower and dressed.

By the time she came downstairs, Susie and Marvella were already seated at the table, talking in hushed tones over coffee and scrambled eggs.

There was enough resemblance between mother and daughter to make Caroline want to smile. Two pretty women with mink-colored hair and big blue eyes, they whispered together like children in the back pew of a church service. They both had bow-shaped mouths like kewpie dolls, that curved into sympathetic smiles when they spotted her.

There was a closeness between them, a simple understanding and re-spect that Caroline had never enjoyed with her own mother. Seeing it, feeling it, she felt herself struck by a hard, unexpected wave of envy.

"We hoped you'd sleep awhile longer." Susie was already up pouring another cup of coffee.

"I feel like I slept a week. Thanks." She took the cup Susie offered. "It was so kind of you to stay, I—"

"That's what neighbors are for. Marvella, fix Caroline a plate."

"Oh, really, I—"

"You have to eat." Susie nudged her into a chair. "When you've had a shock like that, you need fuel."

"Mom makes great eggs," Marvella offered. She tried not to stare at Caroline as she served. She wanted to ask her where she'd gotten her hair cut—though Bobby Lee would just about shit bricks if she had her own shoulder-length curls whacked like that. "You always feel better if you eat. Last time I broke up with Bobby Lee, Mom and I had great chocolate sundaes."

"It's hard to feel blue when you're full of chocolate." Susie smiled and served up a plate of toast. "I got some of your grandma's wild raspberry jam out of the cupboard. Hope you don't mind."

"No." Fascinated, Caroline picked up the hand-labeled jelly jar. "I didn't realize this was around."

"Oh, my, Miss Edith put by every year. Nobody had a hand like hers for jams and jellies. She won the blue ribbon at the fair the last six years running." Bending, Susie opened a bottom cupboard and gestured toward the lines of jars. "You've got a good year's supply here."

"I didn't know." All those pretty colorful jars, so carefully labeled, so lovingly aligned. The sense of loss and shame closed her throat. "I wasn't able to see her often."

"She was so proud of you. Used to talk about her little Caro traveling all around the world, and how you played music for royalty and presidents and all. Showed around the postcards you sent her."

"There was one of Paris, France," Marvella put in. "With the Eiffel Tower off in the back. Miss Edith let me use it for a report."

"Marvella took two years of French." Susie sent her daughter a pleased look. She herself had had to quit school four months before graduation, when she'd begun to show. It never failed to delight her that her daughter already held a high school diploma. She glanced at her watch. "Honey, hadn't you better get on to work?"

"Oh, lordy." Marvella popped out of her seat. "Look at the time."

"Marvella works up in Rosedale as a legal secretary. They said she could come in late today, considering." She glanced over as Marvella freshened her lipstick in the reflection of the toaster. "You go on and take my car, honey. I'll call your daddy to come get me." Rising, she rested her hands on Marvella's shoulders. "You don't stop for anybody, even if you know them."

"I'm not stupid."

Susie pinched her chin. "No, but you're my only girl. I want you to call me if you're going to be later than five-thirty."

"I will."

"And you tell that Bobby Lee there's to be no more parking down on Dog Street Road. If the two of you have to get romantic, you'll do it down in the family room."

"Mom . . ." A slow flush worked its way up her throat to her cheeks.

"You tell him, or I will." She kissed Marvella's pouty lips. "Now, get."

"Yes'm." She smiled at Caroline. "Don't let her bully you, Miss Waverly. Once she starts, she never stops."

"Sassy." Susie chuckled after the front screen door slammed. "Hard to believe she's grown up on me."

"She's a lovely girl."

"Yes, she is that. Hardheaded and sure of what she wants, though. She's wanted Bobby Lee Fuller for the best part of two years, so I guess she'll get him all right." She gave a wistful smile before she picked up her cooling coffee. "Once I set my sights on Burke, he didn't have a prayer. She's the same. Only you worry, because they always seem so much younger than you were at the same age." She frowned at Caroline's plate. "You didn't eat much."

"I'm sorry." With effort, Caroline took another bite. "It all seems so strange—I didn't even know that girl, but it's dreadful just thinking about her." Resigned, she pushed her plate aside. "Susie, I didn't want to ask too many questions with Marvella here, but do I understand this right? This girl was the third murdered?"

"Since February," Susie said with a nod. "They were all three stabbed."

"God."

"Burke won't say much, but I know it's bad, really bad. Some kind of mutilation." She rose to clear the table. "As a mother—as a woman—it scares me. And I worry about Burke, too. He's taking this all on himself, like it was his fault somehow. God knows nobody around here was prepared for this kind of thing, but Burke thinks he should have been able to stop it."

The way, Susie remembered, he'd thought he should have been able to stop his father from putting a noose around his neck.

Caroline filled the sink with soapy water. "No suspects?"

"If so, he's not saying. With Arnette, it seemed like it had to've been a drifter. I mean, when you've got eight or nine hundred people in a town, you get so you know damn near everybody. It just didn't seem possible it could have been one of us. Then when Francie was killed the same way, people began to look around a little. And still, when it came right down to it, none of us wanted to believe it could have been a neighbor, or a friend. But now . . ."

"Now you have to look among your own."

"We do." She picked up a tea towel as Caroline began to wash the breakfast dishes. "Though I think it's more likely we've got some psycho living in the swamp, hiding in there."

Caroline looked out the window toward the trees. Trees that seemed so much closer to the house than before. "Well, that's a comfort."

"I don't mean to scare you, but if you're living out here alone, you need to be careful."

Caroline pressed her lips together. "I heard that Tucker Longstreet and Edda Lou had a fight. That she was pressuring him into marriage."

"Trying to, more like." Susie polished a plate clean, then laughed. "Lordy, you don't know Tucker, or else you wouldn't have that look on your face. The idea of him killing someone, well, it's just laughable. First place, it would take too much effort and emotion. Tucker tends to be lacking in both departments."

Caroline remembered the look on his face when she'd come across him by the pond. There'd been plenty of emotion then. The dangerous kind. "Still . . ."

"I guess Burke'll have to talk to him," Susie said. "And that'll be hard. They're as close as brothers. We all went to school together," she continued as she dried and stacked dishes. "Tucker and Dwayne—that's Tucker's brother—Burke and me. They were all planters' sons, though by that time the Truesdale place was already failing, so private school was out of the question for Burke. Dwayne went off to boarding school for a while, him being the first son and all, but he couldn't keep out of trouble so the school shipped him on home. There'd been talk of sending Tucker off, too, but then old Beau was so pissed about Dwayne, he kept Tuck home." She smiled as she examined a glass for spots. "Tuck always said he owed Dwayne big for that one. I guess that's why he tries to look after him now. He's a good man. And if you'd known Tuck as long as I have, you'd know he could no more work up the gumption to kill a person than he could fly. Not that he doesn't have his faults, God knows, but to take a knife to a woman?" The idea made her laugh despite the horror of it. "Truth be known, he'd be too busy trying to get under her skirts to think about anything else."

Caroline's mouth went grim. "I know the type."

"Believe me, honey, you've never known anyone like Tuck. If I wasn't a happily married woman with four kids, I might have taken after him myself. He's got a way about him, Tuck does." She slanted Caroline a look. "Odds are he'll come sniffing your way before too long."

"Then he'll end up with a foot in his nose."

Susie let out a peal of laughter. "I hope I'm around to see it. Now then." She set the last plate aside. "You and me have work to do."

"Work?"

"I won't feel right leaving you here until I know you're protected."

After drying her hands on the flowered tea towel, she walked over to pick up her purse. Out of the straw bag, she pulled a deadly-looking .38.

"Jesus Christ" was all Caroline could think of to say.

"This is a double-action Smith and Wesson. I like the feel of a revolver rather than an automatic."

"Is that—is it loaded?"

"Why, sure it is, honey." She blinked her big blue eyes. "Hell of a lot of good it would do me empty. I won the Fourth of July target shoot three years straight. Burke can't decide whether to be proud or embarrassed that I can outshoot him."

"In your purse," Caroline said weakly. "You carry it in your purse."

"Since February I have. Have you ever fired a gun?"

"No." Instinctively, Caroline linked her hands behind her back. "No," she repeated.

"And you think you can't," Susie said briskly. "Well, let me tell you, honey, if someone was coming after you or yours, you'd fire quick enough. Now, I know your granddaddy had a collection. Let's go pick one out."

Susie set her .38 on the kitchen table and started out.

"Susie." Baffled, Caroline hurried after her. "I can't pick out a gun the way I would a new dress."

"It's just as interesting." Susie strolled into the den, and tapping a finger against her lips, studied her choices. "We're going to start with a handgun, but I want you to practice loading that shotgun. It makes a statement."

"I bet."

Her eyes bright, she curled a hand around Caroline's arm. "Listen here, if someone comes along and bothers you, you step outside with this dove duster on your shoulder, point it mid-body, and you tell the sonofabitch you don't know diddly about shooting. If he doesn't hightail it fast, he deserves a load of buckshot."

With a half laugh Caroline sat on the arm of the easy chair. "You're serious about this."

"Down here we take care of ourselves. Now, this here's an old beauty." Susie opened the case and took out a handgun. "Colt forty-five, army issue. Bet he used this in the war." She broke open the gun with a finesse Caroline had to admire, and spun the empty chamber. "Clean as a whistle, too." After snapping the barrel back into place, she pointed it at the wall and pressed the trigger. "Good." Pulling open the drawer, she gave a satisfied cluck of her tongue as she saw the ammo. She tucked a box in her back pocket, then grinned at Caroline.

"Let's go kill some cans."

◆ ◆ ◆ ◆

SPECIAL AGENT MATTHEW BURNS wasn't doing cartwheels at the prospect of working in a dusty little delta town. Burns was an urbanite born and bred, one who enjoyed an evening at the opera, a fine Châteauneuf, and a quiet afternoon strolling through the National Gallery.

He'd seen a good deal of ugliness in his ten years with the Bureau, and preferred to cleanse his emotional pallet with a taste of Mozart or Bach. He'd been looking forward to the end of the week, which would have included tickets to the ballet, a civilized dinner at Jean-Louis at the Watergate, and perhaps a tasteful and romantic interlude with his current companion.

Instead, he found himself driving into Innocence with his field kit and garment bag tucked into the trunk of a rental car that had a faulty air-conditioning pump.

Burns knew the case would create a media hullabaloo, and he certainly never doubted he was the appropriate man for the job. He specialized in serial killers. And with all due modesty, he'd be the first one to admit he was damn good.

Still, it irked him that his weekend had been ruined. It upset his sense of order that the Bureau's pathologist assigned to the case had been delayed by thunderstorms in Atlanta. He didn't trust some backwater coroner to perform a decent autopsy.

His irritation grew as he drove through town in the nearly airless car. It was just as he'd suspected—a few sweaty pedestrians, a couple of loose dogs, a huddle of dusty storefronts. There wasn't even a movie theater. He gave a little shudder at the faded hand-printed letters that spelled out CHAT 'N CHEW on the only restaurant in sight. Thank God he'd packed his own Krups coffeemaker.

A job was a job, he reminded himself as he pulled up in front of the sheriff's office. There were times one had to suffer in the pursuit of justice. Taking only his briefcase, and trying not to strangle in the heat, he meticulously locked his car.

When Jed Larsson's dog, Nuisance, wandered up to lift his leg on the front tire, Burns merely shook his head. He didn't doubt he'd find the manners of the two-legged residents equally crude.

"Nice car," Claude Bonny said from his perch in front of the rooming house. And spat.

Burns lifted one dark brow. "It serves."

"You selling something, son?"

"No."

Bonny exchanged looks with Charlie O'Hara and Pete Koons. O'Hara wheezed out a couple of breaths and squinted. "You'd be that FBI man from up north, then."

"Yes." Burns felt sweat slide down his back and prayed the town ran to an adequate dry cleaner.

"I used to watch that show with Efrem Zimbalist on it every week." Koons took a pull on his lemonade. "Damn good show, that one."

"*Dragnet* was better," Bonny stated. "Can't understand why they took it off the air. Don't make shows like that no more."

"If you'll excuse me," Burns said.

"Go on in, son." Bonny waved him on. "Sheriff's inside. Been there all morning. You catch that psycho that's killing our girls, and we'll string 'em up for you."

"Really, I don't—"

"Didn't that guy from *Dragnet* go on over to be a doctor on the *M*A*S*H* show?" O'Hara wondered. "Seems I recollect that."

"Jack Webb never played no doctor," Bonny said, taking it as a personal affront.

"No, t'other one. Little guy. My missus near to bust a gut watching that show."

"Good Lord," Burns said under his breath, and pushed open the door of the sheriff's office.

Burke was at his desk, the phone cupped between his chin and shoulder while he busily scrawled on a legal pad. "Yes, sir, the minute he gets here. I . . ." He looked up and identified Burns as quickly as he'd have separated a quail from a pheasant. "Hold on. You Special Agent Burns?"

"That's right." Following procedure, Burns pulled out his I.D. and flashed it.

"He just walked in," Burke said into the phone, then held it out. "It's your boss."

Burns set his briefcase aside and took the receiver. "Chief Hadley? Yes, sir, my e.t.a. was a bit off. There was a problem with the car in Greenville. Yes, sir. Dr. Rubenstein should be here by three. I'll be sure to do that. Just off the top, I'd say we'll need another phone, this appears to be a single line. And . . ." He placed a hand over the mouthpiece. "Do you have a fax machine?"

Burke ran his tongue around his teeth. "No, sir, I don't."

"And a fax machine," Burns continued into the receiver. "I'll call in as soon as I've done the preliminary and settled in. Yes, sir." He handed the phone back to Burke and checked the seat of the swivel chair before sitting. "Now then, you'd be Sheriff . . ."

"Truesdale, Burke Truesdale." The handshake was brief and formal.

Burke caught a whiff of baby powder. "We've got a mess here, Agent Burns."

"So I'm informed. Three mutilations in four and a half months. No suspects."

"None." Burke barely caught himself before apologizing. "We figured a drifter, but with the last one . . . Then there's that one up in Nashville."

Burns steepled his hands. "You have files, I presume."

"Yeah." Burke started to rise.

"Not quite yet. You can fill me in orally as we go. I'll want to see the body."

"We have her down at the funeral parlor."

"Most appropriate," Burns said dryly. "We'll take a look, then go to the crime scene. You've secured it?"

Burke felt his temper heating. "Kinda hard to secure a swamp."

Burns let out a sigh as he rose. "I'll take your word for that."

♦ ♦ ♦

*I*N THE BACKYARD CAROLINE sucked in her breath, gritted her teeth, and pulled the trigger. The punch jumped up her arm and made her ears ring. She hit a can—though it wasn't the one she'd aimed at.

"Now you're getting somewhere." Susie told her. "But you got to keep your eyes all the way open." She demonstrated, plowing three cans off the log in rapid succession.

"Couldn't I just throw rocks at them?" Caroline yelled when Susie went to reset the cans.

"Did you play a symphony the first time you picked up your fiddle?"

Caroline sighed and rotated her shoulder. "Is this how you intimidate your kids into doing what you want?"

"Damn right." Susie came back to her side. "Now relax, take your time. How's the gun feel in your hand?"

"Actually, it feels . . ." She laughed a little and glanced down at it.

"Sexy, right?" She patted Caroline's back. "It's okay. You're among friends. Thing is, you got the power right here, and the control, and the responsibility. Same as having sex." She grinned. "That's not what I tell my kids. Go ahead now, you sight in on that first can on the left. Make a picture on it. Have an ex-husband?"

"No, thanks."

Susie hooted. "Old boyfriend? One who really pissed you off."

"Luis," Caroline hissed between her teeth.

"Whew, was he Spanish or something?"

"Or something." Her teeth were clenching. "He was a big, sleek

Mexican rat." Caroline pulled the trigger. Her mouth fell open when the can jumped. "I hit it."

"Just needed incentive. Try the next."

"Couldn't you ladies take up needlepoint?" Burke called.

Susie lowered her revolver and smiled. "You're going to have more competition next Fourth of July, darlin'." She skimmed her gaze over Burns before rising on tiptoe to kiss her husband. "You look tired."

"I am tired." He squeezed her hand. "Agent Burns, this is my wife, Susie, and Caroline Waverly. Miss Waverly found the body yesterday."

"Caroline Wavery." Burns said the name reverently. "I can't believe it." Taking her free hand, he brought it to his lips while Susie rolled her eyes at Burke behind the FBI man's back. "I heard you play just a few months ago in New York. And last year at the Kennedy Center. I have several of your recordings."

For a moment Caroline only blinked at him. All that seemed so far away, she almost thought he'd mistaken her for someone else.

"Thank you."

"Oh, no, thank *you*." He was thinking the case might have benefits after all. "I can't tell you how many times you've saved my sanity just by letting me hear you play." His smooth cheeks were flushed with excitement, and his hand continued to grip hers. "This is, well, delightful, despite the circumstances. I must say, it's the last place I'd expect to find the princess of the concert halls."

A little ball of discomfort wedged in her stomach. "This was my grandmother's home, Agent Burns. I've been here for only a few days."

His pale blue eyes clouded with concern. "This must be terribly distressing for you. Be assured I'll do everything in my power to resolve the matter quickly."

Caroline made certain to avoid Susie's eyes and managed a small smile. "That's a comfort to me."

"Anything, anything I can do. Anything at all." He picked up the field kit he'd set at his feet. "I'll take a look at the scene now, Sheriff."

Burke gestured, and after glancing at Burns's shiny Italian loafers, winked at his wife.

"Kinda cute," Susie decided as they walked toward the trees. "If you go for the suit-and-tie type."

"Fortunately, I don't go for any type right now."

"Never know." Susie flapped the bodice of her blouse to stir some air. "Why don't I show you how to clean your gun, then we'll make something cold for the boys." She gave Caroline a curious look. "I didn't know you were really famous and all. I thought it was just Miss Edith bragging."

"Fame all depends on the ground you're standing on, doesn't it?"

"I guess it does." Susie turned toward the house. Because she'd developed a fondness for Caroline, and because it seemed to her Caroline needed a smile just then, Susie swung an arm over her shoulders. "Can you play 'Orange Blossom Special'?"

Caroline had her first real laugh in days. "I don't know why not."

Chapter 6

TUCKER PROPPED HIS FEET on Burke's desk and crossed his ankles. He didn't mind waiting—in fact, waiting was one of the things he did best. What was often interpreted as a bone-deep laziness, even by Tucker himself, was an innate and boundless patience and a clear, untroubled mind.

At the moment his mind wasn't as unfettered as he liked. And the truth was, he hadn't slept well the night before. A little catnap while he waited for Burke to come along seemed like a sensible way to pass the time.

It hadn't taken long for news of the FBI blowing into town to get down to Sweetwater. Tucker already knew that Special Agent Burns dressed like a mortician and drove a tan Mercury. Just as he knew that Burns was down at McNair Pond doing whatever FBI types did at murder scenes.

Murder. With a little grunt Tucker closed his eyes—the better to relax. Sitting there, listening to the creak of the ceiling fan and the whine of the useless window air conditioner, it didn't seem possible that Edda Lou Hatinger was stretched out on a slab a few blocks away at Palmer's Funeral Parlor.

He winced, trying to get beyond the discomfort, the plain creepiness of remembering how ready he'd been to go head to head with her. Worse, he'd been looking forward to the battle, to hearing her wail when she finally got it through her conniving brain that she wasn't going to be the new mistress of Sweetwater.

He wouldn't have to set her straight now. Or salvage some of his pride by hacking at hers.

Now, because he'd made the mistake of finding something sexy about the way she punched keys on the cash register at Larsson's, because he'd indulged himself by sharing her bed and nibbling on that soft skin, he was going to have to make up an alibi to keep himself from being a suspect in her murder.

He'd been accused of many things. Of laziness, which was no sin in Tucker's book. Of carelessness with money, which he readily admitted. Of adultery, which he took objection to. He'd never slept with a married woman—except for Sally Guilford a few years back, and she'd been legally separated. Even of cowardice, which Tucker preferred to think of as discretion.

But murder. Why, it would be laughable if it wasn't so scary. If his father had been alive, he'd have busted a gut laughing. He—the only man Tucker had truly feared—hadn't been able to bully or embarrass his son into shooting anything but thin air on any of their enforced hunting trips.

Of course, Edda Lou hadn't been shot. Not if she'd been killed like the others. Because it was all too easy to slide her face over his image of Francie's, to see what had been done to her smooth, white skin. He fumbled in his pocket for a cigarette.

He pinched off part of the tip—he was up to nearly a quarter of an inch now—and was just lighting it when Burke walked in with a sweaty, annoyed-looking man in a dark suit.

Spending the best part of the day with the FBI hadn't put Burke in the best of moods. He scowled at Tucker's feet as he tossed his hat toward the pole by the door.

"Make yourself at home, son."

"Doing my best." Tucker blew out a stream of smoke. His stomach was jumping, but he sent Burke a lazy smile. "You ought to get yourself some new magazines, Burke. A man needs more to entertain his mind than *Field and Stream* and *Guns and Ammo*."

"I'll see if we can find some issues of *Gentleman's Quarterly* and *People*."

"I'd be obliged." Tucker took another drag while he scanned Burke's companion. The dark suit had wilted in the heat, but the man didn't have the sense to loosen his tie. Though he couldn't have said why, that simple fact had Tucker taking an instant dislike to Burns. "I thought it'd be a good idea for me to come on in and talk to you boys."

Burke nodded, and wanting to take authority, walked behind his desk. "Tucker Longstreet, Special Agent Burns."

"Welcome to Innocence." Tucker didn't get up, but offered a hand. It pleased him that Burns's was soft, and a little clammy from the humidity. "What makes you special, Agent Burns?"

"It's my rank." Burns took a measure of Tucker's scuffed sneakers, his casually expensive cotton slacks, and cocky grin. The dislike was mutual. "What did you want to discuss, Mr. Longstreet?"

"Well now, we could start with the weather." Tucker ignored Burke's warning look. "Looks like we've got a storm rolling in. Might cool things off for a spell. Or we could talk baseball. Orioles're playing the Yankees tonight. Birds got themselves a tight pitching staff this year. Might just pull it off." Tucker sucked in smoke. "You a betting man, Special Agent?"

"I'm afraid I don't take an avid interest in sports."

"Well, that's okay." There was a yawn in Tucker's voice as he angled the chair back. "I don't take an avid interest in much of anything. Avid takes too much effort."

"Let's get to the point, Tuck." Since the look hadn't worked, Burke tried his quiet, cut-the-bullshit tone. "Tucker knew the victim, Edda Lou . . ."

"The word you're scratching for is *intimately*," Tucker provided. His stomach muscles clenched up on him again, so he shifted to crush out the cigarette.

Burns settled in the third chair. In his fussily efficient way, he took a mini recorder and a pad from his pocket. "You wanted to make a statement."

"Like 'The only thing we have to fear is fear itself'?" Tucker stretched his back. "Not particularly. Burke here thought you might want to ask me some questions. And being the cooperative sort, I'm here to answer them."

Unruffled, Burns switched on the recorder. "I'm informed that you and the deceased had a relationship."

"What we had was sex."

"Come on, Tuck."

He shot Burke a look. "That's as honest as it gets, son. Edda Lou and I went out a few times, had some laughs, and tangled some sheets." His eyes hardened, and he had to stop himself from reaching for another cigarette. "Couple weeks back I cut things off because she started talking marriage."

"You ended the affair amicably?" Burns asked.

"I wouldn't say that. I figure you already know about the scene in the diner a few days ago. It's safe to say Edda Lou was pissed."

"Your term, Mr. Longstreet. I have it here"—he tapped his pencil on his pad—"that she was angry and agitated."

"You put those two words together with Edda Lou, and what you get is pissed."

"She claimed you'd made her promises."

Lazily, Tucker lowered his legs. The chair squeaked as he rocked it. "That's the thing about me, Agent Burns, I don't make them, 'cause it's unlikely I'll keep them."

"And she announced publicly that she was pregnant."

"Yeah. She did that."

"After which, you left the . . . Chat 'N Chew, is it? You left abruptly." He smiled thinly. "Would it be safe to say, Mr. Longstreet, that you were . . . pissed?"

"Having her come down on me in the diner, tell me—for the first time, in front of maybe a dozen people—that she was pregnant, and threatening to make me pay for it? Yeah." He gave a slow, considering nod. "It'd be safe to say."

"And you had no intention of marrying her."

"Not a one."

"And being infuriated, embarrassed, and trapped, you had a motive for killing her."

Tucker ran his tongue over his teeth. "Not as long as I've got a checkbook." He leaned forward. Though his face was hard, his voice flowed easily, like honey over corn bread. "Let me give you a clear picture of this, friend. Edda Lou was greedy, she was ambitious, and she was smart. Now, maybe there was a part of her figured she could intimidate me into a double-ring ceremony, but she'd have settled happily enough for a check with enough zeroes on it."

He rose, then forced himself to take a breath and sit on the corner of the desk. "I liked her. Maybe not as much as I once did, but well enough. You don't sleep with a woman one week and slice her up the next."

"It's been done."

Something dark came alive in Tucker's eyes. "Not by me."

Burns shifted the recorder an inch to the right. "You were also acquainted with Arnette Gantrey and Frances Alice Logan."

"Me and most everybody else in Innocence."

"Did you also have relationships with them?"

"Dated them some. Didn't sleep with either." His lips curved a little in memory. "Though with Arnette, it wasn't for lack of trying."

"She rejected you?"

"Hell." In disgust, Tucker pulled out another cigarette. It seemed he'd picked a lousy time to try to quit smoking. "We were friends, and she didn't want to wrestle. Truth is, she'd always had her eye on my brother, Dwayne, but he never picked up the ball. Francie and I were just at the flirt-and-giggle stage." He tossed a bit of paper and tobacco aside. "She was a sweetheart." He shut his eyes. "I don't want to talk about Francie."

"Oh?"

Fury bubbled up. "Look, I was with Burke when he found her. Maybe you're used to seeing that kind of thing, but I'm not. Especially when it's someone I had a fondness for."

"Interesting that you were fond of all three women," Burns said mildly. "And Mrs. Logan was found in Spook Hollow?" He gave a quick snort at the term. "That's just a couple of miles from your home. And Miss Hatinger was found in McNair Pond. Less than a mile from your home. You visited that spot the day you argued with Miss Hatinger."

"That's right. And plenty of other times."

"According to Miss Waverly, you seemed tense, upset, when she came across you."

"I thought we'd settled on pissed. Yeah, I was. That's why I stopped off there. It's a peaceful spot."

"And a secluded one. Can you tell me what you did with the rest of your evening, Mr. Longstreet?"

It wasn't going to be the truth. "I played gin with Josie, my sister," Tucker lied without a blink. "Being as I was distracted, she took me for about thirty or forty dollars, then we had a drink and went on up to bed."

"What time did you leave your sister?"

"I went up about two, two-thirty maybe."

"Agent Burns," Burke broke in, "I'd like to say that on the afternoon Edda Lou was found, Tuck came in to see me. He was worried because he hadn't heard from her, and she wasn't answering the phone."

Burns lifted a brow. "So noted, Sheriff. How did you come by your black eye, Mr. Longstreet?"

"Edda Lou's father gave it to me. That's how I came to realize she was missing. He rode up to the house, figuring I was hiding her. Then he got it into his head I'd talked her into going somewhere for an abortion."

"Did you discuss abortion with the deceased?"

"She was deceased before I had a chance to discuss anything with her." He pushed himself off the desk. "That's all I've got to say. If you have any more questions, you ride on down to Sweetwater and ask. I'll see you around, Burke."

Burke waited until the door slammed. "Agent Burns, I've known Tucker all my life. I can tell you that no matter how het up he was about Edda Lou, he couldn't have killed her."

Burns merely switched off his recorder. "Isn't it fortunate that I have an objective eye? I believe it's time we checked at the funeral parlor, Sheriff. The pathologist is due."

♦ ♦ ♦ ♦

*T*UCKER'D JUST ABOUT HAD IT. He'd done nothing but mind his own business, live his own life, and what did he have to show for it? Sore ribs, a swollen eye, and the novelty of being a murder suspect.

He shot out of Innocence and cranked the car up to eighty.

The way he figured it, it all had to do with women. If it hadn't been for the way Edda Lou had rubbed up against him every blessed time he'd walked into Larsson's, he wouldn't have started dating her. If Della hadn't nagged him, he wouldn't have been in town for Edda Lou to harp on. If that Waverly woman hadn't wandered into the bayou, she wouldn't have seen him sitting by the pond. Looking "tense and upset."

Jesus H. Christ, he'd had a right to look that way.

He was sick about Edda Lou, gut-churning sick. No matter how sneaky she'd been, she didn't deserve to be dead. But dammit, he didn't see why he had to suffer for it. Having to sit there and take it while that stiff-necked Yankee bastard prodded him with questions and gave him those cop looks.

Worse than cop looks, he thought as he swung around a curve. It had been those superior, big-city honcho-to-addled-good-old-boy sneers that burned his ass.

Caroline Waverly had looked at him the same way. She'd probably done handsprings on her way to tell the FBI about coming across the dirty Reb plotting murder in the swamp.

A yard past the McNair lane, Tucker slammed on the brakes. His tires screamed on the pavement as he whipped into a U-turn. Maybe he'd just go have himself a talk with the duchess.

As he sent gravel spitting, he didn't notice the pickup lumbering down the road. Austin's blackened eyes narrowed as he spotted the red flash disappearing into the brush. His lips spread in a smile as he pulled over to the side.

He turned off the ignition, pocketed the keys before reaching for the shoe black. Studying himself in the rearview mirror, he sliced black lines under his eyes, adjusted his camouflage hat. From the rack in the window he chose his weapon, opting for the Remington Woodsmaster, and checked the load. He was still smiling as he stepped out of the truck, wearing full camouflage, with keen-edged hunting knife tucked in his ammo belt.

He was going hunting. For the glory of the Lord.

✦ ✦ ✦ ✦

CAROLINE DIDN'T MIND BEING alone. Though she'd enjoyed Susie's company, the woman's energy pitch had all but exhausted her. Nor did she believe that anyone was going to break into the house and kill her in her sleep. She was a stranger, after all, and no one knew her well enough to wish her harm. Now that the pistol was tucked away, she had no intention of touching it again.

To please herself, she picked up her violin. She'd barely had time to do more than tune it since arriving. Her hands passed over the smooth, polished wood, brushed over the strings. This wasn't practice, she thought as she rosined the bow. It wasn't performance. It was the urge she was often too pressured to remember, to make music for herself.

With her eyes closed, she laid the violin on her shoulder, her head and body shifting automatically into position, as a woman's does to welcome a lover.

She chose Chopin for the beauty, for the peace, and for the hint of a sadness she couldn't quite dispel. As always, the music filled all the voids.

She didn't think of death now, or of fear. She didn't think of Luis and betrayal, of the family she'd lost or done without. She didn't think of the music, but only felt it.

It sounded like tears. That's what Tucker thought as he walked from his car to the porch. Not hot, passionate tears, but slow ones, aching ones. The kind that bled out of the soul.

Though no one could hear them, his thoughts embarrassed him. It was just violin music, the long-haired kind that didn't even make you want to tap your toe. But it sounded so heartbreaking, drifting out of the open windows. He would have sworn he felt it, actually felt the notes shiver over his skin.

He knocked, but so softly be barely heard the rapping himself. Then he reached down, opened the screen, and stepped inside. He moved quietly, following those haunting notes into the front parlor.

She was standing in the center of the room, facing the windows so that he could see her profile, her head tilted slightly toward the instrument. Her eyes were closed, and the smile that curved her lips was as wistful and lovely as the music.

Though he couldn't have said how he knew it, that particular melding of notes came straight from her heart. Like a whispered question, they hung on the air.

He slipped his hands into his pockets, leaned a shoulder against the jamb, and let himself drift along with her. It was odd, and certainly foreign to him, that he could find a woman so restful, so quietly appealing, so deeply arousing, when it had nothing whatsoever to do with sex.

When she stopped, the music fading off into silence, he felt a disappointment so keen it was almost physical. If he'd been wise, he would have slipped out again while her eyes were still dreamy, and knocked. Instead, he went with instinct and clapped.

She jolted, her body snapping into tension, her eyes filling with fear, then sharpening with simple annoyance.

"What the hell are you doing in here?"

"I knocked." He gave her the same little shrug and grin he'd offered by the pond. "Guess you were too involved to hear me."

She lowered the violin but held the bow up, somewhat like a fencer with a blade. "Or it's possible I didn't want to be disturbed."

"Can't say I thought of it. I liked the music. I'm more into R and B myself, a little jazz, but that was something. No wonder you do it for a living."

She kept her eyes on his as she set the violin aside. "What a fascinating compliment."

"Just an honest observation. You reminded me of a knickknack my mama had. It was a pearl caught in a big chunk of amber. It was the prettiest thing, but sad, too. The pearl was all alone in there and could never get out. You looked like that when you were playing. Do you always play sad songs?"

"I play what I like." His bruises had blossomed over the last day. They gave his face a rakish, dangerous look, with just enough of the little boy to make a woman want to press something cool—her lips perhaps—on the swelling. "Do you have a reason for walking into my house uninvited, Mr. Longstreet?"

"You might as well make it Tucker. I'm going to call you Caroline. Or Caro." His teeth flashed. "That's what Miss Edith called you. I like it."

"That doesn't answer my question."

He eased away from the jamb. "We tend to drop by on neighbors around here, but as it happens, I did have a purpose. You going to ask me to sit down?"

She tilted her head. "No."

"Damn. The nastier you are, the more I like you. I'm perverse that way."

"And other ways?"

He chuckled and sat on the arm of the sofa. "We'll have to get to know each other better first. You might hear I'm easy, Caroline, but the thing is, I've got my standards."

"What a relief." She tapped the bow against her open palm. "As to your purpose?"

He cocked a foot on his knee, as thoroughly at home as a hound in a patch of green shade. "Lord, I like the way you talk. As fine and cool as a bowl of peach ice cream. I'm real partial to peach ice cream."

When her lips threatened to quirk, she turned them down in defense. "I'm not terribly interested in your partialities at the moment, nor am I in the mood to entertain company. I've had a difficult couple of days."

The easy humor vanished. "It was rough on you, finding Edda Lou that way."

"Rougher on her, I'd say."

He stood, reaching for a cigarette as he paced. "Being as you've been here a few days, you'll know everything that's been said."

Though she tried, she couldn't prevent a twinge of sympathy. It was never easy to have your private life, your private mistakes the topic of hot speculation. She knew. "If you're saying the gossip around here is as thick as the humidity, I won't argue."

"I can't stop you from thinking what you're inclined to think, but I want my say."

She lifted a brow. "I can't fathom why my thoughts would concern you."

"You jumped fast enough to give them to that shiny-shoed Yankee."

She waited. The way he was pacing up and down the room struck as more frustrated than violent. She relaxed enough to set down the bow. "If you're speaking of Agent Burns, I told him what I'd seen. You were by the pond."

His head whipped around. "Sure I was there, goddammit. Did I look like I was planning to murder somebody?"

"You looked angry," she tossed back. "I have no idea what you were planning."

He stopped, turned, and took a step toward her. "If you think I did that to Edda Lou, why the hell are you standing here talking to me instead of running for your life?"

She jerked up her chin. "I can take care of myself. Since I've already told the police everything I know—which is essentially nothing—you'd have no reason to hurt me."

He balled his hands at his sides. "Lady, you keep looking at me as if I were something you scraped off your shoe, and I might come up with a reason or two."

"Don't threaten me." Adrenaline began to pump through her, pushing her forward until she was nearly nose to nose with him. "I know your kind, Tucker. You just can't stand it that I'm not tripping over myself to get you to blink my way. It galls your male pride when a woman isn't interested. Then when one is, like this Edda Lou, you can't wait to shake her off. One way or another."

It was close enough to the truth to sting. "Honey, women come and women go. Doesn't mean a damn to me. I don't pine away for them, and I sure as hell don't kill them. And as far as tripping over yourself . . . Christ."

She managed one short scream as he grabbed her and tossed her to the floor. Then the breath was knocked out of her when he landed hard on top of her. She heard the explosion, and thought for a moment it was the crack of her head hitting the hardwood.

"What the hell do you think—"

"Stay down. Holy bleeding Jesus." His face was only inches from hers, and she saw something move into his eyes that might have been fear, or cunning.

"If you don't get off me this minute—" Whatever she planned to do next was forgotten as she heard the next shot and watched a hole explode in the cushion of the couch just above their heads. "My God." Her fingers dug into his arms. "Someone's shooting at us."

"You caught on, sugar."

"What are we going to do?"

"We could stay like this and hope he goes away. But he won't." On a sigh, he lowered his forehead to hers in a gesture that was curiously intimate. "Shit. He's crazy enough to kill you, too, and figure it was God's will."

"Who?" She pounded on his back. "Who is it?"

"Edda Lou's daddy." Tucker lifted his head a fraction. Under the circumstances, he didn't dwell on the fact that her mouth was ripe and full and naked. He noticed—but he didn't dwell on it.

"The woman who was killed? Her father is out there shooting at us?"

"At me, mostly. But he wouldn't worry much about hitting you along the way. I got a glimpse of him through the window while he was sighting between my eyes."

"That's crazy. A man can't go around shooting into someone's house."

"I'll be sure to mention that to him if I get the chance." There was only one thing to do, and he hated it. "You got a gun around here?"

"Yes. My grandfather's. In the den, across the hall."

"Here's what I want you to do. Stay down, keep quiet."

She nodded. "I can do that." As he eased down her body, she grabbed his shirt. "Are you going to shoot him?"

"Christ, I hope not." He shimmied back, using the couch as cover, then sucking in a breath when he was forced to crawl out into the open. When he reached the doorway, he figured he was far enough away to keep any strays from hitting Caroline. "Austin, you sonofabitch, there's a woman in here."

"My daughter was a woman." Another .44 slammed through the window, scattering glass. "I'm going to kill you, Longstreet. 'For this is the time of the Lord's vengeance.' I'm going to kill you. Then I'm going to slice you up into pieces, just like you done to Edda Lou."

Tucker pressed the heels of his hands to his eyes and concentrated. "You don't want to hurt the lady."

"Don't know if she's a lady. Might be another of your whores. The Lord's guiding my hand. This here's an eye for an eye. 'For the Lord thy God is a consuming fire. The wages of sin is death.' "

While Austin quoted scripture, Tucker belly-crawled across the hall. Once inside, he moved quickly. He grabbed a Remington and with sweaty hands loaded it, queasy at the knowledge that he might have to use it. He moved to the window, eased out the screen, and crawled through.

The next shot had him babbling his own prayer as he hunched over and darted into the bush.

Austin had picked his spot. Not two yards from the front of the house, he leaned against a lone maple. Sweat streamed off his face and dampened the back of his camo shirt. He called on Jesus, peppering his prayers and threats with rifle fire. All of the front windows were smashed.

He could have rushed the house and ended it. But he wanted, needed, to know Tucker was suffering. For more than thirty years he'd been waiting for a way to pay back a Longstreet. Now he'd found it.

"I'm going to shoot your nuts off, Tucker. Gonna blow away that cock you're so proud of. That's the justice for a fornicator. You'll go to hell dickless. That's God's will. You hear me, you heathen sinner? You hear what I'm saying?"

With little regret Tucker shoved the rifle barrel into Austin's left ear. "I hear you, no need to shout." He hoped Austin didn't notice the gun was wavering in his shaking hands. "Put down the gun, Austin, or I'll have to put a bullet in your brain. Believe me, it'll be hard on me. You'll be dead, but I'll have to throw away this shirt. It's almost brand new."

"I'll kill you." Austin tried to turn his head, but Tucker poled hard with the rifle.

"Not today, you won't. Now, you toss that gun away, then you un-buckle that ammo belt. Slow and easy." When Austin hesitated, Tucker gave him another nudge. He got a ridiculous image of the barrel sliding right through Austin's head and poking out the other ear. "I know I'm not much of a shot, but even I can't miss when I've got the barrel in your ear."

He breathed a little easier when Austin tossed the gun aside. "Caroline," he shouted. "You give Burke a call now, tell him to get his ass down here on the double. Then bring me some rope." The moment the ammo belt hit the dirt, Tucker kicked it aside. "Now, what was that about my dick, Austin?"

Two minutes later Caroline streaked out of the house with a length of clothesline. "He's on his way. I just . . ." She trailed off and stared down at the man sprawled in the grass. His face was battered and grimy with sweat and black streaks. Camouflage wear covered his tanklike torso and steel-girder legs. Despite the fact that Tucker stood over him, pointing a gun at the nape of his neck, the younger man looked toothpick-thin and vulnerable.

"I brought the rope," she said, swallowing when her voice squeaked.

"Good. Honey, you want to scoot around behind him?"

Moistening her lips, she gave Austin a wide berth. "How did you . . . I mean, he's so big."

"Big mouth, too." He couldn't resist giving Austin a little nudge with his foot. "He was so busy screaming his fire and brimstone, he didn't hear the sinner coming up behind him. Can you shoot this thing?"

"Yes." She eyed the rifle. "Sort of."

"Sort of's good. Ain't it, Austin? She's liable to shoot something vital off you if you move too quick. Nothing more dangerous than a female with a loaded gun. Unless it's a Yankee female. Here now. You just keep pointing that right at his head while I tie him up." He balanced the gun in her hands. Their eyes met with twin expressions of giddy relief. For an instant they were the fastest of friends.

"That's the way, sugar. Just don't point it at me. Now, if he moves, you just press your finger. Then close your eyes, 'cause it'll blow his head off, and I wouldn't want you to see something that nasty."

He winked at her so that she understood the warning was for Austin's benefit. "Okay. But I'm a little shaky. I hope I don't press it without meaning to."

Tucker grinned as he hunkered down to tie Austin's hands. "Just do the best you can, Caro. Nobody can ask for better than that. Gonna hogtie you, Austin. Seems to fit." He looped the cord and tugged, bowing Austin's beefy legs. "Don't seem right to me that you blew out all this lady's windows. Ruined her davenport, too. As I recall, Miss Edith was fond of that davenport."

He stepped back to take the gun from Caroline. "Darlin', would you mind fetching me a beer? I've worked up a thirst."

She had an insane urge to laugh. "I don't have any . . . beer, that is. I have some wine. Some chardonnay," she babbled.

"That'd go down nice, too."

"All right. I . . . sure." She started up the steps, then turned back to see Tucker taking out a cigarette. Putting a hand to her giddy head, she watched him pinch off the tip. "Why do you do that?"

"Hmm?" He squinted as he struck a match.

"Tear off the tip?"

"Oh." He drew in smoke with every indication of pleasure. "I'm fixin' to quit. Seems a sensible way to go about it. Figure after a couple weeks, I'll be down to a half a smoke at a time." He smiled at her, wildly attractive and pale as a sheet. "You put that chardonnay in a big glass for me now, okay?"

"Yeah." She let out a shaky breath as she heard the wail of a siren. Tucker was still close enough that she heard the same sigh of relief from him. "You bet." The screen door slammed behind her.

Chapter 7

THUNDER GRUMBLED OVER IN the east. A breeze, the first she'd felt since crossing the Mississippi border, stirred the leaves in the maple where not thirty minutes before, a man had stood with a loaded rifle.

It didn't seem reasonable, or even possible, but Caroline found herself sitting on the porch steps drinking chardonnay out of a water glass, with what was left of the bottle wedged between her hip and Tucker's.

Her life, she decided as she took another long swallow, had certainly taken some interesting twists and turns.

"This is good stuff," Tucker swirled the wine. He was beginning to feel mellow again—a state he preferred.

"It's a particular favorite of mine."

"Mine, too, now." He turned his head and smiled at her. "Nice breeze."

"Very nice."

"We've been needing rain."

"Yes, I suppose."

He leaned back on his elbows, lifting his face to the cool. "The way the wind's coming, it shouldn't blow the wet into your parlor."

Almost absently, she turned to look at her shattered windows. "Well, there's good news. We wouldn't want it to soak the couch. After all, it has only one bullet hole."

He gave her a friendly pat on the back. "You're a good sport, Caro. I expect some women would've gone bawling or screaming or fainting, but you held up fine."

"Right." Since her glass was nearly empty, she refilled it. "Tucker, may I ask you a regional sort of question?"

He held his glass out, enjoying the music of fine wine striking fine wine when she poured. "Right now, sweetie, you can ask me damn near anything."

"I was curious. Are murders and shootouts common in this part of the state, or is this just a phase?"

"Well now." He contemplated the wine in his glass before drinking. "Speaking for Innocence, and since my family's been here since before the war—that's the War Between the States."

"Naturally."

"I feel confident in holding an opinion on it. I have to say we're new to the kind of murder you're thinking of. Now, Whiteford Talbot blew a good-sized hole in Cal Beauford back when I was a kid. But Whiteford caught old Cal shimmying down the drainpipe outside his bedroom window. And Whiteford's wife—that was Ruby Talbot—was buck-ass naked in bed at the time."

"An entirely different matter," Caroline concluded.

"There you go. And not more than five years back, the Bonny boys and the Shivers peppered each other with buckshot. But that was only over a pig. And seeing as they're cousins and crazy, too, nobody paid much attention."

"I see."

By Jesus, Tucker thought, he liked her, liked her in a companionable sort of way that ran a friendly parallel alongside physical attraction.

"But mostly, Innocence is pretty peaceable."

She frowned over the rim of her glass. "Do you put that on?"

"Which is that?"

"That slightly addled, good-ol'-boy routine."

He grinned and drank. "Only if it seems appropriate."

She sighed and looked away. Overhead the sky was darkening, and the occasional rumbles of thunder were closer, as were the quick, sharp flashes of lightning. But it felt good, too good, just to sit.

"Are you worried? When the sheriff took that man away, he kept swearing he was going to kill you."

"No use getting in a lather over it." But the concern in her voice stirred the juices. Smoothly, he slid an arm around her shoulders. "Don't you worry, sweetheart. I wouldn't want you to fret over me."

She turned her head. Again, her face was inches from his. "It's a bit morbid, isn't it? Using a near-death experience as a seduction."

"Ouch." He was good-natured enough to laugh, experienced enough to keep his arm where it was. "Are you always so suspicious of a man?"

"Of a certain kind of man." She lifted a hand and unwrapped his arm from her shoulders.

"That's cold, Caro, after all we've shared." On a sigh of regret he touched his glass to hers. "Don't suppose you'd invite me to supper?"

Her lips twitched. "I don't suppose I would."

"Maybe you'd play me another tune."

She didn't smile now, only shook her head. "I'm taking a break from playing for anyone."

"Now, that's a shame. Tell you what, I'll play for you."

Her brows lifted in surprise. "You play the violin?"

"Hell no. But I play the radio." He stood, and realized abruptly the wine had gone straight to his head. It wasn't a feeling he objected to. Strolling to his car, he pushed through his cassettes. After choosing one, he turned the key to auxiliary and popped it in.

"Fats Domino," he said with proper respect as "Blueberry Hill" slid out. He walked back, holding out a hand. "Come on." Before Caroline could refuse, he was pulling her to her feet and into his arms. "I just can't hear this song and not want to dance with a pretty woman."

She could have protested or broken away. But it was harmless. And after the last twenty-four hours, she needed a little harmless diversion. So she settled against him, enjoying the fluid way he moved from walk to lawn, laughing a little when he eased her back into a dip, appreciating the way the wine spun inside her head.

"Feel good?" he murmured.

"Hmmm. You're smooth, Tucker, maybe too smooth. But it's a lot better than being shot at."

"I was thinking the same thing." He nuzzled his cheek against her hair. It was soft as silk against his skin. Since he'd always had a weakness for texture, he didn't try to prevent himself from feeling the contrast of her butter-smooth cheek against his, or the way her blouse shifted under his guiding hand. How long and slim her thighs were as they brushed and bumped against his.

The sexual pull didn't surprise him. It was as natural as breathing. What did surprise him was the overwhelming desire to toss her over his shoulder and carry her inside, upstairs. He'd always preferred to take it slow and easy with the ladies, savoring the chase, holding on to control. Dancing with her as the air took on that hushed and pearly light before a storm had him jumpy.

Tucker passed it off as due to his being more than half drunk.

"It's raining," Caroline whispered. Her eyes were closed and her body swayed with his.

"Um-hmm." He could smell the rain on her hair, on her skin. And it was driving him crazy.

She smiled, enjoying the way the slow, fat drops soaked through her clothes. There'd been no rifle fire in her life before, she mused. But there'd been no dancing in the rain either. "It's cool. Wonderfully cool."

The way he was starting to feel, he was surprised the rain didn't sizzle as it plopped against his skin. He found his teeth were at her ear, and her quick, surprised shudder when he closed them gently over the lobe sliced straight through him.

Her eyes shot open, glazed for a moment as he nipped his way along her jawline. Something hot and delicious stirred in her gut before she managed to cut it off. An instant before his mouth took hers, she slapped a hand on his chest and leaned back.

"What do you think you're doing?"

He blinked. "Kissing you?"

"No."

He stared at her for a moment, at the rain streaming down her hair, at her eyes which betrayed as much passion as determination. There was an urge to ignore the protesting hand and take what he wanted. The fact that he couldn't had him sighing out an oath.

"Caroline, you're a hard woman."

The alarm bells in her head slowed. Her lips curved a little. He wasn't going to push. "So they say."

"I could hang around awhile, persuade you to change your mind."

"I don't think so."

His eyes laughed. He made one slow pass down her back before releasing her. "Now, that's a challenge, but I figure you had a difficult day, so I'll save it."

"I appreciate that."

"You damn well should." He took her hand, skimmed his thumb over her knuckles. And damn him, she felt the shiver clean down to her toes. "You're going to think about me, Caroline, when you snuggle into your bed tonight."

"What I'm going to think about is getting those windows repaired."

His gaze moved beyond her to the jagged glass stabbing viciously from the worn wooden frame. "I owe you for that," he said. And there was a grimness in his eyes that reminded her how they'd come to be holding hands in the rain.

"I think it's Austin Hatinger who owes me," she said lightly, "but that won't get my windows fixed."

"I'll take care of it." He looked back at her. "You sure are pretty when you're wet. If I stay around much longer, I'm going to try to kiss you again."

"Then you'd better go." She started to tug her hand away, then glanced at his car. Laughter bubbled out. "Tucker, did you know your top's down?"

"Shit." He turned and stared. Rain was bouncing off his white leather upholstery. "That's the trouble with women. They distract you." Before she pulled her hand free, he brought it to his lips for a long kiss that ended with the barest scrape of teeth. "I'll be back, Caroline."

She smiled, stepped back. "Then bring some window glass and a hammer."

He slid into his car without bothering to lift the top. Tucker gunned the engine, blew her a kiss, and started down the lane. In the rearview mirror he watched her, standing in the rain, her hair like wet wheat, her clothes clinging to her curves. Fats belted out "Ain't That a Shame." Tucker could only agree.

Caroline waited until he'd driven out of sight before she walked back to the steps, sat, and downed the rain-diluted wine. Susie had been right, she thought. Tucker Longstreet was no more a killer than she was. And he did indeed have a way about him. She rubbed the hand he'd kissed over her cheek and let out a long, shaky breath.

It was a good thing she wasn't interested. Eyes closed, Caroline lifted her face to the rain. A very good thing.

♦ ♦ ♦ ♦

WHEN SHE AWAKENED THE next morning, it was in a foul mood. She'd slept poorly. And dammit, she had thought of him. Between that and the sound of the rain pattering against the tin roof, she'd tossed and turned the better part of the night. She'd nearly given up and downed one of the sleeping pills left over from Dr. Palamo's last prescription.

But she'd resisted, wanting to prove something to herself: As a result, she opened bleary eyes to steamy sunlight. On top of it, her head was pounding from the wine.

As she swallowed aspirin and stepped under the shower, she knew exactly where to place the blame. If it hadn't been for Tucker, she wouldn't have indulged in too much wine. If it hadn't been for Tucker, she wouldn't have lain awake half the night, taunted by an unwanted sexual ache. And if it hadn't been for Tucker, she wouldn't have holes in her house that had to be dealt with before flies, mosquitoes, and God knew what else decided to come in and live with her.

So much for peace and tranquility, she thought as she stepped out of the shower to dry off. So much for a quiet period of healing. Since she'd had the misfortune to bump into Tucker, her life had been in upheaval. Dead women, crazy men with rifles. Muttering to herself, Caroline pulled on her robe. Why the hell hadn't she gone to the South of France and baked herself whole on a nice crowded beach?

Because she'd wanted to come home, she thought with a sigh. Despite the fact that she'd spent only a few precious days of her childhood in this house, it was as close to home as she had.

Nothing and no one was going to spoil it for her. Caroline marched downstairs, one hand nursing her drumming head. She was going to have her quiet time. She was going to sit on the porch and watch the sunset, tend flowers, listen to music. She was going to be just as peaceful and solitary as she chose. Starting right this minute.

Chin set, she shoved open the front door. And let out a strangled scream.

A black man with a scarred cheek and shoulders like a Brahma bull stood by a broken window. Caroline caught the glint of metal in his hand. Her thoughts tumbled over each other. To dash inside and try for the phone. To streak to her car and hope the keys were inside it. To simply stand and scream.

"Miz Waverly, ma'am?"

After a frantic search, she found her voice. "I've called the sheriff."

"Yes'm, Tuck told me you had yourself some trouble out here."

"I . . . excuse me?"

"Hatinger blew out your windows. Sheriff's got him down in jail. I oughta be able to take care of things right quick."

"Take care?"

She saw his hand move and sucked in air to scream. Let it out again when she saw that the metal in his hand was a tape measure. While she fought to lower her pulse rate, he stretched the tape across the empty space where glass had been.

"You're going to fix the windows."

"Yes'm. Tuck gave me a call last night. Said he'd let you know I'd be by in the morning so's I could measure them up and reglaze." His nut-brown eyes flickered, then filled with quiet amusement. "Guess he didn't let you know."

"No." As relief and annoyance flooded through, Caroline pressed a hand to her speeding heart. "No, he didn't mention it."

"Tuck's not what you call dependable."

"I've come to understand that."

With a nod he jotted figures on a pad. "Guess I gave you a turn."

"That's all right." She managed a smile. "I think I'm getting used to it." Settling, she ran fingers through her damp hair. "You didn't mention your name."

"I'm Toby March." He tugged on the brim of his battered fielder's cap in a kind of salute. "I do handyman kind of work."

"It's nice to meet you, Mr. March."

After a moment's hesitation, he took the offered hand. "Just call me Toby, ma'am. Everybody does."

"Well, Toby, I appreciate you getting to this so quickly."

"I'm grateful for the work. If you was to get me a broom, I might could clear up this broken glass for you."

"All right. Would you like some coffee?"

"No need to trouble."

"It's no trouble. I was just about to make a pot."

"I'd sure be obliged, then. Black with three sugars, if you don't mind."

"I'll bring it out in a minute." The phone began to ring. "Excuse me."

Pressing a hand to her forehead, Caroline hurried down the hall and snatched up the receiver. "Yes?"

"Well, honey, you sure do lead an exciting life."

"Susie." Caroline leaned back against the banister. "Whoever said small towns were uneventful?"

"Nobody who lived in one. Burke said you weren't hurt any. I'd have come down to see for myself, but the boys had a sleepover. Even keeping an eye on them, the place looks like we had a war."

"I'm fine, really." Except for a hangover, shattered nerves, and an unwelcome dose of sexual frustration. "Just a little frazzled."

"Who could blame you, honey? Tell you what. We're having a barbecue tomorrow. You come out here and sit in the shade, eat till you can't walk, and forget all about your troubles."

"That sounds wonderful."

"Five o'clock. You drive into town, go all the way to the end of Market, and turn left on Magnolia. We're the third house on the right. The yellow one with white shutters. You have any trouble finding it, just follow the smell of charring ribs."

"I'll be there. Thanks, Susie."

Caroline hung up and started back to the kitchen. She put the coffee on, popped some bread in the toaster, and took out some of the wild raspberry jam. The sun was sizzling on the wet grass outside, and the wild, hot smell was as appealing as the scent of coffee. She watched a woodpecker settle against the side of a tree to root for breakfast.

From the front porch came Toby's voice, a rich, creamy baritone. It was lifted in a body-swaying gospel tune about finding peace.

Caroline found that her headache had vanished, her eyes were clear.

All in all, it was good to be home.

♦ ♦ ♦ ♦

NOT SO FAR AWAY, someone lay tangled in sweaty sheets and moaned in sleep. Dreams, like dark, twisted rivers, flowed. Dreams of sex, of blood, of power. The dreams were not always remembered in the daylight. Sometimes they flitted in those waking moments, razor-winged butterflies slicing through the mind and leaving shallow wounds that stung.

Women, there were always women. Those brutal, smirking bitches. The need for them—the smooth skin, the soft scent, the hot flavors— was hateful. It could be overcome for long stretches. For days, weeks, even months, there could be a gentleness, a warmth, even a respect. And then, then one of them would do something. Something that required punishment.

The pain would begin, the hunger would grow. And nothing would quench it but blood. But even through the pain, even through the hunger, there was guile. There was a wild satisfaction in knowing that no matter how they looked, how they struggled, no one would find proof.

Madness was alive in Innocence, but it cloaked itself well. As the summer wore on it would fester inside its unwilling host. And smile.

♦ ♦ ♦ ♦

DR. THEODORE RUBENSTEIN—Teddy to his friends— polished off his second cherry danish. He washed the pastry down with lukewarm Pepsi straight from the bottle. He'd never developed a taste for coffee.

Teddy had just skimmed past his fortieth birthday and had begun to comb Grecian Formula 44 through his thick brown hair. He wasn't balding—praise be—but he didn't care for the professorial look the threads of gray gave him.

Teddy considered himself a fun-loving kind of guy. He knew that with his small dark eyes, slightly receding chin, and sallow complexion, he wasn't heart-stirring handsome. He used humor to attract the ladies.

Personality, he liked to tell himself, caught as much pussy as a perfect profile.

Humming to himself, he scrubbed his hands in the sink in Palmer's embalming room, the sink just below the trick picture of Jesus. To amuse himself, Teddy swayed from side to side. When he shifted left, Jesus wore a red robe, a kindly expression, and held an elegant hand up to the valentine-shaped heart prominent on his chest. Shift right, and the face shivered for an instant, then moved to sadness and pain. Understandable, as there was now a crown of thorns perched atop the chestnut hair, thin rivulets of blood marring the intellectual forehead.

Teddy wondered which image Palmer preferred before he reached for his Rock-Hard Cavity Fluid. While he experimented, trying to find that precise point where he could stand and have the two images merge into one, he dried his hands. Behind him, Edda Lou Hatinger lay naked on the porcelain embalming table—the old-fashioned kind, with the run-off grooves along the sides. Her skin was ghastly under the merciless fluorescent lights.

Such things didn't put old Teddy off his danishes. He'd chosen pathology because he'd been expected to go to medical school. He was the fourth generation of Rubensteins with Doctor in front of his name. But long before he'd completed his first year of internship, he'd discovered in himself a nearly obsessive abhorrence of sick people.

Dead was different.

It had never bothered him to work on a cadaver. Hospital rounds with the wheezing, moaning patients had put him off. But the first time he'd been called upon to watch a dissection, he knew he'd found his vocation.

The dead didn't complain, they didn't need to be saved, and they sure as hell weren't going to sue for malpractice.

Instead, they were like a puzzle. You took them apart, figured out what went wrong, and filed your report.

Teddy was good at puzzles, and he knew he was a hell of a lot better with the dead than with the living. Both of his ex-wives would have been more than happy to point out his lack of sensitivity, his selfishness, and his ghoulish, offputting sense of humor. Though Teddy happened to think he was a pretty funny guy.

Putting a joy buzzer in a cadaver's hand was a surefire way to liven up a dull autopsy.

Burns wouldn't think so, but then, Teddy enjoyed irritating Burns. He smiled to himself as he snapped on surgical gloves. He'd been working on a trick for weeks, waiting for the opportunity to pull it on someone like straight-and-narrow Matt Burns. All he'd needed was a suitably mangled victim.

Teddy blew Edda Lou a kiss in thanks as he turned on his tape recorder.

"What we have here," he began, using a thick southern accent, "is a female, Caucasian, mid-twenties. Identified as Edda Lou Hatinger. Got her height as five foot five, weight one twenty-six. And boys and girls, she's built like your old-fashioned brick shithouse."

That, Teddy thought gleefully, would burn Burns.

"Our guest today suffered from multiple stab wounds. Pardon me, Edda Lou," he said as he made his count. "Twenty-two punctures. Concentrated on the areas of breasts, torso, and genitalia. A sharp, smooth-bladed instrument was used to sever her jugular, trachea, and larynx in a horizontal stroke. From the angle and depth, I'd say left to right, indicating a right-handed assailant. In layman's terms, ladies and gentlemen, her throat was slit from ear to ear, probably by a knife with a . . ." He whistled as he measured. "Six- to seven-inch blade. Anybody out there see *Crocodile Dundee?*" He tried on a heavy Aussie accent. "Now, that's a knife! On examination of other traumas, this throat wound was probable cause of death. It would do the job, belive me. I'm a doctor."

He whistled "Theme from *A Summer Place*" as he continued his exam. "A blow to the base of the skull by a heavy, rough-textured instrument." Delicately, he tweezered out fragments. "Bagging fragments that appear to be wood or tree bark for forensic. I think we'll agree that victim was clubbed with a tree branch. Blow issued prior to death. If you detectives out there conclude that the blow rendered the victim unconscious, you win a free trip for two to Barbados and a complete set of Samsonite luggage."

He glanced up as the door opened. Burns nodded at him. Teddy smiled. "Let the record show that Special Agent Matthew Burns has arrived to watch the master at work. How's it hanging, Burnsie?"

"Your progress?"

"Oh, Edda Lou and I are getting to know each other. Thought we'd go dancing later."

Inside Burns's clenched jaw his teeth ground together. "As always, Rubenstein, your humor is revolting and pathetic."

"Edda Lou appreciates it, don't you, dear?" He patted her hand. "Bruises and broken skin at wrists and ankles." Using his tools, he located and removed tiny white fibers, bagged them while he continued to detail, cheerfully, his findings.

Burns suffered through another fifteen minutes. "Was she sexually assaulted?"

"Pretty hard to tell," Teddy said through pursed lips. "I'm going to take tissue samples." Burns averted his eyes as Teddy did so. "I put her in the water for twelve to fifteen hours. A rough guess before I run the tests puts time of death between eleven and three on the night of June sixteenth."

"I want those results asap."

Teddy continued taking his scrapings. "God, I love it when you talk in acronyms."

Burns ignored him. "I want to know everything there is to know about her. What she ate, when she ate it. If she was drugged or had used alcohol. If she had sexual relations. She was supposed to be pregnant. I want to know how many weeks."

"I'll take a look." Teddy turned, ostensibly to exchange instruments. "You might want to check out her left molar. I found it very interesting."

"Her teeth?"

"That's right. I've never seen anything like it."

Intrigued, Burns leaned over. He opened Edda Lou's mouth, narrowed his eyes.

"Kiss me, you fool," she demanded. Burns yelped and stumbled back. "Jesus. Jesus Christ."

As laughter doubled him over, Teddy had to sit down or fall down. He'd spent months studying ventriloquism for just such a moment. The wild-eyed panic on Burn's face had made it all worthwhile.

"You've got some style, Burnsie. Even dead women fall for you."

Fighting for control, Burns clenched his fists at his sides. If he took a swipe at Rubenstein, he'd have no choice but to put himself on report. "You're fucking crazy."

Teddy only pointed at Burns's white face, pointed at Edda Lou's gray one, and whooped.

There wasn't any use threatening, Burns knew. Any official complaint he made would be duly noted, then ignored. Rubenstein was the best. A known lunatic, but the best.

"I want the results of your tests by the end of the day, Rubenstein. You may find it all highly amusing, but I have a psychopath to stop."

Unable to speak, Teddy just nodded and held his aching ribs.

When Burns swung out the door, Teddy wiped his teary eyes and slid off the stool. "Edda Lou, honey," he said in a voice still breathless with mirth. "I can't thank you enough for your cooperation. Believe me, you're going down in the annals of history for this one. The boys back in D.C. are going to love it."

Whistling, he picked up his scalpel and went back to work.

Chapter 8

DARLEEN FULLER TALBOT LISTENED to the sounds of the Truesdale barbecue drifting through her bedroom window. She thought it was a damn shame that uppity Susie Truesdale hadn't even invited her own next-door neighbor to the party.

Darleen would've liked a party to take her mind off her troubles.

Of course Susie didn't socialize with Darleen. She preferred the Longstreets, or the Shayses, or the nose-in-the-air Cunninghams from across the street. And didn't she know for certain that high-and-mighty John Cunningham had cheated on his prissy wife with Josie Longstreet?

It seemed to Darleen that Susie had forgotten she'd had to get married and had waited tables at the Chat 'N Chew while her belly was bulging. Maybe her husband had come from rich, but he hadn't ended up that way. Everybody knew Burke's daddy had killed himself because all he had left was a pile of debts.

The Truesdales were no better than she was, and neither were the Longstreets. Maybe her daddy made his way working at a cotton gin instead of owning one, but he wasn't a drunk. And he wasn't dead.

Darleen thought it was downright unfriendly that Susie would give a party right out in the backyard where the smell of grilling meat and spicy sauce could make someone feel lonely. Why, even her own brother was down there—not that Bobby Lee ever gave his sister's feelings any thought.

The hell with him, the tight-assed Truesdales, and everybody else. She didn't want to go to any damn party anyhow. Even if Junior was working four to midnight down at the gas station. How could she laugh and lick barbecue sauce off her fingers when her very best friend in all the world was going to be set in the ground come Tuesday?

She sighed, and Billy T., who was sucking for all his worth on her rosy breasts, took that to mean she was finally going to start putting some effort into it.

She shifted so he could stick his tongue in her ear. "Come on, baby, you get on top."

"Okay." That perked her interest. Junior not only liked it only in bed these days, but he liked it only in one position.

When they were finished, Billy T. lay puffing contentedly on a Marlboro. Darleen stared at the ceiling, listening to the music from the Truesdales'.

"Billy T.," she said, her mouth moving into a pout. "Don't you figure it's rude to give a party and not ask your next-door neighbors?"

'Shit, Darleen, will you stop worrying about them people?"

"It just ain't right." Piqued by his lack of sympathy, Darleen rose to fetch her rose-scented talcum powder. If she was going to pick up Scooter from her ma's in an hour, it was the quickest way to soak up the scent of sweat and sex. "I mean she thinks she's better'n me. Her snotty Marvella, too. Just 'cause they're friends with the Longstreets." She tugged on her T-shirt and shorts, forgoing underwear as a concession to the heat. Her breasts, high and full and round, bulged against the cotton, distorting the faded picture of Elvis. "That Tucker's down there right now, cozying up to the Waverly woman. Why, Edda Lou ain't even buried yet."

"Tucker's a shithead. Always was."

"Well, Edda Lou loved him to distraction. He brought her perfume." She sent a hopeful look toward Billy T., but he was too busy blowing smoke rings. Darleen turned back to frown out the window. "I just hate them. Hate them all. Why, if Burke Truesdale wasn't Tucker's best friend, that boy would be locked up, same as Austin Hatinger."

"Hell." Billy T. rubbed his damp belly and wondered if they could get in one more poke. "Tucker's a shithead, but he ain't no killer. Everybody knows it was a black that done it. Them blacks the one's who like to carve up white women."

"He broke her heart just the same. It just seems he ought to pay somehow." She looked back at Billy T., one tear slipping out of one eye. "I sure wish someone would get back at him for making her so unhappy before she died." As the laughter rose up form the next yard, infuriating her, Darleen blinked her wet lashes. "Why, I guess I'd do just about anything for somebody who had the guts to pay him back."

Billy T. crushed out his cigarette in the little ashtray that had a picture of the Washington Monument on it. "Well now, honey, if you were to come on over here and show me how much you want it, it might be I could do something to even things out."

"Oh, honey." Darleen tugged Elvis away from her breasts as she rose to kneel between Billy T.'s legs. "You're so good to me."

◆ ◆ ◆ ◆

*W*HILE DARLEEN WAS BUSY bringing a smile to Billy T.'s face, ribs were sizzling on the grill in the yard next door. Burke presided over them, wearing a big apron that sported a cartoon chef and the caption KISS THE COOK OR ELSE! He tipped back a Budweiser with one hand and sauced the ribs with the other. Susie hauled bowls and platters from the kitchen to the picnic table, shooting off orders to her children to grab the potato salad, fetch more ice, to stop sneaking the deviled eggs.

Caroline had to admire the orchestration. One would swing into the kitchen, another would swing out. Although two of the boys—Tommy and Parker, she remembered—would occasionally pause for a few elbow pokes and jostling, the choreography went smoothly. The younger boy, Sam—named after Uncle Sam, as he'd be nine on the Fourth of July—was engrossed in showing his baseball card selection to Tucker.

Tucker was sprawled on the grass, and despite the heat, held Sam in his lap as they perused the album. "I'll trade you my eighty-six Rickey Henderson for that Cal Ripkin."

"Nuh-uh." Sam's mop of sandy hair flopped in his eyes as he shook his head. "This's Cal's rookie year."

"But you've gone and bent the corner, son, and my Henderson's in prime condition. Might even throw in my brand-new Wade Boggs."

"Shoot, that's nothin'." Sam turned his head, and Caroline caught the gleam in his dark eyes. "I want the sixty-three Pete Rose."

"That's robbery, boy. I'm going to have your daddy throw you in jail for even suggesting it. Burke, this boy's a born criminal. Better send him off to reform school now and save yourself the heartache."

"He knows a scam when he hears one," Burke said mildly.

"He's still pissed that I got his Mickey Mantle back in sixty-eight," Tucker murmured to Sam. "The man doesn't understand creative trading. Now, about that Cal Ripkin."

"I'll take twenty-five dollars for it."

"Shit. That does it." He caught Sam in a headlock and hissed in his ear. "You see that guy sitting there working on boring Miss Waverly to death?"

"The one in the suit?"

"Yes, sir, the one in the suit. He's an FBI agent, and asking twenty-five dollars for Cal Ripkin's rookie year is a federal offense."

"Nuh-uh," Sam said, grinning.

"It sure as God is. And your daddy'd be the first to tell you ignorance of the law is no excuse. I'm going to have to turn you in."

Sam studied Matthew Burns, then shrugged. "He looks like a pansy."

Tucker hooted with laughter. "Where do you learn these things?" He decided to try another tack and see if he could torture the card from Sam. He flipped the boy over, hung him upside down, then began to tickle him.

As Caroline watched them wrestle, she lost track of Burns's conversation. Something about the Symphony Ball at the Kennedy Center. She let him drone on, managing an occasional smile or murmur of agreement. She was much more interested in watching the other guests.

A scattering of people were huddled under the shade of an oak. It was the only tree in the yard and a perfect place for a gathering of lawn chairs and lazy conversation. The skinny, swarthy-looking pathologist was making some of the ladies giggle. Caroline wondered how a man could perform an autopsy one day and tell jokes the next.

Josie was posed in a tire swing, flirting with him—and with every other man within reach. Dwayne Longstreet and Doc Shays were sitting on the back porch, rocking and sipping beers. Marvella Truesdale and Bobby Lee Fuller were sending each other long, intimate looks, and the beauty-shop owner, Crystal something, was gossiping with Birdie Shays.

She could see little patches of yard running on either side of the Truesdales'. The clothes strung on lines to bake dry in the yellow sun. There were kitchen gardens in nearly every one, with tomatoes heavy on vines, snap beans, collards, waiting for the pot.

She could smell the beer, the spicy meat, the hot flowers baking in the late afternoon sun. Tommy punched a new cassette in his portable radio and blues drifted out, heavy on the bass, bittersweet, and slow and easy as heartbreak. Caroline didn't recognize Bonnie Raitt, but she recognized excellence.

She wanted to hear it. She wanted to hear Sam squeal and giggle as Tucker wrestled him. She wanted to hear Crystal and Birdie gossip about someone who'd died twenty years earlier in a car wreck.

She wanted to dance to that music, to watch the way Burke kissed his wife through the fragrant smoke of the grill—kissed her as if they were still teenagers sneaking love in shadows. And she wanted to feel what Marvella was feeling when Bobby Lee took her hand and pulled her through the kitchen door.

She wanted to be a part of it, not someone sitting on the sidelines discussing Rachmaninoff.

"Excuse me, Matthew." She offered him a quick smile as she swung her legs over the wooden bench. "I want to see if Susie needs any help."

While Sam bounced on his back, Tucker admired the way Caroline's neat white shorts showed off her legs. He sighed when she bent down to pick up a Frisbee. Then he yanked Sam over his back, gave him a quick pink belly, and rose.

"I think I'll get myself a beer."

Caroline paused by the grill. "Smells great," she said to Burke.

"Five more minutes," he promised, and Susie laughed. "That's what he always says. What can I get you, Caroline?"

"Nothing, I'm fine. I thought you could use some help."

"Honey, that's what I've got four kids for. I just want you to sit down and relax."

"Really, I . . ." She sent a cautious look over her shoulder. Burns was still sitting at the table, his tie ruthlessly knotted as he sipped the chardonnay Caroline had brought as a contribution.

"Oh." Susie had followed her glance. "I guess there are times a woman needs to keep herself occupied. Why don't you run in and fetch the bread-and-butter pickles? There's a fresh jar in the cabinet, left of the refrigerator."

Grateful, Caroline headed off to comply. On the porch Doc Shays tipped his hat. Dwayne gave her the sweet, absent smile of a man already half drunk.

Caroline stepped inside and pulled up short. Bobby Lee and Marvella were locked in a heated embrace in front of the refrigerator. When the screen door slammed, they jumped apart. Marvella flushed and hitched her blouse back into place. Bobby Lee offered a smile that was caught somewhere between prideful and sheepish.

"I'm terribly sorry," Caroline began, uncertain who was the most flustered. "I just came in to get something for Susie." There was enough heat in the kitchen to fry bacon. "I can come back." She nearly backed into the door when Tucker pulled it open.

"Caro, you can't leave these two in here alone." He winked at Bobby Lee. "Kitchens are dangerous places. Y'all get outside where your mamas can keep an eye on you."

"I'm eighteen," Marvella said with a gleam in her eye. "We're both grown-up."

Tucker grinned and pinched her chin. "That's my point, sweetie pie."

"Besides," Marvella went on, "we're getting married."

"Marvella!" The tips of Bobby Lee's ears turned bright red. "I haven't even talked to your daddy yet."

She tossed her head. "We know what we want, don't we?"

"Well, yeah." He swallowed under Tucker's quiet stare. "Sure. But it's only right I talk to him before we say anything."

She hooked an arm through his. "Then you'd better start talking." She pulled him through the back door.

Tucker stared after them. "Jesus." Shaken, he dragged a hand through his hair. "She used to drool on my shoulder, now she's talking about getting married."

"From the look in her eyes, I'd say it was more than talk."

"How the hell'd she get to be eighteen?" Tucker wondered. "I was just eighteen myself a minute ago."

With a light laugh Caroline patted his arm. "Don't worry, Tucker, I have a feeling she'll be giving you another baby to drool on your shoulder in a year or two."

"Holy God." Even the thought had him sputtering. "That'd make me something like a grandfather, wouldn't it? I'm thirty goddamn three. I'm too young to be a grandfather."

"I'd think it would be more of an honorary title."

"Doesn't matter." He looked at the beer in his hand. "I'm not going to think about it."

"I'm sure that's wise." She turned to open the cupboard. "What are bread-and-butter pickles?"

"Hmm?" He turned back to her, and his thoughts about life and aging flitted away. Lord, she did have fine legs, and the sweetest little butt. "Top shelf," he said. "Stretch on up there." He watched the way her shorts rode high on her thighs when she rose to her toes and reached. "That's the way."

Caroline's fingers brushed the jar before she realized what was going on. Dropping back on her heels, she glanced over her shoulder. "You're a sick man, Tucker."

"I do feel a fever coming on." Still grinning, he strolled over. "Here, let me help you with that." His body pressed lightly against hers as he reached for the jar. "You smell good, Caro. Like something a man would be happy to wake up to in the morning."

The instant jolt of reaction forced her to take a slow breath. "Like coffee and bacon?"

He chuckled and pleased himself by nuzzling her neck. "Like soft, lazy sex."

Too much was happening inside her. Too much, too fast. Tingles and pressures and muscles going lax. She hadn't felt anything like it since . . . Luis.

Her muscles tensed again. "You're crowding me, Tucker."

"I'm trying." He plucked the jar out, set it on the counter. Putting his hands on her hips, he turned her toward him. "You ever come across something, like a piece of music, that kept playing through your mind— even when you didn't think you were that fond of it?"

His hands slid up, his thumbs just brushing the sides of her breasts. The blood began to swim in her head. "I suppose I have."

"That's the trouble I'm having with you, Caroline. You just keep playing through my head. You could almost say I'm fixated."

His eyes were level with hers, and so close she saw that there was a faint and fascinating outline of green around his pupils. "Maybe you should think of a different tune."

He leaned closer, and when she stiffened, contented himself with a light, quick nip on her bottom lip. "I've always had the damnedest time doing what I should." He lifted a hand to rub his knuckles over her cheek. She had a way of looking at him, Tucker realized, a straight, unwavering gaze that made him feel defensive, protective, and weak-kneed all at once. "Did he hurt you or just disappoint you?"

"I don't know what you mean."

"You're skittish, Caro. I figure there's a reason."

The liquid warmth that had been spreading through her hardened into iron will. "Skittish is a word better applied to horses. What I am is uninterested. And the reason for that might be that I don't find you appealing."

"Now, that's a lie," he said mildly. "The uninterested part. If we didn't have company right outside the door, I'd show you how I know it's a lie. But I'm a patient man, Caro, and I never blame a woman who likes to be persuaded."

Hot temper streaked to her throat, all but scalding her tongue. "Oh, I'm sure you've persuaded more than your share of women. Like Edda Lou."

Amusement fled from his eyes, to be replaced by anger, then by something else. Something akin to grief. Even as he stepped back she laid a hand on his arm. "Tucker, I'm sorry. That was despicable."

He lifted his beer to swill some of the bitterness out of his throat. "It was close enough to truth."

She shook her head. "You pushed the wrong button, but that's no excuse for saying something like that to you. I am sorry."

"Forget it." He set aside the empty beer, and as much of the hurt as he could manage. They heard Burke shout, and though Tucker's lips curved, she saw that the smile didn't reach his eyes. "Looks like we're finally going to eat. Go on, take that jar out. I'll be along."

"All right." She paused at the door, wishing there was something she could say. But another apology was useless.

When the door swung behind her, Tucker laid his forehead against the refrigerator. He didn't know what he was feeling, didn't have words for it. He hated that. His feelings had always come so easily, even the bad ones. But this morass of emotion that churned inside him at odd times was new, unpleasant, and more than a little frightening.

He'd even dreamed of Edda Lou, and she'd come to him with her body torn and bloated with death. Moss and dank water had dripped from her hair, and her skin had oozed black blood as she pointed a skeletal finger at him.

She had not had to speak for him to know what she meant. His fault. She was dead and it was his fault.

Christ almighty, what was he going to do?

"Tucker? Honey?" Josie slipped into the kitchen to curl an arm around him. "You feeling bad?"

As bad as it gets, he thought, but let out a sigh. "Headache, that's all." He smiled as he turned to her. "Too much beer on an empty stomach."

She stroked his hair. "I've got aspirin in my purse. Extra-strength something or other."

"I'd rather have food."

"Let's go get you a plate." She kept her arm around him as she walked to the door and onto the porch. "Dwayne's already mostly drunk, and I don't want to have to haul both of you home. Especially since I've got a date tonight."

"Who's the winner?"

"That FBI doctor. He's just cute enough to eat." She chuckled and sent Teddy Rubenstein a wave. "I thought I'd try him out for Crystal. She's been sending a lot of looks his way."

"You're a true friend, Josie."

"I know it." She took a deep breath. "Let's get some of those ribs."

◆ ◆ ◆ ◆

*B*EYOND THE OLD SLAVE quarters with their heat-baked stone, beyond the cotton fields smelling of fertilizer and pesticides, was the dark, horseshoe-shaped pond that Sweetwater was named for.

The water wasn't so sweet now, as the poisons used to kill weevils and other crop pests seeped into the ground, generation after generation, and thence into the lake.

But if it wasn't fit to drink, if most would think twice or more about eating any fish caught there, it was still a nice sight under a crescent moon.

Reeds danced languorously in the current and frogs talked and plopped. Cypress knees poked through the surface like old dark bones. The night was clear enough that you could see the gentle ripples on the surface made by mosquitoes and the creatures that snacked on them.

Dwayne had shifted from the beer he'd drunk at Burke's barbecue to his favorite, Wild Turkey. The bottle was only a quarter empty, but he was feeling miserably drunk. He'd have preferred to sit in the house and drink until he passed out, but Della would have laid into him. And he was sick to death of women picking at him.

The letter from Sissy had him eagerly fueling his anger with whiskey. She was going to marry her shoe salesman. He didn't care about that, he told himself. He didn't give a flying fuck if she married some asshole who put his hands all over other people's feet. Christ knew he didn't want her—never had, if it came to that. But he'd be damned if she'd dangle his kids in front of him to try and soak him for more money.

Expensive private schools, expensive clothes. He'd come through, hadn't he, even when Sissy and her slick-haired lawyer had made it next to impossible for him to so much as see either of the boys. "Limited supervised visitations" they called it. Just because he liked to have a drink now and then.

Scowling at the dark water, Dwayne guzzled more whiskey. They'd made him out to be some kind of monster, and he'd never laid a hand on those kids. Sissy either, if it came to that. Though he'd been sorely tempted a time or two, just to show her her place.

But he wasn't a violent man, Dwayne reminded himself. Not like his own daddy had been. He could hold his liquor just fine, and had proven it since he was fifteen. And Sissy Koons had known just what she was getting when she'd spread her legs for him. Had he blamed her for getting pregnant? No sir. He'd married her, bought her a nice house and all the pretty clothes she wanted.

Given her more than she'd deserved, Dwayne told himself now, remembering the letter. If she thought he was going to let that guitar-playing shoe hawker adopt his blood children, she had another think coming. He'd see her in hell first. And he'd be damned if he'd buckle under to that veiled threat that she'd take him back to court if he didn't increase his monthly child support payments.

It wasn't the money. He didn't give a damn about money. Tucker took care of all that. It was the principle. More money, she'd said in her wheedling way, or your sons'll be wearing another man's name.

His children, he thought again, his symbol of his own immortality.

And he had a fondness for them, of course. They were his blood, after all, his link to the future, his shackles to the past. That was why he sent them presents and candy bars. But it was a whole lot different if you had to deal with them face-to-face.

He could still remember how Little Dwayne—who'd been no more than three—had wailed and cried when he walked in on his daddy during a mean drunk. Dwayne had been getting a lot of satisfaction out of smashing Sissy's company glasses against the wall.

Then Sissy had run in, scooping up Little Dwayne as if his father had been tossing *him* against the wall instead of the gold-rimmed tumblers. And the baby had started to bawl.

Dwayne had just stood there, wanting nothing more than to bash all their heads together.

You want something to cry for? By God, I'll give you something to cry for.

That's what his daddy would have said, and the lot of them would have trembled in their boots.

He thought maybe he had said it, too. Maybe he'd screamed it. But Sissy hadn't trembled, she just screamed back at him, her face all red, her eyes full of fury and disgust.

He almost slapped her. Dwayne remembered he came within a hair of knocking her sideways. He even lifted his arm and saw his father's hand on the end of it.

Instead, he stumbled out and drove off to wreck another car.

Sissy had the door bolted when Burke hauled him home the next day. And that had been a powerful humiliation. Not being able to get into his house, and having his wife shout out through the window that she was going down to Greenville to see a lawyer.

Innocence had been ripe with talks for weeks about how Sissy kicked Dwayne out of the house and tossed his clothes through the upstairs window. He had to drink himself into oblivion for days to be able to take it with a shrug.

Women just messed up the natural order of things. Now here was Sissy, popping back to do it again.

What made it worse, what made it bitter, was that Sissy was going to do something with her life. She'd shed Sweetwater as easily as a snake sheds skin, and was moving on. While he—he was bound and mired in generations of Longstreet obligations. The expectations a father passed on to his son. A woman didn't have that to tie her down.

No, a woman could do just as she damn well pleased. It was easy to hate them for that.

Dwayne tipped back the bottle and brooded. He watched the dark water, and as he sometimes did, imagined himself just walking into it, going under, taking a big, deadly drink, and sinking to the bottom with his lungs full of lake.

His eyes still on the surface, he drank, drowning himself in whiskey instead.

◆ ◆ ◆ ◆

*A*T A TABLE AT McGreedy's Tavern, Josie was just heating up. Next to the beauty parlor, the tavern was her favorite spot in town. She loved its dark, whiskey-soaked walls, its sticky floors, its rocky tables. She loved it every bit as much as she loved the equally boozy but much more elegant parties she often attended in Atlanta and Charlotte and Memphis.

It never failed to cheer her up to walk into that smoke- and liquor-tainted air, listen to the country sounds on the juke, to the voices raised in anger or amusement, the snap of pool balls from the room in the back.

She'd brought Teddy here to down a few beers at her favorite table—under the head of the scarred old buck McGreedy had bagged back when people were pinning I like Ike buttons to their lapels.

She slapped Teddy on the back, hooted with laughter at an outrageous joke he'd told her, then reached for her cigarette.

"You're a pistol, Teddy. You sure you haven't got a wife hiding somewhere?"

"Two exes." Teddy grinned through Josie's haze of smoke. He hadn't had so much fun since he'd rigged a cadaver with fishing wire so he could make the arms and legs move in time with "Twist and Shout."

"Now, that's a coincidence. I've got two of my own. First one was a lawyer." Smiling, she drew the word out into two elongated syllables. "A fine, upstanding young man from a fine, upstanding Charleston family. Just the kind of husband my mama wanted me hook on to. Nearly bored me to death before the year was out."

"Stuffy?"

"Oh, honey." She tilted her head back so the cool beer slid straight down. "I tried to shake him out of it. I gave a party, a fancy dress ball for New Year's? I came as Lady Godiva." Cocking a brow, she ran her hand through her wild black hair. "I wore a blond wig." Her eyes glittered as she rested her chin on her hands. "Just the wig. Old Franklin—that was his name—Franklin just couldn't get himself in a partying mood."

Teddy could easily imagine her in nothing more than a fall of blond hair, and figured he'd have partied just fine. "No sense of humor," he commented.

"You said it. So naturally, when I decided to go husband-hunting again, I looked for a different kind. I met a rough, tough cowboy type on a dude ranch up in Oklahoma. We had some high old times." She sighed, reminiscing. "Then I found out he was cheating on me. That wasn't so bad, but it turned out he was cheating with cowboys instead of cowgirls."

"Ouch," Teddy said, wincing in sympathy. "And I thought it was rough just having my wives tell me I had a disgusting job." He gave Josie a wink. "Women don't usually find my work suitable for conversation."

"I think it's fascinating." She signaled for another round, shifting so that she could rub her bare foot over his calf. "You have to be smart, don't you? Running all those tests, finding out who killed someone just by cutting up, you know. A corpse." Her eyes glowed as she leaned closer. "I just don't see how it works, Teddy. I mean, how can you tell about a killer from a dead body?"

"Well." He slurped up some beer. "It's pretty technical, but in easy terms, you just put all the puzzle pieces together. Cause of death, time and place. Fibers, maybe blood that doesn't belong to the victim. Skin scrapings, hair samples."

"Sounds creepy." Josie gave a delicate shudder. "Are you finding out stuff about Edda Lou?"

"We've got the time, the place, and the method." Unlike some of his colleagues, he wasn't bored by shop talk. "Once I conclude my tests, I'm going to correlate my findings with the county coroner's on the other two women." Sympathetic, Teddy patted her hand. "I guess you knew all of them."

"I sure did. Went to school with Francie and Arnette. Arnette and I even double-dated some—in our wild, misspent youth." She grinned into her beer. "And I guess I knew Edda Lou all her life. Not that we were good friends. But it's scary, thinking about her dying."

She cupped her chin on her hands. There was a gypsy look about her, that long, curling black hair, the golden eyes and golden skin. She'd exploited the image that day by adding wide hoops to her ears and baring her shoulders in a red elastic-necked blouse. Teddy's mouth watered just looking at her.

"I guess you can't tell if she suffered much," Josie said softly.

"I can tell you most of the wounds were inflicted after death." He gave her hand a comforting squeeze. "Don't you think about it."

"I can't help it." Her eyes flicked down to her fresh drink, then back to his. "To tell the truth—I can tell you the truth, can't I, Teddy?"

"Sure."

"Death just fascinates me." She gave a quick, embarrassed laugh, then leaned closer. He caught a seductive drift of her perfume, felt the brush of her breast against his arm. "I guess I can tell you, because it's your business. When people get killed, and it's in the papers and on the TV, I just lap it up."

He chuckled. "Everybody does. They just don't say so."

"You're right." She scooted her chair closer to his so that her dark sweep of hair brushed his cheek. "You know when they have that stuff on like *A Current Affair* or *Unsolved Mysteries*? Those shows about, like, psychos and hatchet killers? I just think it's so interesting. I mean, how come they do all that stuff to people, and why they're so hard to catch. I guess we're all a little nervous about having somebody like that roaming around town, but it's exciting, too. You know?"

Teddy lifted his beer in salute. "That's what sells supermarket tabloids."

"Inquiring minds, right?" She chuckled and tapped her bottle against his. "I've got a real inquiring mind. You know, Teddy . . . I've never seen a dead body. I mean, before it's all prettied up and in a casket in church."

He saw the question in her eyes and frowned. "Now, Josie, you don't need to see that."

Her bare foot continued to caress his calf. "I guess it sounds kind of morbid and awful, but, I think it might be kind of . . . educational."

◆ ◆ ◆ ◆

TEDDY KNEW IT WAS a mistake, but it was hard to resist Josie Longstreet when her mind was set. The fact that they were both half drunk and giggly didn't help. After three wavering tries, he stuck the key he'd been given into the lock in Palmer's rear door.

"This the delivery entrance?" Josie said, covering her mouth to hold in the shaky chuckle.

Teddy reached back into childhood. "Palmer's Funeral Parlor. You kill 'em, we chill 'em."

Josie laughed so hard she had to cross her legs. Together, they stumbled through the doorway. "Gosh, it's dark."

"Let me get the light."

"No." Her heart was thudding. To show him, she took his hand and pressed it to her breast. "That would spoil the mood."

Teddy leaned her back against the door and enjoyed a long, sloppy kiss. Pressing himself against her, he worked his hands under her blouse. Her breasts spilled over the flimsy half cups that supported them and filled his palms. Her nipples were long, and hard as stone.

"Jesus." His breath was coming in pants. "You've got terrific muscle tone." He replaced his hands with his mouth and started to struggle with her shorts.

"Hold on, honey. I swear, you're as horny as a two-peckered goat." She laughed and nudged him away. "Let me find a flashlight." Thrusting her hand in her purse, she rooted until she came up with a pen-sized flash. She ran it over the walls, making shadows shake. She felt giddy with fear and excitement, as if she'd been watching the horror flick showing at the Sky View. "Which way?"

To humor her, Teddy danced his fingers up her arm until she shivered. "Walk this way," he invited her, and set off in a shambling gait that made her giggle again.

"You're such a card, Teddy." But she kept close to his back. "Smells like dead roses, and . . . Lord knows."

"That's the ghostly scent of departed souls, my dear." No use telling her it was embalming fluid, formaldehyde, and Mr. Clean. He moved to another door, and using her light, found the next key.

"You're sure?"

She swallowed, nodded.

Teddy pushed open the door, wishing the Palmers were less fastidious. A nice moaning creak would have been perfect. Josie took a deep breath and hit the lights.

"Shit." She rubbed damp palms on her thighs. "It looks sort of like a dentist's office. What do you use those hoses for?"

He smiled, wiggled his eyebrows. "Do you really want to know?"

She moistened her lips. "Maybe not. Is that . . ." She gestured toward the form under the white sheet. "Is that her?"

"The one and only."

Josie felt her insides tremble. "I want to see."

"Okay. But it's look and don't touch." Teddy walked over and eased down the sheet.

Josie's mind spun once, twice, then settled. "Jesus," she whispered. "Jesus. She's gray."

"Haven't had time to fix her makeup."

Pressing a hand to her stomach, Josie took another step. "Her throat . . ."

"Cause of death." He rubbed a palm on Josie's apple-firm bottom. "The knife had a six-, maybe seven-inch blade. Now look here." He eased one of Edda Lou's arms from under the sheet. "See the way this area of the wrist is discolored? The flaking skin? She was tied with a common clothesline."

"Wow."

"She also bit her nails." He tut-tutted and covered the hand again. "This contusion at the base of the skull"—he turned the head—"it shows that she was struck before death. Certainly hard enough to render her unconscious, during which time we would conclude she was bound and gagged. There were fiber traces in her mouth and on her tongue that indicate the use of a red cotton cloth."

"You can tell all that?" Josie found herself hanging on every word.

"All that and more."

"Was she, you know, raped?"

"I'm running tests on that. If we're lucky enough to find a trace of sperm, we can run a DNA."

"Uh-huh." She'd heard the term somewhere. "Whoever did it killed her and the baby."

"The lady died alone," Teddy corrected her. "Hormone levels were flat low."

"Pardon?"

"No buns in her oven."

"Oh, yeah?" Josie looked down at the gray, lifeless face, and her mouth pursed in thought. "I told him she was lying."

"Told who?"

She shook off the thought. This was no time to bring up Tucker's name. Instead, she looked away from Edda Lou and around the room.

The thing was, once you got settled inside, it was fascinating. All those bottles and tubes and slim, shiny instruments. She strolled over to pick up a scalpel, and in testing the blade, sliced the pad of her thumb. "Shit."

"Baby, you shouldn't touch those things." All solicitude, Teddy whipped out a handkerchief and dabbed at the thin line of blood. Over his head, Josie stared at the face on the embalming table. Beer made her head woozy.

"I didn't know it was so sharp."

"Sharp enough to slice little pieces off you." He clucked and dabbed until she smiled. He really was the cutest thing.

"It'll stop quicker if you suck on it." She brought her wounded thumb to his mouth, eased it between his lips. While his tongue laved the wound, she let her eyes close. There was a powerful intimacy, knowing he was tasting her blood. When her eyes opened again, they were heavy with lust.

"I've got something for you, Teddy." As he drew her thumb deep into his mouth, she reached over the tray of keen-edged instruments, her hand wavering, then finding the purse she'd dropped there. While his hand slid up her thigh, hers dug into the bag. It convulsed into a fist as his fingers slid under the hem of her shorts, nipped under the elastic of her panties, and found her.

"Here you go." With a little sigh she pulled out a condom. Her eyes were gold and hot as she yanked down his zipper. "Why don't I put this on for you?"

Teddy shuddered as his pants fell to his ankles. "Be my guest."

◆ ◆ ◆ ◆

*W*HEN JOSIE SHOT DOWN the drive to Sweetwater about two A.M., feeling used up and sated from sex, Billy T. Bonny was crouching behind the front fender of the red Porsche. He swore as the headlights sliced the dark a few inches from his head. Ten more minutes and he'd have been finished and gone.

His heartbeat roared as Josie hit the brakes. Gravel spat out and bounced on the toes of his work boots. His grease-smeared fingers tightened around the handle of his wrench.

As she climbed out of her car, he held himself in a tight ball and watched her feet. They were bare, carmine-tipped, and she wore a thin gold chain around her ankle. He felt a quick rush of sexual interest. Her scent was on the air, darkly sweet, mixed with the deeper tones of recent sex.

She was humming Patsy Cline's "Crazy." She dropped her purse, scattering lipsticks, loose change, a small department store's worth of cosmetics, two mirrors, a handful of foil-wrapped condoms, a bottle of aspirin, a neat little pearl-handled derringer, and three boxes of Tic Tacs. Billy T. bit back an oath as she bent to retrieve her belongings.

From the underbelly of the Porsche, Billy watched the long line of her legs fold up as she crouched, saw her hand scramble around, dumping the contents back into the bag along with a fair share of gravel.

"Hell with it," she muttered. Yawning hugely, she got to her feet and started toward the house.

Billy T. waited a full thirty seconds after the door shut before he went back to work.

Chapter 9

ON SUNDAY MORNINGS MOST of Innocence gathered in one of its three churches. The Church of Redemption was for the Methodists, and made up a large part of the religious pie. It was a small gray box smack in the center of town. It had been built in 1926 on the site of the original First Methodist Church which had washed away—along with Reverend Scottsdale and the church secretary he'd been breaking several commandments with—in flood waters in '25.

On the south end of town was Innocence Bible Church, where the blacks went to worship. There was no law of God or man that segregated the churches. But tradition was often stronger than law.

Every blessed Sunday the sound of rich voices raised in song flowed through the open windows with a clarity the Methodists couldn't compete with.

Across from Redemption and down a block was Trinity Lutheran. It was famous for its bake sales. Della Duncan, being in charge of such matters, was given to bragging that Trinity had raised enough money selling brownies and custard pies to buy a stained glass window. That had inspired Happy Fuller to organize three catfish suppers for Redemption so that they could buy a bigger window.

Those down at the Bible were content with their clear glass and clear voices.

Sundays were a time for prayer, contemplation, and fierce competition in Innocence. From three pulpits the word of God rang out and sin was put in its place. In hard wooden pews old men and children nodded off in the heat, and women wielded their fans. Organs blared and babies wailed. Hard-earned money was dropped into the passing plates. Sweat rolled.

In all three holy places, preachers bowed their heads and reminded the congregation of Edda Lou Hatinger. Prayers were requested for Mavis Hatinger, her husband—in none of the churches was Austin referred to by name—and her remaining children.

In the back pew of Redemption, pale with grief and confusion, Mavis wept silent tears. Three of her five children were with her. Vernon, who'd inherited his father's sullen looks and mean temper, sat beside his wife, Loretta. She hushed their toddler as best she could with a well-used pacifier and practiced knee bounces. Her cotton dress stretched tight across her pregnant belly.

Ruthanne sat beside her, dry-eyed and silent. She was eighteen, and ten days out of Jefferson Davis High School. She was sorry her sister had died, though she hadn't loved Edda Lou. Sitting in the stifling church, all she could think of was how quickly she could make enough money to get out of Innocence.

Bored and wishing he were anywhere else was young Cy. His feet were cramped inside the hard black shoes that were already a size too small, and his neck was chafed from the starch his mother had sprayed into his collar. His family was an embarrassment to him, but at fourteen, he was stuck with them.

He hated the fact that the preacher was talking about them like they were to be pitied and prayed for. Too many of his peers were scattered through the congregation, and his face flamed every time one of them shot a look over a shoulder. It was a great relief to Cy when the service ended and they could stand up. As sachet-scented ladies made their way to his mother to express sympathy, he ducked out the back of the pew and hurried off to have a smoke behind Larsson's.

It all sucked as far as Cy could see. His sister was dead, his father and his brother were in jail. His mama didn't do much more than wring her hands and talk to the Legal Aid guy in Greenville. All Vernon could talk about was paying somebody back. Loretta agreed with every word; she'd learned to agree fast and avoid a fist in the eye. A real quick study, that Loretta.

Cy lighted one of the three Pall Malls he'd swiped from Vernon and tugged at his tie.

Ruthanne had more sense than the rest, Cy decided. But she was always busy counting her money—just like Silas Marner and his coins. Cy knew she hid her cache in a box of sanitary napkins—a place her father would never look. Because Cy had a sense of loyalty—and he'd be just as happy to see her go—he kept Ruthanne's secret to himself.

He'd already figured that the minute he had his high school diploma, he'd be lighting out himself. There would be no chance of college for him. As Cy had a keen and thirsty mind, that hurt more than a little. But he was also a pragmatic sort and accepted what was.

Though he'd yet to find real pleasure in smoking, he took another drag.

"Hey." Jim March sidled around the building. He was a tall boy, gangly, with skin the color of molasses. Like Cy, Jim was in his Sunday best. "Whatcha doing?"

In the way of old friends, he dropped down beside Cy.

"Just having a smoke. You?"

"Nothing." Comfortable with each other, they lapsed into silence. "Sure am glad school's out," Jim said at length.

"Yeah." Cy wasn't about to embarrass himself by admitting he liked school. "Got the whole summer." For Cy, it stretched out interminably.

"Going to get you a job?"

Cy moved his shoulders. "Ain't no work."

Jim carefully folded his bright red tie and put it in his pocket. "My daddy's doing some work for that Miz Waverly." Jim didn't consider it politic to mention that his father had replaced the windows Cy's father had blown out. "Going to paint her whole house. I'm helping."

"Guess you'll be a rich man."

"Shit." Jim grinned and began to draw patterns in the dirt. "Get me some pocket money though. Got two dollars right now."

"That's two more'n I got."

Lips pursed, Jim slanted a look at his friend. They weren't supposed to be friends, not according to Cy's old man. But they'd managed to remain so, on the sly. "I heard tell the Longstreets are hiring on for field work."

Cy hooted and passed the Pall Mall to Jim to finish off. "My daddy'd skin me alive if I went near Sweetwater."

"Guess so."

But his daddy was in jail, Cy remembered. If he could get work, he could start his own secret fund, just like Ruthanne. "You sure they're hiring?"

"What I heard. Miss Della's down at the church bake sale. You could ask her." He smiled at Cy. "They've got lemon pies down there. Might get one for two dollars. Sure would be nice to take some lemon pie down to Gooseneck Creek and catch some cats."

"Sure would." Cy cast a look at his friend. His grin was slow and surprisingly lovely. "I really oughta help you eat it, or else you'll just pig it down and puke it up."

♦ ♦ ♦ ♦

*W*HILE THE BOYS WERE negotiating for pie, and women were showing off their Sunday dresses, Tucker was spread over his bed, luxuriating in a half doze.

He loved Sundays. The house was quiet as a tomb, with Della off to town and everyone else asleep or sprawled somewhere with the Sunday paper.

In his mother's day it had been different. Then the whole house had marched off to church—spit and polish—to take their place in the front pew. His mother would smell of lavender and be wearing her grandmother's pearls.

After service there would be a varied critique of the sermon, talk of weather and crops. New babies would be admired and clucked over. Grown children come back to visit would be shown off by proud parents, and the young would take the opportunity to sashay and flirt.

Afterward, they would sit down to Sunday dinner. Glazed ham, sweet potatoes, fresh biscuits, green beans swimming in pot liquor, and maybe some pecan pie. And flowers, there would always be flowers on the table. His mother had seen to that.

Out of respect for her, Tucker's father never touched a bottle on Sunday, not from sunup to sundown. As a result, those long afternoons took on a pleasant, dreamy quality in retrospect—an illusion perhaps, but a comforting one.

Part of Tucker missed those days. But there was something to be said for snoozing in a quiet house with the chatter of birds piping outside, the hum of the fan stirring air, and the happy notion that there was no place to go and nothing to do.

He heard a car engine and rolled over in bed. The movement revived a few aches. He grunted, waiting for the discomfort and the disturbance to pass.

The knock on the front door had Tucker opening one eye. Sunlight speared it, causing him to hiss through his teeth. He considered playing possum, waiting for Josie or Dwayne to handle things. But Josie's room was on the other side of the house, and Dwayne was probably just as comatose as he'd been last night when Tucker hauled him in from the lake.

"Shit. Go the hell away."

He had snuggled into the pillow and was willing himself back to sleep when the knocking stopped. Before he could congratulate himself, Burke's voice rose from beneath his window.

"Tucker, get your butt up. I gotta talk to you. Dammit, Tuck, it's important."

"Always goddamn important," Tucker muttered as he pushed himself out of bed. All of his aches and pains began to awaken. Naked and irritable, he pushed open the terrace doors.

"Jesus." Burke tossed his cigarette aside and took a long, slow scan of Tucker's body. It was a palette of black, blue, and sickly yellow. "He really worked you over, didn't he, son?"

"Did you come all the way out here and wake me up just to make that stunning observation?"

"You come on out and I'll tell you why I'm here. And put some clothes on before I haul you in for indecent exposure."

"Up yours, Sheriff." Tucker stumbled back into the bedroom, looked at his tangled sheets with some regret, then grabbed some cotton drawstring pants and his sunglasses. That was as close to dressed as he intended to get.

Since he wasn't feeling kindly toward Burke, he took a detour into the bathroom to empty his bladder and brush his teeth.

"Haven't even had a cup of goddamn coffee," he grumbled when he walked out onto the porch. Burke was sitting on one of the rockers. From the shine on his shoes and the crispness of his shirt, it was obvious he'd come straight from service.

"Sorry to get you up so early. Can't be more than a minute past noon."

"Give me a cigarette, you bastard."

Burke obliged, waited until Tucker had finished his little routine. "You really think making them shorter's going to help you quit?"

"Eventually." Tucker pulled in smoke, winced as it burned, then blew it out. He drew again, felt marginally better, and sat. "So Burke, what brings you calling?"

Burke frowned at the peonies Tucker had tried to salvage. "Talked to that Dr. Rubenstein a while ago. He was having breakfast at the Chat 'N Chew. Waved me inside."

"Hmmm." That had Tucker giving some thought to breakfast himself. Maybe he could sweet-talk Della into fixing up some hotcakes.

"He wanted to fill me in on a couple things—mostly because he knows it'll yank Burns's chain. He's strictly by-the-book—Burns, I mean. Damn near taking over my office. Can't say I care for it."

"You've got my sympathy. Can I go back to bed now?"

"Tucker, it's about Edda Lou." Burke fiddled with his sheriff's badge. He knew it wasn't purely professional for him to pass any information along to Tucker, especially since the FBI still considered him a suspect. But some loyalties ran deeper than the law. "There wasn't a baby, Tuck."

"Huh?"

Burke sighed. "She wasn't pregnant. Came out during the autopsy. There was no baby. I thought you had a right to know."

A rushing sound filled Tucker's head as he stared down at the tip of the cigarette. When he spoke, his voice was slow and deliberate. "She wasn't pregnant."

"No."

"For certain?"

"Rubenstein knows what he's doing, and he says she wasn't."

With his eyes closed, Tucker sat back and rocked. He realized a large portion of his guilt and grief had been due to the child. But there wasn't a child, had never been a child, and grief easily transformed into rage.

"She lied to me."

"I'd have to say that's true."

"She stood there, in front of all those people, and lied about something like that."

Feeling useless, Burke rose. "I thought you should know. It didn't seem right for you to think . . . well, I thought you should know."

Thanks didn't seem quite appropriate, so Tucker only nodded, keeping his eyes closed until he heard the cruiser start, listened to it purr down the long, winding drive.

His hands clenched at his sides. There was a black, bubbling rage in him, geysering up from the pit of his stomach until he tasted the vileness of it in his throat. He recognized the signs, and at another time they might have frightened him.

He wanted to hurt something, smash it, pull it apart and grind it to dust.

His eyes were wild when he opened them. In a headlong rush he was racing into the house, up the steps. In his room he grabbed for his keys and gave himself the satisfaction of smashing a lamp. He snatched a shirt from the arm of a chair and shoved his arms through as he stalked out again.

"Tuck?" Heavy-eyed and wrapped in a red silk robe, Josie started down the hallway. "Tuck, I have something to tell you." The one violent glance he sent her before he flung himself down the stairs cleared the sleep from her brain. She streaked after him, calling, "Tuck! Wait!" She caught up with him as he was yanking open the door of his car. "Tucker, what's wrong?"

He shook her off, fighting to hold the animal inside him on a choke chain. "Stay away from me."

"Honey, I just want to help. We're family." She made a grab for the keys, then gasped when his hand clamped tightly around her wrist.

"Get the hell away."

A film of tears coated her eyes. "If you'll just let me talk to you. Tucker, Tucker, I went out with the doctor last night. The FBI doctor." She raised her voice to a shout as the Porsche gunned to life. "Edda Lou wasn't pregnant. There wasn't a baby, Tuck. It was a trap, just like I told you."

His head whipped around, his gaze speared into hers. "I know." He sent gravel flying as he tore up the drive.

Josie hissed and grabbed her calf where one of the stones struck. Furious, she snatched up a handful and flung them after the car.

"Jesus H. Christ. What's all this racket?"

Josie turned to see Dwayne on the porch. His hands were over his eyes. He squinted out from under them, swaying, wearing nothing but his Jockey shorts.

"It's nothing," Josie said on a sigh as she started back up the steps. There didn't seem to be anything she could do for Tucker, but she could tend to Dwayne. "Let's go get us some coffee, honey."

The wheel vibrated under Tucker's hand when he whipped it to make the turn toward town. He was too furious to give a damn when the rear end fishtailed and the tires sang.

She wasn't going to get away with it. That single thought ran circles in his head. She was damn well not going to get away with it. Teeth clenched, he punched the accelerator and jumped up to eighty.

Even with the curves and twists the road took, he could see for miles. The heat waves shimmied up from the patched road and turned distance into a watery mirage. He didn't know where he was going or what he was going to do, but it would be done now. Right now.

He closed a hand over the gearshift, preparing to downshift for the curve just before the McNair place. But when he tugged the wheel, the car stayed arrow straight. He had time to swear, to wrestle the wheel, and to tramp on what turned out to be nearly useless brakes.

♦ ♦ ♦ ♦

WITH ONE OF HER grandmother's wide-brimmed hats shading her face, Caroline attacked the overgrowth beside her lane. Despite the heat and her aching arms, she was having the time of her life. The clippers were sharp as a razor, and their wooden handles were worn smooth by time and use. The short gardening gloves she wore protected her hands from blisters. She imagined her grandmother wearing them to perform this same homey chore.

She knew she could have waited and assigned the task to Toby. But she was enjoying it, the sun, the dusty heat, the verdant smell of green. She was enjoying the simple accomplishment of caring for her own. All around her was a chorus of birds, the hum of the afternoon, the heaviness of solitude. It was precisely what she wanted, and after taking a moment to rub her aching shoulder, she sheared off a vine as thick as her thumb.

She heard the roar of a car engine. Before she shaded her eyes and looked down toward the slice of road she could see at the end of her lane, she knew it was Tucker. The car was coming so fast, and she recognized the powerful purr of his engine.

One of these days, she thought as she put a hand on her hip, he was going to turn that car into a Tinker Toy and put himself in the hospital. And if he was heading her way, she would tell him so. Why the man was . . .

Her thoughts spun off as she heard the high squeal of rubber on pavement. She heard the shout, and though it contained more fury than fear, she was already running before she heard the crash of glass and rending of metal.

The clippers went flying out of her hands. Above the roaring of her heart all she could hear was the bouncy strains of the young Carl Perkins warning everybody off his blue suede shoes.

"Oh my God!" She saw the ruts torn into the grassy shoulder an instant before she spotted the Porsche sitting drunkenly against the post that had held her mailbox. Shattered glass winked like diamonds over the surface of the road. She saw Tucker slumped over the wheel, and screaming his name, ran to the car.

"Oh, God, my God. Tucker."

Terrified to move him, terrified to leave him, she touched gentle hands to his face. She squeaked out a fresh scream when he jerked his head back.

"Fuck."

She inhaled in three shaky gasps. "You *idiot*! I thought you were dead. You should be dead the way you drive. A grown man, tearing down the road like some hyped-up, irresponsible teenager. I don't see how you can—"

"Shut up, Caro." He put a hand to his pounding forehead and discovered he was bleeding. What else was new? When he fumbled for the door handle, she jerked it open herself.

"If you weren't hurt, I'd punch you." But she leaned over to help him to his feet.

"I'm in the mood to punch back." His vision grayed, infuriating him, and he leaned on the undamaged rear fender. "Turn the radio off, will you? Get the keys."

She was still muttering to herself when she ripped them out of the ignition. "You killed my mailbox. I suppose we should be thankful it wasn't another car."

"I'll make sure you have a new one tomorrow."

"It's so easy for you to replace things, isn't it?" Fear sharpened her voice as she put an arm around his waist and took his weight.

"Most things." His fucking head was going to fall off, he thought. That might not be so easy to replace. She was still ripping into him as she guided him down the lane toward the house. The sharp stab of gravel reminded him he'd neglected to stop for shoes. He felt a trickle of blood skim down his temple. "Back off, Caroline."

There was something in his voice—not the anger, but the misery—that made her subside. "Lean on me a little more," she murmured. "I'm stronger than I look."

"You look like something a good breeze would blow away." The house wavered in his vision, and he was afraid he might faint. He squinted, which hurt his bruised eye enough to clear the dizziness. "You've got this fragile look about you. Never appealed to me before."

"I'm sure I'm supposed to be flattered."

"But you're not fragile. You're a tough one, Caro, and you're pissed at me. Just hold off yelling for a little while."

"Why should I yell?" She could tell from the hollowness in his voice that he was close to passing out. Keep him angry, keep the adrenaline up, she told herself. If he went down, she wouldn't be able to get him up. "It certainly wouldn't make a difference to me if you wrecked your car and ended up a smear on the road. I'd prefer you do it somewhere other than next to my lane, though."

"Do what I can. Honey, I gotta sit down."

"Almost to the porch." She half dragged him another foot. "You can sit down there."

"Never liked bossy women."

"Then I'm safe." When she got him to the porch and he was still upright, she pulled him along inside.

"You said I could sit—"

"I lied."

He gave a weak, somehow grim laugh. "Women always do."

"Now you can." She eased him down on the couch with the bullet hole through the cushion. After heaving his legs up, she propped a pillow under his head. "I'm going to call Doc Shays, then I'll clean you up."

He made a grab for her hand, and missed, but the movement stopped her. "Don't call him. It's just a bump and I've got plenty more."

"You could be concussed."

"I could be a lot of things. All he'll do is give me a shot of something. I really hate needles, you know?"

Because she did know, and sympathized, she wavered. The bump didn't seem so bad, and he was certainly lucid. "I'll clean you up, then we'll see."

"Fine. How about a bucket of ice with a beer in it?"

"Ice yes, beer no. Just lie still."

"Woman never will get me a beer," Tucker said under his breath. "I'm lying here bleeding to death and all she does is bitch and nag."

"I heard that," Caroline called from the kitchen.

"They always do." On a sigh, Tucker let his eyes close. He didn't open them again until Caroline pressed a cold cloth to the cut on his forehead. "How come you're wearing that ugly hat?"

"It's not ugly." She felt a trickle of relief as she studied the wound and found it shallow.

"Honey, you may be wearing it, but I'm looking at it, and I'm telling you, it's ugly."

"Fine." Annoyed, she tossed it off, then took a bottle of iodine from the coffee table where she'd set her medical supplies.

Tucker sent the bottle a baleful glance. "Don't do that."

"Baby."

Smiling, he took her wrist. "I think you're real cute, too, sugar."

"That wasn't an endearment." She merely switched the bottle to her other hand and dabbed on the iodine. He yelped and swore. "Oh, get a grip, Tucker."

"Least you can do is blow on it."

She did. His hand snuck from her wrist to her thigh. Caroline gave the cut one last blow, then slapped his hand aside.

"Jesus. Have some respect for the injured."

"Just be still while I bandage this." She snipped some gauze and tape. "And if your hand starts wandering again, I'll give you a lump twice as big as this one."

"Yes, ma'am." Her hands were gentle, and except for the sledgehammer pounding his brain, he was feeling considerably better.

"Are you hurt anywhere else?"

Her hands felt soft and cool as raindrops. "Can't say. Why don't you check?"

She ignored the smirk in his voice and unbuttoned his shirt. "I certainly hope this teaches you . . . oh, God, Tucker."

His eyes jerked open. "What? What?"

"You're all black and blue."

He took a moment to be grateful she hadn't found a rib sticking out. "Those're old. Austin."

"Why, that's hideous." Horror stung her voice and turned her eyes green as emeralds. "He should be locked up."

He had to smile. "He is locked up, darlin'. Right and tight in the county jail. Carl transported him yesterday."

Caroline laid gentle fingers on his bruised ribs. "He really hurt you."

Pride nettled. "He didn't walk away smiling."

"Of course, that makes it all right." Caroline jerked her hands away and popped open a bottle of painkiller Dr. Palamo had prescribed for her stress headaches. "Men are all idiots."

Carefully, Tucker propped himself on his elbows. "I didn't start it. He came after me."

"Just shut up and take one of these."

"What am I taking?"

"Something that won't laugh at that headache I imagine you've got."

He took the pill, grateful, but also scanned the label of the bottle. If it did the job, he'd have to ask Doc Shays to get him some for the rest of his pains. Tucker swallowed it with a sip of the water she offered. "Can I have that beer if I'm able to stand up?"

"No."

He laid his head back against the cushion. "Just as well. Darlin', do me a favor and call Junior Talbot. He's going to have to come on down and tow my car."

"I'll take care of it." She rose, then shot him a warning look. "Don't go to sleep. You're not supposed to sleep if you have a concussion."

"Why not?"

Frustration added an edge to her voice. "I don't know why not, I'm not a doctor. It's just something you hear all the time."

"I won't go to sleep if you promise to come right back and hold my hand."

Caroline lifted a brow. "If you go to sleep, I'm calling Doc Shays and telling him to bring his longest needle."

"Christ, you're a mean one." But his lips curved as she walked out.

She gave him less than three minutes to consider drifting off before she returned with an ice pack. "Junior said he'd be out as soon as he could get away." When he only grunted, she laid the ice pack on his head, and the grunt turned into a long "ah" of gratitude. "I didn't know whether I should call your family."

"Not yet. Della'll be in town awhile longer. I forgot she was running a bake sale today. Josie's not likely to go anywhere, especially if Dwayne wakes up with his usual Sunday head." Lord, he was tired. Not the pleasant, sleepy tired of a lazy afternoon, but tired clean to the bone. "Anyway, wrecking cars is kind of a hobby in my family."

She frowned at him. Since his color was coming back, she felt she had a right to demand an explanation. "Then the lot of you should take up croquet or needlepoint. Where the hell were you going in such a hurry?"

"I don't know. Anywhere."

"Anywhere's a stupid place to go barefoot at a hundred miles an hour."

"More like eighty. You tend to exaggerate."

"You could have killed yourself."

"Since I felt like killing somebody else, it was a better bet." He opened his eyes, and though she could see the pain had misted away—Dr. Palamo's magic worked quickly—there was something else, something deeper and more poignant.

"Did something happen?"

"There wasn't a baby," he heard himself say.

"Excuse me?"

"She wasn't pregnant. She lied to me. She stood there, looked me right in the eye, and told me she had my baby inside her. And it was a lie."

It took Caroline a moment to realize he was talking about Edda Lou—the Edda Lou she had found floating in the pond. "I'm sorry." She folded her hands in her lap, unsure what to say or how to say it.

He didn't know why he was telling her, but once started, he couldn't stem the words. "These last few days . . . it's been eating at me. Thinking about her dying that way. She meant something to me once. Almost meant something to me. Thinking about that, and thinking that a part of me died with her was . . . but there wasn't any part of me in Edda Lou, except for a lie."

"Maybe she made a mistake. She might have thought she was pregnant."

He gave a short laugh. "I hadn't slept with her in nearly two months. A woman like Edda Lou keeps close track of that kind of female business. She knew." He closed his eyes briefly, and when they opened again, a trace of the wild rage glowed in them. "Why am I so mad that there wasn't a baby? She lied, so that means no baby died, and I don't have to hurt thinking about it anymore."

Caroline did hold his hand, even brought it up to her cheek for a moment in comfort. She hadn't realized he had feelings that traveled that deep and difficult a road. The part of her that softened for him would never be able to harden again.

"Sometimes we hurt more for what might have been than for what is."

He turned his palm so that their fingers linked. She had the loveliest and the saddest eyes he'd ever seen. "You sound like you know what I'm talking about."

She smiled, and didn't object when he kissed her knuckles. "I do." Always cautious, she drew her hand free before it lingered too long in his. "Why don't I go out and see if Junior's made it yet?"

He didn't want to break the contact yet, not quite yet. With an effort he pushed himself up. "Why don't we both go?" the room revolved once, slowly, then settled. "If you'll give me a hand."

She looked down at his outstretched hand. It was foolish, she supposed, to think he was asking for more than momentary support. Shaking off the feeling, she reached out and joined her hand with his.

Chapter 10

JUNIOR TALBOT STEPPED OUT of the cab of his tow truck, stuck a finger under his Atlanta Braves fielder's cap, and dug through his tangled mop of red hair to scratch his head. He made a long, slow circle around Tucker's mangled Porsche, his J. C. Penney work boots crunching on shards of glass. His pale blue eyes were sober in his round, powerfully freckled face. Thoughtfully, he pulled at his full bottom lip.

Caroline thought he looked like Howdy Doody on tranquilizers.

"Seems like you got yourself some trouble here," he said at length.

"Little bit," Tucker agreed. "Got a smoke, Junior?"

"Guess so." Junior pulled a pack of Winstons from the breast pocket of his grease-stained work shirt. He shook the pack, shooting a cigarette out to the filter, carefully replacing the pack after Tucker had taken it. Then he crouched down to contemplate the mashed fender. There was another long moment of silence. "Sure used to be a pretty car."

Tucker knew Junior wasn't rubbing his nose in it. It was simply his nature to state the obvious. Leaning over, Tucker opened the glove compartment and found a pack of matches. "I s'pose they can fix her up, down in Jackson."

Junior thought about that awhile. "I s'pose," he decided. "Could be you bent the frame, though. They got a way of straightening them out now. Used to be, you bent the frame and that was all she wrote."

Tucker smiled through a haze of smoke. "You just can't stop progress."

"That's the truth." Taking his time, Junior straightened, then studied the torn grass on the verge of the road, the shower of glass, and the lack of skid marks. After some consideration, he decided to have a cigarette himself. "You know, Tucker, I always said you were the best driver I've seen, outside of the time I went down to Daytona to watch the 500."

Caroline gave a snort, and was politely ignored.

"I recall how you took the Bonny boys for twenty dollars in the drag race down on Highway One—back in July of seventy-six it was. They put their Camaro up against your Mustang." Junior accepted a match from Tucker and lit it with a flick of his thumbnail. "Wasn't no contest."

Tucker remembered the race with pleasure. "Might've been closer if Billy T. had let John Thomas drive."

Junior nodded agreeably. "Closer, maybe. But neither of those boys got the talent for driving you have."

"Idiots," Caroline said under her breath. If Junior heard her, he pretended not to. He'd been a married man more than a year now, and knew when a man should let his ears work and when he shouldn't.

"I gotta ask you," Junior continued in the same slow, quiet voice. "How'd you happen to hit this pole here?"

"Well . . ." Tucker took a considering drag. "You could say the car got away from me. Steering seized up."

Junior nodded and continued to smoke. Caroline nearly asked them if they'd like her to go back and fetch a couple of folding chairs so they could have their conversation in comfort.

"Don't look to me like you even hit the brakes."

"I hit them," Tucker said. "They were out."

Junior eyes came as close to sharp as they ever did. If it had been anyone else, he would have shrugged off the story. But he knew and admired Tucker's skill at the wheel. "Now, that's a puzzle. Bad steering, bad brakes, all at once in a car like this? No more than six months old, is she?"

"Just."

Junior nodded again. "We'll have to take a look."

"I'd be obliged if you would, Junior."

Caroline held her tongue until Junior walked back to his tow truck. "What the hell does a drag race more than fifteen years ago have to do with you crashing into my mail post?"

Tucker smiled. "It was a hell of a night. Get on back from the car now, darlin'. It might shift some when he hooks it on." Careful to keep her sympathy close to the surface, Tucker slid an arm around her shoulders, leaned a little of his weight on her, and allowed her to help him move back a few feet.

"Are you dizzy?"

He wasn't, but there was such sweet concern in her voice. "Maybe a little," he said—bravely, he thought. "It'll pass." He bit back a smile when her arm curved around his waist in support.

"Let's get you back in the car." She'd insisted on driving him to the end of the lane rather than allowing him to walk. "I'll take you home."

Home, hell. He was just starting to make progress. "Maybe I could just stretch out on your couch till I get my strength back."

She was wavering, he could tell. When he heard the blare of a horn, he had to swallow an oath. Dwayne screeched his white Caddy to a stop, dead in the middle of the road. He hadn't shaved yet, and his hair was sticking out at all angles. He had pulled a pair of pants over his Jockeys and had added a muscle shirt.

"Jesus H. Christ, boy."

He glanced at Tucker, saw he was standing on both feet, and gave his attention to the car Junior was hooking up.

"Out for a Sunday drive, Dwayne?"

"Crystal called." Dwayne whistled through his teeth as he took a look at the front end of the Porsche. "Seems Singleton Fuller was in the Mobile when Junior got the call. He ran into Jed Larsson, then Crystal stopped in for a six-pack of Cokes. Good thing I answered the phone before Josie, or she'd've had a hissy fit for sure." His hangover, thanks to Josie's stock of pills and remedies, had backed off enough to make him sympathetic. "Shit on toast, Tuck, you sure did kill that pretty little toy."

Out of patience, Caroline sucked in a breath. "He's doing as well as can be expected," she shot out. "It could have been worse, but as it happens he only rapped his concrete head. It's understandable that you're so concerned about your brother's condition, but let me reassure you. He'll be fine."

Junior had stopped what he was doing to stare, the cigarette dangling from the corner of his mouth. Dwayne blinked. Tucker struggled not to lose his dignity by hooting with laughter.

She was crazy about him, he decided.

"Yes, ma'am," Dwayne said, meticulously polite. "I can see he is. I just rode down so I could take him home."

"What a concerned, close-knit family you must be."

"We do tend to stick together." When he smiled, there was something charming about him despite the bloodshot eyes, the barroom glow.

"I've never known another family like yours," Caroline said sincerely.

"She's all set, Tuck," Junior called. "I'll let you know what's what."

"You do that. Thanks." Tucker had to turn away. He just couldn't watch his car being towed off. It was almost as bad as watching a loved one being carried away on a stretcher.

"Nice to see you again, Caroline," Dwayne began, then headed to his car. "Let's go, Tucker. There was a game starting when Crystal called. I've missed the whole first inning by now."

"In a minute." Tucker turned back to Caroline. "I appreciate the nursing." He touched a hand to her hair. "And the listening. I didn't realize I needed someone to listen."

It took her a moment to understand he was being sincere. There were no teasing lights in his eyes, no trace of mockery in his voice. "You're welcome."

"I'd like to pay you back." When she started to shake her head, Tucker cupped her chin. "I'd like you to come to dinner tonight, at Sweetwater."

"Really, Tucker, you don't have to—"

"It occurs to me that I'd like you to see me under some better circumstances than I've managed so far." His thumb traced along her jawline. "And I'd just like to see you, period."

Her heartbeat skittered for a moment, but her voice was clear. "I'm not interested in starting anything, not with anyone."

"Having neighbors in for Sunday dinner's an old country custom."

She had to smile. "I don't mind being neighborly."

"Shit, Tuck, would you just kiss her and come on?"

Smiling back, Tucker brushed a finger over her lips. "She won't let me. Yet. Come on down around five, Caro. I'll show you around Sweetwater."

"All right."

She watched him walk to the Caddy, ease in carefully beside his brother. He flashed her a quick grin before Dwayne shot toward Sweetwater, the Caddy hugging dead center of the road.

◆ ◆ ◆ ◆

HERE I COME RUSHING home from the bake sale, thinking you've cracked your skull or worse, and you tell me company's coming." Della whacked her rolling pin down on the pie crust. "Now I don't even know how much we took in. Had to leave Susie Truesdale in charge, and she don't know squat about salesmanship."

As this particular refrain had been playing for the best part of three hours, Tucker decided to act. He pulled a twenty out of his pocket and slapped it on the counter. "There. That's my contribution to the Trinity Lutheran bake sale."

"Hmph." But Della's nimble fingers snatched up the bill and tucked it away in the deep pocket of her apron. She was far from through. "Nearly had me a spell when Earleen came running down to tell me you'd gone and wrecked that car. Told you when you bought it, no good comes of buying foreign. Out racing the roads on the Lord's day, too." She flipped the crust into a pie plate. "And when I come hurrying home to see if you're dead or alive, you tell me you've invited a guest for dinner."

Fuming, she trimmed and fluted the edges. "As if that ham in the oven was going to fix itself. Edith's grandbaby, too. I had a great fondness for Edith, and she told me how her grandbaby'd been to Paris, France, and Italy, walked right into Buckingham Palace and even had dinner with the President of the United States in the White House." She pounded out the next crust. "Here she's coming to dinner and I ain't had time to see if the silver needs polishing. Your mama'd turn over in her grave—God rest her—if I weren't to use the good silver." She wiped the back of her wrist over her brow. Her heavy charm bracelet danced and jangled. "It's just like a man to think Sunday dinner makes itself."

Tucker scowled down at the potato he was peeling. "I'm helping you, aren't I?"

She gave a superior sniff and glanced at him. "Fine help you are. You're taking too much meat off them 'taters—and getting peelings all over my clean floor."

"Jesus Christ—"

Della's eyes flashed with the cold ire Tucker respected. "Don't you use the Lord's name in vain—not in my kitchen on Sunday."

"I'll clean up the floor, Della."

"See that you do—and not with one of my good dishrags neither."

"No, ma'am." It was time to pull out the big guns, Tucker decided. He set the bowl of potatoes in the sink, then moved over to wrap his arms around Della's considerable waist. "I just wanted to do something nice for Caroline after she'd patched up my head."

Della grunted. "I've seen what she looks like. I can guess what that something nice is."

He grinned into her wild red curls. "Can't say the thought hasn't passed through my mind."

"Passed under your zipper, more like." But her lips were quirking. "Seems a bit skinny for your taste."

"Well, see, I figured she'd flesh out some, especially after sampling your cooking. You know there's nobody in the county who can set a table compared to yours. I kind of thought I'd like to impress her, and the sure-fire way was to have her taste some of your honey-glazed ham."

Della snorted and shifted, but the flush of pride was creeping up her cheeks. "I guess I don't begrudge giving the girl a decent meal."

"Decent?" He gave Della a squeeze. "Sugar, she won't have had better in the White House. You can take that to the bank."

Della chuckled and slapped his hands away. "She won't get nothing if I don't finish. You drop them 'taters in that kale I got simmering, then clear out. I can do this quicker without you sniffing 'round."

"Yes'm." Tucker pressed a kiss to her cheek that made her grumble and grin. When he walked out of the steamy kitchen a few minutes later, he found Dwayne sprawled in the parlor watching another baseball game. "Wouldn't hurt you to shave."

Dwayne shifted and reached for the bottle of Coke sitting on the floor. "It's Sunday. I never shave on Sunday."

"We've got company coming."

Dwayne took a long swallow, and swore when the shortstop bobbled the ball. "If I shave, she might see that I'm better looking than you. Then where'd you be?"

"I'll risk it."

Dwayne snorted. "They're going to be pulling this pitcher before the inning's up—if they got half a brain. I'll do it then."

Satisfied, Tucker started upstairs. Before he reached his room, Josie called to him.

"Tucker? Is that you, honey?"

"I'm going to take a shower."

"Well, just come on back here for a minute and help me out."

He checked the grandfather clock, saw he had a half hour before Caroline would arrive, and sauntered down the hall to Josie's room.

It looked like a department store after a clearance sale. Blouses, dresses, lingerie, shoes, were tossed over bed, chair, and window seat. A black lace teddy hung suggestively from the trunk of a stuffed pink elephant some forgotten swain had won for her at the state fair.

She was still wearing the little red robe and her head was stuck in her closet as she pawed through what was left hanging there.

As always, there was a scent clinging to the air, a mixture of perfumes, powders, and lotions. The result was something between the perfume counter at Bloomingdale's and a high-class bordello.

Tucker gave the room a brief survey, and came to the obvious conclusion. "Got a date?"

"Teddy's driving me down to the nine o'clock show in Greenville. I told him to come on to dinner, since we're having company anyway. How's this?" She turned, holding a short orange leather skirt up to her waist.

"Too hot for leather."

Josie pouted a minute because she knew the skirt showed off her legs, then tossed it aside. "You're right. I know what I need, that little cotton dress, the pink one. I wore it at a garden party last month in Jackson and got a marriage proposal and three indecent propositions. Now, where the hell is it?"

Tucker watched as she started tossing through clothes already discarded. "I thought you were trying out the doctor for Crystal."

"I did." She glanced up and grinned. "Thing is, I decided he wasn't Crystal's type at all. And he'll be going back north in a day or two, and that would just break her heart. She couldn't afford to visit him if things got serious between them, And I can. Does your head still hurt?"

"Not much."

"Look here." She pointed to a small bruise on her calf. "You went tearing out of here so fast before, you kicked up gravel. Now I'll have to put Erase on that if I want to wear a skirt."

"Sorry."

She shrugged and went back to looking for the pink dress. "I guess it's okay. You were upset. Everybody's going to know she was lying, Tucker. Even before they bury her on Tuesday, everybody'll know."

"I expect so." He spotted a swatch of shell pink and crouched down to pull the dress out from under the pile. "I've calmed down, Josie. Hearing it from Burke just fired me up."

She touched the bandage on his forehead, and they stood close, in a drift of Josie's perfume. They shared more than their mother's face, more than the Longstreet name. Between them was a tie deeper than blood. It went to the heart.

"I'm sorry she hurt you, Tucker."

"Poked a few holes in my pride, that's all." He kissed Josie lightly on the lips. "They'll heal up fast enough."

"You're just too nice to women, Tucker. It makes them fall in love with you, then you've got nothing but trouble. If you were a little harder on them, you wouldn't get their expectations up."

"I'll keep that in mind. Next time I take a woman out, I'll tell her she's ugly."

Josie laughed and stood up to hold the dress in front of her as she twisted and turned in front of her cheval glass. "Don't go reciting any poetry, either."

"Who says I do?"

"Carolanne told me you talked poetry when you took her over to Lake Village to look at stars."

Tucker shoved his hands in his pockets. "How come women always tell the intimate details of their life over a manicure or a permanent?"

"It's the same as men bragging about the size of their wangers over a bottle of beer. How's this look?"

He scowled. "I'm finished handing out compliments to females."

Josie only chuckled as he strode off to shower.

◆ ◆ ◆ ◆

CAROLINE WAS SO STUNNED by Sweetwater that she stopped her car halfway up the drive to stare. The house was pearly white in the afternoon sun, all gracious curves and delicate ironwork, slender columns and glinting windows. It took no imagination at all to picture women in hoop skirts strolling across the grass, or gentlemen in frock coats sitting on the porch discussing the possibility of secession while silent black servants served cool drinks.

Flowers grew everywhere, climbing up trellises, spilling over the borders of brick-edged beds. The heady smells of gardenia, magnolia, and roses perfumed the air.

A Confederate flag, faded and ragged at the edges, hung from a white pole in the center of the front lawn.

Beyond the house, she could see neat stone buildings. What once were slave quarters, smokehouse, summer kitchen—she could guess that much. The lawn stretched back to acre after acre of flat, fertile land thick with cotton. She saw a single tree in the center of one of the fields, a huge old cypress left standing either through laziness or sentiment.

For some reason that—just that single tree—brought tears to her throat. The simple majesty of it, the endurance it symbolized, touched her in some deep corner of her heart. Surely it had stood there for more than a century, watching over the rise and fall of the South, the struggle for a way of life, and the ultimate end of it.

How many spring plantings had it seen, how many summer harvests?

She shifted her gaze back to the house. It, too, symbolized continuity and change, and the stately elegance of the Old South that so many from the north thought of as indolence. Babies had been born there, grown up and died there. And the rhythm of this quiet spot on the delta went on. And on. The slow pulse of their culture and traditions survived.

The proof was here, just as it was in her grandmother's house, in those houses and farms and fields dotting the road into Innocence. And in Innocence itself.

She wondered why she was just beginning to understand that.

When she saw Tucker come out the front doorway to stand on

the porch, she wondered if she was beginning to understand him as well. She got the car moving again, eased it around the island of peonies, and stopped.

"The way you were sitting back there on the drive, I was beginning to think you'd changed your mind."

"No." She opened the car door and stepped out. "I was just looking."

He was doing some looking of his own, and decided not to speak until the fingers squeezing his heart loosened up. She was wearing a thin white dress, with a full skirt he imagined would billow gloriously in a breeze. Two finger-width straps held it over her shoulders and left her arms bare. There was a necklace of polished stones around her throat. Her hair was sleeked back to set off matching stones that dangled from her ears. She'd done something mysterious and female to her face, deepening her eyes, darkening her mouth.

As she mounted the steps toward him, he caught the first whiff of her light, tempting scent.

He took her right hand in his left, and turned her slowly in a circle under the arch of his arm, as if in a dance. It made her laugh. When he saw how low the dress dipped in the back, he swallowed hard.

"I've got to tell you something, Caroline."

"All right."

"You're ugly." He shook his head before she could comment. "That's just something I had to get out of my system."

"It's an interesting approach."

"My sister's idea. It's supposed to keep women from falling in love with me."

Why did he always make her want to smile? "It could work. Are you going to ask me in?"

He traded her left hand for her right. "It seems like I've been waiting a long time to do just that." He led her to the door, opened it. Pausing, he studied her, wanting to see how she looked in the doorway—his doorway—with flowers and magnolia trees at her back. She looked, he realized, perfect.

"Welcome to Sweetwater."

The moment she stepped inside, Caroline heard the shouting.

"If you've gone and asked somebody to come and sit at my table, the least you can do is set it." Della stood at the base of a curving stairway, one hand braced on a mahogany newel post, the other on her sturdy hip.

"I said I would, didn't I?" Josie's voice tumbled down the steps. "I don't know what you're in such a god-awful lather about. I'm going to finish putting my face on, then I'll get to it."

"Way she's messing around with those paints, it'll get set next week." Della turned. The righteous indignation on her face gave way to curiosity when she spotted Caroline. "Well now, you're Edith's grand-baby, aren't you?"

"Yes, I suppose I am."

"Edith and I, we used to have ourselves some nice chats out on her front porch. You favor her a bit, 'round the eyes."

"Thank you."

"This is Della," Tucker announced. "She takes care of us."

"I've been trying for the best part of thirty years, but it ain't done all that much good. You take her on into the guest parlor and give her some of the good sherry. Dinner'll be ready before long." With a last scowl at the stairway, she lifted her voice. "If somebody would stop tarting herself up and come set the table."

"I'd be happy to do it," Caroline began, but Della was already pulling her along the hallway toward the living room.

"No sir, you'll do no such thing. Tucker peeled the potatoes and that girl's going to set out the china. Least she can do after asking that dead doctor to dinner." She patted Caroline's arm then scurried off toward the kitchen.

"Ah . . . dead doctor?"

Tucker grinned, strolling over to an antique walnut server for the sherry. "Pathologist."

"Oh, Teddy. He's certainly an . . . interesting character." She took a slow sweep of the room with its tall windows, lace curtains, Turkey carpets. The twin settees, as she was sure they were called, were in misty pastels. Cool colors predominated in the subtle stripes of the wallpaper, the hand-worked pillows, the plump ottoman. The richness of antiques melded with it. On the mantel above the white marble fireplace was a Waterford vase filled with baby roses.

"This is a lovely house." She took the glass he offered. "Thank you."

"I'll give you the grand tour sometime. Tell you the whole history."

"I'd like to hear it." She walked to the window where she could look out at the garden and beyond to the fields and the old cypress. "I didn't realize you farmed."

"We're planters," he corrected her as he came up behind her. "Long-streets have been planters since the eighteenth century—right after Beau-regard Longstreet cheated Henry Van Haven out of six hundred acres of prime delta farmland in a two-day poker game down in Natchez in 1796. It was in a bawdy house called the Red Starr."

Caroline turned. "You made that up."

"No ma'am, that's just the way my daddy told it to me, and his daddy to him, and so on since that fateful April night in ninety-six.

'Course it's just speculation about the cheating part. The Larssons put in that bit—they're by way of being cousins of the Van Havens."

"Spoilsports," Caroline said, smiling.

"Could be that, or it could be the God's truth, but neither changes the outcome." He was enjoying the way she looked at him, her lips tilted up just a little, her eyes laughing. "Anyhow, Henry got so irritated about losing the land, he tried to ambush old Beau when Beau finished celebrating with one of the Starr's best girls. Her name was Millie Jones."

Caroline sipped and shook her head. "You ought to write short stories, Tuck."

"I'm just telling you the way it was. Now, Millie was pleased with Beau's performance—did I mention that the Longstreets have always been known as exceptional lovers?"

"I don't believe you did."

"Documented, through the ages," Tucker assured her. He loved the way laughter brightened her eyes, softened her mouth. If he hadn't had a story to tell, by God he would've made one up. "And Millie, being grateful for Beau's stamina—and the extra five-dollar gold piece he'd left on the nightstand, went on over to the window to wave him off. It was she who spotted Henry in the bushes with his flintlock loaded and ready. At just the right moment, Millie shouted a warning. The gun went off. Beau's frock coat was singed at the arm, but his reflexes were keen. He pulled out his knife and sent it whipping into the brush where the shot had come from. Hit Henry dead in the pump, as my grandpappy used to say."

"He was, of course, an expert at knife-throwing as well as lovemaking."

"A man of many talents," Tucker agreed. "And being a prudent man as well, he decided it best not to stay around Natchez and answer uncomfortable questions about a deed, a dead man, and an Arkansas Toothpick. Being a romantic, he took pretty young Millie out of that bawdy house, and they traveled to the delta."

"And planted cotton."

"Planted cotton, got rich, and had babies. It was their son who started building this house, in 1825."

Caroline said nothing for a moment. It was much too easy to become caught up in the flow of his words, the easy rhythm of his voice. *It's not really the point—how much is true and how much is made up,* she decided. *It's all in the telling.* She moved away from the window, acutely aware that he was about to touch her again, and less sure if she'd want to stop him. "I don't know much of anything about my family history. And certainly nothing that goes back two hundred years."

"We look back more than forward in the delta. History makes the best gossip. And tomorrow . . . well, tomorrow's going to take care of itself anyway, isn't it?"

He thought he heard her sigh, but the sound was so soft, it might have been silence.

"I've spent my whole life thinking about tomorrow—planning next month, next season. It must be the air here," she said, and this time she did sigh. There was something wistful in the sound. "I've hardly thought of next week since I walked into my grandmother's house. Haven't wanted to, anyway," she said, remembering the phone calls from her manager that she'd been dodging ever since she decided to come to Mississippi.

He had a strong urge to hold her—just to offer her the circle of his arms and the support of his shoulder. But he was afraid the gesture would spoil whatever was happening between them.

"Why are you unhappy, Caro?"

Surprised, she looked back at him. "I'm not." But she knew it was only part of the truth. And part of the truth was a lie.

"I listen almost as well as I talk." His hand was gentle as he touched her face. "Maybe you'll try me sometime."

"Maybe." But she moved back, marking the distance. "Someone's coming."

Now he knew the time wasn't right, and turned to the window again. "The dead doctor," he said, and grinned. "Let's go see if Josie set the table."

Chapter 11

IN THE COUNTY JAIL in Greenville with its scarred, ringless toilet and graffiti-laced walls, Austin Hatinger sat on a board-hard bunk and stared at the bars of sunlight on the floor near his feet.

He knew why he was in a cell, like a common criminal, like an animal. He knew why he was forced to stare at bars, in a cage with filthy sayings painted on the sweaty walls.

It was because Beau Longstreet had been rich. He'd been a God-cursing rich planter and had tossed all his tainted money to his bastard children.

They were bastards, sure enough, Austin thought. Madeline might have worn that traitor's ring on her finger, but in the eyes of God, she had belonged to only one man.

Beau hadn't gone off to the stinking hole of Korea to serve his country and save good Christians from the Yellow Peril, but had stayed behind, in sin and comfort, to make more money. Austin had long suspected that Beau had tricked Madeline into marriage. Not that that excused her betrayal, but women were weak—weak of body, weak of will, weak of mind.

Without a strong guiding force—and the occasional back of the hand—they were prone to foolish behavior and to sin. God was his Witness that he'd done his best to keep Mavis on a straight path.

He'd married her in a blindness of despair, trapped by his own raging

lust. "The woman thou gavest me, she gave me of the tree, and I did eat."
Oh, yes, Mavis had tempted him, and, weak of flesh, he had succumbed.

Austin knew that from Eve down, Satan spoke first to women in his
smooth, seductive voice. They being more open to sin, they fell and with a
wily heart took a man down with them.

But he'd been faithful to her. Only once in thirty-five years had he
turned to another woman.

If there were times when, exercising his marital rights, plunging into
Mavis, he felt, tasted, smelled Madeline in the dark, it was only the Lord's
way of reminding him what had belonged to him.

Madeline had pretended to be indifferent to him. He'd known, all
those years ago he'd known, that she'd gone with Beau only to tease and
torment him, as women did. She'd belonged to him. Only him. Her
shocked denial when he'd made his declaration before shipping out to war
had only been another pretense.

If it hadn't been for Beau, she'd have been waiting for him when he'd
returned. That had been the beginning of the end for him.

Hadn't he worked his fingers raw, broken his back, sweated out his
heart trying to make a decent life for the family he'd taken? And while he'd
worked, and failed, sweated and lost ground, Beau had sat up in his fine
white house and laughed.

And laughed.

But Beau hadn't known. Despite all his money and his fine clothes
and fancy cars, he'd never known that once, on a dusty day in high summer, when the air was thick and still, when the sky was baked white with
heat, Austin Hatinger had taken what was his.

He remembered still how she'd looked that day. And the picture
in his mind was so clear, his hands trembled and his blood pumped hard
and hot.

She'd come to him, carrying a basket up to his porch, a big straw basket filled with charity for him, for his squawling son, for his wife who lay
inside, sweating through the birthing of another child.

She'd been wearing a blue dress and a white hat that had a filmy blue
scarf trailing from the crown. Madeline had always been one for floating
scarves. Her dark hair was curled under the hat so that it framed the creamy
skin of her face—skin she could pamper with the lotions Beau's godless
money could buy.

She'd looked like a spring morning, strolling up the dirt path to his
sagging porch, her eyes soft and smiling, as if she didn't see the poverty, the
broken cinder-block steps, the dingy clothes hanging on the line, the
scrawny chickens pecking in the dust.

Her voice had been so cool as she'd offered him that basket filled with cast-off clothes Beau's money had bought for the babies he'd planted in Austin's woman. He couldn't hear past it, to the weak whine of his own wife calling to him that it was time to fetch the doctor.

He remembered how Madeline had started to go in, concerned for the woman who would never have laid in his bed at all if it hadn't been for betrayal and deceit.

"You fetch the doctor, Austin," she said in that cool, spring-water voice. The kindness in her golden eyes burned a hole in his gut. "Hurry and fetch him, and I'll stay with her and your little one."

It wasn't madness that had gripped him. No, Austin would never accept that. It was righteousness. Right and wrath had filled him when he had dragged Madeline off the porch. Truth had pounded through him when he had pulled her down to the dirt.

Oh, she'd pretended that she didn't want him. She'd screamed and she'd fought, but it had all been a lie. He'd had the right, the God-given right to push himself into her. No matter that she'd worn a mask that had wept and pleaded, she'd recognized that right.

He'd emptied his seed into her, and all these years later, he could still remember the power of that release. The way his body had bucked and shuddered as the part of him that was a man flowed into her.

She'd stopped her weeping. While he'd rolled over in the dirt to stare up at that white sky, she had gotten up, gone away, and left him with the sound of triumph in his ears and the taste of bitterness on his tongue.

So he'd waited, day after day, night after night, for Beau to come. His second son had been born and his wife lay stony-faced in the bed, and Austin waited, his Winchester loaded and ready. And he'd ached with the need to kill.

But Beau had never come. He knew then that Madeline had kept their secret. And had doomed him.

Now Beau was dead. And Madeline. They were buried together in Blessed Peace Cemetery.

It was the son now, the son who had brought the circle twisting back. From generation to generation, he thought. The son had seduced and defiled his daughter. The girl was dead.

Retribution was his right. Retribution was his sword.

Austin blinked and focused on the bars of light again. Bars that came through bars. They had shifted with oncoming dusk. He'd been sitting in the past for more than two hours.

It was time to plan for today. In disgust he stared down at his loose blue pants. Prison clothes. He would be rid of them soon. He would get out. The Lord helped those who helped themselves, and he would find a way.

He would make his way back to Innocence and do what he should have done more than thirty years ago. He would kill the part of Beau that lived in his son.

And balance the scales.

♦ ♦ ♦ ♦

CAROLINE STEPPED OUT ONTO the flower-decked patio and inhaled deeply of summer. The light was gentling, easing quietly toward dusk, and insects stirred in the grass. She had that smug, too-full feeling she'd forgotten could be so pleasant.

The meal had been more than platters of food served on old silver trays. It had been a slow, almost languorous pocket of time filled with scents and tastes and talk. Teddy had done magic tricks with his napkin and the flatware. Dwayne, passably sober, had displayed a remarkable talent for mimicry, moving from old standards like Jimmy Stewart to Jack Nicholson and on to locals like Junior Talbot.

Tucker and Josie had kept her laughing with rambling, often graphic stories of sex scandals, most of which were fifty or sixty years old.

So different, she thought now, from her own family dinners, where her mother would dictate the proper conversation and not a drop would spill on the starched damask cloth. Those dinners had been so stifling and lifeless—more like a corporate meeting than a family meal. The peccadilloes of ancestors would never have been discussed, nor would Georgia McNair Waverly have found it amusing to have a guest pluck a salad fork out of her bodice.

No indeed.

But Caroline had enjoyed the evening more than any she could remember, and was sorry it was nearly over.

"You look happy," Tucker commented.

"Why wouldn't I be?"

"It's just nice to see, that's all." He took her hand, and what he felt when his fingers linked with hers was not so much resistance as uncertainty. "Want to walk?"

It was a pretty evening, a lovely spot, and her mood was mellow. "All right."

It wasn't really a walk, she thought as she wound through rosebushes and the heavy scent of gardenia. It was more of a meander. No hurry, no destination, no problems. She thought meander suited Tucker perfectly.

"Is that a lake?" she asked as she saw the glint of water in the last light of the sun.

"Sweetwater." Obligingly he shifted directions. "Beau built his house there, on the south side of it. You can still see what's left of the foundation."

What Caroline saw was a scattering of stones. "What a view they had. Acres and acres of their own land. How does that feel?"

"I don't know. It just is."

Dissatisfied, she looked out over the wide, flat fields of cotton. She was a child of the city, where even the wealthy held only squares of property and people crowded each other for space. "But to have all this . . ."

"It has you." It surprised him to say it, but he shrugged and finished the thought. "You can't turn away from it, not when it's been handed down to you. You can't see it go fallow when you're reminded that the Longstreets have held Sweetwater for the best part of two centuries."

"Is that what you want? To turn away?"

"Maybe there are some places I'd like to see." His shoulders moved again with a restlessness she recognized and hadn't expected. "Then again, traveling's complicated. It takes a lot of effort."

"Don't do that."

The impatience in her voice nearly made him smile. "I haven't done anything yet." He skimmed a hand up her arm. "But I'm thinking about it."

Frustrated, she broke away. "You know what I mean. One minute you act as though there might be something inside your mind other than a thought for the easiest way out. The next thing, you shut it off."

"I never could see the point in taking the hard way."

"What about the right way?"

It wasn't often he came across a woman who wanted to discuss philosophy. Taking out a cigarette, Tucker settled into the conversation comfortably. "Well, what's right for one isn't necessarily right for the other. Dwayne went off and got a degree he's never done a damn thing with, because he'd rather sit around and brood about how things should have been. Josie runs off and gets married, twice, flies off to anywhere at the drop of a hat, and always ends up back here pretending things are better than they can be."

"What about you? What's your way?"

"My way's to take it as it comes. And yours . . ." He glanced back at her. "Yours is to figure out what's coming before it gets here. That doesn't make either of us wrong."

"But if you figure it out, and it's not the way you want it, you can change it."

"You can try," he agreed. " 'There's a divinity that shapes our ends, rough-hew them how we will.' " He inhaled smoke. *"Hamlet."*

Caroline could only stare. He was the last man on earth she'd have expected to hear quoting Shakespeare.

"You take that field there." He put a companionable arm around her shoulders as he turned her. "Now, that cotton—all things being equal—is going to grow. That topsoil's better than a foot deep and full of fertilizer. We spray off the goddamn weevils and when summer's gone it'll be harvested, bailed, trucked, and sold. And my worrying myself sick about whether all those things are gonna happen won't help the situation one bit. Besides, I've got an overseer to do the worrying."

"There has to be more to it than that—" she began.

"We're taking this down to the basics, Caro. It gets planted, it gets harvested, and somewhere along the line it ends up in a pretty dress like the one you're wearing tonight. Sure, I could sit up nights worrying whether we're going to get enough rain, or too much rain. Whether the truckers are going on strike, or those dimwits up in Washington are going to fuck up again and shuck us into a depression. Or I can get myself a good night's sleep. The results would be exactly the same."

With a half laugh, she turned to him. "Why does that make sense?" She shook her head. "There has to be a flaw in that logic."

"You let me know if you figure it out, but I think it holds solid. Let me give you another example. You won't let me kiss you because you're worried you might like it too much."

Her brows shot up. "That's incredibly egocentric. The reason could very well be that I'm sure I won't like it at all."

"Either way," Tucker said agreeably as his arms slid around her waist. "You're trying to figure out the answer before there's a problem. That's the kind of thing that brings on headaches."

"Really?" Her voice was dry, and she kept her arms at her sides.

"Trust me, Caroline, I've made a study on it. It's like standing on the edge of a swimming hole, worrying about the water being too cold. You'd be better off if somebody put a foot to your butt and pushed you in."

"Is that what you're doing?"

His lips quirked in a grin. "I could tell you I was doing it for you, so you'd just fall in and stop thinking about the what-ifs. But the truth is—" He lowered his head. Something twisted inside her when his warm breath fluttered over her lips. "Thinking about this is keeping me up at night." He gave her chin a playful nip. "And I need my sleep."

Her body was stiff as his lips, light as moth wings, cruised over hers. Practiced seduction, she told herself as her heart began to thud. She hadn't forgotten how clever some men were at exploiting a woman's needs.

"You can kiss me back if you want to," Tucker murmured against her mouth. "If you don't, I'll just please myself."

First, he indulged in a lazy journey of her face, lips tracing along her temples, over her closed lids, down her cheeks. The gentleness in him was too ingrained for him to heed the urgency growing inside him to rush and take. Instead, he concentrated on her first faint shiver, on that gradual, glorious softening of her body against his. On the quickening of her breath as he slowly, quietly, brought his mouth back to hers.

And oh, it was nice, so nice, to feel that slow, female yielding, to hear that quick hitch of her breath, to smell her over the scent of water and shadows as he eased them both into the kiss.

This time her lips parted at the first touch. As he increased the pressure, degree by tormenting degree, her hands shot up to grip his arms. His last coherent thought was that the water wasn't cold, but it was a hell of a lot deeper than he'd expected.

She couldn't think at all, not with this steady roaring in her ears. She had grabbed him for balance, but no matter how desperately she clung, the world kept spinning. Caution had gone up in smoke. With a quick, helpless moan, she dived into the kiss.

His mouth drank and drew from hers. But it wasn't enough. The taste was hot, honeyed, and he craved more. Tongue and teeth drove the kiss into greater intimacies. Still he ached.

He wasn't supposed to ache over a kiss. His head wasn't supposed to swim when she locked herself around him. He wasn't supposed to tremble when she moaned out his name.

He knew what it was to want a woman. It was a natural, pleasurable part of being a man. It didn't rip at you or carve a hole in your gut. It didn't make your knees shake until you were afraid you'd fall down on them and beg.

He felt himself teeter on some high, thin edge. Self-preservation had him windmilling his arms and stumbling back before he could fall. Carefully, he put his hands on her shoulders and drew her away. His brow rested weakly against hers while he struggled to catch his breath.

Caroline let her unsteady hands stay at his hips. Gradually, through the mist of sensation, she forced her thoughts to surface and hold. It had simply been too long since she'd felt the comfort of an embrace, or tasted genuine desire on a man's lips. Those were reasons enough to excuse losing herself for a moment.

But she was back now. The blood was no longer pounding in her head. She could hear the whirl and click of insects, the croak of frogs. The sweet three-note call of a whippoorwill.

The light was shadowed, caught in that final magic moment between day and night. Already day was losing, ebbing away, and taking the passionate heat with it.

"I guess we both could've been wrong," Tucker said.

"About what?"

"You figuring you wouldn't care for it, and me thinking that once I'd kissed you, I'd sleep better." On a long breath, he lifted his head. "I gotta tell you, Caroline, wanting a woman's always been a pleasure for me. Since I was fifteen and Laureen O'Hara and I wrestled off each other's clothes in her daddy's barn. You're the first woman I've come across since that monumental day who's complicated that pleasure."

She wanted to believe him, wanted to believe that what he'd felt here was more difficult, more intimate, more dangerous than anything he'd felt before. And because she did believe him, she was frightened enough to shake him off.

"I think it would be best if we left it alone."

His gaze flicked down to her lips, swollen and soft from his. "In a pig's eyes," he said mildly.

"I mean it, Tucker." A trace of desperation crept into her voice. "I've just ended a destructive relationship and have no intention of starting another. And you . . . your life certainly has enough complications at the moment without adding another."

"Normally I might agree with that. You know, your hair looks just like a halo in this light. Maybe I want a shot at redemption. The angel and the sinner. Christ knows, there's just about that much difference between us."

"That's the most ridiculous—"

His hand shot out quickly, so quickly she swallowed the rest of her words as it fisted into her hair. This time when he spoke, the mild tone was lined with steel. "Something about you, Caroline. I don't know what the hell it is, but it eats at me at the oddest times. There's usually a good reason for a reaction like that. I figure it'll come out sometime."

"My time doesn't flow the way yours does, Tucker." She thought her voice was admirably calm, particularly when her heart was thudding in her throat. "In a few months I'll be in Europe. A quick affair to pass a hot summer isn't in my plans."

The ghost of a smile lit his mouth. "You do make plans. I've noticed that about you." He stepped forward and crushed her lips under his in a hard, brief kiss that rocked her back on her heels. "I'm going to have you, Caroline. Sooner or later we're going to have the hell out of each other. I'll try to leave the timing up to you."

"That's the most outrageously arrogant, despicably male statement I've ever heard."

"Depends on your point of view," he said affably. "I meant it as fair warning. But I don't want to get you so riled up it spoils your digestion." Clamping his hand over hers, he started back toward the house. Lightning bugs were glinting and dancing in the growing dark. "Why don't we sit on the porch awhile?"

"I have no intention of sitting anywhere with you."

"Now, honey, you talk like that, I'm going to think you find me irresistible."

Her quick hoot of laughter made him grin. "The day I can't resist some self-styled delta Don Juan—"

He gave a hoot of his own and scooped her off her feet to swing her in a circle. "I'm crazy about that sassy mouth of yours." He gave it an enthusiastic kiss. "I bet you went to one of those fancy finishing schools in Switzerland."

"I did not, and put me down." She squirmed for a minute. "I mean it, Tucker. Someone's coming."

He didn't put her down, but he did look across the lawn. A pair of headlights were coming fast. "I guess we'll just mosey on over and see who's calling."

He carried her to the drive as much to fluster her as for the pleasure of having that long, slim body cupped in his arms. And he figured once she got over being irritated by it, she'd see the romance.

"First star's out," he said conversationally, and she made a sound suspiciously like a growl.

"You know, you don't weigh much more than a sack full of flour. Feel a lot nicer though."

"The man's a poet," Caroline said between her teeth, and wished she didn't see the humor of it.

He couldn't resist. " 'Fair as a star, when only one is shining in the sky.' " He sent her a smile. "I guess Wordsworth said it better, huh?"

Before she could think of a proper response, he set her on her feet, gave her bottom a friendly pat, then waved at Bobby Lee, who was scrambling out of his rusting Cutlass.

"Hey, boy, shouldn't you be out sparking Marvella?"

"Tucker." Bobby Lee pushed a hand through his drooping pompadour. In the headlights he'd neglected to turn off, his face was pale with fear or excitement. "I rode on out as soon as I finished." He nodded belatedly to Caroline. "Evening, Miz Waverly."

"Hello, Bobby Lee. If you'll excuse me, I'd like to thank Della again for dinner before I leave."

She hadn't even taken the first step when Tucker captured her hand. "It's early yet. What brings you out?" he asked Bobby Lee.

"Junior brought in your car this afternoon. Holy Jesus. It sure was a mess, Tucker."

Tucker grimaced and touched fingers gingerly to his bandaged head. "Yeah, it's a heartbreaker, all right. Barely had five thousand miles on her. Frame's bent, then?"

"Well, yeah. Bent to shit—excuse me, ma'am. We saw that soon as we had her up on the lift. We figured you'd have to have her hauled down to Jackson, but seeing as we haven't had a real good wreck come through since Bucky Larsson creamed his Buick out on sixty-one during that ice storm last January, we wanted a look-see."

Tucker settled his hip against the Cutlass. "That Buick looked like it'd been run over by a tank when you towed it in. Never could figure out how Bucky got off with only a broken collar bone and eighteen stitches."

"Gets a queer look in his eyes sometimes," Bobby Lee added. " 'Course he always did, now that I think on it."

Tucker nodded. "His mama was spooked by a nest of copperheads when she was carrying him. Might have addled him."

Caroline no longer felt the urge to leave. But she did have to resist the urge to cup her head in her hands and bray with laughter. "You came all this way to tell Tucker his car's wrecked?"

The two men looked over at her with identical expressions of puzzlement. To them it was obvious Bobby Lee was only setting the stage for whatever he'd come to say.

"No ma'am," he said politely. "I come out to tell Tucker how his car come to be wrecked. Tucker here drives slick as spit. Everybody knows that."

"Thanks, Bobby Lee."

"Just telling it like it is. Well, the thing is, Junior mentioned as to how there wasn't no skid marks or nothing."

"Brakes were out."

"Yeah. He said. So I got to thinking, and when Junior's old lady kept calling, complaining how he'd promised to take her and the baby on down to Greenville for spaghetti, I told him I'd stay to watch the station. It's quiet on Sundays anyhow, so I figured I'd take a look at those brakes for you."

He pulled a piece of Double Bubble from his pocket, unwrapped it, and popped it into his mouth. "I took a good look at the lines, and at the hydraulics for the power steering, too. Might not've seen it if I hadn't been so curious. But I did."

"See what?" Caroline demanded when Tucker seemed content to let the silence hang.

"Holes poked through the lines. Not rotted or nothing like that, but poked through. Like with an awl, or maybe an ice pick. Fluid would've dribbled on out. That's how your wheel seized up on you, see? You could've wrestled with it if you'da been expecting it, but coming up to a curve at a clip, well, the car's gonna keep going dead ahead. Then you hit the brakes and they're useless as tits on a bull. Beg your pardon, Miz Waverly."

"My God." Her fingers dug into Tucker's arm. "Are you saying someone deliberately sabotaged the car? He could've been killed."

"Could've," Bobby Lee agreed. "But more like busted up some. Everybody 'round here knows Tucker handles a car as good as those Formula One guys."

"I appreciate your coming down to tell me." Tucker flipped his cigarette away, his eyes following the arch of spark. He was angry, blood-pumping angry, and needed to sit on it awhile. "You going by to see Marvella this evening?"

"I was planning on it."

"Then you go on and tell the sheriff what you told me. But nobody else, hear? Don't tell anybody else."

"If that's the way you want it."

"For now. I'd be obliged if we keep it just like that for now. Get on back to town before Marvella lays into you for being so late."

"Guess I will. Be seeing you, Tucker. Evening, Miz Waverly."

Caroline didn't speak until the Cutlass's taillights winked off at the end of the drive. "He could've made a mistake. He's just a boy."

"He's one of the best mechanics in the county. Makes sense anyway. If I hadn't had my brains rattled, I'd've seen it myself. I just have to figure out who's riled enough to give me trouble."

"Trouble?" Caroline echoed. "Tucker, I don't care what Bobby Lee believes about your superhuman skill with a car, you might have been seriously hurt, even killed."

"You worried about me, sugar?" Though his mind was working in other directions, he smiled and ran his hands up and down her arms. "I like it."

"Don't be such a jerk."

"Now, don't get mad, Caro. Though God knows I like the look of you when you get heated up."

Her voice chilled. "I'm not going to stand here while you pat me on the head and put me off like a helpless female. I'm offering to help you."

"That's sweet of you. No—" He grabbed her as she swore and swung away. "I mean it. It's just that until I sift the whole thing through, there's nothing to help with."

"It's obvious to me that it had to be someone close to Edda Lou Hatinger." She tossed her head. "Unless, of course, you've got a list of jealous husbands you need to consider."

"I don't date married ladies. Except that once," he began, and caught her look. "Never mind. Austin's in jail, and I can't picture poor old Mavis scooting under my car with an ice pick."

Caroline angled her chin. "She had brothers."

"True enough." Tucker's lips pursed as he considered. "Vernon wouldn't know a crankshaft from a fence post. He's not the sly kind either. More open, like his daddy. And young Cy . . . there's no meanness in him that I've ever seen."

"They could have hired someone."

Tucker snorted. "With what?" Gently, he pressed his lips to her temple. "Don't fret, honey, I'm going to sleep on it."

Staring, she stepped back. "I think you could," she said slowly. "I believe you could actually close your eyes and sleep like a baby, even after this."

"I already wrecked my car and banged my head," he pointed out. "I don't see why whoever did this should have the pleasure of keeping me from sleeping, too." He got that look in his eye she was beginning to recognize. That gleam that sent off warning signals in her brain and flutters in her heart. "The only thing keeping me up at night is you. Now, if we were to . . ." He trailed off as another set of headlights bounced down the drive. "Christ almighty, we're doing big business tonight."

"I'm going now," Caroline said decisively. "I'll call Della tomorrow and thank her."

"Just hold on." He was trying to make out the type of car. All he could tell for sure was that its muffler had parted ways sometime before. The noise was enough to wake the dead. It was difficult to believe that the sedate black Lincoln that came to a rocky stop in back of Caroline's BMW could be so rude.

When the door opened and a small white-haired woman in a tie-dyed T-shirt, blue jeans, and army boots stepped out, Tucker broke into a hoot and a grin.

"Cousin Lulu."

"That you, Tucker?" She had a voice like a freight train, loud and rattly and full of dust. "What are you doing over there in the dark with that girl?"

"Less than I'd like to." He was beside Lulu in two strides, bending himself nearly in half to kiss her powdered, paper-thin cheek. "Pretty as ever," he pronounced, and she giggled and swatted him.

"You're the pretty one. Look more like your ma than she did herself. You, you there." She signaled to Caroline with one bony finger. "Come on over where I can see you."

"Don't you scare her off," Tucker warned. "Cousin Lulu, this is Caroline Waverly."

"Waverly, Waverly. Not from these parts." She cast her bright bird's eyes up and down. "Not your usual type either, Tucker. Doesn't look top-heavy or pinheaded."

Caroline thought about it. "Thank you."

"Yankee!" Lulu set up a screech that could have shattered crystal. "Christ in a sidecar, she's a Yankee."

"Only half," Tucker said quickly. "She's Miss Edith's granddaughter."

Lulu's eyes narrowed. "Edith McNair? George and Edith?"

"Yes, ma'am," Caroline said with her tongue in her cheek. "I'm staying the summer in my grandparents' house."

"Dead, aren't they? Yes, they're dead, but they were Mississippians born and bred, so that counts for something. That your hair, girl, or a wig?"

"My . . ." Automatically, Caroline lifted a hand to her hair. "It's my hair."

"Good. Don't trust bald-headed women any more than I trust Yankees. So we'll see. Tucker, you take my cases in and get me a brandy. I need you to call that Talbot boy about my car. Lost my muffler somewhere in Tennessee. Maybe it was Arkansas." She paused at the base of the steps. "Well, come on, girl."

"I was . . . I was just leaving."

"Tucker, you tell that girl when I offer to have a brandy with a Yankee, that Yankee better drink."

With that, Lulu clumped up the steps in her army boots.

"She's something, isn't she?" Tucker asked as he switched off the purring ignition.

"Something," Caroline agreed, and decided she could use a brandy at that.

Chapter 12

Cy HATINGER'S PALMS WERE sweating. The rest of him wasn't exactly Arrid-dry either, as they said in the commercials. His armpits dripped, despite his conscientious use of Ban Roll-On. He had hair there now, had for the best part of a year. Between his legs, too. The fact both thrilled and embarrassed him.

His sweat was the sweat of youth, clear and mostly inoffensive. It came from a combination of the thick morning heat and his own fear and excitement. What he was doing would bring his father's holy, belt-flashing wrath down on him.

He was going to ask the Longstreets for work.

Of course, his father was in jail, and that comforted him some. The fact that it did brought on hot little flashes of guilt that made him sweat more.

Aren't you glad you use Dial? he thought. Don't you wish everybody did?

He didn't know why he was thinking in commercials, unless it was because his mother left the flickering old TV on day and night. For company, she would say, wringing her hands and looking at him dully out of red-rimmed eyes. She cried just about all the time now, and hardly seemed aware of him or Ruthanne at all.

He might come across her sitting on the sagging and faded sofa. Still in her bathrobe in the middle of the day, a basket of laundry at her feet while she sniffled and watched *Days of Our Lives*. At this point Cy wasn't sure the tears were for herself or in sympathy for the trials and tribulations of the people in that mythical town of Salem.

To Cy the Hortons and the Bradys of Salem were more real than his mother, who wandered the house like a ghost each night while the TV droned on through Leno's monologue or reruns of sitcoms or commercials for gadgets like the Clapper, that magical boon to society that allowed you to turn on lights or turn off TVs and all you had to do was applaud.

It was like congratulating an electrical appliance, and Cy found it creepy.

He could imagine his mother with one, weeping in the front room and clapping her hands together while the lights jumped and the TV flipped on.

"Thank you, thank you," the dusty screen would say. "And for my next number, here's the Reverend Samuel Harris to show all you sinners the way through those gates of paradise."

Oh, yes, his mama was right fond of all those religion programs with their hypnotic-voiced Reverend this or that, shouting down sin and bartering salvation for social security checks.

After he'd come home from fishing with Jim the day before, he'd followed the sound of organ music and hallelujahs through the kitchen and into the front room, where his mother stared glassy-eyed at the screen. It had scared him more than a little, because for a minute—just a minute—the face of the TV preacher had become his father's face, and his father's all-seeing eyes had stared right at him.

"Got hair between your legs and evil thoughts in your mind," his father had accused. "The next step is fornication. *Fornication!* It's Satan's tool between your legs, boy."

As he walked along the dusty verge of the road, Cy adjusted Satan's tool, which seemed to have shriveled up in memory of his father's voice.

His father couldn't see him, Cy reminded himself, and swiped his forearm over his sweaty brow. He was in jail and would likely stay there for a while. Just like A.J., who had gone from shoplifting packs of cigarettes and Mars Bars to grand theft auto. The minute the cell doors had clanged shut behind his oldest brother, his father had said he'd no longer had a son named Austin Joseph. Now that his father was in the same kind of pickle, Cy wondered if that meant he no longer had a father.

The sweet relief of that possibility had another flash of guilt slicing through his gut.

He wasn't going to think of his father. He was going to think of getting this job. Cy knew his mother would have forbidden him to set foot on Sweetwater. That pale, pasty look would have come over her face—the look she got when his daddy decided she needed punishment.

What sins had his mother committed? Cy asked himself as his hands clenched and unclenched at his sides. What sins that needed to be washed away in her own blood?

And when black eyes or split lips or bruised ribs had saved her from Satan, she would tell the neighbors how she'd fallen. If the sheriff came by, she would get that horrible, terrified smile on her face and insist, over and over, that she'd taken a tumble down the porch steps.

No matter how often or how viciously those thick fists rained down on her, his ma would stay at his daddy's side.

So Cy knew she would have forbidden him to go to Sweetwater. That was why he hadn't told her.

She noticed so little these days, outside her television world and those whining calls to the lawyer, that Cy had had no problem slipping out of the house that morning. He hadn't even hurried down the hard-pack, knowing if she looked out and saw him walking down the road, her eyes would flick over him, then flick back to the screen.

After three miles on the hardpack, he'd hit the gravel on Gooseneck Road, and had been lucky enough to catch a ride for two miles with old Hartford Pruett in the cab of his Chevy pickup. That left a four-mile walk to Sweetwater.

He'd worked up a powerful thirst by the time he reached the crushed mailbox and splintered pole at the McNair place. He could feel the heat beating up through the soles of his shoes. His throat was dry as a picked bone. Through the morning silence he could hear Jim's daddy singing about the sweet by and by.

The longing rushed through him so fast he could only stand help-less. He knew—because Jim had told him—that his friend had felt his daddy's big, callused hand across his butt. He knew that once when Jim had been four and had wandered off into the swamp, his daddy had found him and had laid a switch across his legs that had made the young Jim dance a jig all the way home.

But Jim's father had never come wheeling down with his fists or locked Jim in his room for two full days with nothing but bread and water. According to him, his daddy had never once, not once, raised a hand to his ma.

And he had seen for himself the way Toby's hand could come down to lay gently, and somehow proudly, on Jim's shoulder. The way they would walk off together with fishing rods over their shoulders. And even though they weren't touching, you could tell they were.

His throat ached miserable, and Cy fought back an urge to walk down the lane to watch Jim and his daddy slap paint on the boards of Miss Edith's place. He knew Toby would turn and smile, his teeth white as the moon against his dark skin—skin scarred by Cy's own father nearly twenty years before.

"Look who's here, Jim," he would say. "Looks to me like that boy's ready to paint. We got us some nice tomato sandwiches for lunch. If you was to pick up a brush and get to work, might be I'd find one for you."

Cy yearned toward the lane. He could almost feel his body lean toward it even as his feet stayed planted on the glass-splattered hardtop.

No son of mine is going to run with niggers. Austin's voice cut through Cy's mind like a rusty blade. *If the Lord wanted us to truck with them, he'd've made them white.*

But it wasn't that which had Cy turning away from the lane. It was the knowledge that if he spent the morning painting and eating tomato sandwiches with Jim and his daddy, he would never work up the nerve to walk the last mile to Sweetwater.

His faded checked shirt was clinging to his skin by the time he turned through the iron gates. He'd walked nearly eight miles in the steadily spiraling heat, and wished now he'd taken the time for breakfast. His stomach growled ominously one minute, then churned the next, turning his sweat cold with nausea.

Cy took a faded bandanna out of his back pocket and swiped at his face and neck. Maybe it was best he hadn't had that breakfast, because he was pretty sure if there was anything in his stomach, it would be coming up quick. He'd missed supper the night before, too, half sick on his share of a lemon pie he'd gorged on at the fishing hole.

The thought of that lemon pie had his stomach rising. It took two hard swallows to settle it down again. He looked longingly at the cool green grass beyond the line of magnolias. He could just stretch out there a minute, press his hot face into that sweet grass.

But he thought someone might see him, and he'd never get the job.

He put one foot in front of the other.

He'd seen Sweetwater only a time or two before. Sometimes he thought he'd imagined how grand it was, with its white walls and tall, winking windows. But it was never as grand in his imagination as it was in reality. The thought that people lived there, ate and slept there, was an amazement to Cy, who had lived his whole life in a cramped shack with a dirt yard.

Light-headed from heat and hunger, Cy stared at the house as the sun splashed on those white walls and winking windows. Vapors shimmering up from the gravel made it look as though it were underwater. An underwater palace, he thought, and had some vague recollection of reading about mermen and mermaids who lived under the sea.

He felt as if he were walking through water. His steps were slow and sluggish and the air he breathed in was like thick, warm liquid that filled up his throat instead of soothing it. A little nervous, he looked down at his feet and wasn't sure if he was relieved or disappointed to see his cracked and dusty shoes instead of a shiny green tail.

The scent of flowers was strong as he rounded the peony bed where his father had recently kicked the shit out of Tucker.

Cy hoped Miss Della would come to the door. He liked Miss Della with her wild red hair and colorful jewelry. She'd given him a quarter once just for carrying her bags from the market to her car. And since Miss Della had thick muscles in her arms, Cy knew she could have carried them herself and saved her quarter.

If she came to the door, she might tell him to come on around back. When he got around to the kitchen, she'd give him a cold glass of lemonade, and maybe a biscuit. Then he would thank her, real polite, and ask her if Lucius Gunn was about, so he could ask the overseer about work.

A little dazed, he found himself on the porch, facing the big carved door with its polished brass knocker. He licked his dry lips, lifted his hand.

The door swung open before he'd reached the knocker. Standing in front of him wasn't Miss Della but a small, elderly lady who wore orange lipstick and what looked like an eagle feather in her hair. Cy didn't know that the shiny stones around her crepy neck were Russian diamonds. Her feet were bare, and she carried a set of bongos.

"My great-granddaddy on my mama's side was half Chickasaw," Lulu told the gaping Cy. "Might have been a time when my ancestors scalped the hell out of yours."

"Yes'm," Cy said for lack of anything better.

Lulu's orange-slicked mouth curved. "You sure do have a fine head of hair on you, boy." She threw back her head and let out with a screeching warwhoop that had Cy stumbling back.

"I just—I just—I just—" was all Cy managed to get out.

"Cousin Lulu, you're scaring the spit out of that boy." Tucker strolled up to the door, his grin indulgent. "She's only fooling." It took him a moment to place the boy, then most of the grin faded. "What can I do for you, Cy?"

"I . . . I came down looking for work," he said, then pitched forward in a dead faint.

♦ ♦ ♦ ♦

SOMETHING WAS DRIPPING DOWN Cy's temples as he surfaced. For a horrible moment he thought it was his own blood from where the crazy woman had scalped him. He struggled weakly against the syrupy world of unconsciousness and tried to sit up.

"Just hold on, boy."

It was Miss Della's voice, and Cy was so relieved to hear it that he nearly floated off again. But she slapped her hand lightly against his cheeks until he opened his eyes.

She was wearing painted wooden earrings in the shape of parrots. Cy watched them swing as she cooled his face with a damp cloth.

"Passed clean out," she told him cheerfully. "Tucker hadn't been quick enough to catch you, you'd've bashed your head good on the porch." Cupping a hand behind his neck, she lifted a glass to his lips. "I was coming down the steps and saw it myself. Don't believe Tucker's moved that fast since his daddy found out he broke one of the panes in the sun room."

From over the back of the sofa Lulu leaned down, nearly into his face. She smelled like a lilac bush, Cy discovered.

"Didn't mean to scare you green, boy."

"No, ma'am. I was just . . . I think I had too much sun is all."

Hearing the mortification in the boy's voice, Tucker stepped forward. "Stop fussing over him. He's not the first one to pass out in this house."

Della turned to spit at him, but caught the gentle warning in Tucker's eye and understood. "I got work to do. Cousin Lulu, I'd be obliged if you'd come up with me. I'm thinking of changing the curtains in the Rose Room."

"Don't see why." But Lulu was interested enough to tag along.

When they were alone, Tucker sat down on the coffee table. "Cousin Lulu's developed an interest in her Indian heritage."

"Yes, sir." Since Cy felt he'd humiliated himself beyond redemption, he got shakily to his feet. "I guess I'd best get on."

Tucker looked up at the pale face with its two flags of embarrassment riding high on bony cheeks. "You came a long way to talk about work." Best part of ten miles, Tucker thought. Christ in a sidecar, had the boy hoofed it in all this heat? "Why don't you come on back with me to the kitchen? I was about to get some breakfast. You can join me and say your piece."

Cy felt a splinter of hope prick through the haze. "Yes, sir. I'd be obliged."

He did his best not to gawk as he followed Tucker down the hallway with its gleaming floors. There were paintings on the walls, richer, more elegant than anything he'd seen before. He had an urge to touch one but kept his hands close to his sides.

In the kitchen with its rose-colored counters and shiny white tiles, the light was golden and cool.

Cy's stomach juices started churning the minute Tucker opened the door of the Whirlpool refrigerator and revealed shelf after shelf of food. When he took out a platter of ham, Cy's eyes nearly fell out of his head.

"Have a seat while I fry some of this up."

Cy would have eaten it cold. Hell, he'd have eaten it raw, but he choked down the whimper and sat. "Yes, sir."

"I believe we've got some biscuits around here, too. You want coffee or a Coke?"

Cy rubbed his damp hands on his thighs. "A Coke'd be fine, thank you, Mr. Longstreet."

"I expect you can call me Tucker since you fainted on my porch." Tucker popped the top on a chilled sixteen-ounce bottle and set it in front of Cy.

By the time he'd tossed a couple of slices of ham in a skillet, Cy had downed half the bottle. A belch erupted out of him and had his pale face going red as an American Beauty rose.

"Beg pardon," he muttered, and Tucker bit back a chuckle.

"Them bubbles work on a man." As the ham began to sizzle, tormenting Cy with its aroma, Tucker tossed him a cold biscuit. "Sop some of them up with that. I'm going to heat the rest up in this atomic oven. If I can figure it out."

While Tucker pondered over the microwave, Cy devoured the biscuit in two famished bites. Tucker caught the act out of the corner of his eye and decided to add eggs to the ham. The boy was eating like a starved wolf.

The eggs were a little runny in the center and singed on the edges, but Cy's eyes rounded with gratitude when Tucker set the plate in front of him.

As they ate, he studied the boy who was plowing through ham and eggs.

Good-looking kid, Tucker mused. For some reason Cy reminded him of a picture of the apostle John in the family Bible. Young and frail and lit with some inner light. But he was thin as a rail—not just teenage gangly, but painfully thin, his elbows sharp edges, his wrists like sticks. What the hell was that bastard doing? he wondered. Starving his kids into heaven?

Patient, he waited until Cy had mopped up every trace of egg.

"So, you're looking for work," Tucker began, and Cy nodded, his mouth still full. "Anything particular in mind?"

Cy swallowed gamefully. "Yes, sir. Heard you were hiring on for the fields."

"Lucius is pretty much in charge of hiring field hands," Tucker said. "He's gone to Jackson for a day or two."

Cy felt the strength the good food had put back into him waver. He'd come all this way, only to be told to go home and try again.

"Maybe you could tell me if you're hiring."

Tucker knew they were, but there was no way in hell he was putting this pale, hollow-eyed boy with pencil-thin arms out in a cotton field. He started to tell him they had all the hands they needed, but something in those dark, shadowed eyes stopped him.

This was Edda Lou's brother, he reminded himself. Austin's son. The last thing in this world he needed was to hire on a Hatinger. Christ knew, he had no business caring about one. But those eyes stayed steady on his, full of hope and despair and painful youth.

"You know how to ride a tractor?"

The hope began to deepen. "Yes, sir."

"Can you tell the difference between a weed and a pansy?"

"I think so."

"Can you swing a hammer without hitting your thumb?"

Unexpectedly, Cy felt his lips twitch. "Most times."

"What I need is something more than a field hand. I need somebody to keep things up around here. What you might call a man of all work."

"I—I can do anything you want."

Tucker took out a cigarette. "I can give you four an hour," he said, and pretended not to hear Cy's sputter of amazement. "And Della'd give you your lunch at noon. Or thereabouts. You can take your time eating, but I expect you to watch the clock. I don't pay you for munching on corn bread."

"I won't cheat you, Mr. Longstreet—Mr. Tucker. I swear it."

"No. I don't expect you will." The boy was as unlike the rest of his family as day to night. Tucker had to wonder how such things happened. "You can start now if you want to."

"Sure I can." Cy was already pushing back from the table. "I'll be here every day, first thing. And I can . . ." He trailed off as he remembered Edda's Lou's funeral the next day. "I—uh—tomorrow . . ."

"I know." It was all Tucker could think of to say. "You do this little job for me today, then come on back Wednesday, and that'll be fine."

"Yes, sir, I'll be here. I sure will."

"Come on out here." Tucker led him out the door and across the patio, over the green lawn to a shed. After rapping on the side a few times in case any snakes were napping inside, Tucker pulled open the door. Its hinges squeaked like old bones. "I expect you ought to oil those sometime," Tucker said absently.

He was struck with the scent here, the damp richness of peat that brought back memories of his mother turning it into the ground as she planted. What he was looking for was tilted against the shed wall opposite the garden spades and hoes and pruning sheers. Grinning to himself, Tucker dragged out his old ten-speed Schwinn.

Both tires were dead flat, but there was a pump, and there were patches. The chain needed oiling worse than the hinges on the shed door, and the seat had developed a nice coating of mold.

Tucker flicked back the lever of the bell bolted to the handlebars. It jingled. He could see himself flying down the blacktop toward Innocence—he'd driven fast even then—eating up the miles toward cherry Popsicles and fountain Cokes. The sun at his back, and his whole life ahead.

"I want you to clean this up for me."

"Yes, sir." Cy touched a reverent hand to the handlebars. He'd had a bike once, a wobbly second-hander he'd bartered for with a flute he'd carved out of a birch branch. Then one afternoon he'd forgotten and left it in the driveway and his father had crushed it flat with his pickup.

That'll teach you to put your trust in worldly goods.

"Then I want you to keep it in tune for me," Tucker was saying, and Cy forced himself back. "A good bike's like a good—" Shit, he'd almost said woman. "Horse. Needs to ridden well and ridden often. I figure riding this back and forth from your place to here every day ought to do it."

Cy's mouth opened and closed twice. "You want me to ride it?" Cy let his hand fall away from the handlebars. "I don't think I could do that."

"You don't ride a bike?"

"Yes, sir, I can ride one, but . . . It don't seem right."

"I don't think walking close to twenty miles a day and fainting on my porch is right either." He put his hands on the boy's shoulders. "I've got the bike, I'm not using it. If you're going to work for me, you can't balk on the first thing I ask you."

"No, sir." Cy wet his lips. "If my daddy finds out, he'll be awful mad."

"You look like a smart boy. A smart boy oughta know where he could pull a bike like this off the road someplace close to home, where nobody'd pay much attention to it."

Cy thought of the culvert under Dead Possum Lane where he and Jim used to play soldier. "I guess that's true."

"Fine. Everything you need should be in the shed. Otherwise, ask Della or me. Mark your time. Payday's on Friday."

Cy watched Tucker's retreating back, then looked down at the dull flecks of blue paint under the grime on the crossbars of the Schwinn.

♦ ♦ ♦ ♦

THREE HOURS LATER, AFTER he'd finished all the busy work Tucker could think of on such short notice, Cy was cruising down the blacktop. The ten-speed wasn't the slick racing machine it had been in Tucker's day, but for Cy it was a steed, a stallion, a wind-dancing Pegasus.

This time when he got to the lane leading to the McNair place, he turned in. He tilted dangerously on the gravel, muttered "Whoa, boy" to his trusty mount, and managed to keep upright.

He saw Jim and his daddy, each perched on extension ladders that leaned against the side of the house. Fresh blue paint glistened. Halfway down the lane, he couldn't hold back and let out a hoot and a holler.

Jim's paintbrush stopped in midair. "Holy crow, lookit what Cy's got. Where'd you get that?" he shouted. "You steal it or something?"

"Heck, no." He stopped the bike just short of running over some of the petunias—he was a little out of practice. "It's like a loan of transportation." Sliding off, he toed down the kickstand. "I got me a job over to Sweetwater."

"No shit?" Jim said before he remembered his father. His slip earned him a halfhearted bop on the head. "Sorry." But he was still grinning down at Cy. "You working the fields?"

"Nuh-uh. Mr Tucker said I was going to be his man of all work, and he's paying me four an hour."

"No . . . fooling?"

"Honest to God. And he said—"

"Hold on. God be patient." Toby shook his head. "You two going to stand around shouting all day? Miz Waverly'll send us packing."

"No, she won't." Amused by the whole scene, Caroline stuck her head out of the window between father and son. "But it seems to me it's a good time to take a break. I've been waiting all day for you to offer me another cup of your wife's lemonade."

"I'd be pleased to. Jim, you go on down. Mind your step." The truth was, Toby wanted to see what was doing himself.

By the time he got down, Jim was already ooing over the Schwinn. Toby went to get the two-gallon cooler while Cy related his adventure.

"Fainted?" Jim said, mightily impressed. "Right there on the porch?"

Caroline stepped through the screen door in time to hear. Her brows drew together. She listened, murmuring an absent thanks to Toby as he handed her a paper cup filled with tart lemonade. Tucker had hired the boy, she thought in amazement. As a—for heaven's sake—man of all work. Chores Tucker was too lazy to do himself, she decided. The child was stick-thin and hollow-eyed. She'd been much the same herself not so long ago, and she felt pangs of empathy and annoyance.

"That boy has no business working," she said under her breath.

"Oh, I expect he'd like some pocket money," Toby said easily.

"He looks like he could use a hot meal more." She started to call out, prepared to fix the child a late lunch herself. "What's his name?"

"He's Cy, Miz Waverly. Cy Hatinger."

Her blood froze. "Hatinger?"

Toby's eyes flicked away from the appalled look in hers. "He ain't nothing like his daddy, Miz Waverly." In an old habit, Toby ran a fingertip down the scar on his cheek. "He's a good boy. Hope you don't think I'm overstepping, but I'm partial to him. He's a good friend to Jim."

Caroline struggled with her conscience. He was a child, after all. She had no business having this urge to shout him off her land only because he carried the Hatinger name. And Hatinger blood.

The bike's bell jingled as Cy and Jim took turns ringing it.

The sins of the fathers. That had been Austin's quote. And his threat. She didn't believe it, not when she looked out at the thin-faced boy who smiled like a dreamy angel.

"Cy."

His head came up, not like an angel's but like a wolf's—fast and wary. "Ma'am?"

"I was about to fix myself some lunch. Would you like some?"

"No, ma'am, thank you, ma'am. I had me some breakfast down to Sweetwater. Mr. Tucker, he fixed me up ham and eggs himself."

"He . . . I see." But she didn't see at all. Beside her, Toby let out a bel-low of laughter.

"Tuck cooked, you ate, and you're still standing? Boy, you must have a cast-iron stomach."

"He cooked it good. He has this microwave. He put biscuits in and quick as you blink they came out again steaming." Revving up, Cy went on about how he was going to get lunch fixed for him every day by Miss Della, and about the loan of the bike, and how Mr. Tucker had given him two dollars in advance already.

"And he said I should spend it as I pleased—as was a man's privilege with his first pay—long as it wasn't on whiskey and women." He flushed a little and shot a look at Caroline. "He was only kidding."

Caroline smiled. "I'm sure you're right."

Cy thought she was the prettiest female he'd ever seen. He was afraid if he kept looking at her, his old tool of Satan would start to twitch. So he looked at the ground. "I'm awful sorry about how my daddy shot out your windows."

Caroline hated to see his thin shoulders go tense that way. "They're all fixed now, Cy."

"Yes'm." He was going to say something, maybe offer her the two dollars for the damage, but he heard the car. Seconds before any of the others heard the sound of the engine slowing, the whisper of gravel under tires, he turned. "It's that FBI man," Cy said, his voice expressionless.

They all watched in silence as Matthew Burns drove up and stopped at the end of the lane.

He wasn't terribly pleased to come across the crowd. He'd hoped to find her alone so that they could have a leisurely chat. But he fixed a pleasant enough smile on his face as he stepped from the car.

"Good afternoon, Caroline."

"Hello, Matthew. What can I do for you?"

"Nothing official. I had an hour free, and thought I'd drop by to see how you were."

"I'm fine." But she knew that wouldn't be enough. "Would you like some iced tea?"

"That would be wonderful." He stopped by the bike where Cy had his eyes planted firmly on the ground. "You're the young Hatinger boy, correct?"

"Yessir." Cy remembered Burns coming out to the house, trying to get some sense out of Ma while she wept into her apron. "I'd best be getting home."

"Come on, Jim. Let's get back to work."

"I wish you'd take a longer break, Toby. It's so hot."

"Toby?" Matthew's gaze sharpened on the broad-shouldered black man. "Toby March?"

Muscles tensed, Toby nodded. "That's right."

"Coincidentally, your name's on my list to be interviewed. That scar on your face. Hatinger gave that to you?"

"Matthew," Caroline said, appalled, her gaze locking on Cy's face.

"I gotta go," Cy said again, quickly. "Maybe I'll see you tomorrow, Jim." He hopped on the bike and pedaled furiously.

"Matthew, did you have to do that with the child here?"

Burns spread his hands. "In a town like this, I'm sure the boy knows already. Now, Mr. March, if you have a moment."

"Jim, you go on around and scrape that window trim."

"But, Daddy—"

"Do as I say."

Head down, shoulders slumped, Jim obeyed.

"You wanted to ask me a question, Mr. Burns."

"Agent Burns. Yes. About your scar."

"I've had it going on twenty years, from when Austin Hatinger come down on me for being a thief." Toby bent to lift an unopened bucket of paint and turned it back and forth in his broad hands.

"He accused you of stealing."

"He said I took some rope from his place. But I never took nothing wasn't mine in my life."

"And there've been hard feelings between you since."

Toby continued to shift the can. Caroline could hear the paint slop gently inside. "We ain't been what you'd call neighborly."

Burns took a pad out of his pocket. "Sheriff Truesdale has a report of a cross-burning on your lawn some six months ago. According to your statement, you believed Austin Hatinger and his son, Vernon, were responsible."

Something cold and hard flashed into Toby's eyes. "I couldn't prove it. I couldn't prove it when I came out of Larsson's one evening and found the tires on my truck slashed, either. And Vernon Hatinger was standing across the street paring his fingernails with his pocketknife and grinning. Even when Vernon says to me I should be glad it was my tires this time and not my face, I couldn't prove anything. So I just said what I thought. Hatinger didn't like his boy being seen with mine."

"There was an altercation between you and Austin Hatinger a few weeks later, in the hardware store, where he threatened to harm your son if you didn't keep him away from Cy. Is that true?"

"He come in while I was buying some three-penny nails. He said some things."

"Do you recall what things?"

Toby's jaw set. "He said, 'Nigger, keep your little black bastard away from what's mine or I'll peel the skin off him.' I said if he touched my boy, I'd kill him."

The quiet, dispassionate way Toby said it sent a chill racing up Caroline's spine.

"He said some more things, quoting scripture and talking trash about how us 'coons' forgot where was our place. Then he picked up a hammer. We got to fighting there in the store, and somebody took off for the sheriff, I guess, 'cause he come hauling ass and broke it up."

"And did you say to Hatinger something along the lines of . . ." He consulted his pad again. " 'You'd be better off worrying about how often that girl of yours is spreading her legs than about Cy fishing with my Jim'?"

"I mighta."

And the girl you were referring to was the now-deceased Edda Lou Hatinger?"

Slowly, Toby set down the paint can. "He was saying things about my family. Shouting filth about my Jim and my little Lucy and my wife. Not a week before that Vernon stopped my wife on the street and told her she'd best keep a closer eye on her boy before he got himself a broken arm or leg. A man don't have to take that from nobody."

"And so you brought up Miss Hatinger's sexual habits."

Toby's skin heated with anger. "I was mad. Maybe I shouldn't've brought in his kin since it was him that riled me."

"But I'm curious how you happen to be acquainted with the deceased's sexual habits."

"Everybody knows it didn't take much to get her on her back." He looked at Caroline with mute apology.

"And do you have personal knowledge of that?"

Now the fury flashed, bright as a sword in his eyes. Frightened by it, Caroline stepped forward to lay a warning hand on his arm.

"I took vows to a woman fifteen years ago," Toby said, clenching his fists. "I've been faithful to her."

"Well, Mr. March, I have a witness who claims you visited Edda Lou Hatinger three or four times in her room at the Innocence Boarding House."

"That's a shit-faced lie. I never been in her room—not when she was there."

"But you were in her room?"

Toby began to feel something very much like a noose tighten around his throat. "Mrs. Koons hired me on to do some work there. I retrimmed the windows in all the rooms. Did some painting, too."

"And when you did your work in Edda Lou's room, you were alone?"

"That's right."

"You were never in the room with her?"

Toby stared at Burns for a slow five seconds. "When she came in, I went out," he said simply. "Now I gotta get my work done and see to my boy."

When Toby stepped off the porch and around the side, Caroline realized she was trembling. "That was horrible."

"I'm sorry, Caroline." Burns put his pad away. "Questioning suspects can be difficult."

"You don't believe he killed that girl because of the hateful things her father did." Though she wanted to shout it, she forced herself to speak quietly. "He's a family man. You only have to see him with his son to understand what kind of person he is."

"Believe me, Caroline, a murderer does not often look like a murderer. Particularly a serial killer. I could give you statistics and psychological patterns that would astonish you."

"Please don't," she said coolly.

"I'm sorry you seem to be dragged into this affair again and again." He smiled. "I'd hoped to come by and spend a quiet hour continuing our conversation of the other day. And of course, I'd hoped to persuade you to play for me."

She took three careful breaths. Perhaps, she thought, he couldn't help being an insensitive, arrogant clod. "I'm sorry, Matthew, I'm taking a rest from performing."

"Oh." His face crumpled in disappointment. "Well, perhaps sometime soon. I'm hoping to have some time at the end of the week. From the little research I've done, I'm told there's an adequate seafood restaurant in Greenville. I'd love to take you."

"Thank you, Matthew, but I'm sticking very close to home for now."

He stiffened a bit at the brush-off. "Pity. Well, the work won't wait, I suppose. I'd best get back." He walked to the car, annoyed but not defeated. "I'll take a rain check on the iced tea if I may."

"Yes. Good-bye."

The moment his dust had cleared, she went inside. For the first time in days, she picked up her violin and played.

Chapter 13

OVERNIGHT, A SLOW, DREARY rain had moved in, soaking the thirsty ground. By mid-morning it had moved on sluggishly to Arkansas, having done little more than turn the dirt to a slick mud that would bake dry by afternoon.

Beside the open grave a huddle of people stood, ankle-deep in the tattered fog that was already burning off in the yellow glare of the sun. Some yards away a narrow line of oaks dripped with rain, a distracting monotone that reminded Cy of the rusty faucet in the bathroom that leaked day and night.

Sometimes he would lie in bed at night thinking that steady drip, drip, drip would drive him crazy. Just like that Chinese water torture he had read about. He was Cy Hatinger, Secret Agent, and the water would drip, drip, drip on the center of his forehead, but he would never break, not even if the water wore right through the skin and bone and down to the brain.

No, they would never break him. He was Bond—James Bond. He was Rambo. He was Indiana Jones.

Then he would just be Cy, stuck in his musty-smelling room, and he would get up, stuff a ragged washcloth under the leak so that the drip would muffle to a bearable plop.

This time his didn't try to block out the sound, but concentrated on it instead, using it to turn his mind away from where he was and what he was doing.

The Reverend Slater seemed ancient to Cy, though in truth the good man was not yet sixty. But Cy's young eyes saw only the thin puffs of white hair on a sunburned scalp, the roadmap lines that scored the wind-roughened face, and the loose skin of his throat that hung stringily from bony chin to concave chest.

To Cy's mind the reverend was too old to know much about life. Then again, today was for death, and there he was bound to be an expert.

Reverend Slater's voice rose and ebbed, flowing melodiously over phrases about salvation and eternal life, and that old standard—God's will.

Cy wondered what would happen if he stepped forward and snatched the Bible out of Reverend Slater's hand.

Excuse me, he could say, *but that's a big pile of horseshit. God didn't have anything to do with Edda Lou getting all sliced up. How come we have to put it on Him that she's going into the ground today? How come we just shuck it aside as the will of the Lord when we all know it was a man's hand who held the knife?*

He was sick of having everything bad put off that way. If the hail came and sliced the young cotton plants to ribbons, it was God's will.

He knew where hail came from, and it all had to do with hot air hitting cold and turning rain into hard little balls of ice. Cy couldn't picture God sitting up there on His golden throne and deciding it was time to pitch hail at Austin Hatinger's pitiful cotton crop.

Just as he couldn't picture God willing that Edda Lou be hacked to pieces and tossed in the pond.

He wanted to say so. The words almost burned on his tongue in their need to be spoken. He knew his mother would only cry harder and groan and sway. Ruthanne would hush him, mortally embarrassed. Vernon would cuff him hard enough to make his ears ring. Others might just stare at him. They were mostly ladies who had come, wrapped in their black dresses.

Mrs. Fuller and Mrs. Shays, grouped together with Mrs. Larsson and Mrs. Koons. Darleen was there, too, bawling up a storm so that her mama finally stepped forward and took the baby she was clutching.

There were other women, some who had been friends with Edda Lou, most who'd come out of Christian duty. But men were scarce. Sheriff Truesdale was there, holding his wife's hand. The FBI man stood off to the side, his face solemn and his head bent. But Cy knew that his eyes were watching, watching, watching.

"I am the way, the truth, and the light," Slater intoned, and Mavis swayed so violently into her eldest son that Vernon tipped into his wife and sent a domino reaction around the circle of mourners. Everyone jigged and jogged for a moment while the reverend went on, heedless.

"Whosoever believest in Me will enter the Kingdom."

Cy wanted to shout, to shout at all of them that Edda Lou hadn't believed in anything but Edda Lou. That all this praying and carrying on was only making a bad thing worse. But he kept his silence, and he kept his head down because there was one man attending the graveyard service whom he feared more than he feared the reverend's God.

That was his father.

♦ ♦ ♦ ♦

*A*USTIN HATINGER STOOD STRAIGHT in his shiny Sunday suit, his ankles and wrists shackled, and a glum-faced deputy flanking him at each side.

He listened to the holy word. He watched as the coffin was lowered into its dark, moist home. And he planned.

He heard his wife's long, ululant cry of grief. His eyes flicked up to her face, saw the ravage done by ceaseless tears. And he plotted.

As the last fingers of fog began to burn off the damp grass, he lowered his head. God had provided, he thought. Concentrating, he stared unblinking into the hole dug for his daughter. In reaction his eyes began to tear. Let them think he was weak with grief, he thought. Let them see a weak, helpless man.

He waited, waited through the end of the service, waited, waited while the women moved to his wife to murmur useless words of condolence.

As they began to walk off toward their cars, one of the deputies nudged him. "Hatinger."

"Please." He focused on that hole in the ground and made his voice tremble. "I need to—pray. To pray with my wife."

He could see by the way the deputies shuffled their feet that they had been moved by the service and the women's tears. Masking everything that was in his heart, he lifted his head. All they could see was the shiny-eyed hopelessness of a father with a dead child.

"Please," he repeated. "She was my daughter. My only daughter. It isn't natural for a man to bury his child, is it? You know what he did to her, don't you?" He looked down so they wouldn't see the hate. "I need to comfort my wife. She ain't strong and this is like to kill her. Just let me hold my wife." He held out his hands. "A man's got a right to hold his wife over his daughter's grave, ain't he?"

"Look, I'm sorry—"

"Come on, Lou." The second deputy had a daughter of his own.

"Where the hell can he go with his legs shackled? It's only decent to give him a minute with his wife."

Austin stood, his head bowed and glee in his heart as the key turned on the cuffs. "But we're going to have to stand with you," the deputy who was called Lou said grudgingly. "And you only got five minutes."

"God bless you." Out of the corner of his eye Austin saw that Burke was already in his car and pulling away. A few of the other women had scattered off to older graves to pay respects to family that was gone. Austin took a step forward, opening his arms. Blindly, limply, his wife fell into them.

He held her a moment, waiting, watching as the deputies averted their eyes out of embarrassed respect for the grieving. It was human nature to offer privacy to the mourning. The smattering of people still in the cemetery turned away.

Then he moved fast, so fast that Cy, who had never once seen his parents embrace, stumbled back into the wet grass.

Austin shoved his wife hard against the first deputy, tumbling both him and the screaming Mavis into the open grave. As the other deputy reached for his weapon, Austin rammed him hard in the chest, going in headfirst like a battering ram. The grappling for the gun was brief while Lou, down in the grave, fought to free himself of a flailing, hysterical woman.

Austin rapped the side of the gun across the deputy's head, knocking him unconscious, then snatched a wide-eyed Birdie Shays around the throat.

"I'll kill her," Austin shouted, full of the wrath of God. "I'll kill her dead as my girl, you hear me? You throw out your gun and the keys, or I'll blow a hole in her head fit to drive a truck through."

Birdie made piping sounds and pawed ineffectually at his arm. A few feet away, Ruthanne began to cry, certain she would never live down this newest humiliation.

"Where you gonna go?" Lou demanded, hating the fact that he was crouched on a coffin with a sobbing woman clawing up his back. The guys back in the station were going to ride him about this like a conventioneer rides a twenty-dollar whore. "Think it through, Hatinger. Where you gonna go?"

"Where the Lord leads me." And yes, he could feel the strength and heat of that fierce God pumping through him. His eyes shone with it. " 'Master, I will follow Thee!' " he shouted, cutting off Birdie's air. "Ten seconds, then I do her. After that, I'll just fill that hole you're in with lead, and that'll be that."

Swearing and furious, Lou tossed out the keys.

"Your sidearm, too."

"Goddammit—"

"*Five* seconds." With a jerk of his head, Austin signaled Vernon to unchain him.

"You oughta just kill them, Daddy," Vernon said between his teeth as he turned the key. The idea had blood surging to his face. "Just shoot the Christless bastards and we'll go to Mexico."

"I ain't going nowhere till this is finished."

Lou popped up, hoping to get off one shot, then ducked down again as a piece of sod two inches away was sheared off by a .38 slug.

"Fucking crazy if he thinks I'm going to end up with a hole in my head." Lou tossed the gun out.

Austin shoved the babbling Birdie toward the grave, where she teetered on the edge for a moment, her eyes wide with dreadful concentration, her arms stretched like a diver preparing for a double gainer. She landed spread-eagle on Lou.

By the time everyone had sorted themselves out, Austin Hatinger was gone, driving off in Birdie Shays's Buick. He was carrying two Police Specials and a gutful of hate.

♦ ♦ ♦ ♦

J IM MARCH STOOD PATIENTLY in the hallway, whistling tunelessly through his teeth and waiting for Caroline to come back down so he could ask her if she wanted the braces on her back porch fixed when the painting was done.

His daddy had run into town for a few supplies, and Jim had opted to stay behind. He was supposed to be painting, but he'd noticed the sag and give in the old porch, and thought his daddy would be pleased if the inquiry led to more work.

Caroline had called down to him to come on in when he'd knocked. He'd been careful to wipe his feet. His mama was a fiend about foot wiping and hand washing. Every few whistles he'd edge his paint-splattered Keds a little farther down the hall. He knew the violin was in the parlor, because he'd seen it through the window. Jim wanted a closer look, the same way he might have wanted one if he'd spotted a brand new Wilson ball glove through Larsson's display window.

He reached the parlor doorway, casual like, he thought. And there it was. He shot a quick glance over his shoulder toward the stairs, then made his dash. He was just going to take one little look, was all, he told himself. One peek, then he'd be back in the hallway lickity-split.

He'd been thinking about that violin ever since Caroline had played it the day before. Jim had never heard music like it, not in all his born days. It made him wonder if there was something special about this violin, something different from the old fiddle Rupert Johnson would sometimes saw on summer nights.

Jim fumbled with the catches on the side, then lifted the top. When he saw it, nestled there against coal-black velvet, it *was* different. Oh, it seemed to be the same shape and size as old Rupert's, but it was shiny as a new penny. And when Jim worked up the nerve to touch it, its glossy surface was smooth as silk. Or what he imagined silk would be.

Forgetting his vow to take one quick peek, he gently brushed a thumb over the strings.

Caroline heard the telltale open chord when she reached the bottom of the steps. Her first reaction was of irritation. No one touched her instrument. No one. She tuned and polished it herself, often to the amusement of whatever orchestra she was playing with.

Luis had complained more than once that she spent more time stroking the violin than stroking him. That had made her feel guilty—until she'd discovered he'd been doing quite a bit of extracurricular stroking himself.

She strode toward the parlor, the lecture already heating her tongue. Then she stopped. Jim was kneeling beside the violin case, and his thumb brushed carefully across the strings, as gently as if he were stroking the cheek of an infant. But it was his face that stopped Caroline from speaking the sharp words. He looked as though he'd just discovered some marvelous secret. His smile stretched across his face, not in glee but in profound joy. His eyes shone with it.

"Jim," she said quietly, and he jerked to his feet like a puppet on a string. His eyes widened until Caroline was all but sure they were going to swallow the rest of his face.

"I—I—I was just looking. I beg pardon, Miz Caroline, I know I wasn't supposed to. Don't fire my daddy."

"It's all right," she said, and it was. Wouldn't Luis be surprised, she thought, that it was all right with her if a young black boy handled her violin? She'd never allowed Luis to do more than breathe on it.

"You don't have to pay me for the work or nothing," he barreled on. "I know I shouldn'ta done it."

"I said it's all right, Jim." When she touched a hand to his shoulder, the calm amusement in her voice finally reached his rattled brain.

"You ain't mad?"

"No, but it would have been better if you'd asked to see it."

Of course, if he had, she would have said no. Then she would have missed that glimpse of sheer pleasure. The same pleasure she remembered feeling herself, once upon a time.

"Yes, ma'am, I apologize. I sure do. Had no right coming into your parlor like this." Hardly able to believe his good luck, he started backing out. "I was coming in to ask if you wanted that back porch braced, then I just . . ." It occurred to him he'd be smarter to leave well enough alone.

"What made you want to see it?"

Shoot, he thought, she was going to tell his daddy for sure. Then the shit would be in the fire. "It was just . . . hearing you play it yesterday. I ain't never heard nothing like the way you made that fiddle sing. So I thought . . . well, I wondered if it was something special."

"It is to me." Thoughtfully, she took the violin from its case, as she had too many times to count. The weight, the shape, the texture, all so familiar. How much she loved it. And how much she hated it. "Have you ever held one?"

Jim swallowed hard. "Well, old Rupert—that's Deputy Johnson's grandpappy—he showed me a couple of tunes on his fiddle. It ain't nearly as pretty as yours. Don't make music the same neither."

She doubted old Rupert owned a Stradivarius. She had an impulse that surprised her. Then she reminded herself that blocking her impulses was what had landed her in that hospital in Toronto. Freeing them had brought her to Innocence, for better or worse.

"Why don't you show me what you can do?" She offered the violin, and Jim immediately put both hands behind his back.

"No'm, I couldn't. Wouldn't be right."

"It's right if I ask you, isn't it?"

She watched the boy's eyes latch on to the violin, saw the war in his face between desire and what he considered propriety. His hands came out slowly to take it.

"Holy crow," he whispered. "It do shine, don't it?"

Silently, she took out the bow, rosined it. "I wasn't very much older than you the first time I played this violin." She thought back, so far back to the night her parents had given it to her. In her dressing room at the Academy of Music in Philadelphia, before her first major solo. She'd been sixteen, and had just finished retching—as quietly and discreetly as possible—in the adjoining bath.

Then her parents had come in, her father so full of beaming pride, her mother so full of desperate ambition, that the sickness hadn't had a chance against them.

She'd never been sure if the violin had been a gift or a bribe or a threat. But she hadn't been able to resist it.

What had she played that first time, Caroline wondered, there in the dressing room heavy with the scent of flowers and greasepaint?

Mozart, she remembered, and smiled a little.

"Show me," she said simply, and handed him the bow.

Jim cast his mind around for what might be best. Settling the violin on his shoulder, he eased the bow over the strings in a few testing sweeps, then launched into "Salty Dog."

By the time he'd finished, the dazed look had left his eyes and a grin was splitting his face. He knew he'd never sounded better, and caught up in the music he flowed into "Casey Jones."

Caroline sat on the arm of the chair and watched. Oh, there were a few wrong notes, and his technique could use a little polishing. But she was impressed, not only with his playing, which was clever and bright, but with the look in his eye, the look that told her he was playing for pleasure.

That was something that had been denied her—and that she had denied herself—for nearly twenty-five years.

Jim came back to himself and cleared his throat. The music was still dancing and swaying inside his head, and his fingers vibrated with it. But he was afraid he was pushing his luck.

"That's just some stuff old Rupert showed me. It's nothing like what you played. That was . . . holy, I guess."

She had to smile. "I think we can make a bargain, Jim."

"Ma'am?"

"You show me how to play what old Rupert showed you—"

His eyes bulged out of his head. "You want me to show you how to play those tunes?"

"That's right, and in return I'll show you how to play others."

"Like what you was playing yesterday?"

"Yes, like that."

He knew his hands were sweating and made himself give her back the violin before he smudged it and ruined everything. "I'd have to ask my daddy."

"I'll ask him." Caroline tilted her head. "If you'd like to."

"I'd like it just fine."

"Then come over here and watch." She remained sitting so he could have a good view of her fingers. "This is called the Minute Waltz. It's by Frederic Chopin."

"Chopin," Jim repeated reverently.

"We won't play it in a minute just yet. It's not a race, it's just for—"

"Fun?"

"Yes." She tucked the violin under her chin, relishing that three-letter word. "For fun."

They were well into their first lesson when Deputy Carl Johnson drove by to tell her that Austin Hatinger had escaped.

♦ ♦ ♦ ♦

CAROLINE MADE UP HER mind about two things after Carl Johnson had driven off to pass the word at Sweetwater. First, she was going to renew her target practice. And she was going to get herself a dog. Her initial instinct to pack and run had faded almost before it had begun. What had replaced it was an emotion much stronger and deeper. This was her home now, and she intended to protect it.

Following Jim's advice and directions, she headed down Hog Maw Road toward the Fullers'. Jim had told her that Happy Fuller's bitch Princess had had a litter some two months before.

Happy, changed from her funeral dress to her gardening clothes, greeted her with pleasure. Not only was she pleased to be rid of the single remaining pup, she wanted a new ear to listen to all the excitement.

"I've never been more terrified," Happy was saying as she led Caroline around to the backyard, past a gaggle of ceramic geese and a bed of impatiens. "I was standing aways apart, by my mama's grave. She passed in eighty-five from cancer of the ovaries. Wouldn't see the doctor, Mama wouldn't, so it ran through her like Grant took Richmond. Me, I go into Doc Shays and have a pap smear every six months like clockwork."

"I'm sure that's wise."

"Makes no sense to hide from problems." Happy paused in front of a whirligig of a man sawing wood. The air hung so heavy and still, the little man was getting plenty of rest.

"Anyhow," Happy continued, bending to tug out a weed that had dared intrude on her zinnias, "I'm standing by Mama and I hear all this commotion. Shouting and screaming and what all. Turned around just in time to see that deputy from Greenville go tumbling with Mavis into Edda Lou's grave. Then Austin, he takes a vicious swipe at the other deputy—hardly more than a boy that one—and knocks him clean out with his own pistol. I'm thinking to myself, Holy God in heaven, he's going to open up with that gun. But what does he do? He snatches Birdie 'round the throat and orders that deputy—the one down in the grave—to throw out the key for the leg shackles. Now you could hear Mavis wailing and screaming fit to wake the dead. Lordy, there's plenty to wake there in Blessed Peace. And there's poor Birdie, white as a sheet with a gun right to her head. I thought my heart was going to stop on me. Birdie's a dear friend of mine."

"Yes, I know." Caroline had already heard all this from Carl Johnson, but resigned herself that she would hear it again. And again.

"When Austin let loose with a shot, I'm not ashamed to say I dove behind my mama's headstone. It's a good-sized one, though I had to fight with my brother Dick over the price of it. Dick always was a skinflint. Why, he'll squeeze a penny till Lincoln shouts uncle. Then Vernon—who's just as shifty-eyed as his daddy ever was—unlocked those shackles. Next thing you knew, Austin was shoving poor Birdie into that hole right on top of the deputy from Greenville and poor Mavis. All hell broke loose then, let me tell you. Birdie was screeching, Mavis wailing, and that deputy was cussing like a drunk sailor on a two-day leave."

Happy's lips twitched, and she would have bitten back the smile if she hadn't seen answering amusement in Caroline's eyes.

They stared at each other for a moment, struggling for sobriety. Caroline lost first, with a quick snorting laugh she tried to turn into a cough. Then they were laughing, standing in the bright afternoon sun and howling until Happy had to dig for her hankie and wipe her eyes.

"I tell you, Caroline, it was a sight I'll not forget if I live to a hundred. After Austin took off in Birdie's Buick, I ran over. There they were, all tangled in a heap of arms and legs on top of the coffin. And the first thing I thought—God forgive me—was that it all looked like one of those unnatural sex doings you might see on an X-rated video." Her eyes twinkled. "Not that I've ever seen one, mind you."

"No," Caroline said weakly. "Of course not."

"Birdie's skirts were hiked up nearly to her waist. She's a bit on the heavy side, is Birdie, and I do believe she'd knocked the wind right out of that deputy when she landed on him. His face was red as a raddish. And Mavis, why she was hanging on to his legs and shouting about the hand of God."

"Awful," Caroline managed to say, then dissolved into laughter again. "Oh, it's awful."

Happy honked into her hankie and fought back a fresh spray of giggles. "Then that young deputy woke up, while those of us left at the cemetery were trying to haul Birdie and the rest of them out. Poor boy was stumbling around, and by Jesus, if Cy hadn't caught hold of him, he'd've tumbled right in with them. It was better than watching *I Love Lucy*."

Caroline had a picture of Ricky Ricardo doing a headfirst dive into a grave. *Luuu-cy, I'm home!* She sat down on the little stone wall by the impatiens and hugged her sides.

With a sigh, Happy sat beside her. "Oh, my, I'm glad I got that out. Birdie'd never forgive me for laughing."

"It's terrible. Gruesome."

That added another five minutes to their fight for composure.

"Well now." Breath hitching a bit, Happy put away her hankie. "Let me call that damn dog. While you're looking him over, I'll go get us something cold. Princess! Princess, you get on over here and bring that mutt with you. Only got the one left," Happy said conversationally, "and you're welcome to him. Can't tell you nothing about the father, as Princess ain't too particular. Going to have her spayed this time. Meant to before."

Caroline saw a big, yellow-haired dog, thick-bodied, weary-faced, come ambling across the yard. Running circles around her was a good-sized puppy of the same color. Every few seconds he made a dash under her for one of the floppy tits. Princess, who had obviously had enough of motherhood, would shift cagily away.

"Here now." Happy clapped her hands. At the sound, the pup gave up his quest for mother's milk and cheerfully gamboled over. "You're a useless little cuss, aren't you?"

The pup yipped in agreement, wagging his tail so fast and hard his hind end nearly met his nose.

"I'll leave you to get acquainted." Happy rose. "I'll fetch us some iced tea."

Caroline eyed the pup with a good deal of doubt. Certainly he was cute, and it was sweet the way he plopped his big front paws on her knees. But she was after a guard dog, not a pet. It certainly wouldn't do for her to develop a fondness for an animal she would have to give away in a few months.

And though he was already good-sized, he was hardly fierce-looking with his dopey long ears and lolling tongue. His mother stood nearly as tall as Caroline's waist, but she wondered how long it would take for the son to grow that high.

It was a mistake, she decided. She should have asked for the nearest pound and gone in to liberate some fang-dripping Doberman she could keep chained near the back door.

But the pup's fur was soft and warm. While she frowned over him, he licked her hand and swiped his tail so hard, he tumbled off his perch, then set to chasing it.

Once he'd gotten a good bite of it, he yelped, then raced back to her, his big brown eyes full of wonder and doggy chagrin.

"Dummy," she muttered, and picked him up to cuddle. Ah, hell, she thought as he slobbered all over her cheek and throat.

When Happy came out with the iced tea, Caroline had already named him Useless. She decided he'd look very dapper in a red collar.

◆ ◆ ◆ ◆

SHE BOUGHT HIM ONE at Larsson's, and added a ten-pound bag of puppy food, a leash, a plastic dish with two bowls, and a flowered cushion which would serve as a dog bed.

He howled in her car the entire time she was in the store. She looked out once to see he'd propped his feet up on the dash and was staring at her with accusation and terror in his big brown eyes. The minute she got back in the car he scrambled into her lap.

After a short battle of wills, Caroline left him curled there for the drive home.

"You're not going to do me a damn bit of good," she said as the pup let out a shuddering sigh of contentment. "I can see that already. I know what the problem is. I always wanted a puppy when I was a little girl. We couldn't have one. Dog hairs in the parlor and piddles on the rug. Then, by the time I was eight, I was already traveling on and off during the summer. So, of course, a pet was out of the question."

She stroked him as she drove, enjoying the warm lump of him on her lap. "The thing is, I'm not going to be here for more than another month or two, so it's not really fair for us to develop a close relationship. Not that we can't be friends," she continued when Useless propped his head in the crook of her elbow and looked up soulfully. "I mean, it's certainly all right to have a little affection, some respect, even some mutual enjoyment for as long as it lasts. Just as long as we both know . . ." He cuddled against her breast and licked her chin.

"Shit."

By the time she turned in her drive, she was already in love and berating herself for it.

It didn't help to see Tucker sitting on her front porch steps with a bottle of wine beside him and a spray of yellow roses across his lap.

Chapter 14

"DON'T YOU EVER WORK?" Caroline asked as she struggled to gather up the wiggling puppy, her purse, and some of her purchases.

"Only if they catch me." Tucker set the roses aside, then lazily unfolded himself. "Whatcha got there, Caro?"

"I call it a dog."

He chuckled and wandered over to where she'd managed to squeeze her car next to the boat-sized Oldsmobile. "Cute little fella." He ruffled the pup's fur, then peeked in the back of the BMW. "Need some help?"

She blew her hair out of her eyes. "What do you think?"

"I think you're glad to see me." He took advantage of her loaded arms and kissed her. "And you wish you weren't. Go on and take a load off. I'll haul the rest of this out for you."

She did, mainly to see if he could do anything with his hands other than raise a woman's blood pressure. After she'd sat on the steps, Caroline worked on fastening the new collar around the squirming puppy's neck.

"Looks like you got all the essentials," Tucker commented. He pulled out a bag, tossed the sack of puppy food over his shoulder. There was a faint and interesting ripple of muscle, Caroline noticed. Then he gathered up the bright-flowered cushion. "What's this?"

"He's got to sleep on something."

Your bed, Tucker figured with a grin. The pup didn't look backward. "So . . ." He dumped everything on the porch, then sat next to her. "That one of the Fuller pups?"

"Yes." The pup deserted her to sniff at Tucker's hand. Caroline could smell the roses and determined not to be charmed by them, not to ask about them, not even to look at them.

"Hey, boy." Tucker scratched the pup in a spot that had Useless grinning and slapping a hind foot rhythmically on the step. "That's a good dog, yeah. That's a pretty good dog. So what's his name?"

"Useless," Caroline muttered as the puppy—her puppy, she reminded herself—stretched himself adoringly over Tucker's lap. "I've already figured out he would be, as a guard dog."

Tucker's brows drew together briefly. "Guard dog, huh?" He tickled the puppy into turning over. "Hey, boy, let me see those teeth." Useless obligingly chewed on Tucker's knuckle. "Well, they'll grow soon enough. Just like the rest of him. Couple of months he'll start to grow into his feet."

"In a couple of months I—I'll be in Europe," she finished. "Actually, I may be leaving sooner than that. There's an engagement I might have to take—in September—that would require me to go to D.C. in August to prepare."

"Have to take?"

She hadn't meant to put it that way. "There's an engagement," she said, dismissing the rest. "But I imagine I'll be able to find a good home for the puppy before I leave."

Tucker looked up at her, golden eyes calm and just a little hard. He had a way of looking now and again, she thought, that stripped away all the nonsense and carved down to truth. "I expect you could take a dog along if you wanted to." His voice was quiet, hardly more than a ripple on the hot, still air. "You're a pretty big deal in what you do, aren't you?"

She hated the fact that she had to look away, had to before he saw through to things she was still hiding from herself. "Touring's complicated," she said, and left it at that.

But he didn't.

"Do you like it?"

"It's part of what I do." She started to make a grab for the puppy, when he scrambled off Tucker's lap to go exploring. "He could wander off."

"He's just sniffing the place out. You didn't answer me, Caroline. Do you like it?"

"It's not a matter of like or dislike. When you're performing, you travel." Airport to airport, she thought, city to city, hotel to hotel, rehearsal to rehearsal. She felt the tightening in her stomach, the little pull of a knot being tied. It warned her to ease off unless she wanted to extend an invitation to her old friend Mr. Ulcer.

When a man was rarely tense himself, he recognized the symptoms. Casually, he put a hand to the back of her neck and rubbed. "I never could understand why somebody'd make a habit of doing something they didn't care for."

"I didn't say—"

"Sure you did. You didn't say, Oh my gracious, Tuck, there's nothing like it. Flying off to London, scooting on to Paris, cruising over to Vienna or Venice. Now, I've always wanted to see some of those places myself. But you don't sound like you've piled up a load of fun by doing it."

See? she thought. What did you really see between interviews, rehearsals, performances, and packing? "There are people in this world who don't consider fun their life's ambition." She heard her own voice, recognized it as prim, and pouted in disgust.

"Now, that's a shame." He settled back to light a cigarette. "See that pup there? He's sniffing 'round there, happy as a frog with a belly full of flies. He'll water your grass, chase his tail if it appeals to him, then settle down and take a nice nap. I always figured dogs had the best idea for getting through."

Her lips twitched. "Just let me know if you have an urge to water my grass."

But Tucker didn't smile back. He studied the glowing tip of his cigarette a moment, then shot her that calm, scapel-honed look. "I asked Doc Shays about those pills you gave me. The Percodan? He said they were potent. It caused me to wonder why you'd need them."

She toughened up. The way she drew in reminded him of a porcupine curling up and showing spines to anything curious enough to take a poke. "That's none of your business."

He put a hand on her cheek. "Caroline, I care about you."

She was very aware—they both were—that he'd said that before, to dozens of women. And they were both aware, uncomfortably, that this time it was different.

"I get headaches," she said, hating the fact that her voice was waspish and defensive.

"Regular?"

"What is this? A test? A lot of people get headaches, especially if they do more than sit in a porch rocker all day."

"I prefer a good rope hammock myself," he said equably. "But we were talking about you."

Her eyes went flat and cold. "Back off, Tucker."

Normally he would have. He wasn't one to poke and prod where his hand could get snapped off. "It doesn't sit well with me, thinking about you hurting."

"I'm not hurting." But a headache was coming on as relentlessly as a highballing freight train.

"Or worrying."

"Worrying." She repeated the word twice, then dropped her head in her lap and laughed. There was a tint of hysteria in the sound that had the puppy bellying over to whine at her feet. "Oh, what's to worry about? Just because some maniac's out carving up women and leaving them floating in my pond. Why should I worry that Austin Hatinger's on the loose again, and may decide to come back and blow out my windows? I certainly shouldn't lose any sleep over the fact that he's sure to try to put a few holes in you."

"I'm not looking for more holes than I've already got." He ran a soothing hand up and down her spine. "We Longstreets have a knack for coming out on top."

"Oh, I can see that. With your eye blackened and your head bashed in."

Tucker frowned a little. He'd been thinking his eye was looking a lot better. "By next week the bruises'll go and Austin's likely to be back in jail. Longstreet luck works that way, darlin'. Take Cousin Jeremiah."

Caroline groaned, but he ignored her.

"Now, he was a good friend of Davy Crockett's. A Kentucky boy, you know?" His voice settled naturally into a story-telling mode. "They'd fought together during the War for Independence. 'Course, Jeremiah'd been no more'n a boy then, but he sure did like to fight. After the war he knocked around here and there, not quite sure what the hell to do with himself. Never settled down. It was like he couldn't find himself a purpose. Anyhow, he heard about this ruckus going on in Texas, and figured he'd mosey on over and see his old friend Davy. Maybe shoot a few Mexicans. He was still this side of Louisiana when his horse stepped down in a rabbit hole. Tossed Jeremiah off. Horse broke a leg, so did Jeremiah. Had to shoot the horse, which pained Jeremiah some, as they'd been together the best part of eight years.

"Now, it so happened this farmer came along, hauled Jeremiah back to his place in his wagon. The farmer had a daughter, as any decent farmer should, and between them they set the leg—it was a bad break and nearly did Jeremiah in, but after a couple a weeks he was able to hobble around on a crutch."

"And he fell in love with the farmer's daughter, had a handsome brood of children who got rich planting cotton or whatever they plant in Louisiana."

"That's true enough, but not my point exactly. The point is Jeremiah lost his horse and walked with a limp the rest of his days. But he never did get out there to join Davy in Texas. At the Alamo."

She'd turned her head to rest her cheek on her knees so that she could watch him as he finished the story which was probably a lie. The odd thing was her headache had receded along with those warning jags in her stomach.

"So the point is," she said, "a Longstreet's lucky enough to break a leg to avoid something more fatal."

"There you go. Now, honey, why don't you gather up your dog and whatever you think you need and come on down and stay at Sweetwater for a while?" The instant wariness in her eyes made him smile. "We've got a dozen bedrooms or more, so you don't have to stay in mine." He flicked a finger down her nose. "Unless you're ready to admit you're going to end up there sooner or later anyway."

"I thank you for the graciousness of your offer, but I'll have to decline."

The faintest shadow of impatience flickered in his eyes. "Caroline, you've got plenty of chaperones and a good solid lock on every bedroom door if you're thinking I'll try to sneak under your sheets."

"I'm sure you would," she said, but with a laugh. "And don't flatter yourself by thinking I'm afraid I can't handle you. I have to stay here."

"I'm not proposing you move in permanently." But it surprised him that the idea didn't give him the shivers. "Just for a visit, till Austin's where he belongs."

"I have to stay here," she said again. "Tucker, up until the last couple months I've never taken a stand on anything. My whole life I've done what I was told, gone where I was pointed, and acted as I was expected to act."

"Tell me."

"No, not now." She let out a long sigh. "Maybe some other time. But this is my home, my place, and I'm sticking. My grandmother lived here her entire adult life. My mother was born here, though she'd prefer you didn't mention it. I'd like to think there was enough McNair in me to last one summer." She shook off the mood and smiled. "Are you going to give me those flowers or let them wilt on the step?"

He considered several valid arguments, then let it go. When people weren't allowed to go their own way, they were more likely to break than bend. "These?" All innocence, he held up the roses. The little plastic nipple of water each stem was tucked in kept them fresh. "Did you want them?"

She shrugged. "I wouldn't want them to go to waste."

"Me neither, since I had to drive all the way over to Rosedale to get them—and that wine there. Had to borrow Della's car to do it," he added, taking an indulgent sniff of the blooms. "And with Della, nothing comes free. You should've seen the list of chores she gave me. Dry cleaning and marketing, and since she'd gotten herself a flyer about a dollar sale at Woolworth's, I had to fetch all that stuff, too. I drew the line at picking out a negligee for her sister Sarah's girl, who's engaged to be married and having a wedding shower next week. A man's got to have his standards, and I don't buy fancy underwear for women unless I'm intimately acquainted with them."

"You're a man of substance, Tucker."

"It's a matter of principle." He laid the roses over her lap, where the slender cupped blossoms glowed like little points of sunlight. "I thought yellow ones suited you best."

"They're beautiful." She inhaled the perfume, sweet and strong. "I suppose I'll have to thank you for them, and for all the trouble you went through to get them for me."

"You could kiss me instead. I'd rather you did." He smiled when her brow creased, then tipped up his chin with a fingertip. "Don't think about it, Caroline, just do it. It's better than any pill for curing headaches."

So with the roses glowing between them, she leaned over and touched her lips to his. The taste was as sweet and as strong as the fragrance that floated over to her. And, she discovered, as comforting. A little dreamy-eyed, she started to draw back, but he cupped a hand around the back of her neck.

"You Yankees," he murmured. "Always in a hurry." He nudged her mouth back to his.

He was savoring. She understood that even as her mind began to mist over with emotion. She was aware of how slow, how deep a kiss could be if you just let yourself fall into it. With a little sigh she did just that.

Even when she felt his fingers tense on her skin, she didn't worry. Under the palm she'd pressed to his chest, his heart was beating fast and hard. But the rhythm brought her pleasure rather than taut nerves.

And all the while his lips cruised over hers so that the kiss was like slipping into a cool blue lake dappled with sunlight.

It was he who drew back now. He hadn't touched her, but for those fingers that had grown strong at the back of her neck, he hadn't touched her. Hadn't dared. For he knew once he did, he wouldn't be able to stop.

Something here wasn't playing the tune he was used to. Difficult though it was to stop, Tucker knew he'd better think this through.

"I don't suppose you're going to ask me in."

"No," she said, and let out a long breath. "Not yet."

"I'd better be getting back, then." After a quick internal tug-of-war between stay and go, he rose. "I promised Cousin Lulu a game of Parcheesi. She cheats." He grinned. "But so do I, and I'm quicker."

"Thanks for the flowers. And the wine."

Tucker stepped over the pup, who was snoring at the base of the stairs. Since there was only three inches between Della's Olds and the BMW, he had to get in through the passenger side and slide over. After he'd started the engine, he rolled down the window.

"You keep that wine chilled, sugar. I'll be back."

As Caroline watched him shoot backward down her lane, she wondered why that brief, cocky statement had sounded so much like a threat.

◆ ◆ ◆ ◆

*J*OSIE AND CRYSTAL SAT in their favorite booth in the Chat 'N Chew. Their excuse was dinner, but since both of them were on a perpetual diet, the reason was gossip.

Josie poked at her chicken salad with little interest. What she wanted was a thick steak and a side of nice greasy fries. But she worried about her body. She was past thirty now, and watched vigilantly for any sags or droops or paunches.

Her mama had kept a trim, willowy figure up to the day she'd dropped dead in her roses. Josie intended to do no less.

Since the day she'd realized her mama was different from her daddy, Josie had been in a subtle and constant competition. It had made her feel guilty from time to time, but she hadn't been able to resist the need to be as pretty as her mother. Then prettier. To be as desirable to men. Then more desirable.

She'd never been able to get a handle on her mother's quiet dignity, had failed miserably in trying to emulate it in her first marriage, so she had chosen to copy her father's bold and bawdy talk instead. She felt it suited her—the stunning femme-fatale looks and the earthy personality. As a child she'd fit the pieces of herself together. Now the puzzle of Josie Longstreet was linked tight.

While Josie toyed with her chicken salad, Crystal made short work of her tuna-stuffed tomato. Crystal was chattering the whole time she forked the tuna into her mouth. As she had all of her life, Josie turned the sound on and off.

She was fond of Crystal, had been since they'd made the solemn decision to be best friends back in first grade, when they'd been two privileged little girls with no idea how radically their lives would diverge. Josie going one way—debutante balls and that first, proper marriage. Crystal going another, after her lawyer father ran off to parts unknown with his secretary. Her path had been the work force and a bad marriage that had ended in divorce after a second miscarriage.

But they had remained friends. Whenever Josie swept back into Innocence, she always spent time with Crystal. Josie was sentimental enough to want a childhood friend in her adult life. And she liked the way they complemented each other. Crystal was tiny and nicely rounded while Josie herself was tall and slim. Crystal had white skin dashed with a sprinkle of freckles. She'd spent a fortune on every freckle remover on the market until she'd finally accepted them as a personality trait. She'd learned to care for her skin in Madame Alexandra's Beauty School in Lamont, where she'd graduated third in her class and had the certificate to prove it.

As a result, she had the blooming complexion of a milkmaid, which was the perfect foil for Josie's dusky Gypsy looks. Her hair, which she changed every few months as a kind of walking advertisement for her skills, was currently Clairol's Sparkling Sherry, which she wore in a viciously lacquered modified beehive. Crystal insisted they were coming back.

"And then, when Bea was doing Nancy Koons's nails, that Justine started going on about how Will told her the FBI figured out it was a black that killed Edda Lou and the others. How they knew it 'cause of the way they were killed, and how they'd found this pubic hair and all." Crystal dug into her tomato, daintily tipping the tuna onto her fork with her pinky. "Now, I don't know if that's the way it was or not, but I don't think it was right for her to be going on like that with Bea—who's black as the ace of spades—sitting there filing nails. I was real embarrassed, Josie, but Bea, she just asks Nancy if she wants ridge filler, and keeps on filing."

Josie sucked on her straw. "Justine's so besotted with Will, if he told her a frog shits gold nuggets, she'd be panning for them in Little Hope Creek."

"That's no excuse," Crystal said righteously. "I mean, we all know it probably was a colored, but you won't find me talking about it in front of Bea. Why, Bea's my best operator. So I gave Justine's hair a jerk and when she squealed, I said, just as nice as you please: 'Oh, honey, did that hurt? I'm *awful* sorry. All that talk about murder and all just makes me so nervous. Good thing I didn't clip your earlobe while I was trimming. A clipped ear bleeds worse'n a stuck pig.' " Crystal smiled. "That shut her right up."

"Maybe I'll talk Will into driving me home tonight." Josie tossed back her mane of hair. "That'll give Justine something to squeal about."

Crystal gave one of her quick, birdlike laughs. "Oh, Josie. You're such a one." Her eyes shifted as the diner's door swung open. Poking out her lip, she leaned closer to Josie. "There's that Darleen Talbot coming in with her baby." She sniffed and sucked her Coke dry. "There's trash and there's trash, I say."

Josie's gaze flicked up as Darleen walked by to settle herself in a booth. "Billy T. Bonny, huh?"

"Speaking of trash." And Crystal dearly loved to. "Just like I told you, I saw him saunter right on in Darleen's kitchen door not ten minutes after Junior went out the front. And all she was wearing was a little pink baby-doll nightgown when she let him in. I saw them clear through Susie Truesdale's kitchen window. There I was, rinsing Susie's hair in the sink. Now, that Susie, she keeps a spotless kitchen, let me tell you, even with all those kids. If her youngest hadn't had a sick stomach, she'd have come on in the shop for her usual wash and style, and I wouldn't have seen a thing."

"What did Susie say?"

"Well, her head was in the sink, but when I was blowing her dry, I mentioned it, real casual like. And I could see by the way she looked that she knew. But she just said she never paid any mind to what went on next door."

"So Darleen's cheating on Junior with Billy T." Josie's lips curved around her straw. Her eyes took on that deep, faraway glow that warned Crystal something was up.

"You're thinking, Josie."

"I was doing just that, Crystal. I was thinking that Junior's got a sweet face even if he is a little bit dim. And I'm real fond of him."

"Shoot." Crystal poked at the remains of her tomato. "Far as I know, he's about the only man in town between twenty and fifty you've never looked twice at."

"I can be fond of a man without wanting to do it with him." Josie examined her straw. There was a smear of red on the tip. "Seems to me somebody ought to give him a little hint about what's happening in his own house when he's not around to see it."

"I don't know, Josie."

"I know, and that's enough." She dug in her bag for a pad and pen. "Let's see now. I'll just write him a little note, and you can get it to him."

"Me?" Crystal squeaked, then looked guiltily around. "How come I have to do it?"

"Because everybody knows you stop at the station on your way home to buy yourself a Milky Way bar."

"Well, sure, but—"

"So when you go in," Josie continued, busily writing, "all you have to do is distract Junior while he's got the cash register open. Then you drop this on in and scoot out. Easy as pie."

"You know I always get a rash under my arms when I get nervous." Crystal thought she could already feel her skin prickling.

"Two seconds, and you're all done." When she saw Crystal wavering, Josie brought out the big guns. "I told you, didn't I, how Darleen was saying that color you used on her hair turned brassy and she was going to save her money by doing it herself with Miss Clairol? She said right out that it was a crime for you to charge seventeen fifty for a color job when all anyone had to do was pick up a box for five dollars and do it themselves."

"That little bitch has no right talking that way to my customers." Crystal was fired up now. "Why, she's got hair like a Brillo pad, and if I've told her once, I've told her a thousand times, she's got to have a professional tend to it or else it'll start falling right out of her head." She sniffed. "Hope it does."

Josie smiled and waved the note in front of Crystal's nose. Glaring, Crystal snatched it.

"Just look at her," Crystal continued. "Sitting there putting on lipstick while that baby smears ice cream all over itself."

Casually, Josie turned her head. She started to remark that Darleen would look better herself, smeared with a little cherry vanilla. The glint of the gold case on the tube of lipstick stopped her.

"Now, isn't that funny," she murmured.

"What?"

"Nothing. I'll be right back, Crystal." Josie rose, and trailing a finger over the back of the booths, strolled up to Darleen. "Hey, Darleen. This baby of yours sure is getting big."

"He's eight months now." Surprised and flattered that Josie had come over, Darleen set the lipstick aside to wipe ineffectually at Scooter's face with a paper napkin. Infuriated by the interruption, he howled. Josie eyed the lipstick case while Darleen and the baby fussed at each other.

It wasn't a mistake, she thought. No indeedy. She'd bought that lipstick in Jackson, at the Elizabeth Arden counter. That gold case had caught her eye, and that particular shade of red.

Hers was missing, too. And had been since . . . since the night she'd gotten plowed—in more ways than one—in the embalming room of Palmer's with Teddy Rubenstein. She'd come home, Josie remembered, and had dropped her purse getting out of the car. Everything had spilled out.

And the next day Tucker had wrecked his car because somebody'd poked holes in some lines.

"That's a pretty lipstick you've got there, Darleen. Looks good on you."

Josie's eyes had taken on a hard, hunting edge, but Darleen heard only the compliment. "Red lipstick's sexy, I think. A man likes to see a woman's lips coming."

"I like red myself, and I never saw that shade before. Where'd you get it?"

"Oh." Darleen flushed a little, but was flattered enough to pick up the case and turn it around in the light. "It was a present."

Josie's grin was fiercely jovial. "My, I do love presents. Don't you?"

She turned without waiting for an answer and strode out past a baffled Crystal.

◆ ◆ ◆ ◆

FIFTEEN MINUTES LATER TUCKER, who was resting after three hard-fought games of Parcheesi, had his peace disturbed when Josie shook him awake and poured out her story.

Blinking against the last slants of sunlight, he tried to get his mushy brain around it.

"Just slow down, Jose, for chrissake. I'm not even awake yet."

"Then wake up, goddammit." She gave him a shove that nearly tilted him out of the hammock. "I'm telling you Billy T. Bonny's the one who messed with your car, and I want to know what you're going to do about it."

"You're telling me he used lipstick to poke holes in my hydraulic and brake lines?"

"No, you peabrain." She took a breath and went through the whole business again.

"Honey, just because Darleen had the same color lipstick as you—"

"Tucker." Patience wasn't one of Josie's virtues, and she punched him, hard. "A woman knows her own lipstick when she sees it."

He rubbed his arm, willing to concede the point. "You could've dropped it anyplace."

"I did not drop it anyplace, I dropped it right over there in the drive. I used it the night I went out with Teddy, and I didn't have it the next morning. Or my mother-of-pearl fold-up mirror either." Fury flared in her eyes. "The bitch's probably got that, too."

With a sigh, Tucker rose. It wasn't likely he'd be able to get in another nap. He wasn't mad yet, only because it all seemed a little farfetched.

"Where are you going?"

"I'll go pass this along to Burke."

Josie slapped her hands on her hips. "Daddy'd have gone and stuck a rifle barrel up Billy T.'s ass."

Tucker turned, and though his face remained calm, his eyes weren't. "I'm not Daddy, Josie."

She was sorry immediately and rushed over to throw her arms around him. "Honey, that was awful of me. I didn't mean it, either. It just makes me so mad, that's all."

"I know." He gave her a squeeze. "Let me handle it my own way." He drew back to kiss her. "Next time I'm in Jackson, I'll buy you a new lipstick."

"Ruthless Red."

"You just go on in and relax now. I'm going to take your car."

"Okay. Tuck?" When he turned back, she was smiling again. "Maybe Junior'll shoot his nuts off."

Chapter 15

$\mathcal{T}$UCKER TRIED THE SHERIFF'S office first, but found only Barb Hopkins, the part-time dispatcher, at her little desk in the corner and her six-year-old, Mark, who was playing jailbird in one of the two cells.

"Hey, Tuck." Barb, who'd put on about fifty pounds since she'd graduated with Tucker from Jefferson Davis High, shifted her girth and put down the paperback novel she'd been reading. Her round, jolly face creased into smiles. "We got ourselves some excitement 'round here, don't we?"

"Looks like." Tucker had always had a fondness for Barb, who'd married Lou Hopkins at nineteen and had proceeded to give birth to a boy child every two years thereafter until Mark arrived, at which point she'd told Lou he could either get his dick clipped or take up residence on the sofabed. "Where's the rest of your brood, Barb?"

"Oh, they're running around town, raising hell."

He paused by the cell to look in on the grimy-faced, towheaded Mark. "So, whatcha in for, boy?"

"I kilt 'em." Mark grinned evilly and shook the bars. "I kilt 'em all, but there ain't no jail can hold me."

"I'll bet. We got ourselves a dangerous criminal here, Barb."

"Don't I know it. I come down this morning, and he'd done turned up the heater on the aquarium and fried every living guppy in there. I got a psychopathic fish-murderer on my hands." She dug into the bag of cheese balls on the desk and munched. "So what can I do for you, Tuck?"

"Looking for Burke."

"He deputized a few of the boys, then he and Carl took them out to look for Austin Hatinger. County sheriff come down, too, in his 'copter. We got ourselves a regular manhunt. Wasn't so much him taking a few shots at you and blowing out that Caroline Waverly's windows," Barb said complacently. "But he dented that county deputy's head pretty good, and embarrassed the shit out of the other one. Now Austin's an escaped felon. He's in big trouble."

"The FBI?"

"Oh, Special Agent Suit-and-Tie? Well, he's leaving this business pretty much up to the local boys. Went out with them for form's sake, but he was more interested in his interviews." She took another handful of cheese balls. "I happened to see one of them lists he makes. Looked like he wanted to talk to Vernon Hatinger, Toby March, Darleen Talbot, and Nancy Koons." Barb licked salt off her fingers. "You, too, Tuck."

"Yeah, I figured he'd get around to me again. Can you call Burke up on that thing?" He pointed to her radio. "Find out where he is and if he's got a minute for me?"

"Sure can. They took walkie-talkies." Obligingly, Barb wiped her orange-smeared fingers, fiddled with some dials, cleared her throat, then clicked on her mike. "This is base calling unit one. Base calling unit one. Over." She put her hand over the mike and grinned at Tuck. "That Jed Larsson said how we should use code names like Silver Fox and Big Bear. Ain't he a one?" With a shake of her head she leaned down to the mike again. "Base calling unit one. Burke honey, y'all out there?"

"Unit one, base. Sorry, Barb, had my hands full. Over."

"I got Tucker here in the office, Burke, says he needs to talk to you."

"Well, put him on, then."

Tucker bent down to the mike. "Burke, I got something I need to run by you. Can I come on out?"

There was a sharp whine of feedback, a protesting oath, and a scratching of static. "I'm pretty tied up right now, Tuck, but you can ride on down to where Dog Street Road runs off into Lone Tree. We got a roadblock set up there. Over."

"I'll be right along." He looked doubtfully at the mike. "Ah, over and out."

Barb grinned at him. "If I was you, I'd keep a shotgun across my lap. Austin got himself two Police Specials this morning."

"Yeah, thanks, Barb."

As Tucker walked out, Mark rattled his cage and shouted gleefully: "I kilt 'em. I kilt 'em all!"

Tucker shuddered. He wasn't thinking about fish.

♦ ♦ ♦ ♦

*H*E SPOTTED TWO 'COPTERS circling on his way out of town. A trio of men spread out like a long V over old Stokey's field. Another group was making a sweep of Charlie O'Hara's catfish farm. Every one of them was armed.

It reminded Tucker miserably of the search for Francie. Before he could prevent it, her dead, white face floated into his mind. On an oath he fumbled for a cassette. It was with relief that he realized he hadn't punched in Tammy Wynette or Loretta Lynn—two of Josie's favorites—but Roy Orbison.

The plaintive, silvery notes of "Crying" calmed him. They weren't out looking for a body, he assured himself. The were just hunting up an idiot. An idiot with a pair of .38s.

On the long straight road he could see the barricade five miles before he came to it. It occurred to him that if Austin came tooling down this way in Birdie's Buick, he'd have the same advantage. The wooden blockades were painted bright orange and glowed in the quieting sunlight. Behind them, two county cruisers sat nose to nose like two big black-and-white dogs sniffing each other.

Ranged along the shoulder of the road were Jed Larsson's shiny new Dodge pickup—between the store and the catfish, Jed was doing real well—Sonny Talbot's truck with its big round lights hooked to the roof like a pair of yellow eyes, Burke's cruiser, and Lou Hopkins's Chevy van.

Lou's van was dusty as an old hound. Someone had scrawled WASH ME! through the grime on the rear window.

As Tucker slowed, he noted that two county boys stepped forward, rifles oiled and ready. Though he didn't think they'd shoot first and ask questions later, he was grateful when Burke waved them off.

"You got yourself a real operation here, don't you?" Tucker commented as he stepped out.

"County sheriff's spitting fire," Burke muttered. "He didn't like it that the FBI was around to see this screwup. He thinks Austin's halfway to Mexico by now, but he doesn't want to say so."

Tucker took out his cigarettes, offered one to Burke, then lighted one of his own. "What do you think?"

Burke blew out a long, slow stream of smoke. It had been a hellishly long day, and he was glad to talk to Tucker.

"Seems to me if a man knew the swamps and rivers around here, he could lay low for a good long time. 'Specially if he had a reason to." He eyed Tucker. "We're going to post a couple of uniforms at Sweetwater."

"Shit on that."

"Gotta do it, Tuck. Come on now." He dropped a hand on Tucker's shoulder. "You got women out there."

Tucker looked across to where the long flat gave way to trees, and trees to swamp. "What a fucking mess."

"It is that."

Something in Burke's voice had Tucker looking back at him. "What else is on your mind?"

"Ain't this enough?"

"I've known you too long, son."

Burke glanced behind him, then edged a few more feet away from the county deputies. "Bobby Lee came by the house last night."

"Now, there's news."

Burke looked miserably at Tucker. "He wants to marry Marvella. Got his gumption up and asked to speak to me in private. We went on out on the back porch. Shit, Tuck, it scared me bloodless. I was afraid he was going to tell me he'd gotten her pregnant, then I'd've had to kill him or something." He saw Tucker's grin and answered it weakly. "Yeah, I know, I know. But it's different when it's your little girl. Anyway—" He blew in smoke, chuffed it out. "He didn't get her pregnant. I guess kids're smarter today about being protected and all. I remember driving clear into Greenville to buy rubbers when I was courting Susie." His grin was a little stronger. "Then when we got into the backseat of my daddy's Chevy, I left them in my pocket." The grin faded. "Of course, if I'd have remembered them, we wouldn't have had Marvella."

"What did you tell him, Burke?"

"Shit, what could I tell him?" He rested a hand absently on the butt of his gun. "She's grown up on me. She wants him, and that's that. He's got a decent job at Talbot's, and he's a good boy. He's crazy in love with her, and I've gotta figure he'll do right. But it damn near breaks my heart."

"How'd Susie take it?"

"Cried buckets." On a sigh, Burke tossed down the cigarette and stamped it out. "And when Marvella started in on how they were thinking of moving to Jackson, I thought she'd flood the house. Then she and Marvella cried together awhile. When they dried up, they started talking about bridesmaid's dresses. I left them to it."

"Getting old sucks, huh?"

"That's the truth." But he felt better having gotten it off his chest. "Keep it under your hat for a bit. They're going to break it to the Fullers this evening."

"You got room in your head for something else?"

"It'd be a pure pleasure to push this out for a while."

Tucker leaned back against the hood of Josie's car and told a tale of lipstick and adultery.

"Darleen and Billy T.?" Burke frowned as he thought it through. "I haven't gotten wind of that."

"Ask Susie."

Burke sighed and nodded. "That woman can keep a secret, God knows. She was three months gone with Tommy before she told me. Worried I'd be upset because we were just scraping by. With Marvella being in love with Darleen's brother, I can see how she'd keep it to herself." Thinking, he jingled his keys. "The thing is, Tucker, I can't go up to Billy T. about all this just because Darleen's using the same kind of lipstick as Josie."

"I know you've got a lot going on, Burke. Just figured I should pass it along."

Burke gave a grunt of assent. They would lose the light soon, and God knew where Austin had gone to ground. "I'll talk to Susie tonight. If it turns out Billy T.'s been seeing Darleen on the sly, I'll make some time to feel him out."

"Appreciate it." But now that his duty was done, Tucker figured he would do some feeling out of his own.

◆ ◆ ◆

THE NEXT MORNING, STRUNG out after barely five hours' sleep, Burke was spooning up corn flakes, worrying about having an armed escapee in his territory—they'd found the Buick ditched out on Cottonseed Road, and nobody was thinking Austin was in Mexico now. On top of that, there was the issue of whether he'd have to rent a tuxedo to give his daughter away.

Susie was already on the phone with Happy Fuller, and the two of them were mapping out wedding plans with the intensity and guile of generals mounting a major campaign.

He was wondering how long the county sheriff would be on his back, when the screams and crashes from next door had him jumping to his feet.

Holy Christ, he thought, how could he have forgotten about the Talbots? By the time Susie came rushing in, Burke was already clearing the fence that separated the yards.

"You've killed him! You've killed him!" Darleen screamed. She was backed into a corner of the small, jumbled kitchen, pulling her hair. The elastic bodice of her shortie nightgown was drawn down, cupped beneath one white jiggling breast.

Burke looked politely away from that to the overturned table, the splattered remains of soggy cereal, and the prone figure of Billy T. Bonny, who lay facedown in a pool of grits.

Burke shook his head and looked at Junior Talbot standing over Billy T. with a cast-iron skillet in his hand.

"I sure hope you didn't kill him, Junior."

"Don't figure I did." Junior put the skillet down calmly enough. "Only whacked him once."

"Well, let's take a look." Burke bent down while Darleen continued to scream and yank at her hair. In the playpen, Scooter was raising the roof. "Just knocked him cold," Burke said, taking in the sizable lump coming up on the back of Billy T.'s head. "Should probably get him over to Doc's, though."

"I'll help you haul him."

Still crouched, Burke glanced up. "You want to tell me what went on here, Junior?"

"Well . . ." Junior righted a chair. "Seems I forgot to tell Darleen something. When I came on back, I saw that Billy T. there had snuck into the kitchen and was forcing himself on my wife." He shot Darleen a look that shut off her wailing like a finger on a switch. "Ain't that right, Darleen?"

"I . . ." She sniffled, and her eyes darted from Burke to Billy T. and back to Junior. "That's right. I—he was on me so quick, I didn't know what to do. Then Junior came back, and . . ."

"You go on and see to the baby," Junior said quietly. He reached over with that same unruffled calm and pulled the pink rayon over her breast. "You don't have to worry about Billy T. bothering you again."

She swallowed and her head bobbed twice. "Yes, Junior."

She rushed out and in a moment the baby's wails turned to hiccoughing sobs. Junior looked back at Billy T. He was beginning to stir a little.

"A man has to protect what's his, don't he, Sheriff?"

Burke hooked his arms under Billy T.'s. "I expect he does, Junior. Let's haul him out to my car."

◆ ◆ ◆

CY WAS HAPPY. It shamed him a little to be so happy when his sister had just been put in the ground and the whole town was whispering about his father. But he couldn't help it.

It was almost enough just to be out of the house where his mother was sprawled, glassy-eyed with whatever pills Doc had given her, watching the *Today* show.

But it was better than just getting out of the house, better than walking away from the police car that sat in the yard waiting to see if his daddy would try to come home. Cy was going to work. And he was going in style.

His shoes kicked up dust and his lips whistled a tune. The prospect of walking and biking ten miles didn't daunt him in the least. He was embarking on the Cy Hatinger Freedom Fund. The fund that was going to buy his way out of Innocence on his eighteenth birthday.

The four years stretched painfully long, but not as hopeless as they had been before he'd become a man of all work.

He like the title, and imagined himself with one of those business cards, like that Bible salesman from Vicksburg had given his mother last April. It would read:

Cyrus Hatinger

MAN OF ALL WORK

NO JOB TOO BIG

NO JOB TOO SMALL

Yessir, he was on his way. By the time he was eighteen, he'd have saved enough to buy himself a ticket to Jackson. Maybe even New Orleans. Shitfire! He could go clean to California if he'd a mind to.

Humming "California, Here I Come," he veered off the hardpack to cross the edge of Toby March's east field. He wondered if Jim would be over at Miss Waverly's painting, and if he'd have time to scoot by and say hey.

He crossed Little Hope stream, which was hardly more than a piss trickle at this time of year, and followed it down to the culvert.

He remembered how he and Jim had scrawled their names on the rounded concrete in Crayolas. And how, in more recent times, they'd pored over every page of a *Playboy* magazine Cy had swiped from under his brother A.J.'s mattress.

Those pictures had been something, he remembered. And for Cy, who had never seen a naked female, it had been an awe-inspiring experience. His pecker had gotten hard as a rock. And that night the old tool of Satan had cut loose in his first and fascinating wet dream.

And hadn't his mama been surprised when he'd done the laundry for her?

Grinning a little over the memory—and wondering if he'd have the experience again anytime soon—he slid down the gentle bank of Little Hope and headed into the culvert.

A hand slapped over his mouth, cutting off his cheerful whistle. He didn't try to scream or struggle. He knew that hand, the shape, the texture, even the smell of it. His fear was much too deep, much too hopeless for screams.

"I found your little hole," Austin whispered. "Your den of sin with your filthy book and your nigger writing. You boys come down here to jerk each other off?"

Cy could only shake his head. He grunted when Austin shoved him against the hard, rounded wall of the culvert. He expected the belt to flash, but even as he braced, he saw his father wasn't wearing one.

They take away your belt when they put you in jail, he remembered. Take it away so you can't hang yourself.

He swallowed. His father was crouched over because the culvert was too low to allow him to rise to his full height. But the position didn't diminish him. If anything, it made him seem larger, stronger. With his back rounded, his legs bent and spread, his face and hands blackened with dirt, he looked like something horrible waiting to pounce.

Cy swallowed again, his throat clicking. "They're looking for you, Daddy."

"I know they're looking for me. They ain't found me, have they?"

"No, sir."

"You know why, boy? It's because I got God on my side. Those Christless bastards'll never find me. What we got here's a holy war." He smiled, and Cy felt ice flow into his belly. "They put me in jail, and they left that murdering son of a whore free. She was a whore. Whore of Babylon," he said softly. "Selling herself when she was mine."

Cy didn't know what he was talking about, but nodded. "Yes sir."

"They'll be punished. 'They shall bear the punishment of their iniquity.'" His hands began to clench and unclench slowly. "All of them. Down to the last generation." His eyes cleared and focused on Cy again. "Where'd you get that bike, boy?"

He started to claim it was Jim's, but with his father's eyes on him, feared the lie might burn his tongue off. "It's just loaned to me, is all." He began to shake, knowing there was no choice. "I got me a job. I got work down at Sweetwater."

Austin's eyes went blank as he took a shuffling step forward. Clench, unclench went his big, blackened hands. "You went to that place? That viper's den?"

Cy knew there were worse things than belts. There were fists. Tears sprang to his eyes. "I won't go back, Daddy. I swear. I only thought—" A hand closed over his throat, cutting off words and air.

"Even my son betrays me. Flesh of my flesh, bone of my bone." He tossed Cy aside like a limp sock. The boy's elbows banged painfully on the concrete, but he didn't cry out. For a long time there was only the sound of breathing.

"You will go back," Austin said at length. "You'll go back and you'll watch. You'll tell me what he does, which room he sleeps in. You'll tell me everything you see and hear."

Cy swiped at his eyes. "Yes sir."

"And you'll get me food. Food and water. You bring it here, every morning, every night." He was smiling again when he hunkered down by his son. His breath was bad, foul as a grave. The light seeped through the opening of the culvert hit his irises and turned them almost white. "You don't tell your ma, you don't tell Vernon, you don't tell nobody."

"Yes sir." Cy's head bobbed in desperate agreement. "But Vernon, he'd help you, Daddy. He could get your truck and—"

Austin slapped a hand across Cy's mouth. "I said nobody. They'll be watching Vernon. Watching him day and night because they know he'll stand by me. But you—they won't pay no mind to you. Just remember I'll be watching you. Sometimes I'll be here, waiting. Sometimes I won't. But I'll always be watching you. Understand me? I'll always be watching you, and listening. The Lord will let me see, let me hear. If you make a mistake, His wrath will smite you down, cleave you in two with one mighty blow."

"I'll bring it." Cy's teeth chattered over the words. "I promise. I'll bring it."

He laid his brutal hands on the boy's shoulders. "You tell anyone seen me, and even God Himself won't save you."

◆ ◆ ◆

*I*T TOOK CY ALMOST an hour to bike to Sweetwater. A quarter of the way there he had to stop and toss up his breakfast. When he was empty, he rinsed off his clammy face with the stingy water of the Little Hope. Because his legs were shaking, he had to ride slow or risk a spill. Every few minutes he looked uneasily over his shoulder, almost certain he would see his father behind him, smiling that smile and snapping the belt they'd taken away from him at the county jail.

When he got to Sweetwater, he saw Tucker was on the side terrace, going through the morning mail. Cy parked the bike with deliberate movements.

"Morning, Cy."

"Mr. Tucker." His voice sounded rusty and he coughed to clear it. "I'm sorry about being late. I was—"

"You're calling your own hours, Cy." Tucker glanced absently at a stock report and set it aside. "We got no time clock here."

"Yes sir. If you'll tell me where to start, I'll get right on it."

"Don't rush me," Tucker said pleasantly, and tossed a scrap of bacon to the ever-hopeful Buster. "Had breakfast?"

Cy thought about what he'd lost on the side of the road. His stomach twisted evilly. "Yes sir."

"Then you can come on up here while I finish mine. Then we'll see what's to do."

Reluctantly, Cy climbed the three rounded stairs that led to the terrace. Buster looked up, thumped his tail once in reflex, then burped.

"He's thrilled to have company," Tucker said dryly. He tossed one of Josie's catalogues aside and smiled up at the boy. "Since you're so all-fired—what the hell'd you do to yourself?"

"Sir?" Panic shot into his voice. "I didn't do nothing."

"Hell, boy, your elbows are all scraped to shit." He took Cy's arm, turned it. Blood was still seeping slowly, and there was a scattering of nasty-looking grit in the cuts.

"I just took a spill, is all."

Tuckers eyes narrowed. "Did Vernon do it?" He'd had a few scrapes with Vernon himself, and was well aware the man wouldn't think anything of laying into the boy.

Like father, like son.

"No, sir." Cy felt a rush of relief that at least he could tell the truth. "I swear Vernon didn't touch me. He gets mad sometimes, but I can stay out of his way until he forgets about it. It's not like Daddy—" He broke off, flushing in mortification. "It wasn't Vernon. I just took a spill, is all."

Tucker's brow had lifted during the babbling explanation. There was no use pressing the boy or adding to his embarrassment by making him admit his father and brother used him for a punching bag. "Well, slow down. You go on in, tell Della to clean you up."

"I don't—"

"Boy." Tucker leaned back. "One of the privileges of being an employer is to give orders. You go on in, get cleaned up, and take a Coke out of the refrigerator. When you come back, I'll have figured out how you're earning your keep today."

"Yes sir." Flooded with guilt, Cy rose. He walked into the house with a heavy heart.

Tucker frowned after him. The boy looked like hell, and that was the truth. But who could blame him? Tucker tossed another scrap of bacon to the dog and figured he'd keep Cy busy enough to ease his mind.

By the time the sun was blazing toward noon, Tucker had Cy occupied on the lawn tractor. Word of the Talbot affair had already raced through town, and thanks to Della's hotline to Earleen, had reached Sweetwater while Billy T.'s bandages were still fresh.

Like good, hand-dipped ice cream, the story came in several varieties and was consumed with relish. But with the connection between Darleen and Billy T. confirmed, Tucker was interested in only one story.

Junior had found his wife wrapped around Billy T. Bonny on the kitchen table. Billy T. had ended up with a goose egg on the back of his head, and no charges were being filed on either side.

Until something came along to nudge it aside, it would be Innocence's hot news item.

He took the afternoon to think it through, then had a piece of Della's banana cream pie and thought some more. It was, after all, a matter of principle. A man could walk away from a lot of things, but he didn't get far walking away from his principles.

He bribed Della for the use of her car with the promise of a new pair of earrings and a full tank of gas. He drove past Caroline's land, wondering if he could talk her into a movie that night. Half a mile down, where Old Cypress Road crossed Longstreet, he parked.

To get from town to his house, or from his house to town, Billy T. would have to drive by that spot. As far as Tucker knew, Billy T. hadn't missed an evening at McGreedy's since he could hold a pool cue.

Tucker pulled out a cigarette and settled in to wait.

He was sitting on the hood of Della's car, thinking about lighting a second one, when he saw Caroline being pulled along by the puppy on a red leash.

She nearly stopped her forward progress, and her fruitless attempts to teach the pup to heel, because she thought she caught a flash of annoyance in Tucker's eyes.

Then he was smiling. "Honey," he called out, "where's that dog taking you?"

"We're going for a walk." She was panting a bit by the time she reached the car. Tail wriggling, Useless leapt up to nip at Tucker's ankles.

"This ain't the city." He leaned over enough to scratch the dog's head as Useless hopped on his hind legs. "Around here you just turn 'em loose in the yard."

"I'm trying to teach him to mind the leash."

To show the futility of that, Useless swiveled around and gnawed at it.

"He seems to mind it plenty." He smiled. "You look tired, Caro. Rough night?"

"Well, the puppy cried a lot." And even when he'd settled, she'd had a hard time sleeping, thinking that Austin Hatinger might come rapping at her door.

"Cardboard box and a windup alarm clock."

"I beg your pardon?"

"He's missing his mama. You put him in a box, maybe with that cushion you bought, and tuck an alarm clock in with him. It's like a heartbeat. Lulls them off to sleep."

"Oh." She thought it over and decided not to mention that he'd lulled off just fine when she'd cuddled him into bed with her. "I'll have to give that a try. What are you doing standing on the side of the road?"

"I'm sitting," he corrected her. "Just passing the time."

"It's an odd place to pass it. They haven't caught Hatinger yet, have they?"

"Not so I've heard."

"Tucker, Susie was by earlier and she mentioned Vernon Hatinger. She said he was as bad as his father."

Idly, Tucker snapped his fingers to entertain Useless. "More like he's working up to it, I'd say."

"She said he was always looking to pick a fight, and—"

"Picked a few with me," Tucker interrupted, reminiscing. "Kicked my ass, I'm sorry to say. Then Dwayne kicked his." He grinned, remembering how Dwayne had been before the bottle had taken such a choke hold. "I never could seem to put on muscle as a boy. Even working in the field, I ended up with toothpick arms. But Dwayne, he hulked right up. Used those arms to quarterback on the football team and set all the girls to swooning after him. After Vernon tried to pound some righteousness into my face, Dwayne pounded some sin into his." He let out a long, satisfied breath. "Sin sure as hell won that day."

"I'm sure that's a touching story of male bonding, but my point is, you don't have just Austin to worry about, but Vernon as well."

"There isn't much point worrying about either one of them."

"Why?" she burst out. "Because your big brother will beat them up for you?"

"These days he's too busy beating up himself." He cast a look down Old Cypress Road and saw the telltale plume of gravel dust and the gleam of Billy T.'s souped-up Thunderbird. "It might be best if you walked on back, put this out of your mind. Maybe I'll stop in later and see how that painting's going."

"What is it?" She'd seen that look in his eyes before. When he'd been sprawled on top of her while glass was shattering. When he'd asked her if she had a gun. This man wouldn't need his big brother or anyone else to fight his battles. She heard the roar of Billy T.'s Glasspacks and turned. "What is it, Tucker?"

"Nothing to concern you. Go on home, Caroline." He slid off the hood just as Billy T. screamed to a stop.

She gathered up the puppy and stood her ground.

"Hey, Fucker . . . I mean Tucker." Billy T. grinned around a tooth-pick at his own witticism. He wasn't in a sunny mood. His head still ached, and his pride had suffered a more serious blow than his skull. He was in a kick-ass frame of mind.

"Billy T." Hands snug in his pockets, Tucker strolled across the road. "Heard you had a little incident this morning."

His eyes slitted. "What the fuck's it to you?"

"Just making conversation. You know, as it happens, I was just sit-ting here waiting for you to come along."

"That so?"

"Yeah." Out of the corner of his eye Tucker saw that Caroline had crossed the road as well. Though she stood several feet back, it annoyed the hell out of him. "A little something I'd like to clear up. If you've got the time."

Before Billy T. realized the intention, Tucker had reached in and snatched the keys from the ignition. People often forgot he could move faster than a crawl.

"Or if you don't," Tucker added complacently.

"Shit for brains." Billy T. shoved the door open. "I guess you're hop-ing for another black eye."

"Well, we'll talk about that. Caroline, if you come a step closer, I'm going to be mighty unhappy with you."

Billy T. slanted Caroline a leer, letting his gaze crawl up her legs, slide over her belly and breasts. "Leave her be, Tuck. Maybe after I've finished smearing you over the road, she'd like to come on and have a beer with a real man."

That brought her chin up. "The only thing I see out here are a cou-ple of sulky schoolboys. Tucker, I don't know what's gotten into you, but I'd like you to drive me home. Right now."

Billy T. grinned and flipped away the toothpick. "Got you pussy-whipped already? Getting you plookie regular, Tuck?"

Outraged, Caroline stepped forward, only to be brought up short by the arm Tucker shot out.

"Now, that's no way to talk about a lady, Billy T., but we'll get to that in a minute. I figured we should have a word about my car."

"Heard your car was down in Jackson getting the pleats ironed out of it."

"You heard correctly. You and me, we never got along too well. And I don't figure we'll get along in the future, but I just can't let what you did to my car go by."

Billy T. snorted and spat. "Way I heard it, you wrecked that car."

"Yeah, after you snuck into Sweetwater like a polecat and diddled with it." Tucker knew Billy T.'s brain wasn't his strong point, and lied with clear eyes. "Darleen let on how you poked those holes in the lines. Guess that wasn't very loyal of her, after you gave her Josie's lipstick."

"She's nothing but a lying slut."

"That may be, but I reckon she's telling the truth about this."

Billy T. swung back the hair that fell across his forehead. "And what if she is? You can't prove it." His lips stretched over his teeth in a sneer. "I can stand right here and tell you that I done it. I walked right down your fancy lane and poked holes in your fancy car. Darleen was feeling blue about your breaking Edda Lou's heart, so I did it to make her feel better. And because I hate your ever-fucking guts. But you ain't going to prove it."

As if considering, Tucker took out a cigarette. "You may have a point there, but that doesn't mean you're going to get off clean." He broke off the tip of the cigarette, lighted it. Caroline took a step back. She recognized that tone, and that look. "It occurred to me that maybe somebody in my family might have taken my car out that morning. Maybe one of them who doesn't handle the wheel as well as I do. You know, Billy T., that just pisses me off."

"You want to do something about it?"

Tucker studied the tip of his cigarette. "I guess I do. I gotta say I don't care for the idea of getting my face pounded on again."

"You always was a chickenshit." Grinning, Billy T. spread his arms. "Go ahead, take your best shot."

"Well, since you put it that way." Tucker kicked him squarely in the crotch.

Billy T. doubled over and a sound escaped him like air coming out of a pressure cooker. Still clutching himself, he went down on the side of the road. When Tucker crouched down and took a firm hold on his bruised genitals, Billy T.'s eyes rolled back in his head.

"Don't pass out, boy, not until I finish what I've got to say. You may start thinking again once your nuts slide down from your throat, and I want you to think about this. Listening?"

"Ga" was about the only sound Billy T. could make.

"Good. You know who holds the note on your family's land?

Payment's been late three months running. I'd sure feel bad if I had to foreclose. And that cotton gin where you occasionally find the time to put in a few hours a week? By coincidence, it so happens I own that, too. Now, you want to have a reprisal against me, I guess I can't stop you. But you'll lose your land, and your job, and as God is my witness, I'll do my best to turn you into a soprano while I'm at it." He bore down with his fingers to make his point. All Billy T. could do was moan and roll into a ball. "I was mighty fond of that car," Tucker said with a sigh. "And as it turns out, I'm fond of this lady here that you insulted. So, don't mess with me again, Billy T. I'm not a skinny ten-year-old anymore."

"Leave me alone," Billy T. managed to get out. "You broke something. You broke my works."

"Don't worry, they'll bounce back. That's why they call them balls." When he rose, Tucker noticed that Caroline had dropped the pup, who was now relieving himself on Billy T.'s shoes. He grinned, but gathered the dog up. "Now, that's adding insult to injury."

He turned to where Caroline was standing on the edge of the road, mouth agape, eyes wide. Tucker hitched the pup under his arm. "Come on, sugar. I'll give you that ride home now."

"You're just going to leave him there?" She craned her neck as Tucker pulled her to the Oldsmobile.

"That's the plan. I was thinking we could go take in a movie tonight."

"A movie," she said blankly. "Tucker, I just stood there and watched you kick that man in the . . ."

"We call them privates in polite company. Scoot on over, unless you want to drive."

Rubbing a hand to her temple, she did. "But that's fighting dirty, isn't it?"

"All fighting's dirty, Caroline, which is why I dearly love to avoid it." He leaned over to give her a quick kiss before starting the engine. In an absent move, he tossed Billy T.'s keys across the road. "Now about that movie?"

Caroline let out a long breath. "What's playing?"

Chapter 16

ERHAPS YOU'D LIKE A glass of water, Mrs. Talbot." Darleen looked at Agent Burns through red-rimmed, swollen eyes ruthlessly outlined with Maybelline. "Yes, sir," she said meekly. In the last forty-eight hours, she'd learned a whole lot about meek. "I'd be obliged."

All solicitude, Burns rose to go into the bathroom and pour tepid tap water into a paper cup. He considered himself an expert interviewer— had even instructed a course on the subject. As he would have told his class at the FBI Academy, the first rule of a good interview is to know your subject.

Burns figured he had Darleen Talbot's number.

Sympathy, flattery, and kindly authority. Those were the watch-words here. Burns estimated thirty minutes for the interview, including a four-minute prologue to gain Darleen's confidence. Along with the paper cup, he offered Darleen a kindly smile. "I appreciate your making the time to come in and talk with me this morning, Mrs. Talbot."

Cautiously, she brought the cup to her unpainted lips. She'd lost her affection for red lipstick. "Junior said I had to."

"Well, I know it's difficult for a young mother to find the time out of a demanding schedule. Where is your little one today?" Burns crossed ask about family off his mental checklist.

"Ma's watching Scooter. She likes to sit with him." As her eyes darted around the room, lighting on anything but Special Agent Matthew Burns, she fiddled with the collar of her flowered blouse. "He's her only grandson, you know. My two sisters both have girls."

"A handsome boy, too," Burns said, though he didn't know if he'd ever laid eyes on the youngest Talbot.

"He is pretty. His hair's as curly as a little lamb." A ghost of a smile brightened her eyes. She figured—accurately—that the only reason Junior hadn't tossed her out of the house was his attachment to his son. "He's quick, too. He's like greased lightning on his hands and knees. I don't know how I'll keep up with him once he starts toddling."

"I'm sure he keeps you on your toes."

More relaxed, Darleen set the cup aside. Why, the FBI man wasn't so bad, she decided. People just didn't know him. "Do you have young 'uns?"

"No, I don't." Nor did the fastidious Burns intend to. Ever. "I'm afraid my work keeps me away from home quite a bit."

"Looking for criminals."

"Exactly." He beamed at her, as if she'd just answered a very complex question. "And it's concerned, responsible citizens like yourself who make my job easier." Still smiling, he took out his mini recorder. "This helps me remember accurately."

Darleen eyed the recorder with distrust. She began to twist her hands in her lap. "Shouldn't I have a lawyer or something?"

"Why, certainly, if you wish." Burns sat down behind Burke's cluttered desk. "But I assure you it isn't necessary for this kind of informal chat. I just need a little background information from you, on your friend Edda Lou Hatinger." He stretched out an avuncular hand to hers. "I know this is difficult for you, Darleen. May I call you Darleen?"

Why, he was just as polite as a waiter in a fancy restaurant. Though the comparison would have caused Burns to cringe, it made Darleen respond favorably. "That'll be just fine."

"Losing a friend is always painful, but in such a tragic way . . ." He trailed off, letting his silence offer comfort. "I'll try not to upset you."

It wasn't difficult or even painful so much as terribly exciting, but she pulled out a ragged tissue and dabbed her eyes. "Talking about it just tears me in two. But I want to help," she added bravely. "She was my dearest friend."

"I know." Pleased, Burns switched on the recorder. "Special Agent Matthew Burns, interview with Darleen Talbot re Edda Lou Hatinger. June twenty-five. Now then, Darleen, why don't you tell me something about Edda Lou?"

Darleen blew her nose loudly enough to make Burns wince. "She was my dearest friend," she repeated. "We went to school together, and she was my maid of honor. I guess she was like a sister to me."

"And like sisters, I suppose the two of you exchanged confidences."

"We never had secrets from each other. My own blood sisters, Belle and Starita? Why, I could never talk to them the way I could to Edda Lou." Another tear squeezed out, and she caught it with her knuckle.

"And I'm sure she felt equally sympatico with you."

Darleen frowned over the word. "I expect."

"I can see that you're an understanding, openhearted woman. No doubt Edda Lou depended on you."

The image had her preening a bit. "She did tend to lean on me. I never minded."

"With you being a married woman, I'm sure Edda Lou came to you for advice—advice about the men in her life."

Advice hell, Darleen thought. Edda Lou had liked to brag. But Darleen didn't think she should say so. "We talked a lot. I guess we talked on the phone every single day."

"And at the time of her death, was Edda Lou involved with anyone in particular?"

"Well, sure. Everybody knew she was all wrapped up in Tucker Longstreet. She could've had lots of other boyfriends. Edda Lou kept herself up real nice, you know. She studied pictures in magazines for hairdos and makeup tricks and all, and she wouldn't step out of her room without doing her face up just so. But she'd set her sights on Tucker. Once she hooked him, I was going to . . . I mean to say, once they'd set a date, I was going to be her matron of honor. We went to Greenville and picked out dresses and everything." And wasn't it a shame she'd never have a chance to wear that pretty pink organdy gown with the puffy sleeves and the big bow?

With encouraging nods Burns made neat notations on a legal pad. "Mr. Longstreet and Edda Lou were to be married?"

Darleen licked her lips and stared at the recorder. She was torn between loyalty and truth—with truth standing in for self-preservation. Her episode with Junior had her inching back. "Edda Lou had her mind set on it."

"And Mr. Longstreet?"

"Well . . . she'd've brought him around. Edda Lou wasn't one to let loose once she got her teeth in something."

"So you believe she would have convinced Mr. Longstreet to propose?"

"I guess you could put it like that."

"Pressured him?" Burns was still smiling benignly. "Could she have known about some weakness, some problem, that would have convinced him to, let's say, come up to scratch?"

Darleen thought about that awhile, then to Burns's disappointment shook her head. "No, Tucker's not one for problems. He just shakes them off. Thing is, I tried to tell Edda Lou the reason he cut things off with her was because she was getting too pushy. Men don't like to be shoved into marriage."

Darleen drew from her vast scope of marital bliss. "You take my Junior? I just waited around, real calm and ladylike, for him to scrape up the courage to ask me. If I'd've been the one to bring up marriage, he'd've been off like a shot. Men just naturally resist the idea of settling. And that's what I told her," Darleen said with a knowing nod. "But she wouldn't listen. Stubborn that way. And she was dead set to live at Sweetwater. I mean, to be with Tucker," she corrected herself. "Edda Lou was wild for him."

"I'm sure her feelings ran very deep," Burns murmured, and Darleen smiled through the sarcasm. "She and Mr. Longstreet had an altercation the day she died."

"Edda Lou came to see me right after." Darleen wiggled more comfortably in her chair. It was just like Perry Mason, she thought. "She was spitting fire, too. You see, Tucker'd broke things off with her, and she'd figured on laying back a few weeks, until he couldn't stand being without her anymore. That's just how she put it. She figured with the sex being so good and all, he'd come sniffing back 'round quick enough." She caught herself and flushed. "What I mean to say is, she knew he loved her."

Face expressionless, Burns nodded. "I understand completely."

"She was starting to get a bit itchy. And then Tucker starts seeing Chrissy Fuller—her being divorced now and all. Well, Edda Lou wasn't going to put up with that, not for a New York minute. She tracked Tuck down at the Chat 'N Chew and told him what was what."

"And claimed that she was pregnant."

Darleen pressed her lips together and stared down at her shoes. "I reckon she made a mistake about that. She was that upset, you see, because Tucker was maybe going to slip away."

"Is that what she told you when she came to see you that afternoon?"

"She was that upset." Darleen began to twist her fingers together. "A woman's bound to say things when she's got a broken heart. She was storming up and down my front room. Said he wasn't going to toss her away like used goods. He wasn't going to do to her what his daddy had done to her daddy."

"Excuse me?"

Darleen perked up. It was always rewarding to be the first to pass along gossip—even if the gossip was more than thirty years cold.

"Years ago Edda Lou's daddy had been courting Miss Madeline—Tucker's mama? Or, well, he wasn't courting exactly, as people say who remember. But he wanted to. He really was set on marrying Miss Madeline, even though her daddy was a state senator and all and he was just a dirt farmer. Edda Lou used to say it was like a Cinderella story in reverse. But the thing was that Miss Madeline was crazy for Beau Longstreet. The more in love she was with Mr. Beau, the more Austin Hatinger wanted her. He never had much use for the Longstreets."

"So," Burns interrupted with some hope of making a long story short. "There's been bad blood between the families for some time."

"Real bad. He and Mr. Beau almost took each other apart at a church social. My daddy was one of the ones that pulled them apart, and he tells the story now and then."

Burns cleared his throat. "That's very interesting, Darleen, but—"

"What I'm trying to say is, because of all that, the way her father saw Beau as taking what was his, Edda Lou thought she deserved Sweetwater. And she went after Tuck, 'cause . . . well, he's real good-lookin' and he ain't stingy with his pennies like his daddy was. But mostly I guess she liked the idea of riling her pa. So she was pretty hot about him—Tucker, I mean—telling her right there in public that he didn't want her. So she says to me: 'He's going to eat those words, Darleen. You wait and see.' "

"Did she happen to tell you how she was going to make him eat them?"

"She was going to get him alone somewhere and let nature take its course." Darleen sent Burns a coy wink. "She took real good care of herself, Edda Lou did. Kept herself up and knew how to dress so men would look twice."

"Any men in particular?"

"Before Tucker? She kinda played the field. Had John Thomas Bonny stuck on her last winter, and before that Judson O'Hara and Will Shiver. And there was Ben Koons, too. Though he was a married man and she never took him seriously."

Burns noted down the names in meticulous block printing. "With a woman as attractive as Edda Lou, there might have been a man who remained . . . stuck on her after she'd committed herself to Mr. Longstreet."

"Oh, Edda Lou liked to brag that men didn't get over her in the wink of an eye. She could've had any of them."

"I see. What about Toby March?"

"Oh." Darleen picked up the paper cup and drank the rest of the water. "Well."

"Yes?"

"There is nothing to that, Mr. Burns. No indeed. Edda Lou liked to tease some. That was just her way."

"She teased Mr. March?"

"It was just a little game." Darleen brought her thumb to her mouth and began to gnaw on the nail. "Edda Lou wouldn't be interested in a black man. Curious maybe."

"And she was curious about Mr. March?"

"It was just to hit back at her daddy. He'd walloped Toby some years ago. Gave him that scar. And Edda Lou's brother, Cy, he was friends with Toby's boy. Austin Hatinger raised holy hell about that. So Edda Lou just liked to flirt with Toby because he'd get all stiff and flustered."

"Did she have an affair with him?"

"I can't say." Darleen chewed the nail down to the nub. "It wasn't nothing serious. She was just teasing."

But it might have been serious for a black man, Burns thought. A married black in a small southern town where some lines were deadly to cross.

"When did she tease him, Darleen?"

"Oh, mostly after Tucker cut her off. That's when Toby was doing work at the boardinghouse. But she wouldn't have done anything, really. Why, her daddy would have killed her. He'd have strung Toby up, and he'd have skinned Edda Lou alive. If he didn't get to it himself, Vernon would have done it for him. Edda Lou and Vernon didn't have any use for each other, but Vernon couldn't have held his head up if it got around that Edda Lou'd—you know—with one of Toby's kind."

Burns smiled. That gave him three more suspects. Three more motives. "Thank you, Darleen. You've been a big help."

◆ ◆ ◆ ◆

*W*HILE TOBY AND YOUNG Jim hammered away at the braces on her back porch, Caroline took aim at a chicken-and-rice soup can. And missed.

"Sight a little more to the right," Susie advised. "You jerk toward the left whenever you pull the trigger."

"I don't know why I'm doing this."

"It's comforting. Hold your breath this time. Right before you nudge the trigger." Susie pursed her lips when Caroline fired again, missed again. "You'll do better once you learn to keep both eyes open. But I'd give this year's Fourth of July contest a pass."

"I'm going to hit one, just one, before I move from this spot."

"Maybe it'd help if you thought of that Luis again."

"Nope. I've just about gotten that out of my system."

"Well, hell, here I've been hoping you'd have a weak moment and tell me all the gory details."

"More clichéd than gory. I caught him with another women."

"Oh." Susie pursed her lips and thought about it. "Do you mean caught him with, or *caught* him with?"

"Capital-C caught." She steadied her hand and took aim. "I walked in on him while a big-busted flute player was giving him an oil change."

"My, my. Did you cut off his dipstick?"

The gun wavered as Caroline laughed. "No. I'm afraid this took place during my wimp period."

"You seem to be over it now."

"The wimp period or Luis? I am. Pretty much." She missed again, swore, and buckled down. "Dammit, I'm going to hit one. It's just a matter of practice. Nobody knows more about practice than a musician." She lifted the gun, sighted in. "I'm going to make that goddamn can sing."

She clipped the side, and while it didn't precisely sing, the quick bang was enough to satisfy her.

"Nice going, Dead-eye." Susie gave her a congratulatory pat on the back. "Why don't you take a break?"

"Why don't I?" Caroline meticulously unloaded. Unlike Susie, she was less than comfortable carrying a loaded gun. "I did better than yesterday. It took over two hours for me to hit one of those stupid cans. Today it took"—she checked her watch—"only an hour forty-five." For lack of a better place, she dumped the spare ammo in her pocket. "Want a drink?"

"I thought you'd never ask." They started back toward the house. "You're keeping Toby and Jim busy. I like the new blue paint. Really freshens the place up."

"They're going to do the porches, too. In white. Can we get through here, Toby?"

"Sure, just mind your step. Afternoon, Mrs. Truesdale."

"Hey, Toby. When you're done here, why don't you come on by and shame Burke into fixing my side door? It still sticks."

He grinned, wiping his face with his bandanna. The dirt from under the porch clung to his skin, settled wetly into the creases. "Now, I told him what needed to be done there. Musta been six months ago."

"He tells me he's getting around to it." She stepped around the toolbox. "I guess he's got a lot on his mind."

Toby's smile faded. "Yes'm. Jim, you hold that board steady now." He kept his eyes on his hands as Caroline ushered Susie into the kitchen.

"Well now, there's that little pup I've heard so much about." Susie crouched down to where Useless was huddled under one of the kitchen chairs— a position he'd assumed since the first shot was fired.

"Yeah, my fierce guard dog." Caroline watched as he trembled and whined and licked at Susie's hand. "I must have been crazy."

"No, just softhearted. Thanks." She stood, accepting the glass of iced tea Caroline offered. "I've been meaning to stop on out before. It's been real hectic since Marvella got engaged."

"I heard about that." Noting the look in Susie's eyes, Caroline searched through the cupboards for something high in sugar and low in nutrition. She settled on the cupcakes she'd bought to treat Jim at lunch. "Here, have some chocolate and preservatives."

"Thanks." Susie sniffled and tore at the cellophane. "I swear, I've been as bad as a leaky faucet ever since it happened. I just think about it and off I go." She bit into the cupcake. "I knew it was coming, of course. They've been mooning around each other for two years. When they weren't mooning they were scrapping, and that's a sure sign."

"But she's your little girl."

"Yeah." Susie swiped at a tear. "My baby. My first baby. I'm okay when I get caught up in the wedding plans, but if I just sit and think about it, I start dripping."

Caroline eyed the second cupcake, and decided she deserved it. "Have they set a date?"

"September. Marvella's always been partial to chrysanthemums. She wants the church full of them, and her five bridesmaids in fall-colored dresses. She's got her own ideas, all right. Russet and gold, she says." Firing up, Susie licked crumbs from her fingers. "Now, I say russet's like red, and seems inappropriate for a church wedding, but she's set. Won't even talk about pastels." Susie caught Caroline's look and grinned. "I know, I know, colors aren't so important as why. It's just easier for me to think about them, and the music, and if we're going to have the reception outside at the house or if we should rent out the Moose Hall." She gave a slow sigh. "Burke and I had a justice of the peace wedding."

"I'm sure between you and Marvella everything's going to be beautiful."

"I'd feel better if I could talk her into rose instead of russet." She polished off the cupcake. "We're going down to Jackson this weekend to shop. You're welcome to come along if you'd like."

"I appreciate that. But I don't have anything to shop for."

"When a woman needs an excuse to shop, she must have something on her mind."

Caroline licked some of the sticky white filling off her fingers. "I guess I do. I guess we all do."

"Burke's hardly been home to do more than fall into bed for a couple of hours since Austin took off." She tilted her head. "Honey, you're not worried that he's going to come back here and bother you?"

"I don't know." Restless, Caroline rose. "I can't quite dismiss it, though there isn't a reasonable motive for him to do so." She looked out the window, and her eyes were drawn to the line of trees, and the memory of what lay beyond them. "It's more, Susie. I suppose it feels like everything else has been covered up by this search for Austin Hatinger. I can't forget that just a couple of weeks ago I walked out there by the pond and found his daughter."

"Nobody's forgotten about Edda Lou. Or Francie or Arnette either. It's just if you think about it too much, you go crazy." She lowered her voice. "That Agent Burns is talking to everyone in town. He interviewed Darleen just this morning. Happy told me about it. The thing that's making it hard is he's not working with Burke. He's working around him. Doesn't want the local law messing with his federal case, I suppose, but it's a mistake. Burke knows these people, and they trust him. They don't trust some shiny-shoed Yankee."

Caroline had to smile and look down at her own shoes. "Mine haven't been polished in weeks."

"Oh, it's different with you." Susie waved Caroline's northern connections aside. "Your kin was here. Of course, you could say that you and that Burns fellow speak the same language."

Caroline lifted a brow. "You could, but I don't think it's quite true."

"It seemed to me he had a lot of respect for you."

"For Caroline Waverly, musician. There's a difference." On a sigh, Caroline sat again. "Why don't you tell me what you're dancing around, Susie?"

"It's just that I was thinking, with you and Agent Burns in the same circles, so to speak, he might listen if you made a suggestion."

"What suggestion would that be?"

"He can't keep cutting Burke out like this," Susie blurted out, and scowled down at the chocolate crumbs. "I'm not just speaking as Burke's wife, because I love him and know this is eating at him. I'm speaking as a woman, as part of this community. Whoever killed those girls needs to be caught, and it's going to be a whole lot harder without Burke smoothing the way with people, and getting them to open up."

"I agree with you, Susie. I do. But I really don't see how I can help."

"I just thought you might find the opportunity to mention it. In passing."

"How's this? If the opportunity presents itself, I'll try."

"I guess he didn't do anything for you," Susie said. "Romantically speaking."

Caroline gave a quick laugh and shook her head. "No, he didn't. And no man will again who thinks of my music first and me second."

"Oh. That sounds like a story." All anticipation, Susie propped her chin on her hands.

"Let's just say I was involved with a man who thought of me more as an instrument than as a woman. Agent Burns looks at me the same way."

"Did you get your heart broken?"

Caroline's lips curved. "Cracked, a little."

"Well, the best way to shore it up again is a nice fling with an easy man." She touched her tongue to her top lip. "I heard you went to the movies with Tucker the other night."

"Why am I surprised?"

"Josie mentioned it to Earleen. I'd think Tucker Longstreet'd be a nice, painless cure for a broken heart."

"Cracked," Caroline corrected her. "And we just went to the movies. That doesn't constitute a fling."

"A man who brings a woman roses is laying the groundwork for one." She grinned as Caroline shut her eyes. "He stopped by and took Marvella out for lunch while he was down in Rosedale picking them out."

"They were just a neighborly gesture."

"Uh-huh. Once Burke brought me a real neighborly bunch of violets. Nine months later we had Parker. Now, don't get all flushed and bothered," Susie said with a wave of her hand. "I'm just being nosy. And I thought if you had any . . . neighborly interest in Tucker, you might want to know that Agent Burns is asking a lot of questions about him."

"What kind of questions?"

"Questions that apply to Edda Lou."

"But . . ." Caroline felt her heart give one uncomfortable thud. "But I thought that he wasn't a suspect because he was home the night she was killed."

"Maybe the FBI would like to find a way around that. Of course, he's asking questions about a lot of people." She looked deliberately toward the back door, and the porch beyond where Toby was humming "In the Garden."

"Susie." Caroline bit her lip and lowered her voice. "That's absurd."

"You may think so, and I might, knowing Toby and his Winnie all my life the way I have, but Agent Burns has different ideas." She leaned closer. "He went by and talked to Nancy Koons. Wanted to know if Edda Lou and Tucker had had any fights there in the rooming house. If he'd shown her any violence. And he asked her about Toby, too."

"What did she tell him?"

"Next to nothing, because she didn't like the way he asked." Susie drew lines in the moisture of her glass. "That's why he needs to bring Burke in. Burke knows how to approach people. They'll talk to him. I have to figure he'll be out this way again soon, since you were the one who found the body."

"There's nothing I can tell him."

"Honey, seems to me he might be interested in the fact that Tucker's coming around here."

Caroline rubbed at an ache centered in her forehead. "My personal life is none of his business. That I will tell him."

♦ ♦ ♦

LONG AFTER SUSIE LEFT, Caroline worried over every point of the conversation. She listened to Toby and his son pack up for the day and worried some more. Alone, she wandered through the house, trying to pinpoint her part in the whole picture.

She was a stranger. Yet her family had sprung from Innocence. She hadn't known Edda Lou, yet she had been the one to find her. She'd never spoken a single word to Austin Hatinger. But he'd shot at her.

She didn't know Matthew Burns. Oh, his type certainly, but not him. Still, it was true that they moved in the same circles, knew the same places, spoke the same language. How that could help solve a crime was beyond her. Yet Susie had made her feel responsible.

She was—for lack of a better term—involved with one of the suspects. Another was working for her.

So she felt even more responsible.

Oh, she knew all about responsibilities. They snuck up on you, attached themselves to you like tiny, thirsty leeches until you were sucked dry.

She'd had a responsibility to her parents, to her music, to her teachers, her maestros, her fellow musicians, to her fans. And, as he'd insisted right up to the last, she' had a responsibility to Luis.

Oddly enough, she'd come to Innocence to escape from responsibility for a little while, only to find herself bogged down in it all over again.

She could do nothing. She understood that now. It had always been her choice, and she had always chosen to give in rather than fight back.

But wasn't it different this time? Wouldn't she be giving in by doing nothing? Though she doubted she had anything to offer, she was involved. Not just with Tucker, but with Innocence. And for the time being, Innocence was home.

"All right, all right." She pressed her fingers to her temples. "I'll go talk to him. I'll make a few quiet suggestions, Yankee to Yankee."

She snatched up her purse and was heading out the front door when Matthew Burns turned into her drive.

Well, Caroline thought with a sigh. *It must be fate.*

"I've caught you on your way out," Burns said as he stepped from his car.

"No—that is, yes." Caroline smiled and altered her plans. "But I have a few minutes yet. Would you like to come in?"

"I would. Very much." The moment he stepped onto the porch, Useless began to growl behind the screen door.

"He's just a puppy," Caroline assured Burns. "A little leery of strangers." She opened the door and scooped the dog up.

"Cute," Burns commented, but Caroline heard the word *mongrel* clear as a bell.

"He's excellent company." She decided against setting Useless outside and carried him with her into the parlor. "Can I get you something? Iced tea, coffee?"

"Iced tea would be wonderful. I'm afraid I'll never get used to the heat."

"Heat?" Caroline said with the same amused derision she'd heard from so many of the locals. "Oh, it doesn't get hot until August. Please have a seat. I'll be right back." She snickered to the dog as she went into the kitchen. When she returned, Burns was standing, hands linked behind his back, frowning at the bullet hole in her sofa.

"An interesting conversation piece, isn't it?" She set the tray of drinks down. "I've about decided not to have it repaired."

"It's deplorable. Hatinger shooting into this house without any concern that you might have been hurt. He didn't even know you."

"Fortunately, Tucker thought quickly."

"If he'd thought at all, he wouldn't have put you in such a dangerous position."

Caroline took a seat, understanding that Burns's stiff manners wouldn't permit him to do so first. "Actually, I don't believe Tucker was aware that Austin was out with a rifle. It came as quite a surprise to both of us. Would you like lemon or sugar?"

"Just a little lemon, thank you." He took his place on the couch, shifting slightly to face her. "Caroline, as I've loved your music for years, I feel as if I know you."

Her smile remained pleasant. "It's funny how often people make that mistake. Actually, the music I play belongs to numerous composers and isn't mine at all."

He cleared his throat. "What I mean is, I've admired your talents, and followed your career, so I feel a certain connection. I hope I can speak frankly."

She sipped. "So do I."

"I'm concerned, Caroline, very concerned. I've heard talk around town that you've been seeing Tucker Longstreet."

She settled back in the crook of the couch. "That's the marvelous thing about small towns, don't you think? If you sit in one place for more than five minutes, you hear everything."

He stiffened like a poker. "Personally, I don't care for rumor, gossip, or innuendo." Her quick burst of laughter had him tightening his lips.

"I'm sorry. You made that sound like a rock group or a law firm." She swallowed the next chuckle when he didn't respond in kind. Laughing at him was certainly no way to soften him up so that he'd listen to a suggestion. "Places like this run on gossip, Matthew. I imagine it could even be helpful."

"Indeed. However much I abhor such habits, I must take this professionally. You'd be wise to do the same. Tucker Longstreet is still being questioned regarding a vicious and brutal murder."

Nerves had Caroline passing the glass from hand to hand, but her eyes remained level. "As I understand, several people are being questioned. I suppose that would include me."

"Your involvement with this is merely that of an innocent bystander who happened to find a body."

"There's no merely about it, Matthew. I found the body, and I'm a member of this community. I have . . ." Her lips curved at the truth of it. "I have friends here, and probably numerous cousins of one sort or the other."

"And you consider Tucker Longstreet a friend?"

"I'm not sure exactly what I consider Tucker." She gave him a bland look. "Is that a professional quesiton?"

"I'm investigating a series of murders," he said flatly. "I have not crossed Mr. Longstreet off my list. I consider him someone to be watched, carefully watched. You may not be aware that he had relationships with the other two victims."

"Matthew, I've been here for over two weeks. I'm well aware of it. Just as I'm aware that Woodrow and Sugar Pruett's marriage is in trouble, and that Bea Stokey's boy, LeRoy, got a ticket for speeding out on Route

One. Just as I'm aware that Tucker isn't capable of doing any of those hideous things to those poor women."

A long, patient breath, and Burns set aside his iced tea. It never failed to fascinate him how easily women could be taken in. "People were fooled by Ted Bundy's charm and attractive looks. A serial killer is not someone you recognize as such in the everyday course of things. They are clever, manipulative, and often highly intelligent. And often, yes quite often, they themselves go for periods of time when they have no recollection of what they've done. And if they do, they hide it under a mask of affability or concern. But they lie, Caroline. They lie because what they live for is the kill. The anticipation of it, the skill with which they hunt, stalk, and slay."

He watched her pale and reached for her hand. "I'm frightening you. I mean to. Someone, very likely someone in this small rural community, is hiding behind a mask, and plotting the next kill. I will use all my skill, all my knowledge, to stop him. But it may not be enough. And if it's not, he will kill again."

She had to set the tea aside. She needed nothing cool now, not when her blood had turned to ice. "If that's true—"

"It is."

"If it is," she repeated, "shouldn't you be using all available assistance?"

"I beg your pardon?"

"You're an outsider here, Matthew. Your badge doesn't change that. If anything, the fact that it's federal makes you more of an outsider. If you want to help these people, then use Burke Truesdale."

His smile was tight as he straightened his shoulders. "I appreciate your concern, Caroline, but the simple fact is you don't know what's involved here."

"No, I don't. But I do know about politics and authority. No one could perform with dozens of different orchestras under dozens of different maestros and not understand the food chain. My point is, Matthew, you—as I have been most of my life—are the outsider. Burke knows these people. You don't."

"Which is precisely part of the problem. He knows them, he sympathizes with them. He's related to them or has old friendships to protect."

"You're speaking about Tucker again."

"To be specific. The term is 'good ol' boys,' isn't it? They toss back a few beers together, shoot some rabbits or other small creatures, and sit on their porches and talk about cotton and women." He brushed a speck of lint from his trousers. "No, I don't know these people, Caroline, but I know of them. The last thing I need to solve this case is to enlist Burke Truesdale to pave my way. I believe him to be an honest man. And a loyal one. It's his loyalties that concern me."

"May *I* speak frankly, Matthew?"

He spread his hands. "Please."

"You're behaving like a pompous ass," she said, and watched his face fall. "That might work well in D.C. or Baltimore, but it doesn't cut it here in the delta. If someone else is killed—as you seem to believe—then look to yourself and wonder if it might have been prevented. If you might have prevented it by having a liaison to these people instead of standing back all smug and superior."

He rose stiffly. "I'm sorry, Caroline, that we're unable to see eye to eye on this matter. However you might feel, I must still advise you to curtail your involvement with Tucker Longstreet until this case is resolved."

"I've discovered a terrible habit in myself of ignoring advice."

"Your choice." He inclined his head. "I'll have to ask you to come in to my temporary headquarters tomorrow. Around ten, if that's convenient."

"Why?"

"I have some questions. Official questions."

"Then I'll give you answers. Official answers."

She didn't bother to see him to the door.

Chapter 17

CAROLINE DIDN'T EVEN HAVE to weigh her loyalties. Before Burns's dust had cleared, she was scooping up Useless and heading for her car. The keys were dangling in the ignition, right where she'd left them.

Turning, she looked back at the house. She hadn't locked the doors. Hadn't even thought about it. Foolish, perhaps, considering the recent violence that had tainted Innocence. But to lock the doors without closing and latching the windows was even more foolish. And to do that meant trapping the heat inside.

In less than a month, she'd picked up country habits.

"I'm not going to be afraid in my own home," she told Useless as she set him inside the car. He immediately propped his front paws on the dash, tongue lolling in anticipation of a ride.

"My home," she repeated, studying the house, the fresh paint, the polished windows, the scarred porch rocker. With a sense of satisfaction and purpose she climbed into the car. "Come on, Useless, it's time we took an active part in the grapevine."

She backed down the drive, unaware of the figure that stood, shadowed by the line of trees, watching.

◆ ◆ ◆ ◆

THE STATLER BROTHERS WERE wailing away from a four-foot boom box on the porch at Sweetwater. Keeping them company were Lulu and Dwayne. Lulu still wore her eagle feather and her combat boots. To complete the outfit she wore a splotched painter's smock over Levis and a pair of ruby earrings with stones as big as pullet eggs.

She stood in front of a canvas, feet planted, body braced. More like a prizefighter going into round three, Caroline thought, than an artist. Dwayne was sprawled in the porch rocker, a tumbler full of Wild Turkey in his hand and the mild smile of an affable drunk on his face.

" 'Lo, Caroline." He gestured with the glass in greeting. "Whatcha got there?"

Caroline set Useless down and he immediately streaked off to sniff the bushes Buster had marked. "My dog. Good evening, Miss Lulu."

She grunted, dabbed a little paint on the canvas. "My grandmammy ran a pair of Yankee deserters off her plantation in 1863."

Caroline inclined her head. She'd come prepared. "My grandmother's grandfather lost a leg at Antietam pushing General Burnside's troops off the stone bridge."

Lulu pursed her lips and considered. "And when would that have been?"

"September 17, 1862." Caroline smiled and blessed her grandmother's carefully documented family Bible. "His name was Silas Henry Sweeney."

"Sweeney, Sweeney. Seems to me there were some Sweeney cousins on my husband's side—that'd be my second husband, Maxwell Breezeport." Lulu squinted her eyes at Caroline and liked what she saw. The girl was fresh as a new quart of cream. And there was a sharp, stubborn look in her eyes, in the set of her chin, that Lulu approved of wholeheartedly.

The Yankee blood was probably diluted anyway, Lulu decided, and besides, it was time Tucker settled down.

"You come down here to sashay around Tucker, have you?"

"Certainly not." But Caroline found it impossible to take offense. "I have come to speak with him, though. If he's here."

"Oh, he's around right enough." Lulu studied her palette, then plunged her brush into a pool of virulent green. "Come on up here on the porch, girl, don't be standing down there gawking at me while I'm working. Dwayne, where's that brother of yours? Can't you see this girl's come to seduce him?"

"I have not come—" Caroline broke off and backed up a foot when Lulu leaned over to sniff at her.

"Pretty cagey not wearing perfume." Lulu shook the dripping brush at her. "When a man's used to women tarting themselves up, he'll fall flat for the smell of pure soap and water."

Caroline cocked a brow. "Is that so?"

"You know it's so. You don't get to be . . . how the hell old am I, Dwayne?"

"I think it's eighty-four, Cousin Lulu."

"Eighty-four? Eighty-four?" Paint dripped on her shoes. "You're drunk as a polecat, Dwayne. No southern lady would ever reach the miserable age of eighty-four. It ain't seemly."

Dwayne considered his whiskey. He was well on the way to being sloshed, but he wasn't stupid. "Sixty-eight," he decided. "What I meant to say was sixty-eight."

"That's better." Lulu smudged paint on her cheek. "A dignified age. You go on in, Yankee, work your wiles on that poor, hapless boy. Just so you know I'm on to you."

"I'll keep that in mind." Unable to resist, she took a peek at the painting. It was Dwayne, cocked back in the rocker, clutching a hugely proportioned glass of whiskey. The style was somewhere between Picasso and the caricatures for *Mad* magazine. Dwayne's face was green, his eyes cracked with broken red lines. Poking up from his head were long purple donkey's ears.

"Ah, an interesting concept," Caroline commented.

"My daddy always said anybody who drinks for a living's bound to make an ass of himself."

Caroline looked from the portrait to the artist. In that single silent exchange she realized that Cousin Lulu wasn't as crazy as she pretended to be. "I wonder what reason anyone would have for choosing to drink for a living."

"For some, life's reason enough. Dwayne, where's that brother of yours? This girl's waiting and I can't paint with her breathing down my neck."

"Back in the library." He took a comfortable swallow of whiskey. "Just go on in, Caroline. Third door down on the right of the hall."

Caroline stepped in. The house was so quiet, it immediately crushed her urge to call out and announce herself. The light had that mellow golden quality she associated with museums, but the silence was more like that of a lady's elaborate boudoir while the mistress was drowsing.

She began to have doubts that anyone was there at all. She caught herself tiptoeing down the hall.

The door to the library was shut tight. As she put her hand up to knock, she pictured Tucker inside. Stretched out on the most comfortable flat, cushioned surface, hands cocked behind his head, legs crossed at the ankles. He would, of course, be taking his early evening, post-afternoon, pre-bedtime nap.

She rapped softly and got no answer. With a shrug, she turned the knob and nudged the door open. She'd just wake him up, she told herself. She had things to tell him and the least he could do was stay awake long enough to listen. Because while he was busy sleeping away his life, things were . . .

But he wasn't on the curvy love seat under the west window. Nor was he sprawled in the wing chair facing the stone fireplace. Frowning, Caroline turned a circle, taking a curious scan of the walls of books, an excellent Georgia O'Keeffe, and a dainty Louis XV side table.

And saw him behind a sturdy oak desk, bent over a pile of papers and books, with his fingers skimming casually—no, she realized—*skillfully* over the keyboard of a sleek little office computer.

"Tucker?" There was a world of surprise in the single word. He answered with a grunt, typed in some more data, then glanced up. The distraction on his face cleared instantly.

"Well, hey, Caroline. You're the most welcome thing I've seen all day."

"What are you doing?"

"Just running some figures." He pushed back from the desk to stand, looking lean and lazy in a T-shirt and chinos. "Nothing that can't wait. Why don't we go on out on the back porch, sit, and watch the sun set?"

"It won't set for two hours or more."

He smiled. "I've got time."

She shook her head, evading him when he came around the desk to reach for her. Holding him off with one hand, she moved closer to the desk to see what he'd been up to.

There were ledgers, printouts with columns of figures, invoices, receipts. Eyes narrowed, Caroline ran her finger over files.

LAUNDROMAT, CHAT 'N CHEW, HARDWARE, GOOSENECK UNIT I, ROOMING HOUSE, TRAILER PARK.

There was a pile of paperwork about cotton—seed, pesticide, fertilizer, market prices, trucking companies. Another pile consisted of various prospectus folders and stock reports.

Dragging a hand through her hair, Caroline stepped back. "You're working."

"In a manner of speaking. Are you going to let me kiss you or not?"

She only waved him off, trying to think it through. "Bookkeeping. You're keeping books."

He grinned. "Honey, it's against the law only if you keep two sets. Which my granddaddy did, successfully, for twenty-five years. So I guess it's more accurate to say it's against the law only if you get caught keeping two sets, which he never did and lived to his dying day as a pillar of this community." He sat on the edge of the desk. "If you don't want to sit on the porch and neck awhile, what can I do for you?"

"You use a computer."

"Well now, I admit I was prejudiced about it at first. But these damn little things save buckets of time once you get the hang of them. I'm all for that."

"Do you do all of this?"

"All of what?"

"This!" Frustrated, she grabbed up a pile of papers and shook them at him. "Do you keep all these records, these books? Do you run all of these businesses?"

He stoked a hand over his chin thoughtfully. Then he punched a few buttons, and the monitor winked off. "Mostly they run themselves. I just add the figures."

"You're a fraud." She slapped the papers down again. "All that lazy-southern-wastrel routine—I'd rather sleep than sit. It's just a front!"

"What you see is what there is," he corrected her, amused by the way she was pacing around the room. "It just seems to me that you have a different definition of lazy up north than we do down here. Down here we call it relaxed." He gave her a pained look. "Honey, I sure wish you'd learn to relax. The way you stir up the air in here is tiring me out."

"Every time I think I've got a handle on you, you shift. Like a virus." She turned back. "You're a *businessman*."

"I don't think that description suits me, Caro. Now, when I think of a businessman, I think of somebody like that Donald Trump or Lee Iacocca. All those fancy suits, messy divorces, and bleeding ulcers. Of course, there's Jed Larsson, and he wears a suit only on Sunday as a rule, been married to his Jolette as long as I can remember. But he does suffer from some bad heartburn."

"You're changing the subject."

"No, I was getting around to it. You could say I oversee some ventures now and again. And since I have a gift for figures, it doesn't take much effort."

She dropped down on the love seat and scowled at him. "You're not wasting your life."

"I always figured I was enjoying it." He walked over to join her. "But if it'll make you happy, I could give wasting it a try."

"Oh, just shut up a minute. I'm trying to think." She folded her arms across her chest. Hapless? she thought. Wasn't that what Lulu had called him? What a joke. The man knew exactly what he was doing, and he'd obviously been doing it his own way, in his own time, for years. Hadn't she seen it herself? The way he could give you that sleepy-eyed grin one minute, then drill right into your brain with a look the next?

"The other day, before that business with Bonny, did you say that you and Dwayne worked in the fields?"

"We've been known to."

"And you once mentioned that Dwayne had a degree he didn't use. But you didn't say if you had one."

"Can't say I actually graduated. I never could get the hang of sliding through school like Dwayne did. I studied some business management and accounting, though." He smiled easily. "Didn't take much thought to figure out it's more comfortable behind a desk than sweating in a cotton field. Want me to dig up my college yearbook?"

She only hissed out a breath. "I can't believe I actually came over here to protect you."

"Protect me?" He slid an arm around her shoulders so he could sniff at her hair. "Sugar, that's awful sweet of you. God, you smell good. Better than cherry pie cooling on the windowsill."

"It's soap," she said between her teeth. "Just soap."

"It makes me crazy." He began to nuzzle her neck. "Dead crazy. 'Specially this spot right here."

She shivered as he nipped under her jaw. "I came here to talk to you, Tucker, not to . . . oh." Her words trailed off as he began doing sneaky, seductive things behind her ear.

"You go ahead and talk," he invited her. "I don't mind a bit."

"If you'd just stop that."

"Okay." He switched from her ear back to her neck. "Go ahead."

As her better judgment began to dim, she tilted her head back to give him more access. "Matthew Burns came by." She felt his lips pause, his muscles tense, then gradually, gradually, relax again.

"I can't say as that surprises me. He's had his eye on you. A blind man on a galloping horse could see that."

"It had nothing to do with . . . It wasn't personal." The hell with her fuzzy brain, Caroline decided, and turned her lips to meet Tucker's. She let out a quiet sigh as he pleasured them both with slow, nibbling kisses. "He was warning me off you."

"Hmmm. Much to my frustration, you haven't been on me yet."

"No, he was talking about the case. The murder." A light flashed on in her brain and she jolted back. "The murder," she repeated, then stared down openmouthed at her gaping blouse. "What are you doing?"

He had to take a steadying breath. "I was just working on getting your clothes off. Seems I've been working on that for some time now." He sat back again, studying her. "And it looks like it's going to get put off again."

She fumbled her buttons back into place. "I'll let you know when I want to be undressed."

"Caroline, you were letting me know just fine. Until you started thinking again." To douse some of the fire, he got up to fix a drink. "Want one?" He gestured with the decanter.

"No."

"Well, I do." He poured two fingers of whiskey.

She lifted her chin. "You can be just as annoyed as you like, but—"

"Annoyed?" His eyes flashed to hers before he lifted the glass. "Sugar, that's a mighty mild word for what you work in me. I've never had a woman stir my juices with less effort than you."

"I came here to warn you, not to stir anything."

"My point exactly." He finished off his drink, thought about having another, and opted for half a cigarette instead. "Who's Luis?"

Her mouth opened and closed twice before she managed to speak. "I beg your pardon?"

"No, you don't. You just don't want to answer me. Susie mentioned that there was somebody named Luis you were pissed at." He scowled down at the stub he was smoking. "Hell of a stupid name."

"Tucker's so much more dignified."

He relaxed enough to grin. "Depends on where you're standing, I expect. Who is he, Caro?"

"Somebody I'm pissed at," she said lightly. "Now, if you'd like to hear what I've come to—"

"Did he hurt you?"

Her eyes locked with his. In them she saw patience, compassion, and, unexpectedly, a quiet, steady strength. "Yes."

"I'd like to promise I wouldn't, but I don't guess I can do that."

Something shifted inside her. A door she'd thought she'd locked tight was creeping open. "I don't want promises," she said almost desperately.

"I've never been one for giving them. Dangerous things, promises." He frowned down at his cigarette, then crushed it out. "But I do care about you. I guess you could say I'm about neck-deep in caring about you."

"I think—I'm not ready . . ." She rose and wished she had something to do with her hands. "I care about you, too, Tucker. And that's where it has to stop. I came here because I care about you, and I wanted you to know that Matthew Burns is looking for a way to prove you killed Edda Lou Hatinger."

"He's going to have to look pretty hard." Still watching her, Tucker slipped his hands in his pockets. "I didn't kill Edda Lou, Caroline."

"I know that. I might not understand you, but I know that. Matthew's looking for the connection between Arnette, Francie, and Edda Lou, and you're the front runner. He also dropped some hints about Toby, and that concerns me. I know these are the nineties, but it's still rural Mississippi, and racial tensions . . ." She shrugged.

"Most people around here have a lot of respect for Toby and Winnie. There aren't that many around here like the Hatingers or the Bonny boys."

"But there are some. I don't want to see anything happen to Toby or his family." She took a step forward. "More, I don't want to see anything happen to you."

"Then I'll have to see to it that you don't." He reached out to lift her chin, his eyes sharp and steady. "You've got a headache." Gently he rubbed at the faint line of stress between her brows. "I don't like to think I had a part in bringing that on."

"It's not you." As always, she felt a trace of embarrassment at the weakness she associated with pain. "It's the situation. Not you."

"Then we're not going to think about the situation. We're going to go sit out on the porch and watch for that sunset." He pressed a kiss to her forehead. "And you don't even have to neck with me. Unless you want to."

That made her smile, which was what he'd intended. "What about your work?"

"Honey." He slipped an arm around her waist to lead her out. "There's one sure thing about work. It doesn't go anywhere."

♦ ♦ ♦ ♦

SO THEY SAT ON the porch, talking idly of the weather, of Marvella's wedding, of young Jim's progress on the violin. And while the sun drifted lower in the sky, bleeding red over the horizon, while the frisky puppy tried to convince the aging Buster to play, while the Statler Brothers gave way to the Oak Ridge Boys, neither of them noticed the quick wink of light glazing off the lens of a pair of dented binoculars.

Austin held them to his eyes in taut hands. He watched, his mouth moving silently in fervent and deadly prayer, his mind twisting deeper into madness, and two Police Specials shoved in the waistband of his Sunday trousers.

♦ ♦ ♦ ♦

WHEN CY REACHED THE culvert the next morning, his father was waiting. He grabbed the boy by the shirt while he peered out at the white morning light.

"You didn't tell anybody? I'll know if you lie."

"No, Daddy." It was the same question, the same answer each morning. "I swear I didn't. I brought you some chicken, and a sausage biscuit."

Austin snatched the paper sack. "You bring the rest?"

"Yes sir." Cy handed over the plastic container of water, hoping his father would be content with that. Knowing he wouldn't.

Austin unscrewed the top and took three long swallows before swiping his hand across his mouth. "The rest."

Cy's hands shook. His throat was too full of fear to allow any words through. He unbuckled the leather holder from his belt and held out the hunting knife.

"Daddy, there's police still out by the house, but they got rid of the roadblocks on Route One. You could get clean over to Arkansas if you wanted."

"Anxious to see me gone, boy?" Lips peeled back in a grin, Austin unsheathed the knife. It caught the funnel of light and shone.

"No, sir, I was just—"

"Oh, you'd like me to run, wouldn't you?" He turned the blade, drawing Cy's terrified eyes to the gleam. "You'd like me to go, leave your way clear to sin and debauchery. To buddying up with niggers and kissing Mr. Tucker Longstreet's rosy ass."

"No, sir. I was just . . . I was just . . ." Cy stared at the knife. One swipe, one quick careless swipe of that knife and he'd be dead. "It's just that they're still out hunting for you. Not like they were before, but they're still looking."

"The Lord's my shepherd, boy. He does provide." Still smiling, Austin ran his thumb along the edge of the blade. A thin line of red welled out of his skin. "And sharp is His sword. Now let me tell you what you're going to do."

Austin turned the knife on his son. For one dizzying instant, while his bowels turned to ice, Cy was certain the point was going to plunge into his throat. But it stopped a whisper away.

"Are you listening, boy? Are you listening?"

Cy nodded. He was afraid to swallow. Afraid that the blade would prick his Adam's apple if it bobbed.

"And you're going to do just as I say, aren't you?"

Cy looked above the blade, into his father's eyes. "Yes sir."

♦ ♦ ♦ ♦

CY WORKED HARD ON sweating out his fear. He hauled wheelbarrows full of mulch around the garden, dug holes for the new peony bushes Tucker had bought to replace the ones that had died off from being trampled. He scraped old paint and slapped on fresh. He yanked up weeds until his fingers cramped, but the fear stayed hot and hard in his belly like a bad meal that refused to digest.

He didn't eat the meal Della set out for him—not even the half he usually took for himself. Instead, he packed the thick pork sandwiches and generous slice of lemon cake into his knapsack.

He couldn't even stand to look at them, but he figured his father would eat well that night.

He'd have a rare appetite after he'd finished with Tucker.

Cy wiped sweat out of his eyes and tried not to think of right and wrong or good and bad. All he had to think about was surviving. Of getting through one day and onto the next until he'd finished up all those days that made up four years.

He looked around Sweetwater, the green fields thriving with cotton, the dark, still water, the splashes of color from flowers. Maybe it was true, what his daddy said. Maybe it was only people like the Longstreets who could afford to plant flowers to look at instead of food to eat.

Maybe it was true that they didn't deserve the fine, big house, and all the land and the easy life they lived. Maybe it was their fault that his own family was poor as dirt and had to scrape for every penny.

And Edda Lou had been his sister, his blood. Family took care of family. His daddy said it was Tucker's doing that she was dead.

If he believed that, if he could believe that, then what he had to do wouldn't be so hard.

It didn't matter if it was hard or not, Cy reminded himself as he walked to the side of the house to rinse off his hands and face with the garden hose. It was something he had to do, because if he didn't, his father would come for him. He would find him wherever he tried to hide. And he would come for him with more than a belt, with more than his fists.

"If thy eye offend thee, pluck it out," his father had said. "You're my eye, boy. You're both my eyes."

And he'd held that honed silver point so close, so close to Cy's left eye that he'd been afraid to blink.

"Don't offend me in this. You bring him here, and I'll be waiting."

"You done for the day, son?"

At Tucker's voice, Cy jerked back and managed to soak his shoes. Tucker merely grinned and put a match flame up to half a cigarette.

"Della told me you were jumpy today. Better turn that hose off before you drown yourself."

"Yes sir. I'm all finished." Cy stared at his hand, watched his own fingers curl around the metal and twist.

"Good, 'cause it damn near wears me out watching you. You want a Coke, another piece of that cake?"

"No, sir." Cy kept his head down as he rewound the hose. He felt something perilously like tears in his throat. Maybe it wouldn't work, he thought desperately. Maybe Tucker would just shoo him on his way. Lips pressed together, Cy limped toward his bike.

"What's wrong with your leg?"

Cy kept his back to the house and stared straight ahead.

Make him feel sorry for you, boy. You see that he gives you a ride in one of those fancy cars. And you bring him down here to me.

"It's nothing, Mr. Tucker. Guess I mighta pulled something." He took another couple of limping steps, praying that Tucker would just shrug and turn away.

"Why don't you come on back in here, let Della take a look at it?"

Cy closed his fingers around the handlebars of the bike and darted a look back toward the house. "No, sir, I'd best get on home."

Tucker caught the glint of tears in the boy's eyes and frowned. Adolescent pride was a touchy thing. "Well, I've got to run into town for some things." He strolled off the porch, improvising as he went. "That woman runs me ragged fetching this and picking up that. How come women can't figure out what it is they need all at once?"

Cy stared down at the silver handlebars, focusing on the splotches of rust. "I don't know."

"One of the mysteries of the universe." He laid a friendly hand on Cy's shoulder and felt him flinch. With a guilty start he realized again how thin the boy was, and how hard he'd been working. "Why don't you load that up in the Olds, Cy? I can give you a ride most of the way home."

Cy's knuckles whitened on the handlebars. "I don't want to trouble you, Mr. Tucker."

"I've got to drive right by your turnoff. Come on, let's get to it before she can think of something else to send me for."

"Yes sir." Head down, Cy wheeled the bike over to the drive. His head was ringing like an anvil by the time Tucker had plucked the keys out of the ignition and unlocked the trunk.

"God knows why she drives this old boat," Tucker muttered. "You could fit three dead bodies in the trunk." He shoved some of Della's debris aside. A cardboard box full of old clothes meant to go to the church. Three pair of shoes to be taken in for repair next time she was passing through Greenville, a box of mason jars, and an over-and-under Winchester.

Cy's gaze lit on the gun, then jumped away. Tucker noted the look as he hefted the Schwinn into the truck. "She's been hauling that thing around in there for months. Says she might need to shoot some crazed rapist if the car breaks down somewhere." Tucker pulled out a length of rope and wound it carelessly around the bumper. "I can't quite picture

Della sitting on the hood with a shotgun across her lap, laying for crazed rapists, but there you go."

Cy said nothing, nothing at all, and climbed in the car. Tucker pulled one of his cassettes from the glove compartment. "I hide these in here," he told Cy. "A woman never goes in a glove compartment. How about some Presley?"

"Okay." Cy linked his stiff fingers in his lap. "Fine."

"Boy, Presley's not fine. He's king." Tucker flipped in the cassette and revved the engine to "Heartbreak Hotel." He sang the opening bars along with the King as they headed down the lane. "You getting along all right at home?"

"At home?"

"Your mama doing better?"

"She's . . . she's getting by."

"If you need something—money or something—you can ask me. You don't have to tell her where it came from."

Cy had to stare out of the window. He couldn't face the concern, the simple kindness. "We're getting along." He caught a glimpse of Toby's truck at the end of Caroline's lane and wanted to weep. How could he ever go whistling up to Jim again? After today, he'd be the same as a murderer.

"You want to tell me what's on your mind, Cy?"

"Sir?" Cy swiveled his head back. His heart bobbed up to his throat. "Nothing, Mr. Tucker. I've got nothing on my mind."

"I haven't been fourteen in a while," Tucker said easily. "But I remember what it was like. I remember what it was like to have a father with a heavy hand and a short fuse." Tucker glanced over, and his eyes were so full of understanding, Cy had to turn away again. "You weren't limping when you got into the car, Cy."

The ball of fear in his belly spread. "I guess, I guess my leg's feeling better."

Tucker said nothing for a moment, then moved his shoulders. "If that's the way you want it."

They were driving along the skinny trickle of Little Hope now. Cy knew that they'd be coming up to the culvert in less than a mile. "I—I keep the bike down by the stream. In the culvert."

"All right. I'll drop you there if you want."

"Maybe you could . . ." Help me take it down. Help me wheel it down off the road and into the culvert where my daddy's waiting for you. You'll help me take it down, because you're willing to help when you're asked.

"Could what?"

Almost there. Almost there. Cy wiped the back of his hand over his dry mouth. It wasn't icy fear in his belly now, it was a sick green fist of horror. *I just have to ask him, and he'll do it.* And Cy caught the glint of light—reflected off the lens of binoculars. Or perhaps the knife.

"Stop! Stop the car!" In panic he grabbed at the wheel and nearly sent them into the stream.

"What the hell!" Tucker wrestled the wheel back and left the car diagonally across the road. "You lost your senses?"

"Turn the car around, Mr. Tucker, turn around. Christ almighty, go back." Sobbing, Cy leapt up and tried to turn the motionless car himself. "Please God, turn it around before he comes and kills us. He'll kill us both now."

"Just hold on."

The Olds banked like a ship leaving port, then shot down the road. Cy huddled on his knees, sobbing against his clenched fists and staring out the rear window while the dead King sang about a hunk of burning love.

"He's going to come. I know he's going to come. My eyes, he's going to cut out my eyes." He doubled over, clutching his belly. Hysteria or not, Tucker veered to the shoulder. He yanked the boy out and held Cy's head while his body shuddered.

When Cy was down to dry heaves, Tucker pulled out a handkerchief and mopped the boy's face. "Try to breathe slow. You think you're done?"

Cy nodded, then began to cry. They weren't wild, wailing sobs, but soft, quiet ones that broke the heart. Baffled, Tucker sat in the open car door and patted Cy's head. "Get those out, too. I expect you'll feel better for it."

"I couldn't do it. I just couldn't. He'll kill me now."

"Who's going to kill you?"

Cy turned his blotched miserable face to Tucker's. Tucker thought he looked like a dog who'd already been beaten half to death and was just waiting for the final blow.

"It's my daddy. He told me to bring you down here. He told me I had to on account of Edda Lou, and if your eye offends you, you have to cut it out. I've been bringing him food every day. And I brought him his belt and a fresh shirt, the binoculars. I had to. And today I had to bring him the knife."

Tucker lifted Cy up by the shirtfront and shook some of the hysteria away. "Your father's back there in that culvert?"

"He was going to lay for you. I was supposed to bring you. But I couldn't." Cy's eyes wheeled around. "He could be coming right now. He could be coming. He's got those guns, too."

"Get in the car."

Cy figured he was going to jail for sure. He'd been aiding a fugitive and was an accessory after the fact, or something like it. But jail was better than having that knife carve out his eyes. "What're you going to do, Mr. Tucker?"

"I'm going to take you back to Sweetwater."

"Take me back? But—but—"

"And you're going to go inside, and you're going to call Sheriff Truesdale and tell him the whole thing." He aimed a hard look at Cy. "Aren't you?"

"Yes sir." Cy wiped tears from his cheeks. "I swear I will. I'll tell him where Daddy is. I'll tell him the whole thing."

"And you tell him he better get out here, quick, fast, and in a hurry." He turned through the gates of Sweetwater.

"I'll tell him. I'm sorry, Mr. Tucker, I was so scared."

"We'll talk about that later." Gravel spewed as he swerved to a stop. "Get on in there. If you can't get him at the office, you call him at home. Della's got the number. You can't get Burke, you get Carl."

"Yes sir. What're you going to do?" He watched, wide-eyed, as Tucker popped the hood, tossed out the bike, then pulled out the shotgun. "You going back after him? Are you going after him, Mr. Tucker?"

Tucker broke open the shotgun, checked the load. His eyes lifted and fastened on Cy's. "That's just what I'm doing. You'd best tell Burke I've just deputized myself."

Cy turned and raced into the house.

Chapter 18

TUCKER DIDN'T CARE TO picture himself in a shootout. It just didn't sit right. As he sped back to Dead Possum Road, it occurred to him that this was the second time Austin had put him in the awkward position of carrying a gun.

It was damn irritating.

But he couldn't go back and sit on the porch, waiting for Burke and Carl to handle it. Not when he still had the picture of Cy's terrified face in his mind. Not when the scent of a young boy's fear was still hanging heavy in the car.

He'll cut my eyes out!

Where in Christ had the boy come up with that?

From his crazy, sick old man, Tucker concluded.

His face was set, his eyes the color of burnished bronze as he swung the car to the shoulder. He hefted the gun, then using the car as a shield, reached in the backseat for the binoculars Della, and almost everyone else in Innocence, carried.

When he brought them up and focused, the concrete hump of the culvert jumped in front of his eyes. Slowly, he scanned, but saw nothing at the entrance, no movement along the slope of the Little Hope. Nothing in the field beyond.

He caught the glint of silver from the roofs of the mobile homes in the trailer park three miles away. Lowering his sights, he clearly saw Earleen's sister Laurilee step out of her trailer, take a swing from a can of Mountain Dew, and give a holler.

Calling the kids in for supper, Tucker thought absently, and slowly swung the binoculars away. He saw pigs rooting in the pen at Stokey's farm and the wash hanging on the line at the Marches', and a plume of dust toward town that might have been Burke riding out.

But on the fields and flats, nothing stirred. And the silence hung heavy, disturbed only by the stream croaking its way over rocks and mud and a few birds that sang disinterestedly in the hazy heat of the evening.

If Austin was waiting, he was waiting in the dim, dirty shadows of the culvert. There was only one way to find out.

Tucker took time to shove a few extra shells in his pocket, though he sincerely hoped he wouldn't have to use them. Keeping low, his eyes trained on the shallow entrance, he circled the culvert. When he got within five feet, he dropped down on his belly, the shotgun nestled on his shoulder.

"God, if You want to do me one favor in this lifetime, don't make me have to shoot this thing."

He took a deep breath, exhaled slowly.

"Austin! I reckon you know I'm out here." It wouldn't occur to him until later that his skin was bone dry, his hands rock steady. "You went to a lot of trouble to invite me out for a visit." He bellied his way to the slope of the bank. "Why don't you come on out and we can talk reasonable, or we can wait awhile until Burke comes along."

There was only silence from the culvert and the scream of a crow overhead.

"You're going to make it hard on me, Austin. I'm going to come in there, seeing as how you tormented that boy. I just can't swallow that. Then we're going to start shooting at each other, and one of us is likely to be dead." With a little sigh Tucker reached over and picked up a stone. "I sincerely don't want it to be me."

He tossed the rock down and waited for the ripping report of a gun. Silence.

"Shit on toast," Tucker muttered, and slid down the slope into the stingy trickle of the Little Hope. There was a roaring in his head now, a steady wall of sound that was his heart and his fury. He swung the shotgun around and charged the entrance, fully expecting to be dodging bullets.

But the culvert was empty. Tucker stood there, feeling more than a little foolish with his shotgun at the ready and his heart beating like a brass band. He could hear his own rushing breaths bouncing off the concrete.

"Okay," he said quietly. "Okay, there was nobody around to see you make an ass of yourself." He started back toward the entrance, then stopped short.

Could Austin be hiding somewhere? Somehow have found a hole just big enough to crouch in? Was he waiting, just sitting out there for Tucker to come back out so he could pick him off?

That was stupid, Tucker assured himself, took another step, then stopped and swore.

It was better to be stupid than dead, he supposed, and wondered what the hell to do now.

He had a ridiculous image of the final scene from *Butch Cassidy and the Sundance Kid*, where Newman and Redford had been freeze-framed in that last, hopeless gun battle.

The slick ending didn't fool Beau Longstreet's son Tucker. No indeedy. He knew just what had happened. Guns had fired, and Butch and the Kid had been blown to glory.

He stood in the narrow culvert thinking he was neither outlaw nor hero, but it was mighty hard on the pride just to huddle there and wait.

Before he had to make the decision, he heard the rumble of a car, then the quick, sharp slam of doors. "Tucker! Tuck, you all right?"

"Down here, Burke." Tucker leaned the shotgun against the wall. "He ain't here."

He heard Burke give Carl orders to look around, then the light at the entrance was blocked by the sheriff's broad shoulders. "What the sweet fuck is going on here?"

"Well, son, I'll tell you," Tucker said, and did.

♦ ♦ ♦ ♦

COULDN'T UNDERSTAND HALF OF what that boy was saying." Burke offered Tucker a light for his half cigarette. "But he seemed damned sure you and his daddy were going to kill each other down here."

"I'm not sure if I'm disappointed or relieved we didn't have the chance to try. Cy's a good boy, Burke. Austin threatened him with some nasty shit, but he did what was right." He pulled in smoke, let it out slowly. "I'm thinking it might be best if he stayed on at Sweetwater for a while. Home's no place for him. If Austin didn't manage to get to him, Vernon will make him pay for this. I swear to Christ I don't see how that boy could be kin to either of them."

"With any luck Vernon won't hear about it for a day or two. Right now we'd better concentrate on finding his father." He nodded at Tucker. "I guess we can say you're already deputized."

"I'd just as soon you didn't." Tucker reached for the shotgun. It was then he noticed the scrawl of writing on the wall. "What the hell's this?" He leaned closer, squinting. "You're in my light, Burke," he said, then swore when he made the letters out.

AN EYE FOR AN EYE

"Christ almighty," Burke murmured as he rubbed his thumb against the first A. "Looks like he wrote it in blood. I'm going to call up some men. We'll do a house to house. We'll walk every inch of the county, but we're getting that crazy sonofabitch tonight."

He'll cut my eyes out!

Tucker pressed his fingers to his own eyes as Cy's terrified voice rang in his head. "I guess I'm going with you. Do I get one of those cheap tin stars?"

♦ ♦ ♦ ♦

WITHIN THE HOUR BURKE had fifteen able-bodied and willing men. It gave him some twinges of uneasiness to see Billy T. Bonny and Junior Talbot both standing around with rifles. He had to hope that the excitement of going after a fugitive would put personal feuds on the back burner. For safety's sake, he separated them, sending Junior off with Carl's group and keeping Billy T. with his own. He took a chance and put Jed Larsson, slow but sensible, in charge of a third.

Using a county map, he diced up territories.

"I don't want any hotdogging. Austin's got himself two weapons, and unless he's been taking potshots at rabbits, he's only used one bullet. I'd sure hate to end the day by having to go to somebody's wife or sweetheart and tell her that her man got himself shot by being stupid."

"We got ourselves more sense than those lard-ass county deputies." Billy T. was excited at the prospect of shooting something.

There was a lot of good-natured whooping to relieve nerves. Burke waited until it died down.

"The last time Austin was seen was right down there in that culvert. Now he's got at least an hour on us, and he's on foot. But a man who knows this country could find a lot of places to hide. We want him brought in, all in one piece. If you spot him, you give a call on the two-way. Your weapons are for defense only."

Several of the men slanted sly looks at one another. Austin wasn't a popular fellow.

"If he ends up dead, there'll be plenty of questions some of you might not like answering." He scanned faces, holding gazes just long enough to make his point. "You boys aren't going deer hunting, you are duly deputized public servants. Now, move out, and watch your butts." He turned away to gather his own group. "And God help us."

Five of them piled into the cruiser. Burke, Tucker, Billy T., Singleton Fuller, and Bucky Koons. Singleton immediately lit up one of the cigars Happy wouldn't let him smoke at home.

"You ain't called up the county boys, Burke," he said casually.

Burke's fingers flexed on the wheel. "No. It's our town."

There was a murmur of agreement through the curtain of foul-smelling smoke.

At the intersection of Old Cypress and Longstreet, which Burke had designated as Base A, he pulled to the shoulder. The spot had significance for Tucker, who flicked a glance in the rearview mirror. Billy T. met the look with surly eyes.

They separated there, three to go east with the cautious Singleton in charge, and Burke and Tucker to go west.

"You want to tell me what's cooking between you and Billy T.?" Burke asked as they started the wide circle that would bring them back as a group by McNair Pond.

"Oh, that's already boiled over and been mopped up." He sent an uneasy glance in the direction of Caroline's house. "You really figure he'd have gotten this far?"

"Can't figure. He could be off in any direction, and I could be making a mistake not calling in to county."

"Hell of a lot of good they did us last time."

"Well," Burke said, and left it at that. "Could be he headed off for home." He worried a minute about Carl and his group. "County's still got his house under surveillance, and he'd know it, but it doesn't sound to me like the man's thinking right."

Tucker figured the distance with some satisfaction. "I hope to hell that's just where he goes. They'll snatch him on up and take him off our hands." Tucker turned his head and pondered on the glint of Caroline's second-story windows. "It's not just that he's not thinking right, Burke. It's like he's gone rabid or something. That day we pounded on each other? He got to thinking I was my old man. He didn't want to kill me nearly so much as he wanted to kill old Beau."

He felt a hankering for a cigarette and struggled it back. "I'll tell you what I think. It wasn't me he wanted Cy to bring to that culvert, either."

Burke frowned. He didn't know a hell of a lot about psychology, unless you assumed that was the same as human nature. But he did understand that a man could do desperate things when a woman pushed him to the edge. Like hanging himself in his own barn.

"That's a long time to hold a grudge over a woman."

"Well, around Innocence, we got a surplus of time. My mama would get up and leave the room anytime his name came up. She did that right up until the end of her life." Tucker stopped while Burke scanned with binoculars. "It used to make me wonder. I asked Edda Lou once if Austin acted strange about her. She laughed." Now he did pull out a cigarette. "She said that he'd sometimes call her mama by my mama's name when he was slapping her around." A chill raced up his spine. "See anything?"

"Not a goddamn thing." Burke pulled out his walkie-talkie to check in with the other groups.

Tucker felt the chill again. He puffed on his cigarette and told himself it was only natural to feel uneasy when you were out hunting a man. Yet he caught himself, not looking over his shoulder, or squinting in the distance, but staring back at the glint of sun against Caroline's bedroom window.

Something was wrong. He could almost smell it, like a trace of ozone on the air after a slash of lightning. Something was sure as hell wrong.

"Burke, I want to cross over there to Caroline's."

"I already told you, Susie called her and told her to come on into town. They're probably sitting around the kitchen table talking about flower arrangements and wedding cakes."

"Yeah." Tucker rolled his shoulders as if trying to ease an itch. "But I want to cross over."

He was already moving fast when they heard the shots.

◆ ◆ ◆

CAROLINE HAD CORN BREAD in the oven. Happy Fuller's family recipe. She'd been finishing up the batter when Susie called. She wasn't fooled by the invitation to dinner, or the request that she come help talk some sense into Marvella over her color schemes. Austin Hatinger had been spotted less than ten miles away, and Susie didn't want her to be alone.

She appreciated the concern, and since she'd started to jump at every creak and shadow since the call, Caroline was more than willing to oblige. She didn't think Austin was going to show up on her doorstep. Certainly not. But as the sun dropped toward evening, she liked the idea of spending some time in Susie's safe and noisy kitchen.

She took a sniff of the air and smiled. The corn bread was nearly ready. Then she'd pack it up, along with Useless, and drive into town.

She took a look at the oven timer. Little more than five minutes, she saw, and pushed open the screen door to call her dog.

"Useless. Come on, boy." She clapped her hands as Happy had done and tried to whistle. "Useless, come on, Useless, we're going for a ride." Hearing the whimper under her feet, she got down on her hands and knees to look through the porch slats. And there he was crouched back against the new brace, whining.

"Dumb dog. Come on right now. What's got you so spooked?"

He let out two yips and cringed back against the new brace. Disgusted, Caroline sat back on her heels. "Probably saw a garter snake," she muttered. She decided to lure him out with a Milk Bone—Useless had already proven to have no willpower when it came to Milk Bones—and was pushing herself to her feet when she saw Austin Hatinger.

For an instant she thought it was her imagination. There could be no man walking across her backyard with two guns hitched in his belt and a knife in his hand. There could be no man crushing her newly planted pansies under his heel and smiling at her, smiling through frozen lips, smiling out of crazed, red-rimmed eyes.

She was still on her knees when he spoke.

"God led me to you." The smile seemed to tear his face, like a rip through tattered burlap. "I understood His will. You were with him. I saw you with him, and you're to be sacrificed." He turned the knife blade in the sunlight as he approached the porch. "Like Edda Lou. It has to be just like Edda Lou."

Like a runner coming off the mark, Caroline pushed herself from her knees and slammed through the back door. She shoved it to, turned the bolt. The oven timer went off with a buzz that made her scream. Then Austin's weight rammed against the wood and set her numb legs free.

She didn't think. Fueled by instinct, she snatched up her grandfather's Colt on her flight from the kitchen. She needed to get to the car, but even as she raced through the house, she heard the old kitchen door give way with a splinter of wood.

And she remembered that the gun she held in her slippery hand was empty.

Sobbing, she barreled through the front door, digging in her pocket. Bullets sprayed out of her sweaty fingers and she nearly lost her footing on the steps. She stumbled, righted herself, and saw that all four tires on her car had been slashed.

Austin swung open the screen door. "You can't run from the will of God. You are His instrument. An eye for an eye, saith the Lord."

But Caroline was already fleeing toward the swamp. Another bullet squirted out of her fingers like wet soap to be lost in the grass. Her scream was no more than a harsh breath of air.

"Stop it, stop it!" she ordered her shaking hands as she fought to get one bullet, then two into the chamber. "Oh, God, please." She was nearly to the trees, nearly there, and there was shelter and terror behind them. One desperate look over her shoulder, and he was less than two armspans behind her. With tears blurring her vision, she turned and fired.

The gun clicked on empty. And he smiled.

"Today you are the lamb of God." The knife arched up, glistening silver death. Caroline saw more than madness in his eyes. She saw a terrible glory.

Then Useless shot out like a small gold bullet and latched his puppy teeth into Austin's calf. Austin howled more in fury than pain. It took only one kick to send the dog lying bonelessly on the grass.

"Dear God," Caroline prayed, and with the gun braced in both hands, fired again. This time the kick knocked her limp body back. She lay stunned, staring at the horrible red stain that bloomed over Austin's dirty white shirt.

His smile was back, a rictus of a grin. He took another step toward her, the knife held high.

"Please, please, please," Caroline whimpered as the gun jerked in her hand again. With numbed horror she saw his face disappear. His big, brawny body twitched. To her terror-frozen brain, it seemed he was still coming, still walking implacably toward her. She scrambled back, screams hitching in her throat, heels digging furrows in the grass.

The knife fell at her feet, and Austin followed it.

♦ ♦ ♦ ♦

TUCKER SKIDDED TO A stop on the gravel drive. While his heart slammed in his throat, he watched Caroline weaving across the lawn, carrying the puppy. Beyond her he could see Austin sprawled facedown, and the blood staining the grass.

"He kicked my dog," was all she said, and moved by him into the house.

"Jesus Christ, Burke."

"I'll take care of this out here." Burke holstered his gun and exchanged it for his walkie-talkie. "Go on in with her. See that she stays inside until this is done."

Tucker found her in the parlor, sitting in the rocker with the dazed dog across her lap.

"Honey." He crouched down beside her, stroking her face, her hair. "Honey, did he hurt you?"

"He was going to kill me." She kept rocking, afraid if she stopped she'd go mad. "With the knife. He could have shot me, but he had to do it with the knife. Like Edda Lou, he said." The dog began to stir and whine in her lap. Caroline lifted him up against her breast like a baby. "It's all right now. It's all right."

"Caroline, Caroline, look at me, honey." He waited until she turned her head. Her pupils were so dilated, the irises were hardly more than a green aura around them. "I'm going to take you upstairs. Come on now, I'll carry you up and call the doctor."

"No." She let out a long breath as Useless licked her chin. "I'm not going to be hysterical. I'm not going to fall apart. I fell apart in Toronto. All kinds of pieces. Not again." She swallowed, pressing her cheek against the dog's fur. "I was making corn bread. I'd never made corn bread before. Happy gave me her recipe, and I was going to take it over to Susie's. It feels so good being a part of this place." Useless licked away a tear that trickled down her cheek. "You see, I thought I was coming here just to be alone, but I didn't know how much I needed to be a part of something."

"It's going to be all right," he said helplessly. "I promise it's going to be all right."

"I was making corn bread in my grandmother's oven. And I shot Austin Hatinger with my grandfather's gun. Do you think that's strange?"

"Caroline." He cupped her face. She could see the streaks of violence and fury in his eyes that he so carefully filtered out of his voice. "I'm just going to hold you for a while, is that all right?"

"All right."

She let her head rest on his shoulder when he picked her up. Saying nothing, he carried both her and the pup to the couch and cradled them there. They both ignored the phone when it rang.

"I'm going to stay here tonight," he told her. "Down here on the couch."

"I'm not falling apart, Tucker."

"I know, darlin'."

She let out a sigh. "The oven timer's still buzzing." She bit her lip to try to steady her voice. "I guess I burned the corn bread."

She turned her face into his shoulder and wept.

Chapter 19

CAROLINE CAME DOWNSTAIRS FEELING hollowed-out by the aftereffects of shock and sleeping pills. She had no idea what time it was, only that the sun was strong and her house was quiet as a tomb.

It was already sultry. Even the thin cotton robe seemed too heavy and hot against her skin. She thought she'd take her coffee iced—in her car. With the air-conditioning running.

She'd killed a man.

That single raw fact had her stopping at the base of the stairs, her fist pressed against her heart like a runner catching her wind after a punishing sprint. And like a runner's, her legs went rubbery so that she sat on the landing, propping her head in her hands.

She had pumped two bullets into flesh, exchanging her life for another's. Oh, she knew it was a matter of self-defense. Even without Burke's gentle questions and quiet support, she knew that. Some circuit in Austin Hatinger's brain had snapped and caused him to turn on her.

But circumstances didn't change the result. She'd taken a life. She, whose most violent act had been throwing a champagne flute against the wall in the Hilton Hotel in Baltimore, had ripped two .45 slugs into a man she'd never even had a conversation with.

It was a big leap, she thought, rubbing her hands over her face. And maybe her legs were a little shaky after landing, but she'd discovered something else about herself.

She could live with it.

She would not search for a way to put the blame on herself. She would not agonize over how she could have avoided, prevented, or changed the outcome. That was the old Caroline's weakness, that delusion of self-importance that had made her believe she had the right, the responsibility, the *power* to bear all burdens—whether it was a performance, her mother's needs, a lover's deceit. Or a madman's violent death.

No, Caroline Waverly was not going to listen to that sneaky little voice that crept inside her brain to whisper about blame and fault and mistakes.

She rose, turning toward the kitchen before the scratching at the front door had her heart doing a cartwheel. Even as the scream tickled the back of her throat, she recognized Useless's whimpering. The scream died to a puff of air as she stepped forward to open the door.

Fevered with gratitude, the dog rushed in to make desperate jumps around her, his tail slicing the air in his delight and relief.

"What were you doing out there?" She bent to scratch his ears and accept his loyal licks of affection. "How'd you get outside?"

He yipped, scrambling around her legs, feet skidding in a search for traction on the polished hardwood before he dashed off to the parlor.

"Is this like a Lassie thing?" Caroline asked as she followed him. "I hope you're not taking me to where Timmy's fallen down the well or . . ." She trailed off, spotting Useless sitting smugly on the floor beside the sofa. And Tucker, bare-chested, barefooted, sprawled over it.

He didn't look innocent in sleep, she noted. There was simply too much wit and wickedness in his face for that. But he did look decidedly uncomfortable. His feet hung over one end of the two-seater sofa, and his neck was crinked to accommodate the curve between cushion and arm. His arms were folded across his belly, less for dignity, Caroline decided, than for the fact that he hadn't been able to find any other space for them. Despite the awkward position and the stream of sunlight falling directly in his eyes, his chest rose and fell gently with deep, even breathing.

She'd forgotten he'd stayed, but it came flooding back to her now. How kind he'd been, how tenderly he'd held her while she'd cried out her shock. And the quiet strength he'd offered just by holding her hand while Burke questioned her.

Tucker had been the one to take her up to bed, sliding over her protests as patiently as a father guiding an overtired child. He'd sat with her while the sleeping pill had trickled through her bloodstream. And to chase away those last shadows of fear, he'd remained on the side of the bed, her hand in his, and had told her some silly story about his cousin Ham who ran a used-car dealership in Oxford.

The last thing she remembered was something about a '72 Pinto that had dropped its transmission five feet out of the lot, and a dissatisfied customer with a five-gauge.

She felt the lock on her heart snick open, and sighed.

"You're just full of surprises, aren't you, Tucker?"

Useless perked up at the name, then leapt up to bathe Tucker's face. Tucker grunted, shifted. "Okay, honey. In a minute."

Amused, Caroline stepped closer. "I hope it's worth the wait."

Tucker's lips curved as he reached out to cuddle the dog. "It's always worth . . ." His hand slid down the dog's back to the gleefully swinging tail. Slowly, his lashes fluttered up and he studied the furry face grinning into his. "You're not quite what I had in mind."

Undiscouraged, Useless scrambled his hind legs until he'd gained Tucker's chest. Tucker gave the dog's head an absent scratch, then closed his eyes again. "Didn't I put you out once?"

"He wanted back in."

Tucker's eyes opened again, and pushing Useless's face out of his, he focused on Caroline. The sleepy look was gone quickly, she noted, and understood she was being carefully measured.

"Hey."

"Good morning." When he shifted his hip, she accepted the invitation and sat. "I'm sorry we woke you."

"I figured on getting up sometime today anyway." He reached up to stroke a fingertip down her cheek. "How you doing?"

"I'm all right. Really. I want to thank you for sticking around."

He winced a little as he straightened his neck. "I can sleep anywhere."

"So I see." Touched, she brushed the hair off his brow. "It was sweet of you, Tucker. I'm grateful."

"I'm supposed to say I was just being neighborly." He caught her hand when she started to draw it back. "But the fact is you had me worried sick. You didn't have a lick of color when you finally went off to sleep."

"I'm steadier now." She wished she'd checked the mirror to see if she looked steadier. "You could have used the spare bed upstairs."

"I thought about it." But when he'd checked on her—for the fourth or fifth time during the night—he'd also thought about slipping into bed with her. Just to hold her, just to keep her close and satisfy himself that she was safe. That had shaken him enough that he'd needed to have the full story laid out between them. Now he needed the simplicity of closeness.

"Come here."

She hesitated, then gave in to the urge to curl up beside him. With her head pillowed against his shoulder and the dog stretched across their legs, she sighed.

"I'm glad you're here."

"I'm sorry I wasn't quicker."

"No, Tucker."

He brushed his lips over her head. "I gotta get this out, Caroline. It gave me some hard hours through the night. He wouldn't have come after you if it weren't for me. It was me he wanted, and me who put you in the middle."

She laid a hand over his heart, wondering if she'd ever felt more comforted, more safe. "I used to think that way about things. That I was at the center, and whenever anything went wrong, I was to blame for it. It's an indulgent kind of arrogance, I think. The kind that carves holes in you that you have to fill up with pills and therapy. Don't change on me, Tucker. I'm starting to find your day-to-day way of looking at things appealing."

"It scared me." When his arms tightened around her, she curved into him to give comfort as well as take it. "Nothing's ever scared me more than hearing those shots and knowing I was too far away."

"I've been scared before, so many times. As horrible as this is, it's really the first time I've done anything about my fear." Her hand fisted, and she slowly, deliberately, relaxed it again. "I'm not glad it happened, Tucker, and I guess I'll always remember what it was like to pull that trigger. But I can deal with it."

He stared at dust motes dancing in a sunbeam. There were things he'd never forget either. Like the numb terror of racing over a fallow field with shots echoing in his head. Like the glassy-eyed shock on her face when she'd walked by him to carry the limp dog into the house.

"I'm no hero, Caroline. Christ knows, I don't want to be one, but I'm going to see to it that nothing bad happens to you again."

She smiled. "That's a broad and daring ambition," she began, and tilted her head back to look at him. There was no answering smile in his eyes, and when he took her chin, his fingers were tense.

"You're important to me." He said the words slowly, as if explaining them to himself. "Nobody's ever been as important, and that's hard."

The air was clogging in her lungs, the way it often did when she stood on a darkened stage, the moment before the spotlight found her. "I know. I guess it's hard for both of us."

He saw the shadow of fear in her eyes, though she kept them steady and level on his. And because she was important, because everything about her had suddenly become vitally important, he struggled to lighten his tone.

"It sure is a new one for me." His tensed fingers relaxed to stroke her jaw. "Here I am all wrapped up in a woman and I haven't even managed to get her clothes off yet. This gets around, my reputation's going to suffer."

"Why don't you try it now?"

His finger froze on her cheek. "What's that?"

"I said, why don't you try it now." With her eyes still full of fears and needs and doubts, she lifted her lips to his.

He felt himself sink into her, and that, too, was a change. That slow, lovely drift into sweetness. There was no hot punch of lust that he had always accepted so easily. Instead, there was a gentle shift of sensation, as subtle as a sky lightening toward dawn.

As her body yielded against his, as her breathy sigh slipped intimately from her mouth to his, he understood that she was offering him more than passion. She was giving him her trust. It humbled him. It disturbed him. She was not the kind of woman to offer anything to a man casually. And he—he had always taken whatever a woman chose to give with an easy grin and no backward looks.

"Caroline." He brushed his fingers over her cheeks, combed them through her hair. "I want you."

His heart drummed fast and hard against hers. The quiet seriousness of his statement made her smile even as his lips cruised over her face. "I know."

"No, I mean I really want you." The robe had slipped off her shoulder, and he let his lips wander to that warm, sweet curve. "I guess I've been waiting for you to give me the go-ahead since about thirty seconds after I met you."

Her body trembled and arched under his. Why were they talking? Why were there words when she wanted only to feel? "I know that, too."

"It's just that . . ." Her throat was so white, so smooth. It wasn't in him to resist it. "I haven't been exactly discreet when it comes to women."

She skimmed her hands over his bare back, exploring that intriguing ripple of muscle. "Tell me something I don't know."

"I don't want you to regret this." He rubbed his cheek against hers before he drew away. His eyes were dark with emotions she was afraid to consider. "I don't think I could stand it if you did."

"You're the last person I expected to complicate this."

"It surprises the hell out of me, too." His fingers curled tight in her hair. "It's not simple with you, Caroline. I figured I ought to try to explain that."

He didn't have to explain what she could see so clearly in his eyes. And seeing it had the little licks of fear leaping higher. "I don't want any explanations." Desperate, she dragged his mouth back to hers. "I'm alive. I just need to feel alive."

Her needs swallowed him, pulled him under, sucked him in. She wanted from him what he had always looked for in other women—simple, mutual pleasure. If there was a twinge of regret, he ignored it. Responding to her urgency, he tugged open her robe and feasted on flesh. She was slim and pale and soft as velvet. And if she was not just any woman, not just another woman, he blocked off those troubling thoughts and let himself take.

She streaked mindlessly into heat, gobbling up his desire like a starving woman might devour a crust of bread. Hers was only a body seeking pleasure from another body. No thoughts, she swore. No emotions. She needed the sensations, the liberation of good, cleansing sex. Her cry of release when he drove her to a hard, knife-edged orgasm left her trembling.

She could hear his harsh, strained breathing even as his hands began to slow, to gentle. He murmured something to her, and though she didn't understand the words, the sweetness of the tone had her battling back an urge to wrap herself around him and weep.

The emotions sneaking through terrified her. She wanted none of them and moved quickly, even ruthlessly, to block them off. Even as his lips whispered over hers, she was dragging his jeans down over his hips. His body went rigid as she touched him, fisted him in a hot, greedy hand. The room tilted, and while he struggled to right it again, she locked herself around him.

"Caroline. Wait."

But she was already surrounding him, already drawing him deep into that glorious velvet sheath, already urging him to match her frantic rhythm.

He was trapped in her, in his own body's demands. So he raced with her toward a release he already realized would be empty.

♦ ♦ ♦

SHE LAY VERY STILL, her robe rucked up under her hips. She did feel alive. Sore and swollen and trembly and alive. If only she didn't feel so hollow with it.

If only he would say something. If only he would lift his head and grin and make some silly joke to put this awkwardness behind them.

But the silence dragged on. His heartbeat slowed to normal against hers, and the silence dragged on.

He knew he was heavy, but he put off shifting his body from hers, put off the moment when he would have to face her. And himself.

Good sex, he thought. Yes, it had been good, basic sex, minus all those insidious and baffling emotions. Smart sex, he thought with some disgust. There was no reason for him to feel . . . used was the word, he realized, and wished he could laugh it off.

Was this why Edda Lou had been so bitter at the end? he wondered. With a sigh he opened his eyes and stared out at the empty room. No, Edda Lou hadn't cared about him. About his money, his name, his position, but not about him. Sex had been a means to an end for her.

That was something they'd had in common.

But surely there had been a woman, someone, between his first adolescent tussle and this final, soulless bout with Caroline, who had cared. Who had wanted more and settled for less. Someone who had lain in hurt silence after the storm.

His just deserts, he supposed. The first time he had wanted more, he had run up against a woman who refused to give it, or take it.

Well, he still had pride. However cold that comfort was, it was better than crawling.

He did shift then, hitching up his pants as he sat back.

"You caught me off guard, sugar." The smile curved his lips, but left his eyes flat. "Didn't give me a chance to, well, dress for the party."

It took her a moment to understand that he was talking about the lack of a condom. She made herself shrug. "I suppose this was more of a surprise party." Avoiding his eyes, she sat up and drew her robe around her. "I take the pill."

"Well then." He wanted to reach out, to smooth her touseled hair, but rose instead. "Looks like we bored that pup of yours right to sleep." He gestured to where Useless was curled under a chair, snoring. Tucker thrust his hands in his pockets. "Caroline."

"I think I'll go make some coffee." She popped off the couch as though Tucker's voice had flicked a lever. "And breakfast. I owe you breakfast."

He studied her, the way she gnawed on her bottom lip, the way her eyes, shadowed with strain, kept slipping over his shoulder. "If that's the way you want it. Mind if I grab a shower?"

"No, go ahead." She wasn't sure if her sigh was one of relief or disappointment, and covered it over with a flow of words. "Upstairs, second door on the right. There are fresh towels on the shelf. The water takes a while to heat up."

"I'm not in a hurry," he told her, and strolled out of the room.

♦ ♦ ♦

WASHING WITH HER SOAP put him in a better frame of mind. Using her toothbrush—he couldn't find a spare—left a lingering taste of her in his mouth.

Physical things. It was much more comfortable to concentrate on physical things. He'd had no business brooding over the deeper meaning of a nice, no-strings session of morning sex.

He'd shrugged his shirt over his shoulders by the time he reached the bottom landing. He caught the scents of coffee and bacon. Everyday aromas that shouldn't have had him quivering for her. He was scowling down the hallway toward the kitchen when he heard the sound of a car in the lane.

Shirt open, thumbs tucked in his pockets, he walked to the screen and watched Special Agent Matthew Burns park. They studied each other, one black-suited and silk-tied, the other unshaven and barely dressed. Animosity leapt up like a large rabid dog.

Tucker shoved open the screen door and leaned on it. "Early for visiting, isn't it?"

Burns locked his car door, pocketed the keys. "Official business." He scanned Tucker's bare chest and damp hair. The homey breakfast scents drifting outside had him thinning his lips. "The interruption is quite necessary."

"You're too late to interrupt," Tucker said placidly. "What can we do for you?"

"You take a lot of pride in this, don't you, Longstreet?"

Tucker lifted a brow. "In what?"

"In your southern-fried womanizing."

"Is that why you're here? Looking for pointers?" His smile wasn't charming this time, but wolfish. "If that's the case, it's going to take awhile. You need a lot of work, Burns."

Burns's jaw clenched. The simple fact that a woman like Caroline preferred Tucker over him burned in his gut like an ulcer. "I find your . . . style, I suppose we'll call it, pathetic."

"If that was an insult, you're off target. I'm not looking to impress you."

"No, helpless females are more your style."

"You know"—Tucker rubbed a hand over the stubble of his chin—"I've never once in my life met a female I'd consider helpless. Caroline's not, that's for damn sure. Right now she might be a little shaky. She might need somebody to lean on until she gets her feet back under her again. She's got me as long as she wants. You'd better understand that."

"What I understand is that you have no compunction about using a woman's vulnerabilities to your own end. You're a user, Longstreet, and you've got the emotional maturity of a mushroom. Edda Lou Hatinger was just the last in a long line of your discards. As for Caroline—"

"Caroline can speak for herself." She stepped forward, laying a hand on Tucker's arm. Whether it was in support or restraint, none of them could tell. "Do you need to talk to me, Matthew?"

He struggled against a wave of black, unreasonable anger. She was wearing nothing but a robe, and the way she ranged herself beside Tucker spoke not only of preference, but of intimacy. It galled, destroying his elegant image of her. However brilliant her talent, however delicate her beauty, she had lowered herself to trollop by her choice.

"I thought it would be more comfortable for you to give me your statement here, rather than coming into town."

"Yes, it would. I appreciate it." She would have offered him coffee in the parlor, but she had no intention of leaving him and Tucker alone again. "If we could go back in the kitchen . . . I've just finished fixing breakfast."

"I'd intended to get Mr. Longstreet's statement later," Burns said stiffly.

"Now you can save some time." Caroline kept a wary watch on both of them as they walked down the hall. "Would you like some eggs, Matthew?"

"Thank you, I've already eaten." He took a seat at the table, as out of place in the country kitchen as a tuxedo at a hoedown. "Coffee would be nice, if you don't mind."

Caroline brought the pot to the table, setting it on an iron trivet in the shape of a rooster. Odd, she thought as she dished up bacon and eggs, until that moment she hadn't imagined herself racing through that room, snatching a gun from the counter, screaming as fists beat against the door.

She looked over now. Only the screen remained. Either Burke or Tucker had taken the broken door away, but there were still a few splinters of wood on the floor.

"You want a statement about what happened yesterday." Caroline busied herself adding cream to her coffee. "I've already given one to Burke."

"Yes, I read it."

Tucker noticed her hands were steady, but her gaze shifted back to the door several times. He lifted a hand to her shoulder for a gentle rub. "I don't know much about the law," he began, "but isn't what happened here yesterday a local problem?"

"Ordinarily. If you'd indulge me, Caroline, I'd very much appreciate your going over everything that happened." He switched on his recorder. "For my records."

It wasn't very difficult. Not when it all seemed so dreamlike and distant. She played it back, as if it were a tape in her head. He let her run it through without interruption, making only a few cursory notes on his pad.

"It's odd, don't you think, that Hatinger didn't use either of the guns he carried?" His tone was conversational as he poured a second cup of coffee. "They were both loaded, and from my information he was considered an excellent shot. When you describe your flight, from the rear porch, through this room, and out the front, it would appear that he could have fired at you at any time. But he didn't even draw a weapon."

"He had the knife," she said, and didn't notice the catch in her voice. Tucker did.

"I don't see the point in this, Burns. He'd snapped, obviously. Maybe he didn't even remember he had the guns."

"Maybe." He added a miserly dab of cream to his coffee. "Would you say, Caroline, that he was aware you had a gun?" He lifted the cup, sipped, then went on without waiting for her answer. "You say you grabbed it on the run while he was still outside."

"Yes, I'd been target practicing. I always unloaded it when I'd finished. Sometimes I stuck the bullets in my pockets. I remember thinking it was a bad habit, and I should break it." She set down her fork, clattering it against her plate. The scent of eggs and bacon grease were nauseating. "I guess I'm lucky I didn't."

"You were lucky you had the presence of mind to load the gun at all."

She gave Burns a wan smile. "You could say I'm used to performing under pressure."

He merely nodded. "If we re-create those last moments outside, when you turned and fired, can you hazard an opinion as to whether he realized you were armed? Did he make any move to reach for one of the guns he carried?"

"It happened very quickly."

It hadn't seemed so. It had seemed as though she'd been running through syrup. It didn't take any effort to rerun the scene, that slow-motion film of nightmares and dark fantasies. The wall of heat that made you fight for every gasping breath. The terrifying feeling that the grass had gone boggy and was sucking you down. The silver glint of the knife under the merciless sun. And that grin, that wide, hungry grin.

"I . . ." She pressed her lips together and bore down on the last, nasty remnants of fear. "I tried to shoot, but nothing happened. He just kept coming, holding the knife and smiling at me. Just smiling. I think I was crying or screaming or praying, I don't know, but he kept coming, and kept smiling. I had the gun out in front of me, and he was saying that I was the lamb of God, a sacrifice. That it was going to be like Edda Lou. That it had to be like Edda Lou."

"You're sure of that." Burns held his cup two inches above the saucer. "You're sure he said it had to be like Edda Lou?"

"Yes." She gave in to a shudder, then pushed her uneaten breakfast aside. "I'm not likely to forget anything he said."

"Wait a minute." Tucker put a hand on Caroline's arm, his fingers taut as wire. He'd been doing more than listening, he'd been watching. Burns looked like a man who'd just drawn to an inside straight. "You're not here getting a statement about the shooting of some escaped lunatic. That's small shit, the kind of local dirt that wouldn't interest a federal agent. You sonofabitch."

"Tucker, please."

"No." His eyes were fierce as he turned to Caroline. "Don't you see? It's about Edda Lou, about Edda Lou and the others. It doesn't have diddly to do with you, except you managed not to be the next victim."

"The next?" she began, then stopped. The blood drained from her face. "Oh, God, the knife. He didn't shoot me because—because it had to be like Edda Lou. It had to be the knife."

"Yeah, the knife." Tucker's hand slid down her arm so that she could grip it. "There are users and users, aren't there, Burns?" Tucker's voice had lost its lazy drawl, sharpening to an icy point. "You're using Caroline to help you gather evidence on Hatinger. Using her to solve your case, but you don't bother to let her know."

Burns set his cup meticulously back in the saucer. "I'm conducting a federal investigation on a series of murders. I'm not required to make my views known to the public."

"Fuck that. You know what she's been through. Easing her mind by telling her this might be over wouldn't have cost you."

"Regulations and procedure," Burns said.

Caroline squeezed Tucker's hand before he could speak again. "I can talk for myself." She inhaled and exhaled twice, slowly. "I didn't even know Edda Lou, but I'll see her floating in the pond for the rest of my life. I've never performed a violent act in my life. Oh, I threw a champagne glass at someone once, but I missed, so it hardly counts. Yesterday I killed a man." Her hand fluttered to her stomach to press against the slow, familiar burn. "That may not seem so terrible to you, Matthew, considering your line of work and taking into account that I was saving my own life. But I killed a man. Now you come in here and ask me to bring it all back. And you don't even grant me the courtesy of the truth."

"It's simply speculation, Caroline, and for your own good . . ." He fumbled to a stop when her head snapped up.

"Do you know," she said slowly, "I once threatened to kill a man if he ever, ever used that particular phrase to me again. I didn't mean it literally at the time. It was just one of those typical statements people make before they realize what it's like to kill. But I should warn you not to use that phrase. It tends to set me off."

Delighted, Tucker kicked back in his chair and grinned. "She's got a hot streak. It's a pure pleasure seeing it aimed at somebody else for a change."

"I apologize if I've upset you," Burns said stiffly. "But I'm doing my job as I think best. It is not a foregone conclusion that Austin Hatinger was responsible for the three deaths in the community or the one in Nashville. However, given yesterday's incident, we are focusing our investigation on him."

"Will you be able to tell if it was his knife?" Caroline asked.

"After certain tests are completed, we should be able to determine if it was that style of knife. Off the record," Burns continued grudgingly, "I can say that Hatinger fit certain psychological points in this kind of killing. He had a deep-seated anger toward women, as evidenced by his frequent abuse of his wife. A religious mania which he may have figured absolved him of guilt, or accorded him a mission. We could speculate that his use of water to dispose of the bodies was more than an attempt to wash away evidence, but a kind of baptism. Unfortunately, he can't be questioned about his motives. As it stands, I'll be backtracking, trying to place his whereabouts at the time of all three murders. And while he is my focus, I'll continue along other avenues of investigation."

His gaze lighted on Tucker, and Tucker merely smiled.

"Then you've got your work cut out for you, don't you, son? We wouldn't want to hold you up."

"I'll want to talk to the boy. Cy Hatinger."

Tucker's smile faded. "He's at Sweetwater."

"Well then." He rose, but couldn't resist a parting shot. "Odd how Hatinger went from gunning for you straight to Caroline, isn't it? Some people have a knack for turning bad luck onto others." He was an expert at recognizing guilt. It gave him pleasure to watch it shadow Tucker's face. "If you think of anything else that might help, Caroline, you know where to reach me. Thanks for the coffee. I can see myself out."

"Tucker," Caroline began the moment they were alone, but he shook his head and rose.

"I've got some thinking to do." He ran a hand through his hair. It was dry now, but he caught a whiff of her shampoo. Even so small a thing had his gut tightening. "Will you be all right? Want me to call Josie, or Susie, or someone?"

"No, no, I'll be fine." But she wondered if he would. "Matthew's a rigid sort of man, Tucker. That kind always sees the logic of placing blame."

"There's blame enough. Listen, I need to get back. I don't want Cy having to talk to him on his own." His hands dug into his pockets again. "He's just a kid."

"Go ahead." It would be better, she thought, to be alone. To put off talking about what had happened between them that morning. "I'll be fine, really." She lifted their plates, thinking Useless was going to breakfast like a king.

He put a hand on her shoulder as she turned to the sink. "I'm coming back."

"I know." She waited until he was at the doorway before speaking again. "Tucker. Thanks for telling Matthew I wasn't helpless. When you're used to people seeing you that way, it means a lot."

Her back was to him, her shoulders straight. He knew she was looking out to where the blood had dried on the grass.

"We're going to have to talk, you and me. About a lot of things."

When she didn't answer, he left her alone.

Chapter 20

$\mathcal{H}$IS DADDY WAS DEAD. Miss Della had told him.

His daddy was dead. There would be no more snapping belts or merciless fists. No more shouts to a fever-eyed God to punish the sinners for their transgressions, their laziness, their filthy thoughts.

Miss Della had sat him down in the bright kitchen and told him, and there had been kindness in her eyes.

He was afraid, so afraid that there would be no end for him but hell. The fiery, screaming black pool of hell his father had often gleefully described. How could he expect forgiveness or a place at the Lord's table when he harbored such an evil secret in his soul? The secret whispered through his brain with the devil's rusty chuckle.

His daddy was dead. And he was glad.

When his tears had come, the tears Miss Della patiently waited out then wiped away, they weren't tears of sorrow or grief. They were tears of relief. A river of joy and gratitude and hope.

And it was that, Cy thought as he watered the kitchen garden, that which would consign him to hell for all eternity.

He had been responsible for the death of his father. And he wasn't sorry.

Miss Della had told him he could stay at Sweetwater just as long as he wanted—Mr. Tucker had said so. He didn't have to go home, he didn't have to go back to that house of fear and hopelessness. He didn't have to face Vernon, see his father in his brother's eyes, feel his father's wrath in his brother's fists.

By a single act of cowardice he had wiped out four years of waiting.

His father was dead, and he was free.

Cy hunkered down, the hose soaking grass until it gurgled in a puddle. Rubbing his knuckles into his eyes, he wept in joy for his life, and in terror for his soul.

"Cy."

The sound of his name had the boy jerking to his feet. It was only quick reflexes that had Burns nipping out of range of the garden hose. They stood facing each other a moment, the water squirting between them, a young boy with a puffy face and frightened eyes and a man who wanted to prove that Cy's father had carved up women in his spare time.

Burns tried his most ingratiating smile, which put Cy immediately on edge.

"I'd like to talk with you for a few minutes."

"I've got to water these plants."

Burns glanced at the soaked greens. "You seem to have done that already."

"I've got other work."

Burns reached down to turn off the water himself. Authority was something he wore as habitually as his tie. "This won't take long. Perhaps we could go inside." Out of the blistering heat.

"No, sir, I can't track all over Miss Della's clean floor."

Burns glanced down. Any trace of white on Cy's sneakers had been obliterated with grass and dirt stains. "No, I suppose not. The terrace then, around the side." Before Cy could protest, Burns took him by the arm and led him around the flower beds. "You enjoy working at Sweetwater?"

"Yes sir. I wouldn't want to lose my job 'cause I got caught sitting around talking."

Burns stepped onto the slate terrace and gestured toward one of the padded chairs under a striped umbrella. "Is Mr. Longstreet that hard a taskmaster?"

"Oh, no, sir." Reluctantly, Cy sat. "He never has enough for me to do, to my way of thinking. And he's always telling me to slow it down and take it easy, real considerate like. Sometimes if he's around late in the afternoon at quitting time, he brings me out a Coca Cola himself."

"A liberal employer." Burns took out his pad and recorder. "Then I'm sure he wouldn't mind you taking a short break to answer some questions."

"You can ask him yourself," Tucker suggested. He strolled out of the kitchen door with a chilled bottle of Coke. "Here you go, Cy." He set the bottle down in front of the boy. "Wet your whistle."

"Mr. Burns—he said how I had to come on out here and talk," Cy began. His eyes were as panicked as a rabbit's caught in the white stream of headlights.

"That's all right." Tucker touched a hand to his shoulder briefly before scraping back a chair for himself. "Nobody expected you to work today, Cy."

With his lips pressed tight together, Cy stared down at the white table. "I didn't know what else to do."

"Well, for the next few days you do what suits you." Tucker pulled out his cigarettes. He figured he was down to a half pack a day by his current method and ruthlessly tore off half the tobacco. "Now, Agent Burns here's having himself a busy morning." His eyes stayed on Burns's over the flare of his match. There was a warning there, as clear as the message Hatinger had written in blood. "So, why don't you tell him what you can. Then maybe you'd like to drop a line with me for an hour or two."

Burns curled his lip at the idea of taking the boy fishing the day after his father had been killed. "I'll let you know when we're finished, if you'd like to go tie some flies."

Tucker helped himself to a swig of Cy's Coke. "No. As I figure it, since the boy's working here and staying here for the time being, I'm a kind of guardian. I'll stay, unless Cy wants me to go."

Cy lifted those panic-dazed eyes to Tucker's. "I'd be obliged if you'd stay, Mr. Tucker. I might get something wrong."

"All you have to do is tell the truth. Isn't that right, Agent Burns?"

"That's exactly right. Now—" he broke off as Josie walked out wearing a paper-thin pink robe.

"Well now, it's not often a woman strolls out of her kitchen and finds three men waiting for her." She moved closer to ruffle Cy's hair, but her eyes were all for Burns. "Special Agent, I was beginning to think you'd taken a dislike to me. Why, you haven't been around to talk but one time." She eased a hip onto the arm of Tucker's chair. When she reached over to pluck up one of Tucker's cigarettes, she afforded Burns the best view in the house. "I was about to make something up just so you could investigate me."

He was stuffy, but he wasn't dead. Burns found his throat clogged and his tie too tight. "I'm afraid I have little time for socializing while on a case, Miss Longstreet."

"Now, that surely is a shame." Her voice was as rich and heady as the scent of magnolias. With a flutter of her lashes, she handed Burns the pack

of matches, then steadied his hand with her own when he touched the
flame to the tip. "And here I've been pining away, hoping you'd find time
to tell me all about your adventures. I bet you've had scads of them."

"Actually, I've had a few interesting moments."

"I'm going to have to hear all about them or I'll just explode from
curiosity." She trailed a finger down her throat to where her robe met
loosely over her breasts. If his eyes had been tied by a string to her hand,
Burns couldn't have followed the movement more closely. "Teddy told me
you were the very best."

He managed to swallow. "Teddy?"

"Dr. Rubenstein." She sent him a sultry look under heavy lashes.
"He was telling me you were the absolute expert on serial killings. I just
love talking to brainy men with dangerous jobs."

"Josie." Tucker sent her an arch look. "Weren't you going to get your
nails done or something this morning?"

"Why, yes, honey, I was." She shifted to hold out her hands. Her
robe crept up another inch. "I don't think a woman can be really attractive
if she lets her hands go." She rose then, satisfied that she'd broken Burns's
concentration. "Maybe I'll see you in town later, Special Agent. I'm fond
of stopping for a cold drink at the Chat 'N Chew after my manicure."

She left him with the distracting image of her hips swaying beneath
that thin pink robe.

Tucker tossed his cigarette into a brass bucket filled with sand. "You
going to turn that recorder on?"

Burns gave him a blank look, then shot to attention. "I'll be asking
Cy questions," he began, but his gaze drifted to the kitchen door. "I have
no objection to you being present, but I'll tolerate no prompting."

Tucker gestured with his open hands and sat back.

Burns switched on the recorder, entered the appropriate data, then
turned to Cy with a solemn smile. "I know this is a difficult time for you,
Cy, and I'm sorry for your recent loss."

Cy started to thank him, then realized he wasn't talking about Edda
Lou, but his father. He took refuge in staring at the table again.

"I realize you spoke with Sheriff Truesdale last night, and your information was very helpful. We'll have to talk about that again, but I think
we'll start with a few other things. Did your father ever mention Miss
Caroline Waverly to you?"

"He didn't hardly know her."

"So he never spoke of her to you, or in your hearing?"

Cy darted a look at Tucker. "He mighta said something on one of the
days I brought him breakfast. Some days he said lots of things, like when
his mood came on him."

"Mood?" Burns prompted.

"Those hard moods he had, when he said God was talking to him."

"And did he have these moods regularly?"

"Pretty much." Cy chugged down Coke to ease his dry throat. "A.J. used to say that he just liked to beat up on people and used God as an excuse."

"He was often violent with you and other members of your family?"

"He . . ." Cy remembered Tucker's phrase. "He had a heavy hand." That didn't sound so bad somehow. It was almost like saying he had a head cold. "He didn't tolerate no sass. The Bible says how you're to honor your father."

Tucker said nothing, but he noted that Cy hadn't said father and mother. He didn't imagine Austin had drilled that part of the scripture into his son's brain.

"And he used this heavy hand when he had his moods."

Cy shrugged his thin shoulders. "He used his hands most all the time. It was just worse during the moods."

"I see." Even Burns wasn't unaffected by the casual way the boy described brutality. "And when you were bringing him food and supplies in the culvert, he had these moods."

"I had to do it." Cy's knuckles whitened on the glass bottle. "He'd've killed me if I'd gone against him. I had to do it."

"Agent Burns isn't blaming you, Cy." Again Tucker laid a hand, that soothing, comforting hand on his shoulder. "Nobody is. You didn't do anything wrong."

"No, I'm not blaming you." Burns's voice roughened, and he coughed to clear it. The stark fear on the boy's face appalled him. "No one would. I only want you to tell me if your father spoke of Miss Waverly."

"He said some things." Cy blinked his eyes fast to close off tears. "He said how she was full of sin. How all women were. Like Lot's wife. She got turned into a pillar of salt."

'Yes." Burns folded his hands. "I know. Did he tell you why Miss Waverly was full of sin?"

"He said how . . ." He shot Tucker a miserable look. "Do I have to say?"

"It'd be best," Tucker told him. "You take your time."

Cy took it by gulping down Coke, wiping his hand across his mouth, squirming in his chair. "He said how she was spreading her legs for Mr. Tucker." His face went beet-red. "And how she was no better'n a whore for it. It was time to cast the first stone. I'm sorry, Mr. Tucker."

"It's not your fault, Cy."

"I didn't know he meant he was going to hurt her. I swear I didn't.

He said stuff all the time. It got so you didn't pay much mind to it, as long as he wasn't hitting you. I didn't know he was going after her, Mr. Burns. I swear I didn't."

"No, I'm sure you didn't. Your father hit your mother, didn't he?"

The frantic color in Cy's cheeks ebbed away. "We couldn't do nothing about it. She wouldn't do nothing. She wouldn't let the sheriff help, 'cause a woman's supposed to cleave to her husband. The sheriff'd come by sometimes and she'd just tell him how she'd fallen off the porch or something." His head dropped. Shame weighed almost as heavy as fear. "Ruthanne says how she likes it. She likes getting beat on. But that don't seem right."

Burns decided there was no use trying to explain the psychology and the cycle of abuse. That was a job for social workers and shrinks. "No, it doesn't. Did he hit Ruthanne, too?"

He smirked, the way brothers do over their sisters. "She's pretty good at getting out of the way."

"How about Vernon?"

"They'd whip up on each other sometimes." Cy made a quick, dismissive move of the shoulders. "Mostly they hung together. Vernon was Daddy's favorite. He took the most after Daddy. Inside and out, my ma said. They were alike inside and out."

"How about Edda Lou? Did your father hit her?"

"She was always butting him, daring him, like. She hit back at him. Once she split his head with a bottle when he used the belt on her. That's when she moved out. She moved into town and never came around the house anymore."

"Did he say things about Edda Lou, too? The way he did about Miss Waverly?"

A wasp circled down to investigate Cy's Coke and was batted away. "We weren't supposed to say her name. Sometimes he got worked up and said how she was a whore of Babylon. Vernon would try to get Daddy riled up about her. He wanted to go fetch her from town and bring her home so they could punish her. Vernon would say how it was their duty as her family and as Christians, but I don't think he believed in that like Daddy did. Vernon just likes to hit people." He said it simply, as if he'd just commented that Vernon liked ice cream sundaes. "Then Daddy found out she was seeing Mr. Tucker and he said how she'd be better off dead. And he beat Ma."

Tucker pressed his fingers against his eyes and wondered if the guilt would ever pass.

"Cy, do you remember when your father and Mr. Longstreet argued?"

Tucker dropped his hands. He nearly laughed. The euphemistic "argument" still showed in fading bruises on his ribs.

"I guess I do. Daddy came home with his face all busted up."

"And what about two nights before that." The night Edda Lou was murdered. "Do you recall if he had one of his moods?"

It was the first question Cy had to think about. His eyes lost some of their glassy fear as he considered. Absently, he took another swipe at the persistent wasp. "I can't recollect for sure. When he got wind that Edda Lou was supposed to be pregnant, he was real fired up. But I don't know which night that was."

Burns prodded for a few minutes, trying to jog the boy's memory without tipping him off to the reason. In the end, he backed off. He still had Ruthanne and Mavis Hatinger. Their memories might be keener.

"All right, Cy, just a few more questions. The knife you took to your father. Did he often carry it?"

"Only when he was going hunting and such. A buck's too big to carry as a rule."

"Could you estimate how many times he might have carried it in, say, the last six or seven months?"

"Four or five times. Maybe more. He was partial to squirrel meat."

"Did he ever threaten you or any member of your family with the knife? Did he ever boast about punishing someone with it?"

"He was going to gut Mr. Tucker." Cy covered his face with his hands, muffling his voice. "He said how I had to bring Mr. Tucker back down to the culvert, and he told me he was going to gut him like a rabbit. He was going to carve off his privates. 'Cause it was divine justice. He was going to cut him up like Edda Lou. And if I went against him, if I didn't honor my father, then he'd cut out my eyes because the eye offended him. And the Lord says you're supposed to. Please, Mr. Tucker." He didn't weep, but kept his hands over his face like a kid in a horror movie trying to block out the monster. "Please, I don't want to think about it no more."

"It's all right, Cy." Tucker rose to stand behind him. "Leave him be, Burns."

Burns turned off the recorder, put that and his pad in his pocket. "I'm not heartless, Longstreet." As he pushed back from the table he looked from the trembling boy to the man who stood as his protector. "And I'm very aware that there are more victims here than are buried in the cemetery." He wished fleetingly that he was capable of offering compassion as easily as Tucker, with the touch of a hand. Instead, he nodded at the boy, and though his voice was stiff, the words were sincere. "You did everything that was right, Cy. There's nothing more any man can do. You remember that."

Tucker laid his hands on the boy's shoulders and watched Burns walk away. For the first time since he'd set eyes on the FBI agent, Tucker felt a tug of respect.

"I'm going to get us a couple of poles, Cy. We're taking the rest of the day off."

♦ ♦ ♦ ♦

Now, FISHING," TUCKER SAID as he balanced his pole between his knees and settled back against a cypress stump, "is the thinking man's sport."

"I never used this kind of stuff for bait before." Cy sniffed again at the foil-wrapped package in Tucker's bait box. "What's it called again?"

"Pâté." Tucker grinned and pulled his cap farther down over his eyes. "Duck liver in this case." And wasn't Della going to raise holy hell when she saw it was gone.

"Duck liver." Cy screwed up his face and looked exactly the way a fourteen-year-old boy should. "That's gross."

"An acquired taste, my man. The cats're crazy for it." Tucker smeared some on a cracker for himself, popped it into his mouth, and washed it down with lemonade.

They had settled on the far side of Sweetwater Pond, under the dappled shade of a willow Tucker's mother had planted before he'd been born.

"The cotton looks fine, Mr. Tucker."

"Hmmm." From under the shadow of his cap, Tucker looked at the fields. He spotted his overseer and several hands checking the rows for growth, for weevils. "We've got a good crop this year. The cotton runs this place." He sighed a little. "And running cotton's what spoiled this water here, so we'll have to toss back whatever fish we catch. I've been thinking about getting some of those bugs."

"Bugs, Mr. Tucker?"

"They got these bugs—scientists figured it out. They eat poison and pollution and the God-knows-what that seeps into water and ruins it."

"Poison eating bugs?" Cy gave a snort of laughter. "You're joaning on me, Mr. Tucker."

The boy's chuckle, however weak, lightened Tucker's heart. "It's the God's truth. They put those bugs into the Potomac River and they ate it clean." He looked wistfully out over the dark, deadly water of the lake. "I'll tell you, Cy, it sure would mean something to me to see this water sweet again. My mama used to talk about having a bridge built over it. You know, one of those pretty arching things like they have in Japan. We never got around to it. I'm sorry for that, 'cause she'd've liked it."

Cy didn't know about Japan or arching bridges, but he liked listening to Tucker talk. As far as Cy could tell, he could talk about just anything and make it seem fine.

They fished for a while, drowsily, with Tucker's voice soothing the air like breeze. Cy caught a fish, whooped over it, then tossed it back in.

"I always wanted to go off to places," Tucker said while Cy baited his hook with Della's prize pâté. "I had a scrapbook when I was your age, filled it with pictures out of magazines. Places like Rome and Paris and Moscow. I'm thinking it was a shame I never worked up the energy to go see them for myself." He waited a moment. "You got yourself a wish, Cy? Something you thought about doing?"

"I wish I could go to college." He turned red, waiting for the laughter. When it didn't come, he let the rest out in a flood. "I like school. I'm good at it and all. Mr. Baker, that's my history teacher, he says I got a curious brain and good study habits."

"That so?"

"It's kind of embarrassing when he says it in front of the class and all. But it feels good, too. He even said how maybe I could apply for a scholarship to the state university, but Daddy said I had to quit as soon as the law allowed and work on the farm. He said they taught godlessness in those colleges, and that I wasn't . . ." He trailed off, remembering his father was gone.

In silence, Tucker yanked a fish out of the water. He held it there a moment, watching it flop and struggle against the inevitable. A boy could feel like that as well, he thought, bringing the catch in, gently removing the hook. He tossed it back in the pond with a splash. It wasn't often that a fish, or a young boy, was given a second chance. It wasn't often that a man was given the opportunity to offer that chance.

Cy was going to college, he decided. He'd damn well see to it.

"Mr. Tucker?" Cy felt the tears rising again and hated them. They made him feel like a whining girl.

"Yeah?"

"Do you figure I killed him?"

Tucker bit back a sharp denial. He took a careful breath, then pulled out a cigarette. "How'd you come up with that?"

"I didn't do like he told me. I didn't do it, and he ran off. He probably got crazy mad at me, and he went after Miss Waverly. Now he's dead. I didn't honor my father, and now he's dead."

Tucker struck a match, as if considering. "That may be the how and why of it, and it may not. But you've got to ask yourself one question. Do you think that particular commandment means you've got to honor your father by helping him kill an unarmed man?"

"No, sir, but—"

"You saved my life yesterday, Cy." He waited until the boy's gaze lifted to his. "That's a plain fact. If you'd done what he told you to do, maybe he'd be alive, or maybe he'd have gone off after Caroline just the same. But I'd be dead. There's no way around that one, is there?"

"No, sir, I guess not."

"Austin killed himself. There's no way around that either."

Cy wanted to believe that, was desperate to. He fought to keep his voice from breaking. "I'm not sorry he's dead. I'm not sorry. Now I'm going to hell and burn through all eternity because when the sheriff told me he was dead, I was glad."

Christ, Tucker thought as he dragged on the cigarette. This was getting touchy, and when it came to the realms of heaven and hell, he would make a poor teacher. But the boy needed something more than platitudes.

"I'm not much on religion myself. That was a big disappointment to my mama. Maybe there's a hell all right. Christ knows, there's plenty of people who deserve to do time there. But when I think about it, when I sit down and think real hard about it, I can't see people getting sent to hell for feelings they can't help. How you act, how you are with other people, what you make of yourself—all that counts for more, I think."

"But sinful thoughts—"

This time Tucker laughed, and tipping back his cap grinned at Cy. "Son, if you went to hell for thoughts, heaven would be a mighty lonely place to spend eternity." He sobered and brushed at the boy's hair. "I can't say why your father did the things he did. But he was wrong. Hurting you and your ma, those things weren't right, Cy, no matter how much he quoted scripture while he was at it. There's no sin in feeling glad that's behind you."

The raw lump in Cy's gut began to shrink. "My ma, she's not going to be glad."

"You can't take on her feelings. You've got your own. There's something I want to put to you, something I want you to think about."

"Yes sir."

"I know Della told you you could stay on here as long as you want."

Panic widened the boy's eyes. "I won't be any trouble, Mr. Tucker. I won't eat much, I promise, and I'll work hard. I can—"

"Hold on. Nobody's pushing you out." Wondering how best to phrase it, Tucker tamped out his cigarette. "I figure Vernon will take over the farm and see to your ma's needs. Ruthanne's nearly grown."

"She's saving up to leave." Cy bit his lip. "That's a secret."

"Nothing I like better than keeping a lady's secrets. Now, I'm thinking you could keep working for me, part-time, when school starts up again. Part of your pay could go to your ma to help her out. And I could add room and board."

Something swelled in his throat. He didn't even recognize it as hope. "You mean I could move into Sweetwater? For good?"

"Until there's somewhere else you'd rather go. If it's something you want, Cy, I'll do what I can to make it happen. Your ma would have to agree to it, and there'd probably be some kind of legal work to make me a kind of guardian over you. You'd have to want it, though."

Cy only stared, afraid to hope for so much. "I'd do anything you told me. I wouldn't cause you trouble."

"We'll look into it. I guess I'd better come up with some rules so you can see what you're getting into." To give Cy time to compose himself, he heaped more pâté on a cracker. If he'd done nothing else right this day, he'd taken the boy's mind off his misery. "No drinking till you're of age."

"No, sir."

"No wild parties unless you invite me."

A chuckle escaped Cy, and the sound had him blinking. "No, sir."

"No flirting with my woman." *Women,* he corrected himself silently. He'd meant women. Hadn't he? But he was thinking of Caroline.

Cy's color rose again, "No, sir."

"And I won't flirt with yours." He winked at the boy and grinned. "Got yourself a girl, do you, Cy?"

"No, sir. Not exactly. I just look sometimes, is all."

"You've got plenty of time to do more than look. Any girl in particular?"

Cy wet his lips. There was no way he could lie to Tucker. It wasn't fear, he realized. Not the way it had been with his father. It was love. "I, ah, well, I kind of look at LeeAnne Hardesty. She grew breasts last year. It sure does make a difference."

Tucker choked on the pâté. "By Christ, it does," he agreed. He tiptoed onto boggy ground. "You're just looking?"

"Well . . ." Face burning, Cy ducked his head. "Once in the lunch line she was behind me and somebody shoved her. Her breasts pushed right into my back. They sure were soft. And she put her arms around my waist a minute, just to get her balance back. And I . . ." He swallowed the shame. "I couldn't help it, Mr. Tucker. I just couldn't stop it no matter what."

Tucker had an image of Cy tossing LeeAnne Hardesty down on the tiles of the cafeteria and tearing in. "What was it that you couldn't stop?"

"Well, you know. It just happens sometimes, no matter how I try to stop it. It just gets . . . you know. The tool of Satan."

"The tool of Satan," Tucker repeated slowly. He would have laughed. In fact he was damn sure he'd have rolled on the ground and laughed fit to kill if Cy hadn't had that guilt-stricken look in his eyes.

Austin Hatinger strikes again, Tucker thought, and blew out a long breath.

"I never heard it called that." To hide the grin, Tucker spent a lot of time stroking his chin. "It seems to me since the good Lord put it between your legs, it has more to do with Him than the other one."

"Evil thoughts and wicked women make it hard."

"And thank God for it." Tucker poured more lemonade and wished it were bourbon. "Listen, son, there isn't a man alive who hasn't had his pecker stiffen up on him at an inopportune moment. It's natural." He took a slug and said a quick prayer. "You know, ah, about how babies get hatched and all that, don't you?"

"Yeah." Jim had told him all about it, and he had it from his dad. "She's got the egg and you've got the sperm. It's best if you're in love and all."

"Right." Tucker felt a wave of sweet relief. "It's better, too, if you wait till you're responsible." And wasn't he a fine one to talk? "Looking at LeeAnne and thinking about her breasts, and doing something about it, those are two different things."

"I guess I know." It was fascinating to Cy to say forbidden things right out loud and not get walloped. He edged in a little deeper. "But sometimes, especially at night . . . I even do all the states and capitals to keep my mind clear of it, but it don't always work. And it gets, you know. It feels like if I don't do something about it, I'll just explode." He shot Tucker a quick look. "Sometimes I do. It's evil, isn't it, to work on yourself that way?"

Tucker scratched his head. "Seems to me a man's got to take matters into his own hand—so to speak—now and again. I don't know that I'd recommend it as a habit, but when an itch just won't go away, it makes sense to scratch it."

"But don't things happen to you if you do?"

"You don't go blind or grow hair on your palms, if that's what you mean."

"You sure?"

This time Tucker had to grin. He lifted his hands, examined the palms with care. "Positive," he said, and was gratified when Cy grinned back.

♦ ♦ ♦ ♦

*B*URNS'S ROOM IN INNOCENCE was small and spartan. As accommodations went, it was merely adequate. He was pleased that Nancy Koons kept it spotless, though. And since he always left a few telltales, he was satisfied that no one came in without his knowledge or went through his things. Everything pertinent to the case was locked in his briefcase unless he was actively working.

He had a twin-size bed, a chest of drawers, and a chifforobe. It had taken him three days to convince Nancy Koons to find him a desk and a sturdy chair. The ceiling fan puffed at the hot air. This inadequate system had prompted Burns to procure an electric fan from Larssons's. Since he'd been fortunate enough to be given one of the two rooms with an adjoining bath, he concluded that he had everything necessary for his stay.

He hadn't expected the bonus.

Stretched beneath him on the iron bed was Josie Longstreet. Burns was still shuddering from their second bout. For the life of him, he wasn't sure how they'd gone from sharing a lemonade at the diner to bouncing on the squeaky mattress. But he wasn't complaining.

He hadn't had that kind of wild, ripping sex since . . . Actually, he supposed he'd never had that kind of sex. The women he dated were cool and composed in bed and out. Five seconds after Josie had dashed up the back stairs ahead of him, she'd been pawing at his clothes.

Over his head, Josie held up her newly painted nails. Scarlet Sin this time. She found it wonderfully appropriate. Experimentally, she raked her nails down his back, watching the red enamel flow over his white skin like blood.

"Honey," she said, "you just about wore me out. I knew there was a tiger inside that suit."

"You were fabulous." Burns knew women expected compliments at such times, but words nearly failed him. "Incredible."

"I've had my eye on you, Special Agent. Something about a man with a badge turns me on fierce." She thought of Burke and frowned at the ceiling. "You think I'm sexy?"

"I think—" He lifted his head. "You're the sexiest woman alive."

That made her smile and grant him a nibbling kiss. "And pretty, too?"

"No, not pretty," he said, too busy playing with her hair to see the flash in her eyes. "Gorgeous, like some wild Gypsy."

The flash died into pleasure. "You're just saying that because I'm stark naked and your pecker's twitching."

Normally, his sensibilities would have been offended, but she was quite right about the state of his tool of Satan. "I'm saying it because it's true. You're dazzling, Josie."

"I sure like the way you talk." She sighed as he began to nuzzle her breasts. Sweat and sex made her skin sticky, though the fan was aimed directly at the bed. Still, Josie had always figured the best way to beat the heat was to lie down naked. And if you were going to lie down naked, you might as well do something about it.

"Not all men know how to say what women like to hear. You take my first husband, Franklin? After we'd been married a month or two and the bloom had worn off, so to speak, he'd finish up, grunt, then start snoring. Lots of men are like that. They just take what they want, then pass on."

His response was muffled against her breast. She let him enjoy himself. "A woman's entitled to pretty words. 'Course, all women don't care about that. Some're just after the same thing some men are after. Appreciating pretty words is the difference between a tramp and a lady, I think."

"You're an incredible lady."

Her smile glowed. "And you're a real gentleman. Smart, too. I love hearing you talk about your cases." Lazily, she stroked his flanks. "But I guess you'll be going back north soon." She snuggled down to find his lips with hers. "It's an awful shame that you and I got together right before you have to leave."

"Actually, things do seem to be winding up."

"I knew it. The first time I saw you I knew you'd solve everything. I could just see how smart you were. I said to myself, now that he's here, we women'll be safe again." She danced her tongue over his. "You're a hero, Matthew."

"I'm just doing my job." He preened as she rolled over on top of him. "It's all been very standard, really."

"Catching a murderer?" She skimmed her lips over his chest. Though he was white as a fish, she thought he had a nice build. "Why, nobody had figured out anything before you came along."

"It's simply a matter of having the experience, the proper equipment."

"I just love your equipment," she purred, wrapping her fingers around him. "Tell me how you did it, Matthew. It just makes me shiver."

His breath started to catch as she guided those clever fingers over him. "First you have to understand the psychology of a serial killer. Their patterns, the stages. Statistics. Most murders are committed on impulse, and for a few standard reasons."

"Tell me." She pressed her lips to his belly. "It makes me so hot."

"Passion," he managed as a red haze coated his vision. "Greed, revenge. Those aren't the motives of the serial killer. For him it's control, power, the hunt. The kill itself isn't as important as the anticipation, the stalking."

"Yes." She licked gently along his inner thigh. She was doing some stalking of her own, and the anticipation was rising like a hot river in a summer flood. "Don't stop."

"He plans, feeds on the plan. He chooses, and he hunts. All the time he does, he may lead a perfectly normal life. Have a family, a career, friendships. But the need to kill drives him. After he destroys his victim, the need to kill begins to build again. And the desire for control, of course." His hand fisted in her hair as she took him into her mouth. "Taunting the authorities, even using them." Burns began to pant as she sucked him deep. "He may want to be caught, he may even suffer from guilt, but his hunger outweighs everything."

She slid sinuously up his body, straddling him. "So he kills again. Until you stop him."

"Yes."

"And you're going to stop him this time?"

"He's already been stopped."

She lifted her hands to her hair, combing it back, arching her breasts to him. "How?"

"Unless other evidence comes to the surface, I'll report this case closed with Austin Hatinger's death."

Josie shuddered as she lifted her hips and took him deep inside her. "You're a hero, Special Agent. My hero." She threw back her head and started the hard ride to paradise.

Chapter 21

A STORM WAS MOVING in. The evening was cooling as it approached, and for the first time in days a real breeze ruffled leaves and brought the sweet scent of rain to the air. Dusk came early as the sun hid behind rough pewter clouds. In the west, heat lightning popped and fizzled.

Even knowing the storm might be a nasty one, knocking down power lines and swelling riverbanks, the delta sighed with relief.

Darleen Fuller Talbot left her mother's in a foul temper. Happy had smiled and cuddled Scooter even as she'd raked Darleen to the bone over Billy T. Her father was no better, she thought as she slammed her car door shut. All he could do was shake his head and leave the room. Darleen had suffered through twenty minutes of listening to her mother ramble on about how Junior was a decent man who hadn't deserved to be betrayed in his own home.

Well, it was her home, too, and her signature on the mortage. She pouted, wiping away angry tears before she started the car. Nobody gave any thought to that. No, it was poor Junior this, and poor Junior that. Nobody cared that poor Junior was treating her worse than the dirt you brushed under the rug.

Was it any wonder she was beginning to miss Billy T. to distraction?

Her own husband wouldn't even sleep in the same bed with her anymore. Not that he'd done much *but* sleep in it, even before the trouble started. But now she was going to bed every night as dry and frustrated as an old maiden aunt.

She was going to fix that, all right. As the first fat drops of rain splattered the windshield, she set her chin. Happy would have recognized the look, and though it might have surprised Darleen, would have wholeheartedly approved.

Scooter was going to stay with his grandma overnight. And she was going to see to it that her husband did her duty by her.

If things didn't turn around soon, she might as well become one of those papist nuns and go live in a convent.

Going without was making her jumpy, Darleen thought, switching on the wipers as the rain began to batter her car. Junior had interrupted Billy T. before he'd come close to finishing her off. By her calculations, Darleen had been celibate for more than a week.

It wasn't healthy.

That's why she was so nervous and irritable, she was sure. For days she'd had the edgy feeling someone was watching her. It was more than the smug looks she'd been getting from some of the town biddies as the story made the rounds. It was more like someone was keeping a bead on her. And there were the phone calls, too. The calls when nobody was there after you picked up.

Probably Junior keeping tabs on her, she thought. He probably had one of his buddies watching the house, too, in case Billy T. came around.

As if Billy T. would speak to her now.

It didn't seem fair that she lost her boyfriend, her husband, and had to listen to her mother's lectures all because she'd wanted to have a little fun.

She skidded on the wet road, and slowed to a crawl.

She wasn't going to put up with it anymore. Crying hadn't worked, and she'd cried buckets. Keeping the house nice and putting a hot meal on the table every night hadn't done much good either. Junior just ate whatever she put in front of him and went off to play with Scooter.

Tonight he was going to play with his wife.

She knew just how to set the stage. There was that new nightgown she'd mail-ordered—for Billy T.'s benefit, but that didn't matter. She'd spent the best part of the afternoon in the Style Rite getting her hair washed and set. She'd even suffered through having Betty Pruett wax her eyebrows and the little fuzz over her top lip.

All that was left was to set the stage.

She had that bayberry-scented candle left over from Christmas, a Randy Travis album, and a bottle of cold duck. Junior got positively romantic after a couple of glasses of cold duck.

Once she got him back in bed, he'd forget all about Billy T. and his manly pride. She'd be his devoted wife. And if she ever took on a boyfriend again, she'd be a damn sight more careful.

She almost didn't hit the brakes in time. The curtain of rain obscured the road so that she didn't see the car sitting across it until it was nearly too late. Her tires slipped and skidded. She gave a quick squeal as she fishtailed sideways. When the bumpers barely kissed, she sat back, one hand over her speeding heart.

"Goddamn." She squinted through the windshield but could see no one, just the abandoned car stretched diagonally across the road. "Well, isn't this just fine and dandy." Shakily, she pushed open her door and stepped out into the storm. Instantly her hair was plastered over her eyes so that she had to scrape it back. "Twenty-two seventy-five shot to hell!" she shouted to the rain. "Chrissakes, how'm I supposed to get my husband back if I go home looking like a drowned cat?"

She thought that over, decided it might work to her advantage on the sympathy scale. But if she wanted Junior to fuss and pet because she'd got caught in the rain, she had to get home first. Hands on hips she kicked the tire of the car blocking the road.

"How the hell's anybody supposed to get around that?" The prospect of turning around and going back to her mother's was so daunting, she ignored the rain and walked around the car to find a solution.

She was looking through the window, hoping to see keys in the ignition, when she heard the sound behind her. Her heart leapt into her throat, then settled again when she recognized the familiar form coming through the rain.

"Thought this was your car," she shouted. "These roads are so wet, I nearly plowed right through. Junior'd have skinned me alive if I'd've wrecked this car."

"I'll save him the trouble."

Darleen never saw the tire iron that smashed over her head.

◆ ◆ ◆ ◆

THE POWER FLICKERED ON and off before finally wheezing out during a particularly robust clap of thunder. Caroline had prepared by setting emergency candles and oil lamps in every room.

She didn't mind the dark, or the storm. In fact, she relished them. She was hoping the phone lines would go as well so that she could stop having to answer the sympathetic and curious calls that had hounded her throughout the day. But if the power stayed off through the night, she didn't want to have to stumble blindly through the house, taking a chance on meeting Austin Hatinger's grinning ghost.

She watched the rain and the wind from the cover of the porch while Useless cowered inside, whimpering. It was a powerful show. With barely a tree to stop it, the wind roared across the flats and rattled shingles, jiggled windows, hooted through grass.

She didn't know whether this violent a rain was good or bad for the crops, though she was certain she'd be told all about it when she drove into town. For now, it was enough just to watch, to be awed, to know there was a dry, candlelit house behind her, waiting to offer sanctuary.

Shelter, she corrected herself, and smiled. What would the good doctor Palamo have to say about her use of the word sanctuary? A reflex reaction, she decided. She was no longer running or hiding. For the first time in her life she was just living.

Or trying to.

She'd certainly hidden from Tucker that morning. She'd accepted sex but turned away intimacy. Because she'd needed to prove she was alive, and had been afraid to feel.

Surprised by the chill, she rubbed her arms. It had been enough for both of them. He had wanted her, she had wanted him. It wasn't worth worrying about.

Closing her eyes, she took a deep gulp of air. There was a trace of ozone from the last spear of lightning. Exhilarating. The puppy yelped at the ensuing blast of thunder, and she laughed.

"All right, Useless, I'll save you."

She found him in the parlor with his nose peeking out from the skirt of the couch. Murmuring to him, she gathered him up and walked him like a baby while he shivered.

"It won't last long. Storms never do. They just come along to shake us up and make us appreciate the quiet times. How about some music, huh? I feel like music." She set him in a chair, then picked up her violin. "Passionate, I think." She ran the bow experimentally across the strings, pausing to tune by ear. "Passionate to match the mood."

She started with Tchaikovsky, flowed into a movement from Beethoven's Ninth, then tried out one of the tunes Jim had taught her before ending with her own rousing interpretation of "Lady Madonna."

Dusk had fallen into full dark when she stopped. The knock on the door had her jumping, but it sent Useless streaking out of the room, up the stairs, and under her bed.

"Maybe I should send him into combat training." After setting the violin aside, she walked out in the hall. Tucker stared back at her through the screen.

She found her competent hands suddenly restless and linked them together to keep them still. "It's a rough night to be out."

"I know."

"Aren't you going to come in?"

"Not yet."

She stepped closer. His hair was dripping. It reminded her how he'd looked after his shower that morning. "How long have you been out there?"

"I drove up right before you went from that longhair music into 'Salty Dog.' That was 'Salty Dog,' wasn't it?"

Her smile came and went quickly. "Jim taught me. We're exchanging techniques."

"I heard about that. Toby's real pleased. He's looking into getting the boy a second-hand fiddle."

"He's talented," she said, and felt foolish. Why were they discussing Jim with the screen door between them? "The, ah, power went out."

"I know. Come outside a minute, Caroline."

She hesitated. He seemed so serious, so deliberate. "Has anything happened?"

"Not that I've heard." He pulled open the screen. "Come outside."

"All right." She stepped through, nerves jumping. "I was wondering before if this rain is good or bad. For the crops, I mean."

'I didn't come by to talk about planting, or about music, if it comes to that." He dipped his hands in his pockets, and together they watched lightning stalk the sky. "I have to ask you about this morning."

"Why don't you let me get you a beer?" She stepped back, one hand reaching for the screen. "I picked some up the other day."

"Caroline." His eyes glowed against the dark, stopping her cold. "Why didn't you let me touch you?"

"I don't know what you mean." She pushed a nervous hand through her hair. "I did let you. We made love right in there on that couch."

"You let me have you, but you didn't let me touch you. There's a difference. A great big difference."

She stiffened. The regal look she sent him nearly made him smile. "If you've come out here to criticize my performance—"

"I'm not criticizing. I'm asking." He moved toward her, but didn't reach out. "But I think you just said it. It was a performance. Maybe you needed to act out something that told you you were alive. God knows you had cause to. I'm asking you if that's all you want. I've got more, and I need to give you more. If you'll take it."

"I don't know. Not just if I want to, but if I can."

"I can leave you alone if you need to think about it. Otherwise, you only have to ask me in." He lifted a hand to her cheek. "Just ask me in, Caroline."

Not just into the house, she realized. Into her, physically, emotionally. She closed her eyes for a moment. When she opened them again he was still standing, waiting. "I'm not a good bet."

A smile softened his lips. "Hell, sugar, neither am I."

She took a deep breath, then stepped aside to open the screen. "I'd like you to come in."

He let out the air he'd been holding. The moment he was over the threshold, he turned and swept her off her feet.

"Tucker . . ."

"It was good enough for Rhett Butler." He kissed her into silence before starting up the steps. He might not have had Ashley to worry about, but by God, tonight she wasn't going to think of Luis. Or anyone else.

"You're wet," she told him, then rested her head on his shoulder.

"I'll give you a chance to get me out of my clothes."

She laughed. How easy it was, she thought. If you let it be. "You're so good to me."

"I can be better." He stopped in the doorway to indulge in another long, lingering kiss.

"I can't wait to see how."

"This time you'll have to wait."

Shadows and candlelight danced over the walls. Heat trapped throughout the day settled into the room like an old friend, smugly overriding the wind that whipped the old lace curtains. There was the smell of candle wax, of lavender sachet, of the rain that dampened the screens and rapped fitfully against the tin roof.

With his mouth teasing hers, he laid her on the bed. His fingertips traced lightly over her face, followed by his lips, coaxing the tension away. Then there was only the sound of the rain, of her sigh, of the grumble of thunder as the storm moved east. Her arms rose up to welcome him.

He lingered there, mouth pressed to mouth, the scrape of teeth, the sultry mating of tongues, until she was sunk deep in the peace and pleasure he offered.

There was no choice now but to feel. He was subtly, slowly nudging her emotions to the surface. They were battering at her, making her pulse tremble, her muscles go limp, her heart stutter. A quick flash of panic had her turning her head away. He contented himself with the column of her throat. And his hands, as skillful as any musician's, began to move over her.

He soothed even as he enticed. He could feel the war between need and doubt being waged through her. He could see the same conflict in her face. Keeping his own desire at bay he patiently, even compassionately, seduced. Long, stirring kisses; lazy, languid caresses. As her body melted against his, as his name tumbled from her lips, he realized he wasn't blocking his desire at all. This was exactly what he wanted.

Their eyes met, held, as he undressed her. Naked. Vulnerable. They both understood the two words were interchangeable, and that this single act took what was happening beyond that frantic, half-dressed coupling on the couch.

With unsteady hands she pulled off his damp shirt, let her fingertips trail over his chest, down to his belly. She felt the warm glow of triumph when his muscles quivered under that hesitant touch. After one sharp breath she unsnapped his jeans, sitting up so that she could peel them over his hips and away.

Then they were kneeling in the center of the bed, the mattress groaning as it sagged, the heat pouring back as the wind died and the rain slowed to a patter. Her hands linked around his waist. His dived into her hair. Surprise, and a flicker of fear, flashed into her eyes as he dragged her head back. The look darkened to passion as he crushed her lips with his.

This was the beast that prowled beneath his veneer of lazy affability. She could all but feel it roar through him, snapping at its leash, threatening to devour both of them in one savage gulp.

Her fingers dug into his hips, then went limp as he molded her to him. He was telling her something, but his harsh whisper was lost in the beat of her blood.

Yes, this was what he wanted. Everything he wanted. To feel her go pliant with pleasure. To taste the hot need on her mouth. To hear that soft, helpless sound she made deep in her throat as she lost herself in him. To know that she thought of nothing and no one but him.

"Caroline." He steadied himself by pressing his lips to her shoulder, letting his teeth run over that scented curve. "There's something I need to do."

"Yes." She reached for him, but he caught her wrists.

"No, not that. Not yet." With his eyes on her, he pressed her back so that his body covered hers. He nipped at her lips, tormenting rather than satisfying. "What I need to do now . . ." He caught her chin lightly between his teeth then gently but purposefully captured her hands. "Is drive you crazy."

"Tucker—"

"If I let you run those hands over me just now, this'll all be over much too quickly." He slid down, circling her breasts with slow, openmouthed kisses. "There's an old southern tradition." He rolled his tongue lazily over her nipple and watched her eyes cloud over. "That if something's worth doing, it's worth taking your sweet time."

Her hands flexed desperately under his as he shifted to her other breast. "I can't."

"Sure you can, darlin'." He drew her into his mouth until she cried out, then gently released her. "I'm going to show you. After, if you decide you don't like it, we'll try again."

She writhed, her head turning restlessly on the pillow as the flood of sensation began to rise. With lips and teeth and tongue he savored. The air was too thick to breathe. She fought it into her lungs, hissed it out again through trembling lips. But even as her mind struggled against total submission, her body was betraying her. It reveled in the hot, primal glory of being taken. It shuddered and strained toward the wild release he held just out of reach.

Damp flesh slid over damp flesh as he glided down her, as much a prisoner as she. A moan dragged out of her, seductive on the sultry air. He rubbed his cheek on her belly, the anticipation of intimacy swimming in his head like fine wine. Once he would have said he knew all there was to know about pleasure. Once he would have denied that the pleasure was much different with one woman than with another.

But it was Caroline's scent teasing his senses, her sobbing breaths quickening his heartbeat, her soft, pale skin quivering under his lips.

And everything was different.

She arched and bucked when he slid his tongue over the sensitive crease of her thigh. He lingered inches away from the core of heat, torturing them both until he felt her body stiffen, freeze, then go lax.

The first ragged climax left her limp. She was floating now, weightless, no longer aware of the room or the heat, only of staggering relief. Her lips curved. Freed, her hands stroked down her own dazzled body, skimming over skin slicked with sweat until they brushed through his hair.

"I guess I liked it after all," she managed to say.

"We're not through yet." He cupped his hands under her hips, lifted them, and devoured her.

He shot her from contentment back into the storm so quickly the breath strangled in her throat. Her groping hands slid off his damp shoulders to grip desperately at the sheets. Wave after wave of titanic sensations battered her until there was only greed. His and her own. He was done with the gentle teasing, and the hands that had flowed over her like silk over velvet sought and demanded with a ruthlessness that was as arousing as it was unexpected.

There were dark pleasures here, dark secret pleasures that were born on hot summer nights. Together they thrashed over the bed, wallowing in them as freely as animals coupling in the grass.

He fought the tide back one last time, dragging her with him with hands that shook.

"Look at me." His chest heaved with each breath as he braced himself over her. "Caroline, look at me."

Her eyes fluttered open, the irises dark as midnight.

"This is more." He lowered his mouth to hers and the words were muffled against her lips as he plunged into her. "This is more."

◆ ◆ ◆

SPENT, SHE LAY DROWSING, content with Tucker's weight. There were a few aches beginning to make themselves known, but even that made her smile. She'd always considered herself an adequate lover—though at the end Luis had certainly disagreed—but she'd never felt quite so smug before.

She gave a little sigh and stretched. With a grunt, Tucker rolled to reverse positions. "Better?" he asked when she lay on top of him, her head on his chest.

"It was fine before." She smiled again. "Just fine." Another sigh and she opened heavy eyes. After a moment's bafflement she realized they were sprawled over the foot of the bed. "How did we get down here?"

"Dexterity. Give me a few minutes and we can work our way up to the other end."

"Hmm." She pressed her lips to his chest. "The rain stopped. Only it's even hotter than before."

"We might have had something to do with that."

Caroline roused herself to lift her head. "You know what I want?"

"Honey, once I get my energy back, I'll do my best to give you anything you want."

"I'll remember that. But . . ." She lowered her mouth to his. "What I want right now, what I really need right now, is ice cream." She grinned down at him. "Want some ice cream, Tucker?"

"I might be able to choke some down. Now that you mention it." He had an amusing little fantasy about licking Strawberry Surprise off some interesting parts of her anatomy. "You going to bring it up here?"

"That was my plan." After indulging in another kiss, she slid out of bed to root in the closet for her robe. "One scoop or two?"

His teeth flashed as she crossed the robe over her breasts. "I'm a two-scoop man myself. Want some help?"

"I think I can manage."

"Good." He tucked his hands behind his head and closed his eyes. Caroline walked out, certain he'd take advantage of the lull with a nap.

In the kitchen she scooped up ice cream by lamplight. It occurred to her that this was a moment that would cling in her memory. The sultry kitchen, the smell of rain and lamp oil, the strong, healthy afterglow of loving. Spooning up ice cream to be eaten in bed.

She was humming to herself as she carried the bowls back down the hall. Even the shrill interruption of the phone couldn't dampen her mood. She set down one bowl and, cocking the receiver between her shoulder and ear, dug into the other with her spoon.

"Hello."

"Caroline. Thank goodness."

The spoon stopped on its way to her lips. Caroline dropped it back in the bowl and put the bowl on the table. Apparently there was one thing that could dampen her mood. Her mother's voice.

"Hello, Mother."

"I've been trying to reach you for over an hour. They had trouble with the lines. Which is no surprise, considering the kind of service down there."

"We had a storm. How are you? And Dad?"

"We're both fine. Your father's on a quick trip to New York, but I had several engagements and couldn't accompany him."

Georgia Waverly spoke quickly, without a trace of the delta she'd worked so hard to rid from her voice and her heart.

"It's you I'm worried about," she continued, and Caroline could imagine her at her rosewood desk in the immaculate and tasteful sitting room, checking off her daughter's name on one of her innumerable lists.

Order flowers. Attend charity luncheon. Worry about Caroline.

The image brought a nasty tug of guilt.

"There's nothing to worry about."

"Nothing! I was attending a dinner party at the Fulbrights this evening, and I had to hear from Carter that my daughter was attacked!"

"I wasn't hurt," Caroline said quickly.

"I know that," Georgia snapped back, testy at the interruption. "Carter explained everything, which is more than you bothered to do. I told you all along you had no business going down there, but you refused to listen. Now I'm told—and by the way, I don't appreciate hearing about all of this over my soup!—that you're embroiled in some kind of murder investigation."

"I'm sorry." Caroline closed her eyes. Apologies became the bill of fare when she dealt with her mother.. "It all happened so fast. And it's over."

A movement on the stairs had her glancing up. She saw Tucker and wearily turned away.

"Carter made it quite clear that's simply not true. You know he owns the local NBC affiliate here in Philadelphia. He said the story was already running, and that several news crews were flying down to cover it at the scene. Naturally, when your name was leaked, it became hot news."

"Oh, Christ."

"I beg your pardon?"

"Nothing." She passed a hand through her hair. Be reasonable, she warned herself. Somehow she had to be reasonable. "I am sorry you heard about this from someone else. And I know the publicity will annoy you. I can't help the press, Mother, any more than I can help the reason for it. I'm sorry if this upsets you."

"Of course it upsets me. Wasn't it bad enough that we had to play down the scandal of you being hospitalized, dropping your summer schedule, your public estrangement from Luis?"

"Yes," Caroline said dryly. "That must have been very difficult for you. It was inconsiderate of me to collapse that way."

"Don't use that tone with me. If you hadn't let yourself become overwrought about a minor disagreement with Luis, none of it would have happened. And now this business of going down there, burying yourself in that place—"

"I'm not buried."

"Wasting your talent." Georgia plowed over Caroline's protest like a blade through soft dirt. "Humiliating yourself and your family. Do you think I've had a single restful night knowing you're there, alone, unprotected?"

Caroline began to rub at the ache in her temple. "I've been alone for years."

Georgia never heard the statement, or the wistfulness behind it.

"And now—well, you might have been raped or murdered."

"Oh, yes, and that would have been dreadful publicity."

There was a brief pause. "That was uncalled for, Caroline."

"Yes, it was." She pressed her thumb and forefinger against her eyes and repeated the usual litany. "I'm sorry. Perhaps I'm still shaken by what happened."

Are you going to ask what happened, Mother? Are you going to ask how I feel, what I need, or only how I behaved?

"I understand. And I expect you to understand my feelings as well. I insist that you come home immediately."

"I am home."

"Don't be ridiculous. You don't belong there any more than I did. I raised you better than that, Caroline. Your father and I gave you every advantage. I won't see you throw it all away over some sort of pique."

"Pique? Well, that's an interesting way of putting it, Mother. I can only say I'm sorry I can't do what you want. Or be what you want."

"I don't know how this strain of stubbornness developed, but it's very unattractive. No doubt Luis found it equally so, but he's more tolerant than I. He's terribly concerned."

"He's . . . are you telling me you called him? That you went against my express wishes and called him?"

"A child's wishes aren't always the same as that child's best interests. In any case, I wanted to speak to him about your White House performance in September."

Caroline pressed a hand to her stomach where the knot was tightening. "I stopped being a child the first time you pushed me out onstage. And I don't need his opinion on my performance."

"I'm not surprised by your attitude. I've come to expect this kind of ingratitude." Georgia's voice tightened. Caroline could picture her, drumming her carefully manicured nails on the polished surface of the desk. "I can only hope that when Luis contacts you you'll display better manners. You and I are both well aware that he was the best thing that could have happened to you. He understood your artistic temperament."

"He understood my pitiful naïveté. I suppose it makes no difference to you that I found him boffing the flutist in his dressing room?"

"Your language is as crude as your surroundings."

"It can get cruder."

"I've had enough of this nonsense. I insist you come home. We have no more than a matter of weeks, as it is, to prepare for your appearance at the White House. And of course you gave no thought at all to your dress. I've had to find the time to consult with your designer. Now this new publicity—it's very detrimental."

So's a knife through the heart, Caroline thought. "It isn't necessary for you to take on any work," she said carefully. "I've already spoken to Frances and finalized the plans. I'll be flying into D.C. for the performance, and flying out again the next day. As for my costume, my wardrobe is more than adequate already."

"Have you lost your senses? This is one of the most important steps of your career. I've already started arranging interviews, photo sessions—"

"Then you'll have to unarrange," Caroline said briefly. "And let me assure you, Mother, that I'm alive and well. The man who attacked me is dead. I killed him myself, so I should know."

"Caroline—"

"Please give Dad my love. Good night." Delicately, she set the receiver back on the hook. She waited a full minute, wanting to be sure she could speak without screaming. "The ice cream's melted."

Picking up the bowls, she walked back into the kitchen to dump them in the sink.

Chapter 22

$\mathcal{I}$T SEEMED TO BE his day for soothing feelings and easing guilt. Tucker wondered how a man could get through most of his life riding just above the surface of troubled waters, then find himself neck-deep in the swirl.

Caroline's emotions still sizzled in the air. It was as if someone had tossed a live wire into those churning waters, where it would snap and spark.

He wished he had a cigarette, but the pack was upstairs, probably drenched by his wet shirt.

He looked up those shadowy stairs—not without longing for the peace and solitude of the bedroom—then back toward the kitchen, where the lamplight flickered and tension brewed.

When he went into the kitchen, she was standing at the sink, looking out the window much as she had the morning after Burns's visit. Only this time she was facing the dark.

Tucker didn't want her to face it alone. He walked up behind her, felt a wave of frustration when her shoulders stiffened at his touch.

"You know, my usual routine on finding myself with a broody woman would be to make some joke and talk her back into bed. If that didn't work, I'd find the quickest way to the door." Despite her resistance, he began to knead her rigid shoulders. "The usual doesn't seem to have much to do with you."

"I wouldn't mind a joke right now."

He laid his brow on the back of her head. Wasn't it a damn shame he couldn't think of one, he mused, or of anything except what was hurting her. "Talk to me, Caroline."

With a restless movement she switched on the tap to wash the sink clear. "There's nothing to say."

As he lifted his head, he could see the ghost of their reflection in the black window glass. He knew she could see it, too, but he wondered if she knew how fragile it was, how easily wiped away.

"When you walked downstairs a few minutes ago, I could still feel the way you'd been, lying there with me. All soft and easy. Now you're all tied up in knots. I don't like seeing you this way."

"It's nothing to do with you."

The speed with which he whirled her around surprised them both, as did the barely restrained violence in his voice. "You want to use me for sex and leave out everything else, then make it plain right now. If what went on between us upstairs was just a tussle on hot sheets for you, then say so and we'll play this your way. But it was more for me." He gave her a quick shake, as if to rattle the wall she'd thrown up between them. "Dammit, it's never been like that before."

"Don't pressure me." Eyes blazing, she shoved against his chest. "My whole life I've had to tolerate other people pressuring me. I'm done with that."

"You're not done with me. If you think you can take a few swipes and send me out the door, you're wrong. I'm sticking." To prove his point, he pressed his lips to hers in a hard, possessive kiss. "We're both going to start to get used to it."

"I don't have to get used to anything. I can say yes, or I can say no, or I can—" She broke off, squeezing her eyes shut. "Oh, why am I fighting with you? It's not you." After a deep breath she slipped away from him. "It's not you, Tucker. It's me. Shouting at you isn't going to make it go away."

"I don't mind you shouting—much—if it makes you feel better."

She smiled, rubbing absently at her temple. "I think one of Dr. Palamo's miracle pills would do a better job of it."

"Let's try something else." Catching her hands, he drew her to a chair. "You sit here while I pour us a couple of glasses of that wine I brought you a while back. Then you tell me why that phone call got you all het up."

"Het up." She sat, closing her eyes again. "That expression covers a lot of ground, doesn't it? My mother would say overwrought, but I like het up." When she opened her eyes there was the faintest hint of amusement in them. "I've been het up quite a bit over the last months. That was my mother on the phone."

"I got the drift of that." He drew the cork on the wine. "And that she was—overwrought—about what happened yesterday."

"Yes indeed. Particularly since it was a topic of conversation at a dinner party she attended. Gossip's a habit of Yankees, too—though my mother's crowd would call it socializing. But she was most particularly upset since the press has picked up the scent, and I have an important engagement pending. She's afraid the President and the Soviet Premier might not want to hear Mozart's Violin Concerto Number Five played by a woman who so recently shot someone's face off." She accepted the glass Tucker held out and offered a quick toast. "Georgia Waverly's daughter Caroline isn't supposed to attract unsavory publicity. What would the Women's League think?"

"Could be she was scared for you."

"Could be. Oh, to give her her due, she wouldn't want anything to happen to me. She does love me, in her way. It's just that her way is so difficult to live up to." She sipped her wine, and it was cold and tart and bracing. "She's always wanted the best for me—her idea of the best. I've spent my entire life trying to give her that. Then I had to take a hard look and admit that I couldn't give her that anymore."

"People get comfortable with the way things are." He sat beside her, with the oil lamp flickering on the table between them. "It might take her a while longer to accept that you've changed the rules."

"Or she might never accept it. That's something else I have to understand." Cradling the glass in both hands, Caroline looked around the room. The old refrigerator thudded, then began its whining hum. Rain was dripping musically from the gutter.

Worn linoleum and faded curtains, she thought. The lamplight was kind to the room, as it would have been to a tired woman. Caroline found that incredibly comforting.

"I love this place," she murmured. "Despite everything that's happened, I feel right here. And I need . . ."

"What?"

"I need to belong somewhere. I need the simplicity, the continuity."

"That doesn't sound like something you should apologize for."

So he'd heard it, she thought with a grim little smile. It was still there, that habitual tone of apology whenever she took something for herself.

"No, it's not. I'm working on that. You see, she'd never understand what I'm saying to you, what I'm feeling. And she certainly can't understand what I need."

"Then I guess it comes down to pleasing her, or pleasing yourself."

"I've come to that conclusion myself. But it's difficult, when pleasing myself alienates her so completely. She grew up in this house, Tucker. She's ashamed of that. She's ashamed that her father chopped cotton for a living and that her mother canned jellies. Ashamed of where she came from, and of the two people who gave her life and did the best they could to make that life a good one."

"That's something for her to deal with, not you."

"But it's because of that shame that I'm here at all. It connects us. I guess that's what families do, and you don't really have any choice about your link in the chain."

"Maybe not, but you can choose what comes after you."

"And what comes after is still bound with what came before. She never gave me a chance to know my grandparents. They did without a lot of things so that she could go to college in Philadelphia. I didn't hear that from my mother," she added, and there was bitter regret in her voice. "I heard it from Happy Fuller. My grandmother took in laundry, sewing, did what the ladies call fancy work to sell. All to scrape together pennies for tuition. They didn't have to pay it long, which was a blessing, I suppose. She met my father during the first semester. He's often told me how he'd tried to weasel out of the blind date his roommate had hooked him into. And how, the moment he set eyes on my mother, he fell in love. Do you ever picture your parents that way? On their first date, falling in love?"

"My father set his sights on Mama when she was barely twelve years old. She made him wait six years."

"Mine moved quicker. They were married before my mother finished her first year of college. The Waverlys were an old, established family in Philadelphia. My father was already destined for corporate law. I know it must have been difficult for her, trying to fit into that niche of society. But for as long as I can remember, she's been more of a snob than any of the Waverlys. A house in the best part of town, clothes from the most exclusive designers, the proper vacations at the proper resorts in the proper season."

"Most people tend to overcompensate when they've got something to prove."

"Oh, she had a lot to prove. And in short order, she produced a child to help her prove it. I had a nanny to deal with the messier aspects of child rearing, but Mother took care of decorum, behavior, attitudes. She used to send for me, and I'd go into her sitting room. It always smelled of hothouse roses and Chanel. She would instruct me, patiently, on what was expected of a Waverly."

Tucker reached out to touch her hair. "What was expected of a Waverly?"

"Perfection."

"That's a tough one. Being a Longstreet, my daddy just expected me to 'be a man.' 'Course, that was in big, tall capital letters, and his ideas and mine veered apart after a while. He didn't use the parlor either," Tucker remembered. "The woodshed was his style."

"Oh, Mother never raised a hand to me. She didn't have to. It was her idea that I take up the violin. She thought it was classy. I should be grateful for that," Caroline said with a sigh. "But then, it wasn't enough that I play well. I had to be the best. Fortunately for me, I had talent. A prodigy, they called me. By the time I was ten that word made me cringe. She picked out my music, my instructors, my recital clothes—the same way she picked out my friends. Then I began to tour, just sporadically at first, because of my age. There were tutors, and the touring increased. By the time I was sixteen, the path had been set. For nearly twelve more years I kept to it."

"Did you want to?"

The fact that he would ask made her smile. No one else ever had. "Whenever I began to think I had a choice, she would be there. In person, by phone, in a letter. It was almost as if she could sense that little seed of rebellion beginning to take root. She'd just nip it off. I'd let her."

"Why?"

"I wanted her to love me." Her eyes filled, but she blinked the tears away. "And I was afraid she didn't. I was sure she wouldn't if I wasn't perfect." Ashamed, she brushed at a tear that had crept through her defenses. "That sounds pathetic."

"No." He wiped the tear away himself. "It only sounds sad, for your mother."

She took a shaky breath, like a swimmer struggling toward shore. "About three years ago I met Luis in London. He was the most brilliant maestro I've ever worked with. He was young, thirty-two when I met him, and he'd built a flashy reputation in Europe. He conducted an orchestra the way a matador dominates a bull ring. Decisive, arrogant, sexual. He was physically stunning, and magnetic."

"I get the picture."

She laughed a little. "I was twenty-five. I'd never been with a man."

Tucker had started to drink, but set the glass down. "You'd never . . ."

"Rolled in the hay?" The stunned expression on his face had her lips quirking. But the smile didn't last. "No. When I was growing up, my mother kept me on a very short leash, and I didn't have the nerve to strain against it very often. When I required an escort to some affair, she chose him. You could say that her taste and mine didn't mesh. I wasn't particularly interested in the men she found suitable."

"That's why you like me." He leaned over to give her a kiss. "I'd turn her hair white."

"Actually, I never thought about it. Another first for me." Pleased with the idea, she tapped her wineglass against his. "Later, when I began to tour by myself, my schedule was rugged, and I was . . . the term's 'repressed.'"

He thought about the woman who'd just tumbled over the bed with him. "Uh-huh."

She hadn't realized sarcasm could be soothing. "My sexuality was tied up in my music. I certainly didn't believe I was the kind of woman who'd just fall into bed with the first attractive man who crooked his finger my way." She reached for the wine bottle. "Within thirty-six hours of my first rehearsal with Luis, he proved me wrong."

She shrugged and drank. "He overwhelmed me. Flowers, soulful looks, desperate promises of undying love. He couldn't exist without me. His life had been meaningless before I'd come into it. He gave me the works. I should add that my mother adored him. He came from Spanish aristocracy."

"Suitable," Tucker said.

"Oh, eminently. When I had to leave London for Paris, he phoned me every day, sent small, charming gifts, gorgeous flowers. He rushed to Berlin to join me for a weekend. It continued that way for more than a year, and if I heard rumors that he was romancing some actress or cuddling with a socialite, I ignored it. I thought it was vicious gossip. Oh, maybe I suspected something, but if I so much as hinted to him that I'd heard something, he flew into a rage at my unwarranted jealousy, my possessiveness, my lack of self-esteem. And my work kept me occupied. I'd just signed a contract for a brutal six-month tour."

She lapsed into silence, thinking back. The airports, hotels, rehearsals, performances. The flu she'd picked up in Sydney and hadn't shaken off until Tokyo. The strained conversations with Luis. The promises, the disappointments. And the news clipping someone had left on her dressing room table. With the picture of Luis embracing a gorgeous French actress.

"There's no point in going into every miserable detail, but the tour was relentless, my relationship with Luis began to unravel, and my confidence—my personal confidence—hit the skids. Luis and I ended things with an ugly scene full of accusations and tears. His accusations, my tears. At that point in my life I hadn't learned to fight well."

Tucker laid a hand over hers. "Then you learned fast."

"Once I make up my mind, I'm a quick study. Too bad it took me nearly twenty-eight years to make up my mind. When Luis and I parted ways, I wanted to take some time off, but I'd already been committed to all these guest appearances and a special for cable TV. My health . . ." It was difficult to admit it, even now. No matter how illogical it was, she was still embarrassed by the illness. "Well, it deteriorated. And I—"

"Wait. What do you mean deteriorated?"

Uncomfortable, she shifted and began to toy with the stem of her glass. "Headaches. I was used to having headaches, but they became more chronic and severe. I lost some weight. My appetite suffered because nothing seemed to settle well. Insomnia, and the resulting fatigue."

"Why didn't you take care of yourself?"

"I thought I was just being indulgent. Temperamental. And I had responsibilities. People were depending on me to perform, and to perform well. I couldn't just—" She cut herself off with a short laugh. "Excuses, as the wise Dr. Palamo would say. Truth—I was hiding out. Using my work to escape. The repression wasn't just sexual. I'd been taught to behave 'properly.' To present a certain image and to live up to my potential. And, as my mother would say, feeling unwell is no reason for a lady to act unwell. It was easier to ignore the symptoms than to face them. When I was taping the TV special in New York, my mother came up. Escorted by Luis. I was so angry, so hurt, I walked off the set." She smiled a little, then the smile became a laugh. "I'd never done a thing like that in my life. Beneath the anger and hurt was this little nugget of triumph. I had taken control. I'd acted on impulse, on pure emotion, and the world hadn't come to a screeching halt. It was a very heady five minutes."

She couldn't sit any longer, simply couldn't, and pushed away from the table to roam the room.

"That was how long it took her to swirl into my dressing room and read me her version of the riot act. I was behaving like a spoiled child, an insufferable artist, a prima donna. I tried to tell her that I felt betrayed that she'd brought him along, but she just ran right over me—I was rude, foolish, ungrateful. . . . Luis was ready to forgive me for being willful and overly sensitive and mindlessly jealous, and here I was turning up my nose. Of course, I apologized."

"For what?"

"For whatever she wanted me to apologize for," Caroline said with a wave of her hand. "After all, she wanted only the best for me. She'd seen that I had the best. She'd worked and sacrificed so that I could have a brilliant career."

"I guess your talent didn't count."

Caroline let out a deep breath, trying to expel some of the bitterness along with the air. "She can't help it, Tucker. I'm still working on accepting that, and I'm almost there. There was a time *I* couldn't help it either. Luis came to my hotel suite that evening. He was charming, sweet, full of regrets and explanations. It had been the strain of being without me for so long—not that that was an excuse for his unfaithfulness, he assured me. But he'd been so lonely, so vulnerable, and my doubts and questions had only added to the strain. The other women, they had only been substitutes for me."

She snatched her glass off the table. "Can you imagine a woman with a single working brain cell falling for that?"

Tucker took a chance and smiled at her. "Yeah."

She stopped, stared at him, then began to laugh. "Of course you would. And, of course I did. He was still the only man who'd ever made love to me. Maybe if I'd had a few flings myself, I wouldn't have been so ready to fall back into the pattern. Maybe if I'd had the same confidence in myself as a woman that I had as a musician, I'd have shown him the door. But I agreed to put all the mistakes behind us, to start fresh. We even talked about marriage. Oh, in a very distant, diluted sort of way. When the time was right, he would say. When things fell into place. And because he asked me, I committed to another tour."

A little surprised, she looked down at her wine. "I'm getting drunk."

"That's all right, I'll drive. Tell me the rest."

She leaned back against the counter. "Luis would be the conductor, I the featured artist. It would be grueling, of course, but we'd be together. And wasn't that the important thing? Dr. Palamo—I had just started to see him—advised against it. What I needed was rest and quiet. I had this nasty little ulcer, you see. And the headaches, insomnia, fatigue. It was all stress, and he made it quite clear that going right back on the road would only make matters worse. I didn't listen."

"He should have tossed you into a hospital and chained you to a bed."

"He'd like you." Amused, she sipped more wine. "My mother threw a party the night before we left. She was in her element and had a grand time, hinting that it was really an engagement party. Luis responded to that with a lot of winking and hearty laughter. And off we went. As I said, Luis is a brilliant conductor, demanding, moody, but absolutely brilliant. We started in Europe, triumphant. After the first week he moved into his own suite—my insomnia made it difficult for him to get much rest."

"Slimy bastard."

"Not slimy," Caroline corrected him meticulously. "Slick. Very slick. The rest I'll go along with. On a professional level he was a tremendous asset to me. He pushed me musically. He said I was the finest artist he'd ever worked with, but I could be better. He would mold me, sculpt me."

"Why didn't he buy himself some Play-Doh?"

She chuckled. "I wish I'd asked. To give him his due, he never once stinted on his dedication to improving my performance. He did start to slide when it came to treating me like a woman. I started to feel like an instrument, something he would tune and polish and restring. I was so tired, and sick, and unsure. It annoyed the hell out of him when I'd turn up for rehearsal looking exhausted and frail. It annoyed me, too. It annoyed me to see those pitying glances from the other musicians, the road crew.

"I performed well, really well. Most of the tour is just a haze of theaters and hotel rooms, but I know I performed as well as I ever had, perhaps better than I ever will again. I picked up some sort of infection along the way and lived on antibiotics and fruit juice and music. We stopped sleeping together completely. He said I was simply not giving him my best. And he was right. Then he assured me that when the tour was over, we'd go away. So I lived on that. The end of the tour, the two of us lying on some warm beach together.

"But I didn't make it to the end of the tour. We were in Toronto, three-quarters done. I was awfully sick, and I was afraid I wouldn't get through the night's performance. I'd fainted in my dressing room. It scared me to wake up and find myself lying on the floor."

"Jesus Christ, Caroline." He started to get up, but she shook her head.

"It sounds worse than it was. I wasn't an invalid, I was just so tired. And I had one of those vicious headaches that make you want to curl up in a ball and cry. I kept thinking it was only one performance, only one, and if I went to him, if I explained, he'd understand. So I went to him, but he was also lying on his dressing room floor. Only he was lying on top of the flutist. They never even saw me," she said half to herself, then shrugged. "Just as well. I wasn't strong enough to face a confrontation. Anyway, I went on that night. A stellar performance. Three encores, standing ovations, six curtain calls. There might have been more, but when the curtain came down the last time, so did I. The next thing I remember, I was waking up in the hospital."

"Someone should have put him in the hospital."

"It wasn't him. He was just one more symptom. It was me. Me and my pitiful need to do what was expected of me. Luis hadn't made me sick. I had done it. Diagnosis—exhaustion." With a restless movement of her shoulders she walked back to the table to pour more wine, carefully shak-

ing out the last drops. "I found that humiliating. Somehow it wouldn't
have been as bad if I'd had a tumor or some rare exotic disease. They ran
scads of tests, poked and prodded and scanned, but it all came down to
plain old exhaustion complicated by stress. Dr. Palamo flew up to treat me
himself. No 'I-told-you-so's' from him. Just competent, compassionate
care. He actually booted Luis out of the room once."

Tucker lifted his glass. "Here's to Dr. Palamo."

"He was good to me, good for me. If I needed to cry, he just let me
cry. And when I needed to talk, he listened. He isn't a psychiatrist, and
though he recommended one, I felt so comfortable talking just to him.
When he felt the time was right, he had me transferred to a hospital in
Philadelphia. It was really more like what they used to call a rest home. My
mother told everyone I was recuperating at a villa on the Riviera. So much
more sophisticated."

"Caroline, I have to tell you, I don't think I like your mother."

"That's all right, she wouldn't like you either. She did her duty,
though. She came to see me three times a week. My father would call every
night, even if he'd been to visit. The tour went on without me, and the
press played up the collapse, and the fact that Luis was now snuggled up
tight with the flutist. He did send flowers, along with romantic little
notes. He didn't have any idea I'd seen him with her.

"It took about three months before I was well enough to go home. I
guess I was still a little wobbly, but I felt stronger than I ever had in my
life. I began to understand that I'd allowed myself to be treated like a victim. That I'd permitted the exploitation of what should have been cher-
ished as a gift. My talent was mine, my life was mine. My feelings were
mine. God, I can't tell you what an epiphany that was. When the lawyers
contacted me about my grandmother, I knew what I wanted to do. What
I was going to do.

"When I told my mother, she was livid. I didn't just stand up to her,
Tucker, which was really all I'd hoped for. I stood in that damn, prissy sitting room of hers and I shouted, I raged, I demanded. Naturally, I apologized. Old habits die hard, but I stuck with what I needed for myself. And
I headed south."

"To Innocence."

"By way of Baltimore. I knew Luis was there, doing some guest-
conducting. I called ahead, so he'd be expecting me. Oh, he was thrilled,
delighted. When I got to his suite, he had an intimate dinner set up. I
threw a glass of champagne at him, then I really cut loose. It felt wonderful. He was incensed enough to follow me out into the hall when I left.
The man in the room across the hall—I never did get his name—came

out and saw Luis trying to drag me back into the room. He decked him."
With her eyes half closed, she pantomimed a right jab. "One shot to that
perfectly chiseled jaw, and Luis was down for the count."

"Buy that man a drink."

"That would have been proper, I suppose, but I was still revving on
instinct. I did something else I'd never done in my life. I grabbed him—a
complete stranger—and kissed him full on the lips. Then I walked away."

"And how did you feel?"

"Free." With a sigh she sat again. There was no trace of the headache,
she realized. Her stomach wasn't knotted, her muscles weren't tense. "I still
have moments, like with that phone call, when I lose that feeling. You don't
dump all your baggage at once. But I know I'm never going back to the
way I was."

"Good." He lifted her hand to kiss her knuckles. "I like the way you
are now."

"So do I, mostly." Her glass had sweated a ring on the table. Caroline
traced patterns in the moisture. "I may never heal the rift with my mother,
and that's hard. But I've found something here."

"Peace and quiet?" he said, and made her smile.

"Right. There's nothing like a few murders to calm things down.
Roots," she said, glancing up. "I know that sounds silly since I spent only
a few days here as a child. But shallow roots are better than none."

"They aren't shallow. Things grow fast and deep in the delta. Even
when people leave, they can't pull those roots out."

"My mother did."

"No, she only sprouted them in you. Caroline." He said her name
softly and reached out to frame her face in his hands. "I hate what you
went through. No, look at me," he insisted when she dropped her gaze.
"Part of you still wants to be ashamed of it. And you don't want me or anybody feeling sorry for you. But I've never made a habit of repressing my
feelings, so you'll have to take them as they come. I don't like thinking
about you being hurt or sick or unhappy, but if all those things brought
you here—right here where we're sitting—I can't be too sorry."

Here, right here, she thought, and smiled. "Neither can I."

She looked so fragile. Those fine bones, that pale skin. Fragile, until
you saw what was in her eyes. There were depths there, he realized,
strengths she hadn't even begun to tap. And he very much wanted to be
around while she continued her self-discovery.

"There are some things I want to tell you. I'm not sure how."

She brought her hands to his wrists. "Maybe, when I'm feeling more
settled, I'd like to hear them. Right now I think it might be better to let
things stay as they are."

He'd always been patient, he reminded himself. But it was hard to be patient when you felt as though you were standing on a narrow ledge with the ground crumbling from under your feet. "All right." He leaned forward to touch his lips to hers. "Let me stay with you tonight."

Her lips curved under his. "I thought you'd never ask." She rose, taking his hands in hers. "Didn't you mention that if I didn't like it your way, we'd try again?"

"You didn't like it?"

"Well . . . I'm not quite sure. Maybe if you showed me again, I'd be able to form a more definite opinion."

"Seems fair." He eyed the kitchen table and grinned. "Why don't we start right here?" He unknotted the belt of her robe. "And we can work our way—shit."

The phone rang, and Caroline dropped her head on his shoulder. "I'd say don't answer it, but she'll just keep calling."

"I'll answer it."

"No, I—"

He caught her hands before she could tie her robe again. "Let me answer it. If I can't charm her into cutting loose for the night, you can take over."

She hesitated, then decided there was some sense in the idea. "Why not?"

He gave her a brief kiss. "Clear the table," he called over his shoulder, and made her laugh.

"Grandma," Caroline murmured as she picked up the rooster trivet, "I hope you won't be shocked." She took the empty glasses and bottle to the sink and decided her grandmother might have liked the idea of love in her kitchen.

"That was quick," she said when she heard Tucker come back in. "I've never known her to give up so easily. What did you . . ." The words died as she turned and saw his face. "What is it? What's happened?"

"It wasn't your mother, it was Burke." He walked to her, putting his arms around her as much to brace himself as Caroline. "Darleen Talbot's missing." He stared at their reflections again, in the shadowed window. Through a glass darkly, he thought, and shut his eyes. "We'll start the search at first light."

Chapter 23

"I WISH YOU'D TRY to get some more sleep." Tucker stood by, frustrated, while Caroline used a woman's tools to disguise the results of a long, restless night.

"I couldn't." She dabbed more concealer under her eyes and blended. "I'd just sit around and wait for the phone to ring."

"Go down to Sweetwater." He stood behind her, watching her in the tiny bathroom mirror. Despite the circumstances, he felt an odd and powerful sense of intimacy at sharing this private space, being a witness to this ageless female ritual. "Take a nap in my hammock."

"Tucker, don't worry about me. It's Darleen we all should be concerned about. And the Fullers—Junior. That little baby. God." Struggling to hold on, she stabbed the mascara brush in and out of the tube. "How could this happen?"

"We're not sure anything happened yet. She might have just run off somewhere. Billy T. said he hadn't seen her, but after Junior walloped him, he'd be apt to lie if he had."

"Then why did she leave her car on the side of the road?"

They'd been over this again and again. "Maybe she was going to meet somebody. That stretch is pretty lonely. She could have left her car and gone off with somebody else just to give Junior a bad night or two."

"I hope you're right." She dragged a comb through her hair, then turned. "I hope to God you're right, because if you're not, it might be like the others. And if it is, that would mean that—"

"Don't take it any further until it has to go there." Gently, he curled his fingers around her forearms. "Day to day, remember?"

"I'm trying." She leaned against him a moment. The tiny room was still steamy from their shower. Outside the single high window, first light was blooming. "If my mother's right, the press should be here before the day's over. I can deal with that." On a long breath she pulled back. "I can. But I feel I have to go to the Fullers to offer Happy some sort of support. I'm not sure I can deal with that."

"There'll be plenty of others there for her. You don't have to go."

"I do. I can be an outsider, or I can belong. It comes down to how you treat others, doesn't it?"

Hadn't he said something very similar to Cy just the day before? It was hard to argue with yourself. "I'll come by when I can. If I can."

She nodded, glancing out the doorway when she heard the toot of a horn. "That's probably Burke. It's nearly dawn."

"I'd better go, then."

"Tucker." She took his shirtsleeve when he turned away, then kissed him. Soft, quiet, comforting. "That's all."

He rested his cheek on hers for one last moment. "That's enough."

◆ ◆ ◆ ◆

THOUGH IT WAS STILL shy of eight A.M. when Caroline arrived at the Fullers', Happy wasn't alone. Friends and family had closed ranks. There was coffee brewing to replace the pots already consumed. Though no one thought of food, women gathered in the kitchen, that time-honored space of comfort.

Caroline hesitated in the doorway, beyond the murmur of conversation, the circle of support and worry and reassurances. She recognized the faces: Susie jiggling Scooter on her hip. Josie standing restless, by the back door, Toby's wife, Winnie, rinsing out cups in the sink, Birdie Shays stationed staunchly beside Happy, Marvella quietly ripping apart a paper napkin.

The sense of intrusion was so great, Caroline nearly turned around and walked out again. It was Josie who saw her, who offered her a tired smile of understanding.

"Caroline. You look like a whipped dog. Come on in and we'll pump you full of coffee."

"I just . . ." She looked helplessly from one woman to the other. "I wanted to stop by and see if there was anything I could do."

"Nothing but wait." Happy held out a hand. Reaching for it, Caroline stepped into the circle.

So they waited, in a melding of perfumes and soft voices, with talk about children and men and a baby's restless crying. Della joined them mid-morning, with jangling jewelry and a basket of sandwiches. She bullied Happy into eating half of one, scolded Josie for making the coffee too strong, and quieted Scooter by giving him one of her bright plastic bracelets to chew on.

"That child's got muddy diapers," she declared. "I can scent 'em a mile off."

"I'll change him." Susie picked him up off the floor, where he was busy banging Della's bracelet on the tile. "He's tired, too. Aren't you tired, little man? I'll just put him down in the daybed, Happy."

"He likes that little yellow teddy bear," Happy told her, pressing her trembling lips together. "Darleen left it for him yesterday."

"Why don't you find it for her, Happy?" Della shot Birdie a warning look before the woman could protest. "She needs something to do," Della said quietly when Happy went out. "Worrying'll eat her up. We all need something. Birdie, see if you can find the makings for one of your Jell-O parfaits. That'll go down cool by afternoon. Marvella, you stop wringing your hands and use 'em to squeeze some lemons. We'll have lemonade instead of this goddamn coffee. Winnie, I think you should mix up one of your potions for Happy. Get her to sleep awhile."

"I thought about it, Miss Della. I didn't believe she'd drink it."

Della smiled grimly. "She will if I tell her to. That woman's been going head to head with me for years, but I've been holding back. Josie, you and Caroline clean up these dishes."

"A woman as bossy as you ought to have a platoon of marines to order around." Even as she complained, Josie stacked dishes.

Now there was purpose in the room as well as a sense of unity. Caroline found herself smiling at Della. "How can I get to be you when I grow up?"

Highly pleased, Della fussed with the big gold buttons of her blouse. "Why, child, you just learn how to use your mean. We all got it, but not everybody knows how to use it constructive like."

"Happy's other girls ought to be here," Birdie said, slamming cupboard doors. "They ought to."

"You know they'll come if there's need. Marvella, is that how your mama taught you to squeeze a lemon? Bear down, girl." Satisfied, Della began to rewrap uneaten sandwiches. "Those girls got families, Birdie. Jobs and homes of their own. Wouldn't it be foolish of them to travel all this way if Darleen's just kicking up her heels?"

"Miss Della?" Winnie sprinkled herbs into a pot on the stove. Her hands were small and dainty. She was a quiet women, given more to doing then to talking. But when she spoke, her voice was cool and smooth, like cream. "I'm going to brew this up like a tea. I ain't making it strong, just enough to ease."

"Let's have a look." Della joined her at the stove, where they muttered and sniffed. Birdie ignored their conversation. As a doctor's wife, she didn't think it quite proper for her to approve of folk medicines.

"There's nothing more I can do here." Josie wiped her hands dry on a tea towel. "I'm going out to hunt around some myself."

"There's more than a dozen men taking care of that," Birdie said. Her tone was sharp enough to have Josie lift a brow, but Birdie had to put her frustration somewhere.

"Men don't always know best where to look for a woman." Josie picked up her purse. "I'm going to check on Cousin Lulu first, Della, then I'm going to ride over to see Billy T. If he knows anything, he'd be more likely to tell me than he would a man."

"Don't see as that's anything to brag on," Della muttered.

Josie shrugged. "Fact's a fact. Besides, Happy's better off knowing whatever there is to know sooner rather than later. She'll make herself sick if this goes on too long."

No one could think of an argument to that. She left by the back door. Moments later they heard the roar of her car engine springing to life.

"If that Billy T. knows where Darleen took off to—" Birdie began.

"If he does, Josie'll find out sure as God made little green apples." Della handed Winnie a cup for the sedative she'd brewed.

"He went off to sleep just like an angel," Happy said as she walked back into the room. Her famous smile was ragged at the edges. "Not a thing like his mama. Why, she used to fight sleep like it was Satan come to steal her soul. I must've walked a million miles of floor with . . ." Rubbing at her eyes, she trailed off.

"You sit on down here, Priscilla," Della ordered, using Happy's given name to get her moving. "This is just making you sick, is all." Using her big, broad hands, she pushed Happy into a chair. "You let us do the worrying awhile. Nobody better at it than a room full of women. Winnie, bring me that cup."

"It's a might hot, Miz Fuller. You gotta blow on it first." Winnie set the cup in front of her, then stayed, resting a hand on the back of the chair. Winnie had gone to school with Happy's eldest daughter, and Belle Fuller had been the first white girl ever to invite Winnie into her home to play with dolls.

"What is it?"

"It's what's good for you," Della said, and waved Winnie aside.

"I don't want one of Winnie's magic potions," she said petulantly. "I'm not sick, I'm just—"

"Scared and miserable," Della finished. "By the look of you, you didn't get a wink of sleep last night. You know Winnie wouldn't give you anything wasn't helpful. You drink up now and get some rest."

"What I need is coffee." When Happy started to rise, Della shoved her back.

"Now you listen to me. Being stubborn's not gonna change a thing. God willing, your Darleen'll be back here preening herself over the ruckus she caused. But right now you've got a child upstairs sleeping who's going to need you one way or the other. What good can you do him if you're worn out."

"I just want her back." When the tears started, she laid her head against Della's cushioning breast. "I just want my girl back. I was so hard on her, Della."

"You never gave her nothing she didn't need."

"She was always so fretful. Even as a baby, the minute she got one thing she wanted something else. I wanted what was best for her, but I never could seem to find it."

Needing to help, Caroline stepped forward. "Here, Happy." She lifted the cup. "Drink a little."

Happy took a swallow, then two, before grabbing Caroline's hand. "She doesn't think I love her, but I do. Somehow you always love in a special way the one who gives you the most grief. All I can think is that when she was here yesterday, wanting me to side with her about what happened with Junior and that Bonny boy, I couldn't do it. She was wrong. Darleen never could figure out what was right and what was wrong, but she came here wanting her mother to stick up for her. And I didn't. We just ended up fighting like always, with her stomping off. I didn't even watch her drive away."

She began to sob then, and Della rocked her and stroked her hair. Susie had come back in to put her arm around Marvella.

"Those other girls." Happy's fingers convulsed on Caroline's. "Oh, sweet Jesus, I keep thinking about those other girls."

"Hush now." Della lifted the cup to Happy's lips. "Aren't they saying that was Austin, and he's dead as a doornail. Why, Caroline here shot him in the head, and every woman in Innocence is grateful to her. Except maybe Mavis Hatinger, and she would be if she had a lick of sense. Now, you come on with me, darling. I'm going to take you up for a nice lie-down."

"Just for a little while." With Winnie's brew making her eyelids heavy, Happy let Della lead her out of the kitchen.

"Oh, Mama." Marvella turned into Susie's shoulder to weep.

"Shush now, don't you start." But Susie patted her back. "We don't know that anything's happened."

"We have to have faith," Winnie added. "And while we're having it, I'm going to fix some food in case others come by. I'll fry up some chicken."

"Good." Susie gave Marvella a last pat. "Honey, you peel some potatoes and put them on to boil for potato salad. No use anybody going hungry. No telling how long we'll have to wait."

♦ ♦ ♦ ♦

TUCKER STOOD ON THE banks of Gooseneck Creek and wiped his damp face with a bandanna. The temperature had soared to a hundred and two with the air so thick it felt as if you could grab a fistful and wring it out. The sky was a pale blue, bleached by the merciless white sun.

He imagined himself taking a quick, relieving dunk in the water. The picture helped a little, but he settled for soaking his bandanna in the creek and cooling his face and neck.

He remembered that Arnette had been found here—by Darleen's brother. While he was hunkered down, Tucker took time to say a prayer.

Please God, don't let me find her.

Someone would, he was sure. He'd discounted the hopeful theory that she'd taken off with someone. It didn't make sense. She hadn't had time to hook up with anyone but Billy T., and he, along with all of her women friends, insisted he hadn't heard from her.

Tucker believed him. Male pride was at stake. Billy T. wasn't likely to take up with a woman whose husband had bested him with a frying pan. Darleen hadn't been of particular importance to Billy T. One woman was the same as another to him.

The inevitable comparison with himself left Tucker with a bad taste in his mouth.

Darleen hadn't left her car on the side of the road during a thunderstorm to hop into another with some new lover or new friend. Not when Junior claimed none of her clothes were missing, and that the housekeeping money was still tucked away in the coffee can, where she'd kept it.

Someone would find her, Tucker thought again. And again he prayed it would be someone else.

He rose to move among the reeds. His part of the search party was ranged along the banks, slopping through the weeds and mud, hoping,

Tucker was sure, that they found nothing but some old beer bottles and maybe a used condom.

They were all armed, which made him a little edgy. Junior had already blasted away a water moccasin. Since it had seemed to make him feel better, no one had commented.

The fact was, there was very little conversation. The men worked silently, like soldiers setting up an ambush. Or walking into one. One of the helicopters called up from County swept by now and again, chopping at the hot air, and the two-way radios each group leader carried on their belts would squawk and buzz with talk or static. The FBI was holding back from taking over. But then, they didn't know Innocence or its people. Burns was convinced Darleen was just another dissatisfied wife who'd taken off for greener pastures.

Tucker figured he wasn't ready to admit another murder had taken place while he was in charge.

He swiped at mosquitoes, finding himself testy enough to want to shoot at the whining bloodsuckers instead of slapping at them. When he heard the long, echoing whistle of the train, he wished he were on it. Going anywhere.

When he'd finished his assigned area, he walked back to join Burke, Junior, Toby, and the others who'd taken this side of the creek.

"They're nearly done on the other bank," Burke said. He was keeping a wary eye on Junior, ready to move in if Darleen's husband started to relieve his anxiety by shooting at something more than a snake. "Singleton and Carl called in from McNair swamp. It's all clear so far."

Toby March laid his rifle in the bed of the pickup. He thought of his own wife, his own daughter, and though it shamed him, in his heart he was grateful whoever was killing was choosing white skin.

"We still got about six hours of good daylight left," he said to no one in particular. "I was thinking maybe some of us could ride down to Rosedale and Greenville and such. Ask around."

"I've got Barb Hopkins calling all the motels, hospitals, the local police." Burke took Junior's gun and laid it with his own in the truck. "County's sending her picture out."

"There you go." Will Shiver gave Junior a hearty slap on the back. "They'll find her holed up in some motel, sitting on the bed, painting her toenails and watching TV."

Saying nothing, Junior shrugged off the hand and walked away.

"Give him a minute," Burke murmured.

The men shifted their gazes politely away. Toby squinted, adjusting the brim of his hat to cut the glare of the sun. "Somebody's coming."

It took several seconds before anyone else could make out the plume of gravel dust or the faint glint of metal through the waves of heat rising from the road.

"You black boys got eyes like hawks," Will Shiver said good-naturedly. "That car must be two miles away yet."

"The eyes're organs," Toby returned with a sarcasm so subtle and smooth that Tucker had to bite the inside of his cheek to keep from grinning. "You know what they say about our organs."

Interested, Will cocked his head. "I heard tell that was a wives' tale."

"Yes, sir," Toby said blandly. "There's plenty of wives who'll attest to it."

Tucker coughed and turned away to light a cigarette. It didn't seem quite right to laugh out loud with Junior suffering so close by. But my, it was good to smile for a minute.

He recognized the car a moment later, by the color and the speed with which it was traveling.

"It's Josie." He shot a glance at Burke. "Looks like she's earning herself another speeding ticket."

She skidded to a halt, spitting gravel and waving a hand out of the window. "Barb told us we'd find y'all here. Earleen and I brought you boys some supper."

She slid out of the car, looking cool and fresh in shorts and a halter that left her midriff bare. Her hair was tied back with a chiffon scarf, reminding Tucker of their mother.

"That's real obliging of you ladies." Will slanted Josie a smile that would have earned him a sharp slap from his fiancée.

"We like to take care of our men, don't we, Earleen?" After answering Will's smile, Josie turned to Burke. "Honey, you look worn out. You come on and have a glass of this iced tea. We brought two jugs."

"Got a pile of ham sandwiches, too." Earleen hefted a hamper out of the backseat. She set it on the shoulder and threw back the lid. "Y'all have to keep up your strength in this heat."

"Yes, sir, meals on wheels." Josie kept up a bright chatter as she dug into the hamper. "Earleen and I got this together so fast, we're thinking we might go into the catering business. Junior, you come on and get one of these now, or you'll hurt my feelings."

When he didn't even turn around, she gestured to her brother. "Tucker, pour me a cup of that tea." While she waited, Josie unwrapped a sandwich and laid it on a paper napkin. "Earleen, you see that these boys leave enough for our next stop, you hear?" She rose, took the cup Tucker held out, then skirted around the truck.

Junior continued to stare down the road. Josie could see a muscle in his cheek twitch. She set the sandwich on the hood of the truck, then pressed the cup of tea into his hands.

"Now, you drink that, Junior. This heat steals all your fluids. A man could drink a gallon and not piss an ounce. Come on." Gently, she rubbed a hand up and down his back. "Getting heat stroke's not going to help."

"We didn't find her."

"I know, honey. Take a drink." She nudged the cup closer to his lips. "I was down at your mother-in-law's before. When I left, your little boy was sleeping like an angel. He's got a sweet disposition, that boy, and I do believe he has your eyes."

She paused when Junior took two big gulps of tea. She took the cup from him and passed him the sandwich. He ate mechanically, his eyes glazed with fatigue and worry. Josie slipped an arm around him, knowing there were few things more comforting than human contact.

"It's going to be all right, Junior. I promise. Everything's going to be just fine. You wait and see."

His eyes filled, spilled over, running rivulets through the sweat and grime on his face. But he kept eating. "I thought I fell out of love with her when I walked into the kitchen and found her with Billy T. Seemed like my heart just closed off toward her. It don't feel like that now."

Moved by his grief, she pressed a kiss to his cheek. "It'll work out, honey. You trust Josie."

He struggled to compose himself. "I don't want my son to grow up without a mother."

"He won't have to." Josie's eyes darkened as she wiped Junior's tears with the paper napkin. "You believe that, Junior, and it'll all be fine."

♦ ♦ ♦ ♦

THEY SEARCHED UNTIL IT was too dark for the 'copters to fly or the men to see. When Tucker arrived home, he was greeted by a weary Buster, who had tried, and failed, to avoid the puppy throughout the day.

"I'll take him off your hands." Tucker gave Buster an absent pat before scooping up Useless. The pup wiggled and licked and barked as Tucker carried him into the house. "If you've been like this all day, I'm surprised you didn't give my old hound a stroke."

He headed for the kitchen, dreaming of a beer, a cold shower, and Caroline. He found Della slicing roast beef and Cousin Lulu playing solitaire.

"What do you think you're doing, bringing that dog into my kitchen?"

"Giving Buster a break." Tucker set the dog down and he immediately scooted under Lulu's chair. "Have you heard from Caroline?"

"She called not ten minutes ago. She was going to stay with Happy until Singleton or Bobby Lee got home." Della arranged another slice of roast beef on the platter. Because she could see how tired Tucker was, she didn't slap at his hand when he stole it. "She's coming by here to pick up this fleabag."

Tucker grunted over a mouthful of beef, and pulled a beer out of the fridge.

"I'll have one of those," Lulu said without looking up. "Cards're thirsty work."

Tucker popped the lid on a second bottle, then scanned the hand she'd dealt. "You can't put a black three on a black five. You need a red four between."

"I'll put it there when I get one." Lulu tipped back the beer, studying him over it. "You look like something that's been dragged through the swamp."

"I guess I have been."

"That youngest Fuller girl still missing?" Lulu cheated a red ten out of her pile and played it. "Della's been half the day over at Happy's. I'm reduced to solitaire."

"I got a duty—" Della began, but Lulu waved her off.

"Nobody's criticizing. I'd've gone myself, but nobody thought to ask me."

"I told you I was going." Della thwacked the knife down on the cutting board.

"Not the same as being asked." Lulu did some more creative cheating. "People come and go so much around here, it makes my blood tired. Josie in and out all hours of the day and night, Tucker here gone for a day at a stretch. Dwayne wasn't back five minutes before he takes a bottle of Wild Turkey and goes out again."

Della started to defend her brood, then frowned. "When did Dwayne get back?"

"Half hour ago. Looked as muddy and worn-out as Tucker. Went out the same way."

"He take his car?"

"Don't see how he could." Lulu reached in her pocket and drew out a set of keys. "He took the bottle, so I took these."

Della nodded in approval. "Where do you think you're going?" she asked Tucker as he tried to edge out of the room.

"I need a shower."

"You've lived with that sweat all day, you can live with it awhile longer. Go on down and see if Dwayne's at the pond."

"Shit, Della, I've already walked a hundred miles today."

"Then you can walk one more. I'm not having him fall in and drown. You bring him up here, where he can get cleaned up and eat. They'll want him out there tomorrow just like they'll want you."

Grumbling, Tucker sat down his half-finished beer and started out the back door. "I hope to Christ he hasn't had time to get drunk yet."

♦ ♦ ♦ ♦

*H*E WAS ONLY HALF drunk, which was exactly the way Dwayne liked it best. The fatigue of the day had faded into a nice, friendly buzz. Slogging through McNair swamp with Bobby Lee and Carl and the others had been a miserable way to spend a day.

He'd gone willingly enough, and would go again in the morning. He didn't begrudge the time or the effort, and didn't see that anyone would begrudge him a little time with the bottle to wash the day away.

He'd felt for Bobby Lee especially. Whenever he'd looked into the boy's face and seen the strain and fear, he'd wondered what it would be like to be searching for his own sister.

That thought had him burning his throat with more whiskey.

He wanted to think of pleasant things now. Of how nice the crickets sounded in counterpoint with the buzzing in his ears. How soft the grass felt under his bare feet. He thought he might spend the night there, watching the moon rise and the stars come out.

When Tucker sat down beside him, Dwayne obligingly passed him the bottle. Tucker took it, but didn't drink.

"This stuff'll kill you, son."

Dwayne only smiled. "It takes it's sweet time doing it, though."

"You know it worries Della when you do this."

"I'm not doing it to worry her."

"Why are you doing it, Dwayne?" Tucker expected no response and continued without one. He gauged his brother's condition and knew he was sober enough to be coherent, drunk enough to talk. " 'Drunkenness is a voluntary madness.' Can't think right off who said that, but it rings true."

"I'm not drunk yet, or mad either," Dwayne said placidly. "Just working on both."

Wanting to choose his words carefully, Tucker took time to light half a cigarette. "It's getting bad. The past couple of years it's been getting real bad. First I thought it was because so many things went wrong so close together. Daddy dying, then Mama. Sissy taking off. Then I thought it was because Daddy drank so heavy and you just picked up on whatever genes it takes to have you follow him along."

Annoyed, and not wanting to be, Dwayne took the bottle back. "You do your share of drinking."

"Yeah. But I'm not making it my life's work."

"We do what we do best." Dwayne lifted the bottle and drank. "Of all the things I've tried, getting drunk's the one thing I don't worry about screwing up."

"That's bullshit." The fury rushed out so quick and sharp, it shocked them both. He hadn't known it had been preying on him, eating at him from the inside—this reality of what his big brother had become, layered over the image of the one Tucker had once admired and envied. "That's just bullshit." Tucker snatched the bottle and, springing to his feet, flung it into the water. "I'm tired of this, goddammit. I'm fucking tired of carrying you home, making up excuses for you in my head, of watching you kill yourself one bottle at a time. That's what he did. Flying that goddamn plane while he was shitfaced. The old man killed himself sure as if he'd put a gun in his mouth and pulled the trigger."

Dwayne got shakily to his feet. He weaved a little, but his eyes were steady. "You've got no reason to talk to me like this. You've got no right to talk about him either."

Tucker grabbed Dwayne by the shirtfront, tearing seams. "Who the hell has the right if not me, when I grew up loving both of you? Being hurt by both of you?"

A muscle in Dwayne's cheek began to twitch. "I'm not Daddy."

"No, you're not. But he was a fucking drunk, and so are you. The only difference is he got mean with it and you just get pathetic."

"Who the hell are you?" His mouth moved into a snarl as he grabbed Tucker's shirt in turn. "I'm the oldest. It was always me he jumped on first. I was supposed to take care of things, to fucking carry on the Longstreet legacy. It was me who got shipped off to school, me who got put in charge of the fields. Not you. Never you, Tuck. I never wanted it, but he wouldn't let me go my own way. Now he's dead and I can do what I want."

"You're not doing anything but sliding into a bottle. You've got two sons of your own. At least he was here. At least he acted like a father."

Dwayne let out a howl, and then they were wrestling on the grass, grunting and growling like a pair of dogs looking for a soft spot to sink fangs into. Tucker took a short glancing blow to his still-sore ribs. The fresh pain brought a burst of wild fury into his blood. Even as they went tumbling into the pond, he was bloodying his brother's lip.

They went under grappling, came up sputtering and cursing. They kicked and shoved, but the water softened the blows and began to make them both feel foolish.

Tucker scissored his legs, holding Dwayne by his torn shirt, one fist reared back. Dwayne mirrored his position so exactly, the two of them stared, panting.

"Shit," Tucker said, warily eyeing his brother as he lowered his fist. "You used to hit harder."

Gingerly, Dwayne touched the back of his hand to his swollen lip. "You used to be slower."

They released each other to tread water. "I wanted a shower, but this isn't half bad." Tucker swiped the hair out of his eyes. "Though Christ knows what's in this water."

"A half pint of Wild Turkey, for sure," Dwayne said, and smiled. "Remember when we used to swim here, when we were kids?"

"Yeah. Still think you can beat me to the other bank?"

"Shit." Dwayne's smile widened to a grin. He rolled over in the water and struck out. Too many years of the bottle had slowed him. Tucker streaked by like an eel. In tacit agreement, they raced back, then floated awhile under the rising moon.

"Yeah," Dwayne said after they'd stopped panting. "You used to be slower. I guess things've changed."

"Lots of things."

"I guess I've messed things up."

"Some things."

"I get scared, Tuck." Dwayne fisted a hand in the water, but there was nothing there to hold on to. "The drinking—I know when I should stop, but I get so I don't see the point in it. Sometimes I can't remember what I've been up to. I'll wake up sick and headachy, and it's like I've been dreaming. I can't make it out."

"We can do something about it, Dwayne. They've got places that take care of it."

"I like how I feel right now." Through half-closed eyes, Dwayne watched the stars wink into life. "Just a nice little buzz on, so nothing seems too goddamn important. Thing to do is to catch myself right here, where I like it best."

"It doesn't work that way."

"Sometimes I wish I could go back, see where I turned off wrong so I could fix it."

"You could always fix things, Dwayne. Remember that model airplane I got for my birthday? I wracked it up the second time I used it. I knew Daddy'd skin me when he found out, but you fixed it all up. Mama always said you had a talent for putting things together."

"I used to think I'd be an engineer."

Surprised, Tucker shifted to treading again. "You never told me that."

Dwayne merely stared up at the sky. "Wasn't any point. Longstreets are planters and businessmen. You could have done something different maybe. But I was the oldest son. He never gave me a choice."

"No reason not to do what you want now."

"Hell, Tuck, I'm thirty-five years old. That's no time to go back to school and learn a trade."

"People do, if they want it bad enough."

"I wanted it bad enough ten, fifteen years ago. That's behind me. A lot of things are behind me." He tried to make out the stars, but they were a hazy blur of light. "Sissy's going to marry that shoe salesman."

"I guess we had to figure she would—him or somebody."

"Says he wants to adopt my kids. Give them his name. 'Course she'd forget that soon enough if I upped the support payments."

"You don't have to take that, Dwayne. Those kids are yours. They're always going to be yours no matter what game she's playing."

"Nope, don't have to take it," Dwayne said lazily. "And I'm not going to. Sissy's going to have to learn that a man has his limits. Even me." He sighed, letting his gaze drift over sky and water. "I got comfortable, Tucker." Out of the corner of his eye Dwayne saw something bob in the water. An empty bottle, he thought, for an empty life. "Drinking makes things that way."

"The way you're doing it, drinking makes you dead."

"Don't start on me again."

"Dammit, Dwayne." He started to move closer when his legs brushed against something soft and slick that made him yelp. "Damn cats," he said. "Scared the shit out of me." He kicked away, glancing over his shoulder.

He, too, saw something bob in the water. But he didn't mistake it for a bottle. As the spit dried to dust in his mouth, as his blood slowed to a crawl, he stared at the trailing white hand.

"Jesus. Oh my Jesus."

"Catfish won't do any more than nibble," Dwayne said placidly. He swore when Tucker gripped his arm. "What's got into you now?"

"I think we found Darleen," he managed to say, then closed his eyes. Some prayers, he thought, just weren't meant to be answered.

Chapter 24

SOBER AND SHAKEN, DWAYNE dragged himself out of the water. On his hands and knees he crouched on the grass, fighting his rebellious stomach.

"Christ, Tuck. Jesus bleeding Christ. What're we going to do?"

Tucker didn't answer. He lay on his back, staring up at heat-hazed stars. It took enough effort just to concentrate on breathing when he was so cold, so bitterly cold.

"In the pond," Dwayne said, his throat clicking as he swallowed. "Somebody dropped her in our pond. We were in there with her. Jesus, we were *swimming* with her."

"She's past being bothered by it." He wanted to toss an arm over his eyes. Maybe that would help block out the image of that hand sticking out of the dark water, its fingers curled. As if it had been reaching for him. As if it would grab hold and pull him under.

It had been worse because he'd felt obliged to be certain. To be certain it was Darleen Talbot, and to assure himself that she was beyond help.

So he'd gritted his teeth and had taken that stiff, dead wrist, tugging against the weight that held the body down. And the head had bobbed up. He'd seen—oh, God, he'd seen what the knife had begun and what the fish were already ending.

The human form was so frail, he thought now. So vulnerable. So easily whittled away into something hideous.

"We can't just leave her in there, Tuck." But Dwayne shuddered at the prospect of going back into the water and touching what had once been Darleen Talbot. "It's not decent."

"I think we have to." Tucker thought regretfully of the bottle he'd tossed away. A few swallows of sour mash would do him some good just now. "At least until Burke gets here. You go in and call him, Dwayne. One of us ought to stay here. Call Burke, and tell him what we found. Tell him Agent Burns better come along." Tucker sat up to drag off his wet shirt. "And bring me out some dry smokes, will you? I wouldn't say no to a beer either," he began, then swore when he caught sight of Caroline walking toward them. Tucker scrambled up, intercepting her after three long strides.

"Glad to see me?" Caroline laughed and gave him a quick, hard hug. "You two decide to take a swim? Della sent me down to—"

"Go on back up with Dwayne." Tucker wanted her as far away from death and misery as possible. "Go on up and wait for me."

"I'll wait for you." Drawing back, she saw by his face that there was trouble. Cautious, she looked from Tucker to his brother. Dwayne's lip had opened up again, and the blood was dark against his pale face. "Have you been fighting? Dwayne, you've got a split lip."

He ducked his head. Della'd give him hell about it. "I'll call Burke."

"Burke?" Caroline grabbed Tucker's arm when he tried to nudge her along. "Why do you need Burke?" Her heart did a slow roll in her chest. "Tucker?"

She'd know soon enough, and it might as well come from him. "We found her, Caroline. In the pond."

"Oh, God." Instinctively, she looked toward the water, but Tucker shifted to block her vision.

"Dwayne's going up to call Burke. You go with him."

"I'll stay with you." She shook her head before he could protest. "I'll stay, Tucker."

When Tucker merely shrugged, Dwayne took off in a half run. A whippoorwill began to call, sweet and insistent, for a mate.

"Are you sure?" Even as she asked, Caroline knew the question was foolish.

"Yeah." He blew out a long breath. "I'm sure."

"God, poor Happy." She had to ask the rest, but it took a moment to force the words from her throat. "Was it like the others?" Caroline took his hand, holding tight until his gaze shifted to hers. "I want to know."

"It was like the others." Firmly, he turned her away from the lake. With his arm around her waist they listened to the night bird's song and watched the lights of Sweetwater glow against the dark.

♦ ♦ ♦ ♦

THE OFFICIAL PROCESS WORKED with callous efficiency. Men crowded around the pond, their faces washed white by the harsh spotlights hooked to Burke's truck. Pictures were taken to record the scene.

"All right." Burns nodded toward the water. "Let's pull her out."

For a moment no one spoke. Burke pressed his lips together and unhooked his gun belt.

"I'll do it." Surprising himself, Tucker stepped forward. "I'm already wet."

Burke set his gun belt aside. "It's not your job, Tuck."

"It's my land." Turning, he took Caroline by the shoulders. "Go inside."

"We'll go in together when it's finished." She kissed his cheek. "You're a good man, Tucker."

He didn't know about that, but as he slipped into the water, he was certain he was a stupid one. Burke was right, it wasn't his job. He didn't get paid to deal with this kind of horror.

He eased his way through the cool, dark water toward the hand, white as bone, fingers curved beckoningly.

Why did he feel it was his responsibility to drag a dead woman out of the water? She'd been nothing to him in life, shouldn't she be less than nothing to him now?

Because the pond was Sweetwater, he realized. And he was a Longstreet.

For the second time, he curled his fingers around the lifeless wrist. As the head rose, he watched her hair float and spread toward the surface. His stomach lurched. He tasted acid in the back of his throat and ruthlessly forced it down. Using his feet to tread, Tucker hooked an arm around the torso.

There was silence on the bank, the kind so deep you could hear your own heartbeat. A graveyard silence, he thought while he struggled against the weight that was trying to drag him and his burden down.

His grip slipped, and when he shifted and tightened it, her head lolled back on his shoulder. Tucker stiffened, but it wasn't revulsion that filled him. It was pity.

Tucker looked toward the bank. White faces stared back at him. He saw Dwayne, with an arm around Josie. Their eyes looked huge in the flood of light. Burke and Carl already hunkered down, ready to reach out and take the burden Tucker was dragging over. Caroline, her face wet, stood with her hand resting on Cy's shoulder. Burns stood back, observing, as though it were a moderately interesting play.

"Something's tied to her legs," Tucker called out. "I need a knife."

"That's evidence, Longstreet." Burns stepped forward. "I want it intact."

"You son of a bitch." Tucker managed to haul her another foot. "Why don't you come on in and get your fucking evidence yourself?"

"I'll help you, Mr. Tucker." Before anyone could stop him, Cy was running over and slipping into the water.

"Christ, boy, get back from here."

"I can help." Slick as an otter, Cy paddled over. "I'm strong enough." His face blanched when he swam close, but he reached down to take part of the weight. "We can do it."

"Keep your eye on the bank," Tucker told him. "And try not to think."

Cy scissored his feet. "I'm thinking about what an asshole that FBI man is."

"Even better."

It was a short and grisly swim. When they reached the bank, both Carl and Burke hooked hands under Darleen's arms.

"Look the other way," Tucker ordered Cy. "There's no shame in it." He would have done so himself, but the angle was wrong. So he saw what had been done to the body. As it was dragged effortfully out and onto the grass, he saw everything. "Go on over with Caroline now, Cy. No." He caught the boy's head before Cy could turn it. "Don't look this way. Go over with Caroline. You did good."

"Yessir."

Tucker hauled himself out. He sat there a moment, his feet dangling in the water. "Dwayne, give me a smoke."

It was Josie who brought him a cigarette, already lighted. "After that, I figure you deserve a whole one." She laid her cheek against his. "I'm sorry it had to be you, Tuck."

"So'm I." He took a greedy drag. "Burke, don't you have a blanket to put over her? This isn't right."

"If you civilians would go into the house," Burns began, "this area will remain off limits until the investigation is completed."

"Goddammit, we knew her," Tucker said warily. "You didn't. Least you can do for her is cover her."

"Go on, Tuck." Burke reached down to help Tucker to his feet. "There are things we gotta do. It's best if you went on while we get to it. We'll be as quick as we can."

"I saw what was done to her, Burke," Tucker said in a raw voice. "You can't be quick enough."

"You will stay available," Burns put in. "You and your brother. I'll need to question you shortly."

Saying nothing, Tucker turned away to walk with Caroline and Cy back to the house.

♦ ♦ ♦ ♦

CAROLINE WASN'T MUCH OF a cook, but she heated up some soup to go with the roast beef Della had sliced. Soup, it seemed to her, was one of those nerve-soothing foods. By the way Cy plowed through his, she decided it worked.

Dwayne scraped his bowl clean, then seemed embarrassed by his appetite. "That was mighty tasty, Caroline. I appreciate you putting a meal together."

"Della did most of it before she left for the Fullers'."

"We do appreciate it," Josie put in. "Though I don't know how Dwayne can eat with that fat lip. Run into a door, honey?"

"Tucker and I had a tussle." He reached for his iced tea. He didn't feel much like getting drunk tonight after all.

"Tucker hit you?" Smiling a little, Josie rested her chin on her hand. "That man's been using his fists more these past few weeks than he has his whole life. Now, what could y'all be fighting about? Don't tell me you've taken a shine to Caroline here?"

Josie winked at Caroline to include her in the joke.

"Nothing like that." Uncomfortable, Dwayne shifted in his chair. "We just had a disagreement, that's all. That's how it happened. We started wrestling and ended up in the pond. Guess we stirred up the water quite a bit between that and racing to the far bank and back. Then Tucker . . . he practically bumped right into her."

"Don't think about it." Josie rose to put her arms around his neck. "It was just bad luck. Bad luck all around."

"That's a mighty cold way of putting it," Tucker said as he stepped into the kitchen.

Josie kept her cheek against Dwayne's hair. "It's the truth. Sometimes the truth's cold. If you hadn't been wrestling around in the pond, you wouldn't have found her. She'd still be dead, but she might've stayed down. Then the two of you wouldn't be looking so peaked."

Tucker dropped into a chair. He knew his temper was on edge, but

Josie's carelessness pushed a dangerous button. "We won't look 'peaked' for long. Darleen's going to be dead forever."

"That's just my point. Finding her like that only made things hard on you."

"Christ, Josie, you've got the sensitivity of a codfish."

She straightened at that, eyes hot, cheeks pale. "I've got plenty of sensitivity when it comes to my family. Maybe I don't give two hoots about what happened to that little slut—"

"Josie." Wincing, Dwayne reached for her hand, but she shook him off.

"That's just what she was, and her being dead doesn't change it. I'm sorry for Happy and the rest, but I'm just sick about how you and Dwayne came to be involved. If you think that makes me cold, Tucker Longstreet, that's fine. I'll just save my sensitivity for someone who appreciates it."

She slammed out, leaving the smoke of her temper lingering in the air.

"Maybe I'll go after her." Dwayne rose awkwardly. "Smooth her feathers."

"Tell her I'm sorry, if you think it'll help." Resigned, Tucker rubbed his hands over his face. "No use slicing at her for being what she is."

"Mr. Tucker, you want a beer?"

Tucker lowered his hands and gave Cy a wan smile. "About as much as I want to breathe right now. But I think I'd do better with coffee."

"I'll get it." Caroline opened a cupboard for a cup. "We're all on edge, Tucker. She's just worried about you."

"I know. Did Della go over to the Fullers'?"

"Yes, she and Birdie were going to stay the night with Happy. Help take care of the baby. Cousin Lulu's upstairs watching a movie."

She didn't add that the lady had commented that murders were much more interesting on TV than in real life, and had settled back with a bowl of popcorn and a bottle of Dixie beer.

"Why don't you go on up with her, Cy?" Tucker suggested. "She likes company."

"Can I take the pup with me?" He hauled Useless out from the dog's spot beneath the table.

"Sure." Caroline smiled. "Don't let Cousin Lulu give him too much beer."

"No, ma'am. 'Night, Mr. Tucker."

"'Night, Cy." He touched the boy's arm. "Thanks for helping out."

"I'd do anything for you, Mr. Tucker." The words came out in a rush. Then Cy colored deep and hurried from the room.

"Devotion like that's a precious gift." Caroline ladled out soup. "You'll be careful with him, won't you?"

"I'm going to try." Tucker rubbed a hand over his rough chin. He hadn't shaved, though he'd showered twice. "I guess I wish he wouldn't look at me like I was Hercules, Plato, and Clark Kent all rolled into one."

Caroline set the bowl in front of him, brushed a hand through his hair. "It's tough being a hero."

"It's tougher trying to be one when you haven't got the makings."

"Oh, I think you'll surprise yourself." Smiling, she sat beside him. "I made you soup."

"So I see." He took her hand. "You sure are handy to have around, Caroline."

"I've been pretty busy surprising myself lately. I'm glad you didn't know me before, Tucker."

"Before doesn't mean diddly."

"This from a man who'll—at the drop of a hat—tell me stories about people who've been dead for a hundred years."

"That's different." He started to eat, more to please her than because he was hungry. After the first few spoonfuls, he discovered he was ravenous. "What happened before matters because it shapes things. But who you were a year ago isn't as important as who you are now."

"I like the way you think. Tucker?"

"Hmmm."

"Do you want me to stay tonight?"

His gaze came back to hers, fastened there with a wealth of feeling and need. "I want you to stay."

With a nod, she rose. "Let me fix you a sandwich."

♦ ♦ ♦ ♦

TEDDY WAS BACK. JOSIE knew he was expected since she'd spent the evening in Burns's bed and the FBI agent had told her so. The idea of having a pathologist and a special agent to juggle had eased her hurt and anger at Tucker's words.

She'd decided she wouldn't speak to her brother for a day or two—at least until he'd apologized in person rather than sending Dwayne scrambling after her as proxy.

She was still brooding over it the following afternoon. While the rest of Innocence was reeling in shock over the latest murder, Josie sat at the counter of the Chat 'N Chew, freshening her lipstick in her new purse mirror. Teddy had promised to join her for lunch as soon as he'd finished his preliminary examination of the body.

"Earleen." Pouting, Josie tilted the mirror back to fluff at her hair. "Do you think I'm a coldhearted woman?"

"Coldhearted?" Earleen leaned on the counter and flexed her aching feet. "Kinda hard to be hot-blooded and coldhearted all at once."

Pleased, Josie smiled. "That's true. Being honest about things and not pretending otherwise doesn't make you cold. Why, it makes you true to yourself, don't you think?"

"That's a fact."

Using the mirror, Josie scanned the diner without turning around. Several of the booths were occupied. Beneath the crooning of Reba McIntire from the juke, the conversation was all about Darleen.

"You know, half the people in here didn't have a minute's use for Darleen while she was alive." Josie snapped the mirror closed. "Now that she's dead, they can't say enough."

"That's human nature," Earleen declared. "It's like one of them artists whose paintings ain't worth shit while he's alive to paint 'em, then once he kills himself or gets hit by a truck, people fall all over themselves to pay a fortune for them. Human nature."

Josie appreciated the analogy. "So Darleen's worth more dead than she was alive."

While she might have agreed, Earleen was superstitious enough not to speak ill of the dead. "It's Junior I'm sorry for. And that dear little boy." With a sigh, Earleen reached back to take an order off the shelf. "And Happy and Singleton, too. The living's who suffers."

While Earleen walked off to serve a customer, Josie murmured in agreement. She dug through her purse for her atomizer of perfume, then squirted scent liberally on her wrists and throat.

When Carl walked in, the conversation died, then picked up again in murmurs. Josie patted the stool beside her.

"Come on over here and sit. You look worn out."

"Thank you, Josie, but I can't. Just come by to get some food to take back to the office."

"What can I get for you, Carl?" Earleen popped back behind the counter, hoping to exchange food for news.

"I need a half-dozen hamburgers. Maybe a quart of your potato salad and some cole slaw. Make it a gallon of iced tea."

"How're you going to want them burgers?"

"Make them all medium, Earleen, and load 'em up."

Josie picked up her Diet Coke. "Y'all must be busy as one-armed paperhangers down at the office if you can't even break for lunch."

"We are that, Josie." He was so tired himself he could have slept standing up. Belatedly, he remembered to take off his hat. "County sheriff and a couple of his boys're down. Agent Burns has had that fax machine clicking all morning. It's hot enough in that office to smoke a ham."

"With all of you working so hard, you must have some clues."

"We got a thing or two." He glanced over as Earleen turned expectantly from the grill. "Now, I can't tell you what we got, official like. But y'all know Darleen was killed like the others. We gotta figure it was the same person using the same weapon."

"It ain't right," Earleen said. "We got some psychopathic killer running loose, and not a woman in the county can feel safe."

"No, it ain't right. But we're going to stop him. You can take that to the bank."

"Matthew says serial killers're different." Josie sucked on the straw. "He says they can look and act just like regular people. It makes them hard to catch."

"We'll find this one." He leaned closer. "I figure I should tell you, Josie, since you'll be finding out soon anyway. Looks like Darleen was killed right there, right by the pond."

"Sweet Jesus." Earleen was torn between excitement and terror. "You mean to say he did it over to Sweetwater?"

"We got reason to think so. I don't mean to scare you, Josie, but you want to be mighty careful."

She took a cigarette from the pack on the counter and her fingers shook lightly. "I will be, Carl. You can take *that* to the bank."

Slowly, she blew out a stream of smoke. And she intended to find out exactly what they knew the minute she could get Teddy alone.

◆ ◆ ◆ ◆

𝒯HERE WERE REPORTERS CAMPED out in her yard. Caroline had stopped answering the phone. Invariably, it was another inquisitive newsman or -woman on the other end. To distract herself, she took out the scrapbook she'd found in her grandmother's trunk.

Caroline could see most of her own life on those pages. Her parents' wedding announcement clipped from the Philadelphia and Greenville papers. The studied, professional photographs taken at the wedding where her mother had worn an heirloom bridal gown—from the Waverly side. The card announcing the birth of Caroline Louisa Waverly. She'd been named for her paternal grandmother.

A few photographs, again professionally done, of the proud parents with their little bundle of joy. Then, of Caroline alone, one studio portrait for each year of her life.

No snapshots, she noted, no out-of-focus or candid shots, except for the few her grandparents had taken themselves on her brief visit all those years ago.

Newspaper clippings marking her musical career, showing her at six and twelve and twenty, and the years between and after.

It was one of the few things her grandparents had had of her, Caroline thought as she set the book back inside the trunk. Now it was one of the few things she had of her grandparents.

"I'm so sorry," she murmured, and drew deeply of the scent of lavender and cedar that wafted from the trunk. "I wish I'd known you better."

She reached in and took out a cardboard box. Inside, wrapped in tissue, was a tiny christening gown trimmed with white ribbons and yellowing lace.

Perhaps her grandmother or grandfather had worn it, Caroline thought as she ran her fingers over the soft white lawn. Surely her mother had.

"You saved it for me." Touched, she brushed her cheek over it. "I couldn't wear it when my turn came, but you saved it for me."

Carefully, she wrapped it back into its bed of tissue. One day, she vowed, her child would wear it.

Useless raced out of the room to stand at the top of the steps, then raced back again as someone hammered on the door. Caroline set the box back in the trunk, then took out a pair of bronzed baby shoes. She smiled over them.

"Don't bother, Useless. It's just one of the idiot reporters."

"Caroline! Dammit, open up before I have to kill one of these jackasses."

"Tucker." Jumping up, she ran downstairs with the dog at her heels. "Sorry." As she unlocked the door, she could see the reporters crowding behind him, thrusting out their mikes, snapping pictures and shouting questions. She dragged Tucker in by the arm, then planted herself in the doorway.

"Get off my porch."

"Ms. Waverly, how does it feel to find yourself living a real life murder mystery?"

"Ms. Waverly, is it true you came to Mississippi to mend a broken heart?"

"Did you really collapse in—"

"Is it true you killed—"

"Were you acquainted with—"

"Get off my porch!" she bellowed. "And get off my land while you're at it. You're trespassing, the lot of you, and we have laws down here. And if one of you so much as sets a toe over my boundary line without invitation,

I'll shoot it off." She slammed the door, threw the bolt, and started to turn when Tucker scooped her up in a quick circle.

"Honey, you sounded just like my mama did when she got her dander up." He kissed her before setting her on her feet. "You're losing the Yankee in your speech, too. Pretty soon you'll be saying 'y'all' and 'fix'n to' just like a native."

She laughed, but shook her head. "I will not." She touched a hand to his cheek. He hadn't shaved, but most of the fatigue had drained out of his eyes. "You look better than you did this morning."

"That's not saying much, seeing as I looked like death warmed over this morning. Felt like it, too."

"You didn't sleep."

"I caught an hour in the hammock this afternoon. Felt like old times." He drew her close again, but this time when he kissed her it was slow and easy. "So does that. I sure wish you'd lowered your standards of respectability and shared my bed last night. I still wouldn't have slept, but I'd've felt better about being awake."

"It didn't seem right, with the house full of your family, and—"

"And the police poking 'round the pond half the night," he finished. Turning away, he walked into the parlor and glanced out of the window. "Do something for me, Caro."

"I'll try."

"Go up and pack what you need, and come back to Sweetwater with me."

"Tucker, I told you—"

"You stayed last night."

"You needed me to."

"I still need you." When she said nothing, he spun around. "This isn't the time for poetry and romance. And I'm not asking because I want you in bed with me. I'd stay here with you if that was all."

"Stay anyway."

"I can't. Don't ask me to choose between you and my family, Caroline, because I can't."

"I don't know what you mean."

"If I go home without you, I'll be eaten up with worry over you. If I stay, it'll be the same for Josie and Della and the rest." He pulled her back to him, held her close. Then, restless, he yanked away to pace the room. "He's still out there somewhere, Caroline. And he was at Sweetwater."

"I understand that, Tucker. I know he left the body there."

"He killed her there." Eyes filled with turmoil, he turned back. "He killed her there, in sight of my house, by the trees where I fished with Cy only days ago. A tree my mother planted. Burke told me enough, maybe too much. I'm going to tell you. I don't want to, but I'm going to so you understand that I've got to go back there, and I'm not going without you."

He took a long, measuring breath. "He staked her out on the ground under the tree. They found the holes where he'd staked her hands and feet. And the blood the rain didn't wash away. I saw what he did to her. I'm not likely to forget what she looked like when I helped pull her out of the water. I'm not likely to forget it was done where my mother planted a willow tree, where I used to play with my brother and sister, across the water from where I kissed you the first time. I'm not likely to forget any of that. He's not going to touch anything else that's important to me. Now I'm asking you to get what you need and come with me."

She stepped forward to take the hands he'd balled into fists. "I don't need much."

Chapter 25

CAROLINE WAS USED TO restless nights. Over the past few years she'd developed a grudging envy for people who could climb into bed, close their eyes, and slip effortlessly into sleep. Since settling in Innocence, she'd come close to joining the ranks of those privileged dreamers. Now it seemed she was back at square one, facing long, dark hours in the frustrating pursuit of sleep.

The tricks of the insomniac were routine to her. Hot baths, warm brandy, dull books. The first two relaxed her body, but when she tried reading, her mind kept drifting away from the words on paper. There was a television cleverly concealed in a cherrywood armoire, but none of the late night shows caught her interest or bored her enough to trick her brain into sleep.

She couldn't complain about the heat, not here in the lovely cool of her room at Sweetwater. And she was used to strange rooms and strange beds. The one she'd been given was as gracious as any she'd found in the fine hotels of Europe. The bed was delicately feminine with its draping canopy and lacy pillows piled high. If that didn't seduce sleep, there was a plump daybed in misty blue satin that angled toward the french doors and offered a view of moonlight.

Vases of flowers fresh from the garden sweetened the air. Charming watercolors were scattered over the warm rose-tinted walls. A lady's dressing table held elegant antique bottles that glistened in the lamplight. There was a small fireplace of blue stone that would provide warmth and comfort on chill winter nights. She could picture herself cuddled under thick handworked quilts on some windy February midnight, watching the flames crackle and shoot shadows up the walls.

With Tucker.

It seemed wrong to think of being nestled up against him, in absolute peace, when there was so much grief and heatbreak around them. Another woman was dead, and she lay alone in some cold, dark room while her family was left to weep and wonder.

It had to be wrong to feel this soft glow of happiness, this insistent spring of hope when death hovered so close.

But she was in love.

Sighing, she curled on the window seat, where she could see the moonlight stream into the garden. The flowers were silver-edged and still, a touch of magic waiting to be plucked. Beyond, far beyond, was the glint of the pond that was Sweetwater. She couldn't see the willows, and was glad. If that was hiding from pain, then for one night she would hide. For now it was only a beautiful spot laced by moonlight.

And she was in love.

It wasn't possible to choose the time and the place to lose your heart. Caroline had come to believe it wasn't possible to choose the person who would take it. Surely if she could have chosen, it wouldn't have been here and now. It wouldn't have been Tucker.

It was a mistake to fall in love now, when she was just beginning to understand her own needs and capabilities. Now, when she had only begun to learn she could stand on her own, in charge of her life. It was foolish to fall in love here, in a place torn apart by tragedy and senseless violence, a place she would have to leave in a matter of weeks.

It was ridiculous to fall in love with a man who had made a study of romance and seduction. A charmingly lazy womanizer. A murder suspect. A poetry-spouting wastrel.

Hadn't she told herself he was just another Luis with a southern twist? And that by falling for him, she was proving herself to be the kind of woman who always chooses poorly and lives to regret the results?

But she couldn't make herself believe it, as much as she'd once wanted to. There was more to him than that, more than he admitted to himself. She'd seen it in the way he cared for Cy, in his loyalty to family, in the way he quietly held the reins of Sweetwater and a dozen businesses without strutting his power or demanding gratitude.

With Tucker it wasn't self-deprecation, it was simply his way. Here was a man who did what needed to be done, and did what was right without thinking about it. And who did it without stirring up the air with demands and worries and desperation about tomorrow.

No, the air around Tucker Longstreet was as calm and placid as the naps he was so fond of taking in the summer shade. As peaceful as a long, lazy tale spoken in a drawl to the music of a porch rocker. And as smooth as a cold beer savored on a hot night.

That was what she needed, Caroline thought as she rested her head against the window glass. That basic acceptance that life was usually a joke, and a person should be able to smile her way through it.

She needed to smile right now, Caroline thought. She needed that island of serenity he so effortlessly carried with him.

She needed him.

So why was she sitting here, searching for sleep, when what she wanted was within reach?

On impulse she uncurled from the window seat. On her way to the terrace doors she plucked a sprig of freesia from a vase. She stopped by the gilt-framed mirror long enough to smooth her hair. Just as she touched her hand to the knob of the doors, they opened to the sultry night. And to Tucker.

Her heart gave a quick, giddy leap that had her stepping back.

"Oh, you startled me."

"I saw your light." He wore loose cotton pants and carried a blade of sweet peas. "Figured you couldn't sleep either."

"No, I couldn't." She looked down at the freesia in her hand, then smiled and held it out to him. "I was coming to you."

The gold of his eyes deepened as he took her flower and offered Caroline his. "Isn't that something? Here I was thinking that since your notions of propriety wouldn't let you come to my room, I'd have to come to yours." He skimmed his fingers through her hair, then cupped her neck. Against her cool skin, his hand was hot and firm. " 'Desire hath no rest.' "

She stepped forward, into him. "I don't want rest."

Reaching behind, he pulled the door closed. "Then I won't give you any."

He caught her against him, and the first kiss was hungry, as if it had been years rather than hours since they'd tasted. The flavor of need was potent and addicting. They fed on it, enhancing appetites with murmurs and sighs.

Breathless, she pressed her lips to his throat, clinging to him as they stumbled toward the bed. He caught her hand as she reached for the lamp, drew her fingers to his mouth to nibble and suck.

"We don't need the dark." Then he smiled and covered her body with his.

◆ ◆ ◆ ◆

WHILE THEY MADE LOVE in the light, and most of Innocence slept uneasily, McGreedy's bar was hopping. It was the beginning of a long weekend that would culminate in Fourth of July celebrations. The town council, which consisted of Jed Larsson, Sonny Talbot, Nancy Koons, and Dwayne, had—after heated debate—decided against canceling the annual parade, carnival, and fireworks display.

Patriotism and economics had swayed the vote. FunTime, Inc., had already been paid a hefty deposit for the carnival's two-night stand, and the fireworks had cost the town treasury a pretty penny. As Nancy had pointed out, the Jefferson Davis High School band and the Twinkling Batons majorettes had been practicing for weeks. To cancel the celebration at this late date would disappoint the kids and lower everyone's morale.

It was pointed out that it was unseemly and disrespectful to ride Crack the Whips and have pie-eating contests with Darleen Talbot barely cold. It was argued back that the Fourth was a national holiday, and that Innocence had ordered up its own patriotic celebration for more than a hundred years.

It was finally decided that a short speech honoring Darleen and the other victims would be given from the bandstand, and a moment of silence would be observed.

So banners and bunting had been hung while Teddy autopsied Darleen in Palmer's embalming room.

In McGreedy's some of the patrons had already begun the celebration. If the laughter was a bit wild or forced, if tempers were edgy, McGreedy was content in the knowledge that his Louisville Slugger was handy behind the bar.

He kept an eye on Dwayne, who was drinking quietly and steadily at the end of the bar. Since he was sticking to beer tonight, McGreedy didn't worry overmuch. It was whiskey that set Dwayne off, and at this point Dwayne looked more unhappy than drunk.

He knew he'd probably have to swing his bat and kick a few butts before the weekend was over. Tonight seemed friendly enough, though there were a few hard cases huddled in the corner, tossing them back and talking quiet. Whatever they were planning, he'd see that they took it elsewhere.

Billy T. Bonny took a slug of house whiskey. It pissed him off that McGreedy watered it down, but tonight he had other things on his mind.

Every damn body in town knew he'd been seeing Darleen on the sly. It was a matter of pride that he do something about her murder.

The more he drank, the more it seemed to him that he and Darleen had been in love.

He was among friends, half a dozen like-thinking men, including his brother, who were tanking up on liquor and hate. They spoke in undertones, wanting to keep their circle closed.

"It ain't right," Billy T. muttered again. "We're supposed to sit around with our fingers up our asses while some jerkoff from the FBI takes care of things. Well, he sure as fuck didn't take care of Darleen."

There was a general murmur of agreement. Cigarettes were lit. Deep thoughts were considered.

"What the hell good did some Yankee lawman do her?" Billy T. demanded. "Him and Burke and the rest of them're running around in circles while somebody hacks up our women. Oh, we're good enough to go out and look for bodies, but we're not supposed to do anything to protect what's ours."

"Probably raped 'em, too," Will said to his beer. "Probably raped the shit out of 'em before he sliced 'em. You gotta figure it."

Wood Palmer, cousin to the undertaking Palmers, nodded sagely. "Them psychos always do. It's 'cause they hate their mothers and want to screw them all at the same time, so they use other women."

"That's bull." Billy T. finished off his whiskey and signaled the waitress for another. His blood was already so pumped with alcohol, he could have opened a vein and fueled his gas tank. "It's 'cause they hate women. White women."

"There ain't been no black woman killed, has there?" his brother piped up. John Thomas had been drinking shooters for the best part of two hours, and was raring for hell. "Four women dead and not one of them colored."

"That's a fact," Billy T. said, and snatched up his whiskey the minute it was served. "And I guess that tells the tale."

Wood scratched the stubble of his beard while the others grunted in agreement. What Billy T. was saying made good sense to him, especially filtered through a haze of tequila. "I heard tell their heads was nearly cut clean off and their sex organs was carved up. That's psycho stuff."

"The cops want us to think like that." Billy T. struck a match, watched it burn. There was fire in his blood tonight, and it needed someplace to spread. "Like they wanted us to think it was Austin Hatinger killed his own daughter. Well, we know it wasn't." As the match fizzed out between his thumb and forefinger, he shifted his gaze from face to face, and what he saw pleased him. "We know it was a nigger. But we got us a

Yankee fed, a nigger deputy, and a sheriff who'd sooner lock up a white man than a colored."

Will cracked a peanut. He was drinking beer and drinking slow. Justine was already giving him grief about spending so much of his pay on drink and pool. "Come on, Billy T., Sheriff Truesdale's okay."

"If he's so okay, how come we got four women dead and nobody paying for it?"

As all eyes turned on him, Will, sober enough to be prudent, decided to keep his own counsel.

"I'll tell you why," Billy T. continued. " 'Cause they know who did it, sure as Christ. They know but they don't want any trouble from the N.A.A.C.P. or any of those other egg-sucking groups. It's the niggers and the ever-fucking liberals responsible."

"They ain't hardly talked to no coloreds either," Wood muttered. "Don't seem right."

"That's 'cause it ain't," Billy T. said viciously. "But there's been one they've talked to right enough." He struck another match for the pleasure of watching it burn. "They've been over to talk to Toby March. That special fucking agent asked plenty of questions about him."

"Talking's all they do," Wood mumbled. "And we got another woman dead."

"Talk's all they're gonna do." Billy T. nodded as the others began to shift restlessly in their chairs. He could feel it, the hate, the fear, the frustration all melded together in a pot simmering with the summer heat and flavored by whiskey. "They'll keep talking and asking questions, and he'll do it again. Maybe one of our women next time."

"We got a right to protect our own."

"It's time somebody put a stop to it. One way or the other."

"That's right." Billy T. wet his lips and leaned in. "And I think we know what needs to be done. It's that March bastard doing it. They homed right in on him, then backed off. They even know he has a taste for white meat."

"He was sniffing around Edda Lou, that's for sure," John Thomas put in. "Somebody shoulda fixed him then. Fixed him good."

"And you know what he's doing?" They all turned to listen to Billy T. "He's laughing at them. Laughing at us. He knows they don't want no race trouble down here in Mississippi that those Yankee papers can turn all inside out. He knows they're going to look the other way 'lest they catch him with a knife in some white woman's throat."

"It's him all right," his brother agreed. "Didn't I see him standing at Edda Lou's window?"

"He was working at the rooming house," Will began.

"That's right." Billy T. sneered. "Working on how he was going to get Edda Lou out to the swamp so he could rape and kill her. He done work for Darleen, too. She told me how he came to patch her roof."

"He done work out to the trailer court where Arnette and Francie lived, too," Wood put in. "I seen him having a soda pop with Francie and laughing."

"That's how they tie all together." Billy T. took a last drag on his cigarette. "He got around them that way, and starting thinking how he'd like to do it to them. How he hated them for being women. White women. The cops don't want to see it, but I do. I see it plain, and I'm not giving that black bastard the chance to kill another of our women." He leaned forward, sensing the moment was right. "I got me some nice strong rope in the back of my car. Every one of us here's got a rifle he knows how to use. I say we kick off our Independence Day by ridding Innocence of a killer."

He pushed back from the table and stood. "Anybody's with me, get your gun and meet at my place. We got us a murderer to hang."

Chairs scraped against the scarred wooden floor. Men started out with an air of purpose tinged with vengeance, their pulses pounding with a sense of right sweetened by the anticipation of violence.

As they trooped out into the hot, sweaty night, McGreedy noted that they looked as though they were hunting for trouble. But as they were hunting it elsewhere, he went back to drawing drafts.

At the door, Wood glanced back to Will, who was standing by the empty table. "You coming, boy?"

"You bet." Will lifted his beer and sloshed it down his dry throat. "I'll be right along."

With a nod that was as much warning as assent, Wood went off to fetch his Remington.

"Oh, Jesus." Will gulped down more beer. He didn't want the other men to think he was pussy. That was the worst thing a man had to live down. But he was thinking, now, maybe there was something worse yet.

Hanging somebody.

He wasn't quite drunk enough to see it as justice. Nor was he sober enough to see it as murder. What he saw was Toby March twitching at the end of a robe—eyes rolling and bulging, face going purple, feet kicking empty air.

He didn't have the stomach to watch, and that was the sad truth. And if he didn't, he'd lose the respect of the men he drank with most every week. There was only one way to solve the problem as he saw it. That was to stop it before it happened.

Wiping his mouth dry, he walked over to Dwayne.

"Dwayne? You gotta listen to me."

"Go on, Will. I told you I'd wait another week on the rent."

"It's not about that. You see those boys that just left?"

Annoyed with the interruption to his drinking, Dwayne scowled into his beer. "I'm making it a point not to see anything."

"They're going out to the March place. They're going out there with a rope."

Slowly, Dwayne lifted his head and focused. "What do they want to do that for?"

"They mean to hang Toby March. They're going to string him right up, Dwayne, for killing all those women."

"Shit, boy. Toby's never killed anything but a possum in his life."

"Maybe, maybe not, but they went off to get their guns. Billy T.'s dead certain Toby done it, and he's fired up for a lynching."

"Shit." Dwayne rubbed his hands hard over his face. "Then I guess we'd better stop them."

"I can't do that." Shaking his head, Will backed up. "They'll ride me from now to next year if they think I chickened out. I've done all I'm going to."

People had come to expect sudden outbursts from Dwayne when a bottle was nearby. That was why no one did more than glance his way when he shoved the table aside and grabbed Will by the throat.

"The fuck you have. Toby gets hurt tonight, I'll see that you pay for it, same as the others do."

"Chrissakes, Dwayne. I can't go against my own kind any more than I have."

"You want to keep that roof over your head, and the job that's paying for it"—Dwayne lifted Will up on his toes and shook—"you get your ass over to the sheriff's office. You don't find Burke or Carl there, you go find them at home, and you tell them what you told me."

"Dwayne, Billy T. finds out I did, he'll kill me."

"Bonny ain't going to be killing anybody." He tossed Will toward the door. "Do it."

♦ ♦ ♦ ♦

HALF-ASLEEP AND LIMP WITH pleasure, Caroline snuggled up to Tucker. She roused herself to trail a lazy line of kisses up his chest to his chin.

"I always thought propriety was overrated."

"Stick with me, darlin'." He curved a hand over her hip. "You'll forget there ever was such a thing."

"I think I already have." Her lips curved against his shoulder before she rested her cheek there. "Can we sleep like this?"

"Like babies," he promised, idly rubbing her back. He didn't pay much attention to the roar of the car down the lane, or the slamming of doors, the pounding of feet up the stairs. If Dwayne was drunk, or Josie was peeved at whomever she'd been sleeping with, it could wait until morning.

But Caroline stirred and started to speak even as Dwayne began to shout Tucker's name.

"Shitfire. He does pick his times." He kissed Caroline's shoulder as he rolled over and grabbed up his pants. "Just wait right here and I'll go quiet him down."

Tucker listened to his brother banging on doors and swore. He swung the door open and stepped out into the hall. "Jesus H. Christ, Dwayne, you're going to wake up the whole house."

"Already has," Cousin Lulu said from her doorway. She was wearing a Redskins football jersey and a headful of purple curlers. "I was having a right good dream about Mel Gibson and Frank Sinatra, too."

"Go back to sleep, Cousin Lulu. I'll handle him."

Wild-eyed, Dwayne burst out of Tucker's room. "Doesn't anybody sleep in their own bed anymore? Get your gun, boy. We've got trouble."

"The only trouble here is the beer you've been slopping down in Mc-Greedy's." Della grabbed his arm and tried to haul him to his own room. "What you need's a face full of ice to cool you off."

Dwayne shook her off and rushed to Tucker. "I don't know how much time we have. They're going to lynch Toby March."

"What the hell are you talking about?"

"I'm talking about the Bonny boys and a bunch of their asshole friends going after Toby right this holy minute with a rope."

"Oh, Christ." Tucker saw Caroline come to the doorway, clutching her robe at her throat. "Wait for me," he said.

"I'm going with you." Della was halfway down the hall in her red-feathered peignoir before Tucker stopped her.

"You're staying right here. I don't have time to argue with you. Call Burke. Tell him fireworks are starting ahead of schedule."

Della stood as they clattered down the steps. She bristled until the feathers rustled.

"There are only two of them," Caroline said from behind her. "If Burke doesn't get there with help, it'll be only Tucker and Dwayne."

Cousin Lulu examined her nails. "I can still shoot Lincoln's face off a one-cent piece at five yards."

Della turned back, nodded. "Get some pants on."

♦ ♦ ♦

TOBY ROLLED OVER IN bed when their old mutt Custer began to bark. "Damn dog," he muttered.

" 'S your turn," Winnie said sleepily.

"How do you figure?"

"I'm the one who got up every night to nurse two babies." She opened her eyes and smiled at him in the moonlight. "Just like I'm going to get up with this next one in about six more months."

Toby skimmed a hand over her still-flat tummy. "Guess it's only fair I deal with the dog."

"Get me a glass of that orange soda pop while you're up." She patted his bare butt before he pulled on his undershorts. "A pregnant woman's got cravings."

"You sure did have them a couple hours ago."

That earned him a giggle and another slap. Toby stumbled, yawning, out of the room.

He saw the reflection of the fire in the front room window, that glitter of gold and red on the glass that made his heart sink and his blood boil.

He bit back an oath, hoping to get rid of the obscenity on the lawn before any of his family could be hurt by it. He was a man of deep faith and did his best to love his fellow man. But in his heart was a cold hate for whoever had lit the cross on his land.

He pushed open his door, stepped out on his porch. And found a gun poked into his naked belly.

"It's Judgment Day, nigger." Billy T.'s lips spread in a grin. "We just come by to send you to hell."

Enjoying the power, he jabbed with the rifle barrel. "Toby March, you've been tried and convicted for the rape and murder of Darleen Talbot, Edda Lou Hatinger, Francie Logan, and Arnette Gantry."

"You're crazy." Toby could barely get the words through his lips. The dog was quiet now, and he could see old Custer crumpled on the grass—dead or stunned. Rage came quickly, then he saw the rope John Thomas Bonny and Wood Palmer were swinging over the branch of a gnarled oak. Fear followed. "I never killed nobody."

"Listen to this, boys." Billy T. gave a cackle while his eyes stayed dark and flat on Toby's. "He says he didn't do it."

Even through terror, Toby recognized that they were all piss-yourself drunk. That only made them more dangerous.

One of the others leaned on his shotgun and brought a pint of Black Velvet to his lips. "Might as well hang him for a liar, too."

"His neck'll stretch just the same. You nigger boys can dance, can't you?" Billy T. grinned until his eyes turned to slits. "You're going to do some dancing tonight. Why, your feet ain't even going to touch the ground. When you finish dancing, we're going to burn your place to the ground."

Fear turned Toby's bowels to ice. They would kill him. He could see that in their eyes. He would fight them, and he would lose. But he couldn't lose his family as well.

He shoved the rifle, felt the bullet sear his rib cage as it exploded. "Winnie!" He shouted in despair and terror. "Run. Get the children and run!" As he clutched at his wounded side, Billy T. brought the rifle butt down in his face.

"Coulda killed him." On a nervous giggle, Billy T. wiped the back of his hand over his mouth. "Coulda blown a hole in his belly, but that's not the way. We're gonna hang him," he yelled to the others. "Drag him on over."

He saw the woman rush out, shotgun blasting. In her terror, Winnie fired wide. Billy T. backhanded her and knocked the gun clear. "Lookie here." He snatched the struggling woman around the waist. "She's going to protect her man." When she clawed at him, he struck her again so that she fell dazed to the porch. "Hold on to her, Woody. Truss her up. When that cocksucker wakes up, we'll show him how it feels to have his woman raped."

"I ain't raping no woman," Wood muttered, already having doubts about the whole night's work.

"Then you can watch, too." Billy T. reached down and yanked Winnie down the steps by the hair. "Take hold of her, goddammit. John Thomas, you go in and bring those nigger kids out here. They got a lesson to learn."

Winnie began to scream, one keening wail after another. She kicked and bit and clawed as Wood bound her hands behind her back.

There was a shout from the house, a curse and a crash. John Thomas staggered back out to the doorway, his shoulder seeping blood. "He cut me." Holding out one bloody hand, he stumbled to his knees. "The little fucker cut me."

"Christ almighty, can't even handle a kid." Billy T. walked over to examine his brother's wound. "You're bleeding like a stuck pig. One of y'all bind this up. Keep an eye on the house. That boy comes out, do what you have to do." Near where the cross burned, Toby began to groan and stir. "I'm going to do this myself. For Darleen." He leaned over. One of Toby's eyes had swollen shut, but there was fear in the other. Billy T. fed on it.

It was power. He tasted it and found it heady. All his life he'd been second rate. Now he was about to do something important, even heroic. No one would ever look at him the same way again.

"I'm going to put this noose around your neck, boy." He reached up and snagged it. Dragging Toby to a kneeling position, he pulled the loop of rope around Toby's neck. "I'm going to tug it nice and tight." He slid the knot down until it pressed evilly against flesh. "But we're not going to string you yet. First I'm going to do to your wife what you did to those white women." He grinned as Toby fought against the rope and gag. "Only I bet I can make her like it. And when she's yelling for more, we're going to hang you."

"I don't hold with raping no woman," Wood said, firmly this time. Snarling, Billy T. whirled, bringing the gun up with him.

"You just shut the fuck up, then. It ain't rape, it's justice."

"I can't stop this bleeding."

Billy T. glanced over to where one of the men tried to staunch the wound on his brother's shoulder. "Well then, let him bleed for a goddamn minute. Won't kill him." He was losing them. He could feel it in the way the men were shifting their feet, shifting their eyes away from the woman who lay bleeding on the ground.

He set his gun down and unbuckled his belt. He was already hard at the idea of taking a woman by force. Once they saw how it was, what kind of man he was, they'd be behind him again.

"Somebody's coming, Billy."

"Probably that Will. Always was a day late and a dollar short."

He stepped over to Winnie, straddled her. He hooked a hand in the bodice of her nightgown when the car fishtailed to a halt, kicking dust as rifle fire split the air.

"I got this pointed right at your balls, Billy T." Tucker stepped out of the car, skin twitching at the idea of having guns aimed at him. "It's got more of a kick than I do, I guarantee."

"This ain't your concern." Billy T. straightened, cursing himself for setting his weapon aside. "We come out here to do what should have been done already."

"Yeah, burning crosses is your style. Like killing an unarmed man." He saw the blood on Winnie's face and was sickened. "Hitting women. It takes a lot of guts to come out here, what, six of you against one man, a woman, and a couple of kids."

"This nigger's been killing our women."

Tucker merely lifted a brow. "For all I know, you've been doing it."

"We're hanging us a killer tonight. You think you can stop us? You and your drunken brother?" He hauled Winnie up in front of him and took two backward steps to reach his gun. "Seems to me there's six of us and two of you."

Another set of headlights sliced the dark, and Della's Olds cruised to a halt. Three women stepped out with rifles.

"Remind me to give them all hell later," Tucker muttered to Dwayne. "Looks like the odds just changed," he said to Billy T. "Evened up quite a bit."

"You think we're worried about a bunch of women?"

To show her feelings about that, Della let off a shot that plowed the earth between Wood's feet. "Y'all know I can shoot. And these two ladies here, well, they're liable to get lucky. Caroline, you aim that Winchester at that asshole bleeding by the porch. He ain't liable to be moving around too much, so you should get a clean shot."

Caroline swallowed, then shouldered the rifle.

"Fuck this." Wood tossed down his gun. "I ain't shooting at no women any more than I'd be raping one."

"Then you might want to step out of the line of fire," Tucker advised him. "Looks like it's five to five." His lips curved as he heard the siren. "And that's about to change. Now, if I were you, Billy T., I'd set that woman down, real gentle like. Otherwise, my finger's going to slip and I'm going to blow a hole through your brother."

"Jesus Christ, Billy, put her down." John Thomas scrambled back against the steps.

Billy T. licked his lips. "Maybe I'll put one through you."

"I expect you could. But since you can't work that rifle one-handed, you'll have to put her down just the same. Then we'll take our chances."

"Put her down, Billy," Wood said quietly. "The gun, too. This is crazy business here." He turned to the others. "This is crazy business."

In agreement, they tossed down their guns.

"You're standing alone now," Tucker pointed out. "You can die alone, too. Doesn't make a damn bit of difference to me."

In disgust, Billy T. dropped Winnie to the ground, where she began to sob and crawl toward her husband. After tossing his gun aside, he started to walk toward his car.

"I'd stand where you are," Tucker said quietly.

"You won't shoot me in the back."

Tucker squeezed off a round that shattered the windshield. "The hell I wouldn't."

"Go ahead and do it," Cousin Lulu suggested. "Save the taxpayers money."

"That's enough." Caroline wiped sweaty hands on her jeans and hurried over to Winnie. "There's nothing to worry about now."

"My babies."

"I'll go to them in just a minute." She fought the knot loose from Winnie's wrists, hoping to free her before the children saw it. But they were already racing out of the house, Jim still carrying the butcher knife stained with John Thomas's blood, and the little girl tripping over the hem of her nightgown.

"Here now." Caroline dragged the noose over Toby's head. Her vision wavered with tears as she took the bloody knife to cut his bonds. "You're hurt." Her fingers came away wet as she touched his side. "Somebody call the doctor."

"We'll get him to the hospital." Tucker knelt down. Burke and Carl were already reading Billy T. and the others their rights. "What do you say, Toby? Up to a ride?"

He was holding his family, his good eye leaking tears as he gathered them close. "Guess I could stir myself." He tried a wan smile while Winnie wept against his chest. "You driving?"

"You bet."

"We'll get there fast anyway."

"There you go. Dwayne, give me a hand here. Della, you take the kids on down to Sweetwater. Caroline." Tucker looked around as she stood and walked away. "Where are you going?"

She didn't look back. "To get a hose and put out this obscenity."

Chapter 26

SCREAMS SHIMMIED ON THE hot air. High pitched howls echoed, chased by shrieks of wild laughter. Colored lights flashed and blinked and whirled, turning the fallow Eustis Field into a fantasy of motion.

The carnival had come to Innocence.

People readily dug out their spare change to be caught by the Octopus, whirled by the Zipper, and scrambled by the Round-Up.

Kids went racing by, their shouts and squeals rising above the piping calliope music, their fingers sticky with cotton candy, their cheeks puffed out with corn dogs or stuffed with fried dough. Teenagers scrambled to impress one another by knocking down bottles, ringing bells, or—in the words of one daredevil—riding the Scrambler till they puked.

Many of the older set settled for bingo at a quarter a card. Others touched by gambling fever lost their paychecks trying to outsmart the Wheel of Fortune.

To anyone traveling over Old Longstreet Bridge, it would look like an ordinary summer carnival on the outskirts of an ordinary small, southern town. The lights and the echo of that calliope might bring a tug of nostalgia to the travelers as they passed by.

But for Caroline, the magic wasn't working.

"I don't know why I let you talk me into coming here."

Tucker swung his arm over her shoulders. "Because you can't resist my fatal southern charm."

She stopped to watch hopefuls pitching coins at glassware that could be had at any respectable yard sale for half the price. "It doesn't seem right, with everything that's happened."

"I don't see what a night at a carnival's going to change. Unless it's to make you smile a little."

"Darleen's going to be buried on Tuesday."

"She's going to be buried Tuesday whether you're here tonight or not."

"Everything that happened last night—"

"Has been taken care of," he finished. "Billy T. and his asshole friends are in jail. Doc says Toby and Winnie are doing just fine. And look here." He pointed to where Cy and Jim were squished together in a cup of the Scrambler, eyes wide, mouths open in laughing howls as they were spun in mad circles. "Those two are smart enough to grab a little fun when it's offered."

Tucker pressed a kiss to her hair and continued to walk. "You know why we call this Eustis Field?"

"No." A smile ghosted around her lips. "But I'm sure you're about to tell me."

"Well, Cousin Eustis—actually, he'd have been an uncle, but there're so many greats in there it gets confusing—he wasn't what you'd call a tolerant man. He ran Sweetwater from 1842 until 1856, and it prospered. Not just the cotton. He had six children—legitimately—and about a dozen more on the other side of the sheets. Word was he liked to try out the female slaves when they came of age. That age being about thirteen, fourteen."

"That's despicable. You named a field for him?"

"I'm not finished." He paused to light half a cigarette. "Now, Eustis, he wasn't what you'd call an admirable man. It didn't bother him at all to sell off his own children—the dark-skinned ones. His wife was a papist, a devoted one, who used to beg him to repent his sins and save his soul from a fiery hell. But Eustis just kept doing what came naturally to him."

"Naturally?"

"To him," Tucker said. Behind him, a bell clanged as some hotshot proved his strength and impressed his girl into rapturous squeals. "One day a young female slave took off. She had the baby Eustis had fathered with her. Eustis didn't tolerate runaways. No indeed. He set out the men and the dogs, and rode out himself to hunt her down. He was riding across this field when he shouted out that he'd spotted her. She wouldn't have had much of a chance with him on horseback and a whip in his hand. Then his horse reared. Nobody knows why—might've been spooked by a snake or rabbit. Or maybe it was that fiery hell reaching out to grab old Eustis. But he broke his neck." Tucker took a last drag on his cigarette, then flung it away. "Right about there, where that Ferris wheel's standing. Seems fitting somehow, don't you think? That all these people, black and white—maybe some with a dribble or two of Eustis Longstreet's blood—should be kicking up their heels on this field where he met his Maker."

She leaned her head against his shoulder. "What happened to the girl, and her baby?"

"Funny thing about that. Nobody else saw them. Not that day or any day after."

She took a deep breath of candy-scented air. "I'd like a ride on the Ferris wheel."

"Wouldn't mind it myself. Afterward, how'd you like me to win you one of those black velvet paintings of Elvis?"

Laughing, she hooked an arm around his waist. "Words fail me."

♦ ♦ ♦ ♦

*D*ON'T YOU WANT TO play some bingo, Cousin Lulu?" Ever hopeful, Dwayne pressed a hand to his jittery stomach.

"What the hell do I want to sit around putting beans on a card for?" Lulu stomped up to the ticket booth to buy another roll. "We only been on the Round-Up once, and missed the Scrambler altogether. That Crack the Whip's worth another go or two." She stuffed the tickets in the pocket of her army surplus slacks. "You're looking a might green, boy. Indigestion?"

He swallowed gamely. "You could call it that."

"Shouldn't have eaten all that fried dough before we took a spin. Best thing to do is bring it up, empty your stomach." She grinned. "A round on the Scrambler'll take care of that."

Which was exactly what he feared. "Cousin Lulu, why don't we take a turn down the midway, win some prizes?"

"Sucker's games."

"Who's a sucker?" Josie strolled up, carrying a huge purple elephant. "I shot twelve ducks, ten rabbits, four moose, and a snarling grizzly bear to win this grand prize."

"Don't know what a grown woman's going to do with a stuffed elephant," Lulu grumbled, but she took a shine to the rhinestone collar around the purple pachyderm's neck.

"It's a souvenir," she said, and shoved it into Teddy Rubenstein's arms so she could light a cigarette. "What's the matter, Dwayne? You're looking a little sickly."

"Weak stomach," Lulu announced, and poked a finger into Dwayne's midsection. "Corn dogs and fried dough. Boy's got all that grease floating around inside." She narrowed her eyes at Teddy. "I know you. You're that Yankee doctor who makes a living cutting dead people up. Do you keep the innards in bottles?"

With a strangled sound Dwayne shambled away, one hand clamped over his mouth.

"Best thing for him," Lulu declared.

"I guess I'd better go hold his head." With a sigh Josie turned back to Teddy. "Honey, why don't you take Cousin Lulu for a ride? I'll catch up."

"It would be my pleasure." Teddy held out his arm. "What's your poison, Cousin Lulu?"

Pleased, she hooked her arm through his. "I had my mind set on the Scrambler."

"Allow me to escort you."

"What's your given name, boy?" she asked as they wound through the crowd. "I may as well call you by it, as you're sleeping with my kin."

He gave a throat-clearing cough. "It's Theodore, ma'am. My friends call me Teddy."

"All right, Teddy. We'll take us a walk on the wild side here, and you can tell me all you know about these murders." Graciously, she handed him the tickets to pay their way through the gate.

♦ ♦ ♦ ♦

THAT MISS LULU." SLURPING on a Snow-Kone, Jim nodded in respect. "She sure is something."

Cy wiped purple juice from his mouth and watched as Lulu sat regally in the jerking, spinning car of the Scrambler. "I seen her standing on her head in her room."

"What she do that for?"

"Don't rightly know. Something about having the blood slosh into her brain so she don't go senile. One day I found her lying on the lawn. I thought she'd had a spell or was dead or something. She said she was pretending to be a cat for a day, and gave me hell for disturbing her nap."

Jim grinned and crunched ice. "My granny mostly sits in a rocker and knits."

They started to walk, taking time to stop by some of the booths and watch balls being tossed, darts being thrown, wheels being spun. They each spent a quarter at the Duck Pond, where Jim won a rubber spider and Cy a plastic whistle.

They debated having their fortunes told by Madame Mystique, then passed her up for a look at the Amazing Voltura, who absorbed a thousand volts of electricity while miniature light bulbs fizzed and popped all over her curvaceous body.

"Pretty fakey," Cy decided, and gave his whistle a toot.

"Yeah, I bet they use batteries or something."

Cy scuffed his shoe in the dirt. "Can I ask you something?"

"Sure."

"I was wondering. Well, how did it feel, stabbing John Thomas Bonny?"

Frowning, Jim dangled his rubber spider by the string. He figured he could get at least one good squeal out of little Lucy with it. "It didn't feel at all, I guess. I was all numb and my ears were ringing. I had Lucy hiding in the closet like Ma told me, but I figured he'd find her. And I didn't know what they were going to do to my ma, and my daddy."

"Were they . . ." Cy wet his lips. "Were they really going to string him up?"

"They had a rope, and guns." Jim didn't say anything about the burning cross. Somehow that was the worst part of all. "They kept saying he killed them women. But he didn't."

"They were saying my daddy killed them, too." Cy bent for something shiny, but it was only a piece of foil from a pack of cigarettes. "I guess he didn't do it either."

"Somebody did," Jim said, and the two boys gazed silently at the flow of people. "Might even be somebody we know."

"Almost has to be, if you think about it."

"Cy?"

"Yeah?"

"When I stuck that knife into John Thomas Bonny? Made me feel sorta sick at my stomach watching it go in. I don't see how anybody could stick people again and again. Less they was crazy."

"Guess they are, then." Cy remembered his father's eyes, and thought he knew all about crazy. Shaking off the sense of dread, he dug in his pocket. "I still got three tickets left."

With a grin, Jim dug in his own. "The Round-Up."

"Last one there pukes on his shoes."

With a war cry, both boys dashed off, making a beeline for the whirling lights of the Round-Up. Both Cy and his innocent pleasure came to a skidding halt when Vernon stepped out in front of him.

"Having yourself a high old time, ain't you, boy?"

Cy stared up at his brother, into the face that was a ghost image of their father, eyes glazed with anger as hard and cold as ice skimmed over a pond. He hadn't seen Vernon since Austin's funeral. There, his brother hadn't spoken to him at all, only stared at him across the hole in the ground where their father would spend his eternity.

The lights of the midway suddenly seemed to brighten, burning hot on Cy's face while the rest of Innocence played in the dark.

"I'm not doing anything."

"You're always doing something." Vernon stepped forward. From behind them Loretta clutched one child to the mound made by another and made a small sound of distress that was ignored by all. "Getting yourself a job over to Sweetwater on the sly. Spending all your time with this kind." He jerked his head toward Jim. "Don't matter to you that them colored's plotting against white Christians, killing white women, and your own sister among 'em. You got bigger fish to fry."

"Jim's my friend." Cy didn't take his eyes off his brother's face. But he knew those big hands were fisted, just as he knew they would pummel him to the ground. And because they were blood, there were many who would turn away rather than interfere. "We weren't doing anything."

"You got your colored friends." Vernon's lips twisted as he snagged Cy's collar. "Maybe you helped them get Edda Lou out there in the swamp where they could rape and kill her. Maybe you held the knife yourself and murdered her same as you murdered Daddy."

"I didn't kill anybody." Cy shoved at Vernon's hand even as he was dragged up to his toes. "I didn't. Daddy was going to hurt Miss Caroline and she had to shoot him."

"That's a filthy lie." Vernon slammed his free hand against Cy's head, and white stars exploded in front of the boy's eyes. "You sent him out to die and they hunted him down like a dog. Used their godless money to cover it all up. You think I don't know how it was? You think I don't know how you fixed it so you could live in that fine, big house, trading your father's life for a soft bed and a life of sin." His eyes flattened like a snake's as he shook Cy off his feet. "You got the evil inside you, boy. With Daddy gone, it's up to me to crush it out."

His arm reared back. Even as Cy was covering his face in defense, Jim was leaping. He grabbed Vernon's arm with both hands and hung on, kicking. Between the two of them, they were still fifty pounds short of Vernon's weight, but fear and loyalty added sinew. Vernon was forced to drop Cy in a heap so that he could buck Jim off. The minute he dragged Cy up, Jim was on him again, agile as a ferret. This time he hitched on to Vernon's back, hooking an arm around the thick neck.

"Run, Cy." Jim clung like a leech while Vernon struggled to yank him off. "Run! I got him."

But Cy wasn't going anywhere. After shaking his head clear, he got back to his feet. His nose was bleeding a little from his last fall, and he swiped a hand under it. He thought he understood now what Jim had meant when he'd said he'd been numb. Cy was numb. His ears were ringing—either from the blow or from adrenaline. Inside his thin chest his heart was banging against his ribs like a spoon against a kettle.

The lights were all on him. Beyond the circle made by him, his brother, and Jim, all was shadowy to his vision. The music of the calliope had slowed to a funeral dirge.

He swiped more blood away, then fisted his smeared hands. "I ain't going to run." He'd run from his father. It felt as though he'd been running all of his life. And here and now was the time to take his stand. What was left of his innocence had fled, and he was a man. "I ain't going to run," he repeated, and hefted his bloody fists.

Vernon shook Jim off and grinned. "Think you can take me on, you little shit?"

"I ain't going to run," Cy said again quietly. "And you ain't going to whip up on me anymore either."

Still grinning, Vernon spread his arms. "Take your best shot. It'll be your last."

Cy's fist snaked out. He would think later that it had been as if he'd had no control over it. His arm, his clenched hand, and the fire behind it had been something apart. And its aim was deadly keen.

Blood spurted from Vernon's nose. There was a roar from the crowd that had gathered, that blood-lust roar that humans seem unable to prevent when one of their kind wars with another. Cy heard it as a tidal wave of satisfaction even as the power of the punch shot pain up his own arm.

"Well, well." Tucker stepped out of the shadows misting Cy's vision, and stepped between them. "Y'all putting on a side show? What's the price of admission?"

Blood dripped down his face as Vernon bared his teeth. "Get the hell out of my way, Longstreet, or I'll cut right through you."

"You'll have to, to get to him." There was a trace of that lust in Tucker's eyes as well. The midway lights glinted on them, turning them gold as a cat's. "Taking a page out of your father's book, Vernon? Slapping down what's smaller than you?"

"He's my kin."

"That'll always be a mystery to me." Tucker threw out an arm when Cy started to move around him. "You just hold on, son. I'm not going to tell you twice." He could feel the air tremble between him and Cy. Not with fear; fear had a different rhythm. This was energy. The boy would have gotten a few good shots in, Tucker mused. Before Vernon broke him to pieces. "You're not laying another hand on him, Vernon."

"And who's going to stop me?"

The thought of having his face battered again made Tucker sigh. The last bruises had barely faded. "I reckon I am."

"And me." Sweaty and far from steady, Dwayne stepped beside his brother.

One by one, men moved out of the crowd and ranged themselves beside the Longstreets. Cy had been wrong—there were more than a few who would have come forward, and they did now. Black and white, forming a silent wall that spoke eloquently of justice.

Vernon flexed frustrated fists. "He can't hide all the time."

"He isn't hiding now," Tucker said. "I think he's proved that. He may be half your size, Vernon, but he's twice the man you are. And he's under my protection. Your mother signed a paper that makes it so. You'd best leave it alone."

"Whatever you paid her to sign him away, he's still my blood. You got too much of my blood on your hands."

Tucker stepped forward, lowering his voice so only Vernon could hear. "He's nothing to you. We both know it. Kinship's just an excuse you use to hurt and call it family business. There's nobody standing with you on this, Vernon. Nobody. Going after him's only going to make it hard for you around here. Your family's had enough grief."

"And you brought it on us." He leaned his face close to Tucker's. "This ain't over."

"I don't expect it is. But it's done for the night." Turning, Tucker walked through the line to where Caroline was dealing calmly with Cy's bloody nose. "I sure do love a carnival," he said. The squeeze he gave Cy's shoulder transmitted both approval and reassurance.

"I was going to fight him, Mr. Tucker."

"You did what you had to do."

Furious, Caroline balled bloody tissues in her hand. "Men. You always think the way to handle any problem is with your fists."

"And women like to talk them away." He winked at Cy, then pulled Caroline close for a quick kiss. "Now, personally, I prefer loving my way out of a problem. But it takes all kinds."

"Don't it just?" Josie strolled up, snapping her purse shut. She carried her pretty little pearl-handled derringer inside among her other necessities. Right now she was almost disappointed that she hadn't had cause to use it. She kept her back to Tucker, whom she'd yet to forgive. "Cy, honey, you're going to be the talk of the annual Innocence Fourth of July Carnival." She kissed his cheek and made him blush. "You bleeding anywhere, Jim?"

"No, ma'am. I landed on my butt, is all." He was busy brushing himself off with hands that shook from excitement. "Me and Cy, we coulda took him."

"I'll just bet you could." Josie squeezed Jim's bicep and rolled her eyes appreciatively. "We got us a couple of strapping young boys here, Caroline. I wonder if I could impose on you two to accompany me to the lemonade stand? It seems my gentleman escort has deserted me for another woman." She nodded toward the Scrambler, where Teddy and Cousin Lulu were taking another round. "Men are such fickle creatures."

Jim puffed out his chest. "We'll go with you, Miss Josie. Won't we, Cy?"

"Is it all right, Mr. Tucker?"

"It's just fine." He passed a hand over Cy's hair, left it lie there a moment. "It is just fine, Cy."

Cy took a deep breath and let it out slowly. "I know it. I didn't run. I'm not running from him or anybody anymore."

Tucker let his hand slide off Cy's shoulder. He thought it was a pity that youth and its simplicity were so soon and permanently lost. "Running away and walking are two different things. Keeping clear of Vernon won't change what you did for yourself tonight. But it might keep your mama from any more grief. You think about that."

"I guess I will."

"Go on with Josie." He watched them walk away with some regret, and something colder, that was suspicion.

"I guess I'm going home," Dwayne said, narrowing his eyes against the spinning lights.

"You sober enough to find the house?" Tucker asked him.

"I haven't had much—and tossed up what I did." Dwayne offered a weak smile. "I never did have the head for those whirly rides."

"Or the stomach," Tucker agreed. "You get sick every blessed year."

"I don't like to mess with tradition. Della and Cousin Lulu came with me, but I don't think they're ready to leave just yet."

"Caro and I'll get them home."

"That's fine, then. 'Night, Caroline." He sauntered off alone, moving beyond the lights and music and into the shadows. Tucker nearly called him back. It didn't seem right that his brother should look so lonely. Then Dwayne was gone, and the moment passed.

"Well . . ." Caroline tossed the bloody tissues into a trash basket. "You certainly show a woman an interesting evening."

"I do what I can." Hearing the strain in her voice, he slipped an arm around her. "You're upset?"

"Upset?" she countered. "You could say so. It upsets me to see that boy have to fight his own brother. He's lost two members of his family and is estranged from the rest of them just because he's different. It's hard to see him have to face those kinds of demands and pressures, those choices, when he's only half-grown."

Tucker drew her around to face him. "Who are we talking about, Caro? You or Cy?"

"It has nothing to do with me."

"Maybe you're shifting things around. Looking at him and seeing yourself at his age, facing something you couldn't fight with your fists."

"I didn't fight at all."

"You took your stand later, and in a different way. That doesn't make it any harder when what you're standing against is family." He led her back a little, where they could stand and watch the lights and the colors and the knots of people. "You want to make it up with your mother."

"There's nothing—"

"You want to make it up," he said again with a quiet assurance in his voice that stopped her from arguing. "I know what I'm saying. I never settled things with my father. I never let him know what I thought or felt or wanted. I don't know if he'd have given a damn. And that's just it. I don't know because I never worked up the gumption to say it all to his face."

"She knows how I feel."

"So you start from there. On your terms. I don't like to see you sad, Caroline. And I know what kind of pull family brings."

"I'll think about it." She tilted her head back to study him. He was looking beyond the midway, into the lights. There was something in his eyes that had her moving closer. "What are you thinking about?"

"Family," he murmured. "And what runs through the blood." Deliberately, he smiled, but that glint in his eye remained. "Let's go check out that Ferris wheel."

Tucker pulled her back into the crowd and the noise. But he was thinking. If Austin had been capable of murder, perhaps Austin's son was equally capable.

The sins of the father, he mused. It was a quotation that would have suited Austin down to the ground. Perhaps Vernon carried that same violent and twisted gene.

As the Ferris wheel began its slow backward arch, Tucker draped an arm around Caroline's shoulders.

He was sure of one thing. Among the laughter and lights of the carnival, a murderer hunted.

Chapter 27

"THERE'S COFFEE ON THE stove, Tuck." Burke yawned over his bowl of raisin bran. "I don't believe I've seen you up and around this early in twenty years."

"I wanted to catch you before you went into your office."

"My office." Burke's lips twisted into a grimace as he held out his morning mug so that Tucker could top it up with hot coffee. "Don't you mean Burns's office? My butt hasn't felt the seat of my own chair in three days."

"Is he getting anywhere, or is he just blowing smoke?"

"He's generated more paperwork than the Bank of England. Faxes, Federal Express packages, conference calls to Washington, D.C. We got us a bulletin board with pictures of all the victims tacked to it. Vital statistics, time and place of death. He's got stuff referenced and cross-referenced till your head spins."

Tucker sat down. "You're not telling me anything, Burke."

Burke met Tucker's gaze. "There's not much I'm free to tell you. We've got a list of suspects."

Nodding, Tucker took a sip of coffee. "Am I still on it?"

"You've got an alibi for Edda Lou." Burke took a spoonful of cereal, hesitated, then set it down again. "I guess you know Burns has taken a real dislike to you. He doesn't think much of your sister saying you were up playing cards with her half the night."

"I'm not too worried about that."

"You should be." Burke broke off when he heard someone moving around in the living room. A moment later the Looney Tunes theme warbled from the television. "Eight o'clock," he said with a smile. "That kid's got it down to a science." He picked up his coffee. "I'll tell you this, Tuck. Burns would like nothing better than to hang this whole thing around your neck. He won't do anything that's not straight and legal, but if he can find a way to reel you in, it would give him a lot of pleasure."

"What we got here's a personality clash," Tucker said with a thin smile. "They got a time of death on Darleen yet?"

"Teddy's putting it at between nine P.M. and midnight."

"Since I was with Caroline from about nine on, the night Darleen was killed, that ought to ease me out of the running."

"With a series of murders like this, it's not just a matter of motive and opportunity. He's got a head doctor who worked up a psychiatric profile. We're looking for someone with a grudge against women—especially women who might be a bit free with their favors. Someone who knew each victim well enough to get them alone."

Burke's flakes were getting soggy. He scooped them up more for fuel than enjoyment. "Darleen's a puzzle," he went on. "Maybe it was just chance that he came across her on the road that way. Could have been impulse. But chance and impulse don't follow the pattern."

Tucker let that settle for a minute. There was a pattern, he mused, but he didn't think anybody had put all the lines and checks together just yet. "I want to get back to that psychiatric stuff. You've got somebody with a grudge against women—maybe because they hated their mama, or some woman let them down along the way."

"That's the idea."

"Before Darleen, you'd pretty well settled on Austin."

"He fit the profile," Burke agreed. "And after he went after Caroline with a buck knife, it looked rock solid."

"But unless Austin came back from the dead, he couldn't have killed Darleen." Tucker shifted in his chair. "What do you think about heredity, Burke? About blood and genes and bad seeds?"

"Anybody with kids thinks about it some. Anybody with parents, I should say," he added, and shoved his bowl aside. "I spent a lot of years wondering if I'd make all the wrong moves the way my father did, push myself into corners or let myself get pushed there, like him."

"I'm sorry. I should have thought before I asked."

"No, it was a long time ago. Almost twenty years now. It's better to look to your own kids. That one out there." He pointed a spoon toward the living room, where his youngest watched Bugs outwit Elmer Fudd. "He looks like me. I got pictures of myself at his age, and it's almost spooky how much he looks like me."

"Vernon favors his daddy," Tucker said. He waited while Burke set his spoon aside. "It can go deeper than coloring and the shape of a nose, Burke. It can go to personality and tendencies, gestures, habits. I've had reason to think on this because of my own family." It was something he didn't like to talk about, not even with Burke. "Dwayne's got the same sickness that killed our father. Maybe he's got a better disposition, but it's there, rooted inside. All I have to do is look in the mirror, or at Dwayne and Josie, and I see our mother. She's stamped right on our faces. And she had a love of books, poetry especially. I got that, too. I didn't ask for it, it's just there."

"I won't argue that. Marvella's got a way of tilting her head the same way, the same angle as Susie does. And she's got Susie's stubborn streak—'I want it and I'll find a way to get it.' We pass things on, good and bad, whether we aim to or not."

"Vernon's not gentle with his wife, any more than Austin was gentle with his."

"What brought this on, Tucker?"

"You heard about the ruckus at the carnival last night?"

"That young Cy bloodied his brother's nose? Marvella and Bobby Lee were there. Nobody thought it was a shame."

"Vernon's not a popular man. His daddy wasn't either. They've got the same look about them, in the eyes, Burke." Tucker kicked back in the chair to stretch his legs. "My mama bought me this picture book once. A Bible stories book. I remember this one picture. It was of Isaiah or Ezekiel or somebody. One of those prophets who strolled off into the wasteland for forty days to fast and meet the Lord? This was supposed to be a picture of him after he came back spouting prophesies and speaking in tongues. Whatever the hell they did when they'd cooked their brains in the desert. He had this look in his eyes, this wild, rolling look like a weasel gets when he smells chicken feathers. I always wondered why the Lord chose to speak through crazy people. I expect it was because they wouldn't question whatever voice they heard inside their head. Seems to me they might hear something else inside there, too. Something not so full of light and good will."

Saying nothing, Burke rose to pour more coffee. Burns had said something about voices. About how some serial killers claim to have been told what to do and how to do it. The Son of Sam had claimed his neighbor's dog had ordered him to kill.

For himself, Burke didn't go in for the mystical. He figured David Berkowitz had juggled psychiatry against the law to cop an insanity plea. But Tucker's theory made him uneasy.

"Are you trying to tell me you think Vernon hears voices?"

"I don't know what's inside his head, but I know what I saw in his eyes last night. The same thing I saw in Austin's when he was choking me and calling me by my father's name. That prophet look. If he could have broken Cy in two, he would've done it. And I'd stake Sweetwater against the fact that he'd have considered it holy work."

"I don't know that he had more than a passing acquaintance with any of the victims other than Edda Lou."

"This is Innocence. Nobody gets through their life without knowing what there is to know about everybody else. What's that saying about the apple not falling far from the tree? If Austin had it in him to kill, his son might have the same."

"I'll talk to him."

Satisfied, Tucker nodded. When the phone rang, they both ignored it. From upstairs, Susie answered it on the second ring. "You're going to be at Sweetwater tonight, for the fireworks?"

"Unless I want my wife and kids to leave me."

"Carl, too?"

"No reason for him to stay in town when everybody'll be out at your place. Why?"

Tucker moved his shoulders restlessly. "A lot of people, a lot of noise and confusion. I'm worried, especially about Josie and Caroline. I'd feel better knowing you and Carl are close."

"Burke." Susie came in. She was still in her robe, smelling of her shower with carnation-scented soap. Studying her, Burke thought she looked no more than twenty.

"Was that the office?" he asked her.

"No, it was Della." She laid her hand over Tucker's. "Matthew Burns had Dwayne brought in for questioning."

◆ ◆ ◆ ◆

IF HE HADN'T BEEN so infuriated, Tucker would have been amused. The idea of Dwayne, softhearted, bleary-eyed Dwayne, as a murder suspect was certainly laughable. The fact that his brother had been yanked out of bed and driven into town to be questioned by some smugfaced FBI agent was not.

Struggling with his temper, Tucker walked into the sheriff's office with Burke. He wouldn't lose it, he promised himself. It would suit Burns too well to kick him out. Instead, he flipped his brother a cigarette, then lighted one for himself.

"You're getting an early start today, Burns," Tucker said mildly. "Guess you forgot today's a national holiday."

"I'm aware of the date." Burns stretched his legs behind Burke's desk and kept his hands folded on top. "I'm also aware that you have a parade scheduled for noon. My business won't interfere with your town's celebrations. Sheriff, I'm told you'll be blocking off the main drag by ten."

"That's right."

"I'd like my car moved where I'll be able to get in and out of town as necessary." Taking out his keys, he set them on the edge of the desk.

Carl saw the flare in Burke's eyes and stepped forward. "I'll move it on down to Magnolia." Jingling the keys in his hand, he stopped by Tucker. "I'm sorry, Tuck. I had orders to bring him in."

"It's all right, Carl. It shouldn't take long to straighten this out. Heard your girl's going to be twirling today."

"She's been practicing day and night. Her grandpappy bought one of those video recorders so he can shoot her whole routine as she marches."

"I'm sure that's fascinating, Deputy," Burns put in, "but we have business to conduct here." His gaze shifted to Tucker. "Official business."

"I'll be sure to watch for her myself, Carl," Tucker said. He waited until the deputy went out before taking another drag. "Dwayne, did they read you your rights?"

"Mr. Longstreet isn't under arrest. Yet," Burns interrupted. "He's merely being questioned."

"He's got a right to a lawyer, doesn't he?"

"Naturally." Burns spread his hands. "If you're concerned that your rights might be abused, Mr. Longstreet, or that you may incriminate yourself, please feel free to call your attorney. We'll be happy to wait."

"I'd just as soon get it done." Dwayne looked miserably at Tucker. "Sure could use some coffee, though, and a bottle of aspirin."

"We'll fix you up." Burke patted his shoulder as he walked into the bathroom.

"This is official business, Longstreet." Burns inclined his head in dismissal. "You have no place here."

"Burke deputized me." Tucker's lips spread in a slow smile. Though Burke paused, lifting his brows as he came back in with the aspirin, he said nothing to contradict the statement. "He can always use some extra help on the Fourth."

"That's the truth," Burke commented as he shook tablets from the plastic bottle. "And seeing as my youngest has a birthday today on top of it, I'd be obliged if we could get things moving."

"Very well." Burns punched in his recorder. "Mr. Longstreet, you reside at the property known as Sweetwater, in the county of Bolivar, Mississippi?"

"That's right." Dwayne accepted the mug of coffee and the aspirin. "The Longstreets have been at Sweetwater nearly two hundred years."

"Yes." History and family legacies didn't interest Burns. "You live there with your brother and your sister."

"And Della. She's been housekeeper at Sweetwater for more than thirty years. And right now Cousin Lulu's visiting." Dwayne singed his tongue with the hot coffee, but the aspirin went down. "She's a cousin on my mama's side. No telling how long she'll stay. Cousin Lulu's been coming and going as she pleases as long as anyone can remember. I recollect once—"

"If you'll save the home-boy routine," Burns said, "I'd like to finish before the brass bands and batons."

Dwayne caught Tucker's grin and shrugged. "Just answering your question. Oh, and we've got Cy and Caroline with us now, too. That what you want to know?"

"Your marital status?"

"I'm divorced. Two years come October. That's when the papers came through, wasn't it, Tucker?"

"That's right."

"And your ex-wife now lives where?"

"Up in Nashville. Rosebank Avenue. She's got a nice little house there, close enough to school that the boys can walk."

"And she is the former Adalaide Koons?"

"Sissy," Dwayne corrected him. "Her little brother never could say Adalaide, so she was Sissy."

"And Mrs. Longstreet was pregnant with your first son when you married?"

Dwayne frowned into his coffee. "I don't see that it's any of your business, but it's no secret, I guess."

"You married her to give the child a name."

"We got married 'cause we figured it was best."

With a murmur of agreement, Burns steepled his hands. "And shortly after the birth of your second child, your wife left you."

Dwayne drained his coffee. Over the rim, his bloodshot eyes hardened. "That's no secret either."

"You'll agree it was an unpleasant scene?" Burns shifted forward to read some notes. "Your wife locked you out of the house after a violent argument—I believe you'd been drinking heavily—and threw your belongings out of an upstairs window. She then took your children to Nashville, where she took up residence with a shoe salesman who moonlighted as a musician."

Dwayne examined the cigarette Tucker had tossed him. "I guess that's about right."

"How did it make you feel, Mr. Longstreet, when the woman you had married under duress left you, taking your children, and turned to a second-rate guitar player?"

Dwayne took his time lighting the cigarette. "I guess she had to do what suited her best."

"So you were amenable to the situation?"

"I didn't try to stop her, if that's what you mean. Didn't seem like I was much good at being married anyway."

"The divorce suit she filed against you accused you of emotional cruelty, violence, erratic and unstable behavior, and stated you were a physical risk to both her and your children. Did that seem harsh?"

Dwayne dragged deep on tobacco and wished desperately for whiskey. "I expect she was feeling harsh. I can't say I did right by her, or the boys either."

"You don't have to do this, Dwayne." When his control broke, Tucker stepped forward to take his brother's arm. "You don't have to answer this fucker's questions about a marriage that's over, or your feelings about it."

Burns inclined his head. "Is there a reason your brother shouldn't confirm what I already know?"

Tucker let go of Dwayne to slap his hands on the desk. "I can't think of one. Just like I can't think of a reason I shouldn't kick your skinny butt all the way back to D.C."

"We can discuss that on our own time, Longstreet. Right now you're interfering with a federal investigation. If you persist, you'll do your complaining from one of those cells."

Tucker grabbed Burns's pinstriped tie and yanked upward. "Why don't I show you how we handle things down here in the delta?"

"Leave him alone." Dwayne stirred himself to snag Tucker's wrist.

"The hell I will."

"I said leave him alone." Dwayne stuck his face close to Tucker's. "I've got nothing to hide. This Yankee sonofabitch can ask questions from now to doomsday and that won't change. Leave him be so we can get it done."

Reluctantly, Tucker loosened his grip. "We're going to finish this, you and me."

Stone-faced, Burns straightened his tie. "It'll be a pleasure." He remained standing, turning to the bulletin board at his back. "Mr. Longstreet, were you acquainted with Arnette Gantrey?" Burns tapped a finger against the space between a photo of a smiling blond woman and a black-and-white police photo taken at Gooseneck Creek.

"I knew Arnette. We went to school together, dated a few times."

"And Francie Logan?" Burns slid his finger to the next set of photos.

"I knew Francie." Dwayne averted his eyes. "Everybody knew Francie. She grew up here. Lived in Jackson for a while, then came back after getting divorced."

"And you were acquainted with Edda Lou Hatinger?"

Dwayne forced himself to look back, but focused on the tip of Burns's finger. "Yeah. I knew Darleen, too, if that's what you're getting at."

"Did you know a woman named Barbara Kinsdale?"

"I don't think so." Dwayne's brow creased as he tried out the name in his head. "Nobody around here named Kinsdale."

"Are you quite sure?" Burns unpinned a photo from the board. "Take a look."

Dwayne picked up the photo from the desk, grateful it was a shot of a live woman. She was a pretty brunette, perhaps thirty, with straight hair sweeping slight shoulders. "I've never seen her before."

"Haven't you?" Burns picked up his notes. "Barbara Kinsdale, five foot two, a hundred three pounds, brown hair, blue eyes. Age thirty-one. Does that description sound familiar?"

"I can't say."

"You should be able to say," Burns continued. "It's almost a perfect description of your ex-wife. Mrs. Kinsdale was a cocktail waitress at the Stars and Bars Club in Nashville. Residence 3043 Eastland Avenue. That's about three blocks away from your ex-wife's home. Emmett Cotrain, your ex-wife's fiancé, performed at the Stars and bars on weekends. An interesting coincidence, isn't it?"

A thin bead of sweat dripped down Dwayne's back. "I guess it is."

"It's more interesting that Mrs. Kinsdale was found floating in the Percy Priest Lake, outside of Nashville, late this spring. She was naked, her throat had been slit, and her body mutilated."

Burns tossed another photo across the desk, but in this one, Barbara Kinsdale was very dead. "Where were you on the night of May 22 of this year, Mr. Longstreet?"

"Oh, Jesus." Dwayne shut his eyes. The body hadn't been covered in the police shot, but had been laid out, gray and tortured, for the cold camera lens.

"I should tell you that my information places you in Nashville from the twenty-first to the twenty-third."

"I took my boys to the zoo." Dwayne rubbed shaking hands over his eyes. It did look like Sissy. God almighty, especially dead it looked like Sissy. "I took them to the zoo and to a pizza parlor. They stayed with me at the hotel."

"On the night of the twenty-second you were seen in the hotel bar at approximately ten-thirty. Your children weren't with you."

"They were asleep. I left them in the room and went down and had a drink. Couple drinks," he said with a sigh. "Sissy'd been on me about doing more for them, and wanting a bigger house once she and the guy she was with got married. I didn't have more than two drinks because I didn't want to forget the boys were asleep upstairs."

"And didn't you call your wife from the bar just before midnight?" Burns continued. "You argued with her, threatened her."

"I called her. I was sitting there in the room while the boys slept. My boys. It didn't seem right that I was to help her buy a new house so she could live in it with another man my sons would think of as a father." Pale, shaken, Dwayne looked over at Tucker. "It wasn't the money."

"It was the humiliation," Burns suggested. "The humiliation at the hands of a woman. She'd already made you a laughingstock by locking you out of your own house, leaving you for another man. Now she was demanding more money so she could live a better life with that man."

"I didn't care who she lived with. It just didn't seem right—"

"No, it didn't seem right," Burns agreed. "So you told her there'd be no more money, and that you'd take her to court if she didn't watch her step. That you'd pay her back."

"I don't know what I said exactly."

"She does. Oh, despite your estrangement, she's loyal enough to add that you were always full of bluster when you'd been drinking. She didn't take anything you said seriously, and went back to listen to the next set at the bar. Even stayed on after it closed, since she didn't have the boys to get home to. But Barbara Kinsdale left about two. She walked out into a deserted parking lot. A dark parking lot, where she was knocked unconscious and dragged to a waiting car. She was driven to the lake and slaughtered."

Burns waited a beat. "Do you own a knife, Mr. Longstreet? A long-bladed hunting knife?"

"This is crazy." Dwayne dropped his hands into his lap. "I didn't kill anybody."

"Where were you on the night of June thirtieth, between nine P.M. and midnight?"

"For chrissakes." He stumbled to his feet. "Burke, for chrissakes."

"I think he should have a lawyer." Strain had etched lines around Burke's mouth when he turned to Burns. "I don't think he should answer any more questions without a lawyer."

Well satisfied, Burns spread his hands. "That's his right, of course."

"I was just driving around," Dwayne blurted out. "It was raining and I didn't want to go home. I had a flask in the car and I just drove around."

"And on the night of June twelfth?" Burns asked, working back to the night of Edda Lou's murder.

"I don't know. How the fuck is a man supposed to remember where he is every night of the year?"

"Don't say anything else." Tucker stepped forward to take both of Dwayne's arms. "Don't say anything. You hear me?"

"Tucker, I didn't—you know I didn't."

"I know. Be quiet." He turned to stand between Burns and his brother. "Are you bringing charges?"

The holiday weekend had bogged down his paperwork. Not everyone was as dedicated to justice as Matthew Burns. "I'll have a warrant within twenty-four hours."

"Fine. In the meantime you can fuck yourself. Let's get you home, Dwayne."

"Mr. Longstreet," Burns rose with a nod to each brother. "I'd advise that neither of you think of leaving the area. The federal government has a very long arm."

◆ ◆ ◆ ◆

I NEED A DRINK."

"You need to keep a clear head," Tucker contradicted him, and punched Josie's car up to seventy. "You stay clear of the bottle, Dwayne." He took his eyes off the road long enough to shoot his brother a warning. "Until we get this mess straightened out, you stay clear. I mean it."

"They think I did it." Dwayne rubbed his hands over his face until he was afraid he'd scrub off a layer of skin. "They think I killed all those women, Tuck. Even the one I'd never seen before. She looked like Sissy. Christ, she did look like Sissy."

"We're going to call our lawyer," Tucker said calmly even as his knuckles whitened on the wheel. "And you're going to keep your head clear so you can think back. Think back real carefully until you find out what you were doing, who you were with when Arnette, Francie, and Edda Lou were killed. One's all you need. One of those nights you had to be somewhere with somebody. They won't have a case then. They know it was the same person killed them all. You just have to think."

"Don't you think I want to? Don't you think I'm trying?" Teeth gritted, Dwayne pounded his fists on the dash. "Goddammit, you don't know what it's like once I start in drinking. I told you I forget things. I fucking blank out." Moaning, he dropped his head between his knees. "I blank out, Tucker. Oh, God, I don't know what I'm doing when that happens. I could've done it." Terrified, he squeezed his eyes tight. "Jesus help me, I could've killed them all and not even know."

"That's bullshit." Furious, Tucker swerved to the shoulder. Dwayne opened his runny eyes as the car jerked to a halt. He stared under the seat. Stared and stared until Tucker jerked him upright. "That's fucking bullshit and I don't want to hear any more of it." He shoved Dwayne back, pushing his livid face into his brother's pale one. "You didn't kill anybody, and you get that plain in your head right now. I got an idea who did."

Dwayne swallowed. His head was reeling along with his stomach, but he tried to grip on to that one sentence. "You know?"

"I said I have an idea. I'm going to check into it as soon as we call the lawyer and get him doing whatever the hell lawyers do." He kept his grip tight on Dwayne's shirt. "Now, you listen to me. You're not going to go home and upset Della and Josie and everybody with talk about this. You're going to hold on to yourself, you understand me? You're going to tough this out until it's fixed. If there was one thing the old man had right in his whole miserable ass-kicking life, it was that we've got a responsibility to the family. We're going to stay whole, Dwayne."

"To the family," Dwayne repeated, and shuddered. "I won't let you down."

"All right." He let Dwayne go, then sat back a minute to calm his jittery stomach. "We'll show that Yankee bastard what Longstreets can do once they're riled. I'll call the governor. That ought to rattle Burns's cage a bit. We'll see how quick he gets his fucking warrant."

"I want to go home." Dwayne closed his eyes again when Tucker started the car. "I'll be all right when I get home."

A few minutes later they turned through the gates of Sweetwater. "You just tell them Burns asked you a bunch of stupid questions and that's that," Tucker advised. "Don't say anything about Sissy or that business in Nashville."

"I won't." Dwayne stared at the house, white and lovely and graceful as a woman in the morning sunlight. "I'm going to figure it out, Tucker. And I'll fix it, like I used to."

"This time you let me do the fixing."

As Tucker parked by the steps, Josie came out. She was still in her robe and her hair was tousled about the shoulders. It didn't take Tucker longer than ten seconds to measure her mood as dangerous. She strutted down the steps to greet them, slapping a hairbrush against her palm.

"Looks like I'm going to have to start locking my car and taking my keys inside with me."

With a shrug, Tucker pulled her keys out and tossed them to her. "I had business in town. You were asleep."

"You'll notice, Mr. Longstreet, it's my name on the registration of this vehicle. I don't appreciate you commandeering it whenever you have the whim." She poked the brush into his chest. "It's common courtesy to ask for the use of someone else's property."

"I said you were asleep."

Fluttering her lashes, she scanned the driveway. "Mine is not the only car here."

"It was the first one I came to." He checked his temper and tried a smile. "You sure did wake up on the wrong side of the bed, darling."

She met charm with a haughty look. "I might suggest you consider getting yourself alternate transportation until that toy of yours is repaired."

"Yes, ma'am." He kissed her cheek. "You sound just like Mama."

Josie sniffed and stepped back. "What are you staring at, Dwayne?" Automatically, she fluffed at her hair, then her eyes changed. "Why, honey, you look just awful. What've you boys been up to so early?"

"Just some business in town," Tucker repeated before Dwayne could answer. "You'd better get yourself prettied up if you're going to the parade."

" 'Course I'm going. The Longstreets never miss a Fourth of July parade. Dwayne, you come inside and get yourself something to eat. You're green around the gills."

"He hasn't recovered from the carnival."

"Aw." Instantly solicitous, Josie took her brother's arm. "You go in and have Della fix you up something. Cousin Lulu shouldn't have teased you into going on that Round-Up."

"I'm all right." He put his arms around her, holding her close. "Josie. It's going to be all right."

"Of course it is, honey." She patted his back. "It's a fine day for a parade, and it'll be a finer night for fireworks. Go on now, so I can paint my face." She waved him inside, but held up a hand to stop Tucker. She forgot all about being annoyed with him. "What's wrong with Dwayne?"

"They had him in for questioning this morning."

Her eyes lit. "Dwayne?"

"They'll call us all in, I imagine. It's just standard."

She began to tap the brush against her palm again. "Why, I might have to give Matthew Burns a piece of my mind."

"Let it go, Jose. It's nothing to worry about. He'll feel better once we get this holiday started."

"All right, but I'm going to keep an eye on him." She patted the keys in her pockets as she started into the house. "Next time you ask, you hear?" She passed Caroline in the doorway. "You watch out for that one, Caro. He's a scoundrel."

"I already know." Caroline stepped out on the porch, then, to please herself, turned a showy circle. The skirt of her pale blue sundress swirled out, then settled softly around her legs.

Tucker stayed on the step below and took her hands. The dress had flirty laces at the bodice and a back cut to the waist. "You sure do look a picture."

"I heard I was going on a picnic after the parade."

"That's a fact." He kissed the palm of her hand, then held it against his cheek a moment. They said you didn't know what you had until you'd lost it. Tucker thought he'd discovered something that was equally true. You didn't know what had been missing from your life until you found it. "Caroline?"

She turned her hands to link her fingers with his. "What is it?"

"I've got a lot of things to say to you." He moved up the steps until their mouths were level and the kiss could be sweet. "I sure as hell hope you're ready to hear them when I do. Right now I've got some business to see to. You mind riding to the parade with Della? I'll meet you there."

"I could wait."

He shook his head and kissed her again. "I'd rather you went on."

"All right, then. I'll pile in with Della and Cy and Cousin Lulu— who's going to be the hit of the day. She's wearing trousers with the Confederate flag on one leg and the American flag on the other. The flag of the Revolution, I should say."

"You can always count on Cousin Lulu."

"Tucker." Caroline cupped his face in her hands. "If you have trouble, I wish you'd share it with me."

"I will soon enough. You look just right here, Caroline. Standing on the porch with your blue dress, the door open behind you and bees buzzing in the flowers. You look just right." He wrapped his arms around her, held her there a moment while he wished the world would stay like this, pretty and peaceful and as gracious as a lovely woman dressed in blue.

"You be ready for those fireworks tonight," he told her. "And for what I want to say to you after." His arms tightened. "Caroline, I want—"

"God sakes," Lulu muttered from the doorway. "Tucker, are you going to stand around all day smooching with that Yankee? We got to get on or we won't get a decent spot to watch the parade."

"There's time yet." But Tucker released Caroline. "You keep an eye on this Yankee till I get there," he began, then his face split with a grin. "I declare, Cousin Lulu, you look good enough to run up the flagpole. Where'd you get those pants?"

"Had 'em made special." She spread her scrawny, flag-bedecked legs. "Got me a jacket to match, but it's too cursed hot to wear it." She stuck an eagle feather into her hair, where it drooped over one ear. "I'm ready to go."

"Then you'd better get." He gave Caroline a quick kiss before heading inside. "I'll send the others out. Cousin Lulu, you make sure Caroline doesn't go wandering off with some smooth talker."

Lulu snorted. "She's not about to go far."

Caroline smiled. "No, I'm not."

Chapter 28

"Just how many of these lunatics you figure'll drop from heat stroke before two o'clock?" Cousin Lulu posed the question from the comfort of her personalized director's chair. A red, white, and blue umbrella was hooked to the back and tilted to a jaunty angle, while a thermos of mint juleps snuggled between her feet.

"We never have more than five or six faint on us," Della said placidly from the web chair beside her. She didn't think she could outdo Lulu's pants, but she'd stuck a miniature American flag in her bushy hair in an attempt. "Most of them are young."

As a marching band strutted by blaring Sousa, Lulu played along on a plastic zither. She enjoyed the wall of sound, the glint of brass in bright sun, but she couldn't help but think that a couple of swooning piccolo players would add some zip.

"That tuba blower there, the husky one with the pimples? He looks a bit glassy-eyed to me. Ten bucks says he drops in the next block."

Della's natural competitive instinct had her studying the boy. He was sweating freely, and she imagined his natty uniform was going to smell like wet goat before the day was up. But he looked hardy enough. "You're on."

"I dearly love a parade." Lulu tucked her zither behind her ear like a pencil so she could pour another drink. "Next to weddings, funerals, and poker games, I can't think of anything more entertaining."

Della snorted and cooled her face with a palm-sized battery-operated fan. "You can have yourself a funeral tomorrow if you want. We've been having us a regular plague of funerals lately." Sighing, Della helped herself to some of the contents of Lulu's thermos. "I reckon this is the first time in fifteen years that Happy hasn't marched on by with the Ladies Garden Club."

"Why ain't she marching?"

"Her daughter's going in the ground tomorrow."

Lulu watched the pom-pom division of Jefferson Davis High shake by to the tune of "It's a Grand Old Flag."

"A good, whopping funeral'll set her to rights," Lulu predicted. "What're you making for after the burying?"

"My coconut ambrosia." Della shaded her eyes and grinned. "Why, look there, Cousin Lulu. Look at Carl Johnson's baby twirl that baton. She's a regular whirling dervish."

"She's a pistol, all right." Lulu enjoyed a cackle and another sip of julep. "You know, Della, life's like one of them batons. You can spin it around your fingers if you've got the talent for it. You can toss it right up in the air and snatch it back if you're quick. Or you can let it fly and conk somebody on the head." She smiled and plucked the zither from behind her ear. "I do dearly love a parade."

From behind Lulu, Caroline thought over the analogy and shook her head. It made a spooky kind of sense. She wasn't sure if she'd ever conked anyone on the head with the baton of life, but she'd certainly dropped it a few times. Right now she was doing her best to make it spin.

"That there's the Cotton Princess and her court," Cy told Caroline. "The whole high school votes on her every year. She was supposed to ride in back of Mr. Tucker's car, but since it got banged up, they rented that convertible from Avis in Greenville."

"She's lovely." Caroline smiled at the girl in her puffy-sleeved white dress and sweat-sheened face.

"She's Kerry Sue Hardesty." Watching her made Cy think of Kerry's younger sister, LeeAnne. She of the soft, fascinating breasts. As the car cruised by, Cy scanned the crowd, hoping for a glimpse. He didn't spot LeeAnne, but he did spot Jim, and waved desperately.

"Why don't you go over and see your friend, Cy? You can meet us at the car when the parade's finished."

He yearned, but shook his head and stood firm. Mr. Tucker was counting on him to stay close to Miss Caroline. They'd had a real man-to-man talk about it. "No, ma'am. I'm fine right here. There's Miss Josie and that FBI doctor. He's got one of those lapel flowers that squirts water in your face. He sure is a caution."

"He certainly is." Caroline was scanning the crowd herself. "I wonder what's keeping Tucker."

"Nothing." From behind, Tucker slipped his arms around her waist. "You didn't think I'd miss watching a parade with a pretty woman, did you?"

Content, she leaned back against him. "No."

"You want me to fetch you and Miss Caroline cold drinks, Mr. Tucker? I got pocket money."

"That's all right, Cy. I think Cousin Lulu's got what the doctor ordered in that jug down there."

Cy jumped forward to take the cup Lulu poured and pass it back. "That FBI man's watching from in front of the sheriff's office."

"So I see." Tucker sipped, savored, and handed the cup to Caroline.

Caroline took her first taste of mint julep and let it slide sweet down her throat. "He doesn't look as though he thinks much of the parade."

"Looks more like he smells dead skunk," Cy commented.

"He just doesn't understand." Tucker kept one arm around Caroline's waist, set his other hand on Cy's shoulder. "Here comes Jed Larsson and his boys."

When the fife and drum corps led by Larsson marched by playing "Dixie," the crowd roared. Those seated rose to their feet and cheered.

Caroline smiled and laid her head on Tucker's shoulder. She understood.

♦ ♦ ♦ ♦

*T*HE FOURTH OF JULY meant fried chicken, potato salad, and smoking barbecues. It was a day for flag waving and pie eating and drinking cold beer in the shade. There were those gathered close in mourning, and the law continued its grinding quest, but on this bright summer day, Innocence tossed a cloak of red, white, and blue over murder and celebrated.

After the parade there were contests along Market Street and over in the town square. Pie eating, target shooting, foot racing, egg tossing, and—always a favorite—watermelon-seed spitting.

In silent amazement Caroline gawked at the junior division pie-eating contest, where seven- to fourteen-year-olds buried their faces in blueberry, slurping and swallowing to the cheers of the crowd. Pie after pie was consumed, and more glistening tins shoved under purple-stained faces. Encouragement and gastronomic advice were shouted out as one by one the young entrants fell by the wayside. Groaning.

"Look at Cy." Caroline pressed a hand to her own stomach in sympathy. "He must have eaten a dozen by now."

"Nine and a half," Tucker corrected her. "But he's leading. Come on, boy, don't chew. Just let it slide on down."

"I don't see how he can breathe," she murmured as Cy buried his face in number ten. "He's going to be sick."

" 'Course he is. That's the way, Cy! Don't hold back now. He's got himself a nice rhythm," Tucker said to Caroline. "He doesn't just smash his face into it and hope for the best, he works in a nice steady circle from the outside in."

She didn't know how Tucker could tell. All she saw was a boy buried to the neck in blueberries while the crowd cheered and stomped. She told herself it was a silly game, messy and certainly undignified. But she was rocking back and forth from toes to heels, pulled in to the simple excitement.

"Come on, Cy! Swallow it whole. Leave them in the dust. Look! He's going for twelve. Oh, Jesus, he's got it sewed up now. Just—" She glanced up at Tucker and found him grinning at her. "What?"

"I'm crazy about you." He kissed her hard and long as Cy, a little green beneath the purple splotches, was declared champion. "Plum crazy."

"Good." She brushed her fingers over his cheeks and into his hair. "That's good. Now maybe I should help the winner scrub blueberry juice off his face."

"Let him get his own girl," Tucker decided, and pulled her along to the next event.

They'd cleared the parking lot of the Lutheran Church for the target shoot. McGreedy's had supplied the beer bottles, and Hunters' Friend the ammo. The elimination rounds went quickly with frustrated hopefuls unloading their weapons and taking a place on the sidelines.

Tucker was pleased to see Dwayne preparing for the second round. It had taken a lot of fast, hard talk to convince his brother to participate in the day's events. He didn't want any gossip until it was impossible to avoid it. And he wanted Dwayne to continue acting normally. In Tucker's mind, normal equaled innocent.

"Both Dwayne and Josie are entered," Caroline commented.

"We were all taught to shoot early. Old Beau insisted on it."

"What about you? You're not after the grand prize of a smoked ham and a blue ribbon?"

He shrugged. "I never cared much for guns. There goes Susie." He waited until she'd blasted away three bottles with three shots. "Lordy, she's a cool hand. Good thing she married a lawman. With that aim she could've taken up a life of crime."

"Cousin Lulu." Concerned, Caroline put a hand on Tucker's arm. Lulu swaggered up with a pair of Colts snug in a leather holster riding low on her bony hips. "Do you really think she should—" She broke off as the old lady drew and fired. The three bottles seemed to explode as one. "Oh, my."

"She can handle anything from a .22 to an AK-47." He watched, entertained, as Lulu twirled a Colt around her finger in three fast circles, then shot it back home. "But if she asks you to stand with an apple on your head, I'd decline. She's not as young as she once was."

It ended with Lulu edging out Susie and a very annoyed Will Shiver. The crowd began to gather back on the street for foot races.

"Sweetwater's doing well for itself." Caroline accepted the cold bottle of Coke Tucker passed her. "Aren't you going to run?"

"Run?" Tucker lighted a cigarette and flipped away the match. "Darlin', why would I want to get all tired and sweaty just to get from one point to another?"

"Of course." She smiled to herself. "I don't know what got into me." Sighing, she settled back against his chest while the first runners took their marks. "So, you don't enter any event?"

"Well now, there is one I usually go for."

She turned her head to look back at him. "Which?"

"Wait and see."

◆ ◆ ◆ ◆

GREASED PIGS? CAROLINE HAD thought she'd gotten into the spirit of things, but when she stood behind the temporary paddock in the town square listening to the porcine squeals, she realized she hadn't come close.

Tucker had bowed off from eating pies, he didn't choose to shoot, and he yawned at the thought of racing. But he was standing in the paddock, stripped to the waist, waiting for the signal to go catch a lard-coated pig.

Baffled, Caroline rested an elbow on Cy's shoulder. "How are you feeling?"

"Oh, just fine now," he assured her. "I chucked most of it up, and the rest is settling all right." He fingered the blue ribbon pinned proudly to his T-shirt. "Mr. Tucker's going to win."

"Is that right?"

"Always does. He can move real quick when he's a mind to." He let out a whoop with the rest of the crowd. "Here they go!"

The shouts and laughter from the onlookers were as wild as the squeaks from the pigs and the curses from the men pursuing them. As an extra incentive, the ground had been watered and churned to mud. Men slipped and sloshed in it, belly-flopped and back-flipped. Pigs squirted out of questing hands.

"Oh, why don't I have a camera?" Caroline let out a crow of laughter when Tucker skidded on his backside. He twisted when a pig raced across his knees, but came up empty.

"That FBI doctor's good!" Cy shouted, cheering when Teddy tackled a pig and nearly held on. "Might've had it if Bobby Lee hadn't tripped over him. Mr. Tucker's going for the big one. Come on, Mr. Tucker! Haul 'em up!"

"An interesting contest," Burns said as he stopped beside them. "I suppose dignity is sacrificed for the thrill of the hunt."

Caroline nearly shot him an impatient look, but she didn't want to miss anything. "You're keeping your dignity, I see."

"I'm afraid I don't see the point in wallowing in mud and chasing pigs."

"You wouldn't. It's called fun."

"Oh, I agree. In fact, I've never been more entertained." He smiled down at Tucker, who was currently sprawled face first in the dirt. "Longstreet looks quite natural, don't you think?"

"I'll tell you what I think," she began, but Cy grabbed her arm.

"Look! He's got him! He's got him, Miss Caroline."

And there was Tucker, slicked with mud and grease, holding a squirming pig over his head. When he grinned up at Caroline, she wished she'd had a dozen roses to throw.

No spangle-suited matador had ever looked more charming.

" 'To the victor go the spoils,' " Burns noted. "Tell me, does he get to keep the pig?"

Caroline tucked her tongue in her cheek. "Until the butchering and pot luck supper next winter. Excuse me. I want to go congratulate the winner."

"One moment." He blocked her way. "Are you still staying at Sweetwater?"

"For the time being."

"You might want to reconsider. It isn't wise sleeping under the same roof with a murderer."

"What are you talking about?"

Burns glanced over to where Dwayne and Tucker were washing

down mud with a beer. "Perhaps you should ask your host. I can tell you that I'll be making an arrest tomorrow, and the Longstreets won't have much to cheer about. Enjoy the rest of the festivities."

Saying nothing, Caroline latched on to Cy and pushed by him.

"What did he mean, Miss Caroline?"

"I don't know, but I'm going to find out." By the time she'd worked her way through the crowd, Tucker was gone. "Where did he go?"

"He probably went down to McGreedy's to hose off with the others. Most everybody'll be packing up to go down to Sweetwater for picnics before the fireworks. They'll be opening the carnival, too."

Frustrated, Caroline stopped. She couldn't talk to him surrounded by a bunch of wet, back-slapping men. She needed him alone. Rising on her toes, she scanned heads and faces. "There's Della. Why don't you catch up with her, ride back to Sweetwater? I'll wait for Tucker."

"No'm. Mr. Tucker said I was to stay with you when he wasn't around."

"That's not necessary, Cy. I don't . . ." A look at the boy's set jaw and she swallowed a sigh. "All right, then. We'll park ourselves somewhere and wait."

Sitting on the stoop in front of Larsson's, they watched the exodus from town.

"You shouldn't let that FBI man worry you, Miss Caroline."

"He doesn't. I'm just concerned."

Cy tugged his ribbon around so he could read it again. "He's like Vernon."

Surprised, Caroline turned to study Cy. "Agent Burns is like your brother?"

"I don't mean he goes around starting fights or hitting women. But he thinks he's smarter and better than everyone else. Figures his way's the only way. And he likes having his foot on your throat."

Caroline rested her chin on her hand and considered. Burns would detest the comparison, but it was eerily apt. With Vernon it was Scripture—his interpretation. With Burns it was the law—his interpretation. In either case it was the using of something right and just for personal power.

"They're the ones who lose in the end." She thought of her mother as well, a great wielder of power, a master of carving out her own will. "Because no one who doesn't have to stays with them. That's sad. It's better if people care about you even if you aren't always smarter, even if you aren't always sure you're right." She stood. Tucker was strolling down the street, his shirt flung over his shoulder, his hair dripping, his jeans soaking wet. "Looks like we're going home."

She crossed the street to slip her arms around him. Laughing, he tried to nudge her back. "Honey, I'm not as clean as I might be."

"Doesn't matter." She turned her head to murmur in his ear. "I need to talk to you. Alone."

He would have liked to have interpreted the demand as romantic, but he heard the tension, felt the nerves in the line of her body.

"All right. Soon as we can." He kept one arm around her as they began to walk. "Let's get a move on, Cy. I heard Della's cooked up a regular feast. Probably baked a few pies, too."

Cy grinned good-naturedly. "I ain't looking at another pie till next Fourth of July."

"Got to keep in practice, boy." Tucker flipped a finger down the boy's blue ribbon. "You know why I'm so good at latching on to those slippery critters?" He swung Caroline off her feet. " 'Cause I'm always grabbing some wriggly female."

Caroline relaxed enough to smile. "Are you comparing me with a sow?"

"Why, no, indeed, darlin'. I'm just saying if a man puts his mind to it, he can keep what he wants from slipping out of his hold."

♦ ♦ ♦

BACK AT SWEETWATER, there were blankets spread on the grass, and the calliope was piping its siren song from over in Eustis Field. Near the pond where death had so recently floated, music twanged out from a fiddle, a banjo, and a guitar.

Here and there exhausted children napped, many of them sprawled where they'd dropped. An impromptu softball game was under way, and now and then the crack of the bat set up a cheer. Old men sat in folding chairs to root and gossip and wish for strong, young legs that could pump toward home. Young people drifted toward the carnival, where the rides were half-price until six.

"Is it like this every year?" Caroline asked. She was close enough to the music to appreciate, far enough from the carnival not to dwell on how tawdry it looked in the daylight.

"Just about." Tucker lay on his back, debating if he had room for one more drumstick. "What do you usually do on the Fourth?"

"It depends. If I'm out of the country, the day goes by like any other. When I'm in the States, we usually tie the concert to a fireworks display." The fiddler took up "Little Brown Jug," and Caroline began playing it in her head. "Tucker, I have to ask you about something Matthew said to me earlier."

The agent's name had Tucker deciding against another drumstick. "I should have figured he'd find a way to ruin things."

"He said he was going to make an arrest tomorrow." She closed her hand over his. "Tucker, are you in trouble?"

He shut his eyes briefly, then rolled, folding his legs under him to sit. "It's Dwayne, Caro."

"Dwayne?" Stunned, she shook her head. "He's going to arrest Dwayne?"

"I don't know that he can," Tucker said slowly. "The lawyer thinks Burns is blustering, that maybe he was trying to get Dwayne to say something he shouldn't. All he's got is speculation. No physical evidence."

"What kind of speculation?"

"He can put Dwayne in the same area as the killings, without any alibis so far. And he's using Dwayne's trouble with Sissy as a kind of motive."

"Divorce as a motive for killing other women?" Caroline arched her brows. "That gives about half the adult male population of the country a motive."

"Seems pretty thin, doesn't it?"

"Then why do you look so worried?"

"Because Burns may be a first-class asshole, but he's not stupid. He knows Dwayne drinks, he knows how he was embarrassed by Sissy. And he knows Dwayne had an acquaintance with the victims. The one up in Nashville's the kicker."

"Nashville?" Letting out a long breath, she nodded. "Tell me."

He'd hoped to keep it all from her for at least one day. But once he began, the words streamed out. Under them, she could sense the anger and a very real fear.

"What did your lawyer advise?"

"That we just go on as usual. Wait and see. Of course, if Dwayne could come up with an alibi for one of the nights, that would cool things off." He popped open a beer, frowned into it. "I got a call in to the governor. He's a little hard to reach today, but I expect he'll call me back tomorrow."

She tried a smile, hoping to coax one from Tucker. "He's a cousin, I suppose?"

"The governor?" He did smile, fleetingly. "No. But his wife is. Odds are Burns is going to need a lot more to put the cuffs on Dwayne."

"I can talk to my father if you like. He's corporate, but he knows some excellent criminal attorneys."

Tucker tilted back the beer. "Let's hope I don't have to take you up on it. The worst of it is, Caro, Dwayne's so scared he's doubting himself."

"What do you mean?"

"He's worried that maybe when he was drunk, when he wasn't think-ing straight, he might have—"

Her heartbeat skipped. "My God, Tucker, you don't think—"

"No, I don't," he said with a barely restrained fury. "Jesus, Caroline, Dwayne's harmless as a puppy. He may flap around and scuffle when he's drunk, but he hurts only himself. And think," he added, because he had been, and he'd been thinking hard. "The way those women were killed. It was vicious, yeah. And sort of primal and wild, but it was also planned. Thought out clean and clever. A man's not clever with a head full of whiskey. He gets sloppy and stupid."

"You don't have to convince me, Tucker," she said quietly. But she wondered if he was trying to convince himself.

"He's my brother." For Tucker, that said it all. He could see Dwayne now, sitting with old Mr. O'Hara. Tucker figured the jug they were pass-ing was of O'Hara's own brew. And it wasn't lemonade. "He'll be drunk as a skunk before nightfall. I haven't got the heart to cut him off."

"Sooner or later you'll have to, won't you?" She put a hand on his cheek. "Otherwise, you'll just be cutting him out. I've been thinking about what you said about families. Not just about taking a stand, but about making things right. I'm going to call my mother."

"I guess what you're telling me is, if my advice is good enough for you, it ought to be good enough for me."

She smiled. "Something like that."

With a nod, he looked back toward Dwayne. "There's a place up in Memphis. It has a good reputation for helping people shake themselves loose of the bottle. I think if I work it right, I could talk him into giving it a try."

"Darling," she said, easing into a delta drawl, "with your talent you could talk a starving man out of his last crust of bread."

"That so?"

"That's so."

He leaned over to touch his lips to hers. "That being the case, maybe I could talk you into doing something for me. Something I've had a han-kering for."

Caroline thought of the cool, empty house behind them, of the big canopied bed. "I imagine you could persuade me." More than willing, she melted into the kiss. "What did you have in mind?"

"Well, you see, I've had this craving." He turned his head to nip at her ear.

"I'm delighted to hear it."

"I don't want to offend you."

She chuckled against his throat. "Please do."

"I thought you might be a little shy, doing it out here in front of all these people."

"I can—what?" With a half laugh, she pulled away. "Do what in front of all these people?"

"Why, play a few tunes, darlin'." His lips curved. "What did you think I was talking about?" As his smile spread wickedly, he lifted a brow. "Why, Caroline, I'm going to start thinking you have a one-track mind."

"Yours certainly takes some interesting curves." Blowing out a breath, she combed fingers through her hair. "You want me to play?"

"Probably nearly as much as you'd like to be playing."

She started to speak, then stopped and shook her head. "You're right. I would like to."

Tucker gave her a quick kiss. "I'll go fetch your fiddle."

Chapter 29

SHE WAS WELCOMED INTO the little band, but dubiously. People settled back politely, very much, Caroline thought, as a class might when they were about to listen to a boring but respected lecturer.

It occurred to her that she'd grown accustomed to ovations when she took the stage. Obviously too accustomed, she thought now as her nerves began to jump. This little patch of grass beside Sweetwater Pond wasn't Carnegie Hall, but it was a stage of sorts. And her current audience was reserving judgment.

She felt ridiculous, absurdly out of place with her gleaming Stradivarius and Juilliard training. She was ready to babble an excuse and crawl away when she saw young Jim grinning at her.

"Well now, little lady." Old Mr. Koons ran his fingers down his banjo strings and made them twang. He couldn't see more than three feet in front of himself, but he could still pick with the best of them. "What's your pleasure?"

"How about 'Whiskey for Breakfast'?"

"That'll do her." He tapped his foot for time. "We'll get her going, missy, and you just come on in when you've a mind to."

Caroline let the first few bars rolls by. It was a good sound, full and cluttered. When the rhythm had caught, she tucked the violin on her shoulder, sucked in a deep breath, and cut loose.

And the feeling was good—full and cluttered. As fun was supposed to be. The hand-clapping from the audience kept time sharply. There was plenty of hooting, and when someone picked up the lyrics, they were given a shout of approval.

"I do believe that fiddle of yours is smoking," Koons told her, then took a moment to spit out a chaw. "Let's keep her going."

"I know only a few," Caroline began, but Koons waved her protest aside.

"You'll pick her up. Let's try 'Rolling in My Sweet Baby's Arms.' "

She did pick it up. Her ear and instinct were keen enough. When the trio segued into the blues, then bounced back with a raucous rendition of "The Orange Blossom Special," she was right there with them.

She lost herself in the pleasure of it. Even so, she noted Burns watching her—and watching Dwayne. She saw Bobby Lee cuddle Marvella into a dance when they slowed things down with "The Tennessee Waltz." The music poured through her, but she noted that Tucker had his head together with Burke in what looked like a private and very serious discussion. And she saw Dwayne, sitting gloomily, a bottle at his feet and his eyes on the ground.

Things were happening, Caroline mused. Even as the sun was lowering, the carnival rides whirling, the shadows lengthening, things were happening. Beneath the whistles and the laughter, nerves were jangling as fast as Koons's banjo strings.

And she was just another player, after all. Just one more player in the odd, uneasy game. Fate had dropped her down into this messy stew of heat and murder and madness. She was surviving. More, she was doing. The summer was half over and she was whole. She was even beginning to believe she was healed.

If she left Innocence with only that, it would be enough. Her gaze shifted back to Tucker. It would be enough, she thought again with a slow smile. But it didn't hurt to hope for more.

"Well, kick me in the head and call me addled." With a wheezy laugh, Koons laid his banjo over his lap. "You sure can make that fiddle dance, little girl. You ain't no la-di-da neither."

"Why, thank you, Mr. Koons."

"It's time we went and had ourselves a beer." He got creakily to his feet. "You sure you're a Yankee?"

She smiled, taking it for the compliment it was meant as. "No, sir, I'm not. I'm not sure at all."

He slapped his knee at that, then hobbled off, shouting for his daughter to get him a beer.

"That sure was some pretty playing, Miss Caroline." Jim hurried over to get a peek at the violin before she closed it in the case.

"Then I'll have to thank my teacher."

He stared, then dropped his gaze to the ground. But even with his head down, Caroline could see his grin spread from ear to ear. "Shoot, I didn't do nothing."

"It's us want to thank you," Toby said, cupping an arm around his wife's shoulders. He held himself stiffly, favoring his bandaged side. "You stood up for us the other night. I know you were a comfort to Winnie."

"I'm ashamed I haven't thanked you properly, Caroline," Winnie added. "I might've gone crazy if I hadn't known you and Miss Della were looking after my kids while Toby was being patched up at the hospital. I'm obliged to you."

"Don't be. I'm told that's what neighbors are for."

"Miss Caroline." Lucy tugged on Caroline's skirt. "My daddy's going to sing the National Anthem before the fireworks. Mr. Tucker asked him special."

"That's wonderful. I'll look forward to it."

"Come on now." Toby hitched his daughter onto his hip. "If I know Tuck, he's going to be looking for this lady here, and we'd better get ourselves situated for those fireworks. It's getting on toward dark."

"How much longer?" Lucy wanted to know.

"Oh, no more'n a half hour."

"But I've waited all day . . ."

Caroline chuckled over the universal complaint as Toby and Winnie toted Lucy away.

"She's such a baby," Jim said with a superior smirk.

Caroline sighed at the derision in his voice. She knew he'd defended his sister at the risk of his own life, but that was forgotten now. "You know what occurs to me, Jim?"

"No, ma'am."

"That I'm an only child." She laughed at his puzzled look, then picked up her case. "Go along with your family. If you see Tucker, tell him I'll be right back."

"I might could take that inside for you, Miss Caroline. It wouldn't be no trouble."

"That's all right. I have to make a quick phone call before it gets dark."

And wouldn't her mother be surprised? Caroline thought as she started across the green lawn, through the green shadows toward the white columns of the house. She would wish her mother a happy Independence Day. For both of them.

I'm free of you, Mother, and you can be free of me. Maybe, maybe if we face each other without all those thin, taut strings between us, we can find something.

Caroline turned around to take a last sweep of the fields of Sweetwater. Though it was barely dusk, the lights on the midway and on the rides were winking in the distance. They didn't look tawdry now, but hopeful. If she listened carefully, she could just hear the piping music and laughter as the Crack the Whip whirled its latest passengers.

Before long, night would fall, then the sky would explode with light and the air would shake from the cracking booms. Turning back to Sweetwater, she quickened her pace. She didn't want to miss a moment of it.

Her mind was so full of what was to come, she paid little attention to the voices. It wasn't until she heard the fury in them that she stopped, wondering how she could avoid walking in on an argument.

When she saw Josie and Dwayne standing in the front drive beside Josie's car, Caroline automatically stepped back, thinking she could hurry around to the side terrace. She hesitated just long enough to see the knife Dwayne held.

She froze where she was, beside the end column on the graceful front porch, watching, stunned, as brother and sister faced each other over the blade. Across the lawn, beyond the cotton field, revelers waited impatiently for full dark and celebration. Here, where the crickets were just beginning their chorus in the grass and a whippoorwill perched in a magnolia and called for a mate, the two were unaware of being observed.

"You just can't do it. You just can't,' Josie said furiously. "You have to see that, Dwayne."

"I see the knife. Jesus, Josie." He turned it in his hand, staring at the dull glint as if hypnotized.

"Give it to me." She struggled to keep her voice calm and even. "Just give it to me, and I'll take care of everything."

"I can't. Name of God, Josie, you have to see that I can't. It's gone too far now. Sweet Jesus, Arnette . . . Francie. I can see them. I can see them, Josie. It's like some sort of awful dream. But it isn't a dream."

"Stop it." Leaning her face close to his, she closed her fingers around the wrist of his knife hand. "You stop it right now. What you're talking about doing is crazy, just crazy. I'm not going to allow it."

"I have to—"

"You have to listen to me. And that's goddamn all you have to do. Look at me, Dwayne. I want you to look at me." When his gaze locked on hers, she spoke quietly again. "We're family, Dwayne. That means we stick together."

His sweaty fingers loosened on the hasp of the knife. "I'd do anything for you, Josie. You know that. But this is—"

"That's good." Smiling a little, she eased the knife away. From her stance by the column, Caroline nearly groaned with relief. "Here's what you're going to do for me now. You're going to trust me to take care of things."

Shaking his head, Dwayne covered his face. "How can you?"

"Just leave it to me. You trust Josie, Dwayne. You go on back down to the field and watch those fireworks. Put this all right out of your mind. That's important. You just put it aside, and I'll take care of the knife."

He let his hands drop. Uncovered, his face was gray and stricken. "I'd never hurt you, Josie. You know I wouldn't. But I'm scared. If it happens again—"

"It won't." After dropping the knife into her voluminous purse she looked back at him. "It's not going to happen again." Gently, she laid her hands on his shoulders. "We're going to put it all behind us."

"I want to believe that. Maybe we should tell Tucker, and he—"

"No." Impatient, Josie gave him a quick shake. "I don't want him to know, and telling him isn't going to clean your conscience, Dwayne, so leave it be. Just leave it be," she repeated. "Go on back down, and I'll do what needs to be done."

He pressed the heels of his hands against his eyes, as if trying to block out the horror. "I can't think. I just can't think straight."

"Then don't think. Just do what I say. Go on. I'll be along soon as I can."

He took two steps away before turning, then stopped, his head down, his shoulders bowed. "Josie, why did it happen?"

She reached out, but her fingers stopped short of touching him. "We'll talk about it, Dwayne. Don't worry anymore."

He didn't see Caroline as he walked away, but she could see the devastation and torment on his face. The shadows swallowed him.

For another moment she stood still as a statue, her heart throbbing hard and slow in her throat, the scent of roses and fear swimming in her head.

Dwayne was responsible for the brutal deaths of five women. The brother of the man she loved was a murderer. A brother, Caroline knew, whom Tucker was deeply devoted to.

And she ached for them, ached for them all. For the pain that was already felt, and the pain yet to come. With all of her heart she wished she could turn and walk away, pretend she had never heard, never seen. Never knew.

But Josie was wrong. Tucker had to be told. No matter how deep and strong the family ties, this was not something to be handled by a loving sister. Tucker had to be told, and prepared for what must happen next. Josie needed to be there. They would all need to be there.

Quietly, Caroline moved to the porch and up, through the door and into the house. The silence was already oppressive as she climbed the stairs to the second floor. No matter how she tried, she couldn't find the right words. She stopped at Josie's doorway and looked in.

The chaos of the room was in marked opposition to the stillness of the woman who stood at the open french doors. The cheerful clash of scents and mixed colors was overpowered by the encroaching dark and the sense of gloom.

"Josie." Though Caroline spoke softly, she saw Josie stiffen before she turned. In the shadows, her face was pale as a ghost's.

"They'll be shooting off those fireworks in a minute, Caroline. You don't want to miss them."

"I'm sorry." When she realized she was still carrying her violin case, she set it aside and gestured helplessly with her hands. "Josie, I'm so sorry. I don't know if I can help, but I'll do what I can."

"What are you sorry about, Caroline?"

"I heard. You and Dwayne." After one shuddering breath, she stepped into the room. "I heard you. I saw him with the knife, Josie."

"Oh, God." On a moan of despair, Josie sunk into a chair to cover her face with her hands. "Oh, God, why?"

"I'm sorry." Caroline crossed the room to crouch at Josie's feet. "I can't even imagine how you must be feeling, but I do want to help."

"Just stay out of it." Voice edgy, Josie dropped her hands to her lap. Though her eyes were wet, the heat behind them would dry tears quickly. "If you want to help, stay out of it."

"You know I can't. Not just because of Tucker and the way I feel about him."

"That's just why you should stay out of it." Josie grabbed her hands, the slim, tense fingers wrapping like wires around Caroline's. "I know you care about him, you don't want him hurt. You've got to leave this to me."

"If I did, what then?"

"Then it'll be done with. It'll be forgotten."

"Josie, those women are dead. No matter how ill Dwayne is, that can't be ignored. It can't be forgotten."

"Bringing it all out, tearing the family apart, isn't going to make them any less dead."

"It's a matter of right, Josie. And of helping Dwayne."

"Help?" Her voice rose as she pushed herself out of the chair. "Going to prison won't help."

"His mind isn't right." Wearily, Caroline rose. It was growing too dark to see. She turned on Josie's bedside lamp and chased away some of the shadows with a rosy glow. "Loving him's a start, but he's going to need professional help. Not only to find out why, but to prevent him from doing it again."

"Maybe they deserved to die." As she paced, Josie rubbed hard at her pounding temples. "People do, and it isn't cold to say so. You didn't know any of them the way I did, so who are you to judge?"

"I'm not judging, but I don't think you believe anyone deserved to die that way. If something isn't done, someone else might die. You can't stop it, Josie."

"I think you're right about that." She passed her hand over her eyes. "I'd hoped, with Dwayne so miserable—but I guess I knew all along. It's blood," she murmured, lifting her head to stare at her own face in the mirror. "Like a wild dog, once you've tasted it, there's no going back. There's just no going back, Caro."

Caroline moved over to her so that their eyes met in the glass. "We'll find good doctors for him. I know one who'll help."

"Doctors." Josie tugged the chiffon scarf out of her hair and gave a short laugh. "What bullshit. Did you hate your mother? Love your father?"

"It's never that simple."

"Sometimes it is. Listen to that." Smiling a little, she closed her eyes. "That's Toby March singing. They must've hooked him up to a mike down at the carnival. That's a sound that carries nice on a hot summer night."

"Josie, we have to go tell Tucker. And we have to see that Dwayne turns himself in. I'm sorry. It's the only way."

"I know you're sorry." With a sigh, Josie reached into her bag. "I'm sorry, too. Sorrier than I can say." Turning, she aimed her derringer at Caroline. "It's you or the family, Caroline. You or the Longstreets. So there's really only one way after all."

"Josie—"

"Do you see this gun?" she interrupted. "My daddy gave it to me for my sixteenth birthday. Sweet Sixteen, he called me. He was a great believer in taking care of your own. I did love him. I hated my father, but I did love my daddy."

Caroline moistened her lips. She wasn't afraid yet. Her brain was too scrambled with shock for fear to take hold. "Josie, put it down. You can't help Dwayne this way."

"It's not just Dwayne, it's all of us. All the fine, upstanding Longstreets."

"Miss Caroline?" Cy's voice echoed up the stairs and had both women jolting. "Miss Caroline, you in here?"

Caroline saw the panic shoot into Josie's eyes. "You tell him to go on. Tell him, Caro. See that he goes outside again. I don't want to hurt that boy."

"I'm up here, Cy," Caroline called out, her gaze fastened to the short, shiny gun barrel. "You go on out. I'll be along in a minute."

"Mr. Tucker said I should stay with you."

She could almost see him, hesitating at the foot of the steps, torn between manners and loyalties. "I said I'd be along," she repeated, the first true licks of fear sharpening her voice. "Now go on out."

"Yes, ma'am. The fireworks are going to start any minute."

"That's fine. You go watch."

She waited, hardly breathing until she heard the door shut.

"I wouldn't want to hurt that boy," Josie said again. "I've got a real fondness for him." Her lips twisted in a mockery of a smile. "A real family feeling."

"Josie . . ." Caroline struggled to keep her voice calm. "You know this isn't the way to solve things. And you know I don't want to hurt Dwayne."

"No, but you'll do what you have to do. Just like me." She slipped a hand into her purse again, and pulled out the knife. "This was my daddy's. He dearly loved to hunt. Dressed the kill himself. Daddy wasn't afraid to get a little blood and guts on his hands. No, sir. I used to go with him when he'd let me. I got quite a taste for hunting myself."

"Josie, please put the knife away."

"Now, Tucker," Josie went on, lips pursed as she turned the blade in the light. "He never cared much for killing things, so he mostly missed—on purpose." As if baffled by the waste, she shook her head. "Lordy, did Daddy wail into him for it. Dwayne, he didn't have any problem bringing down a deer or a rabbit, but when it came time to dress 'em, he'd go green. Squeamish. That's what Daddy used to say. 'Josie, you come on over here and show this boy how it's done.'" She laughed a little. "So I would. Blood never turned my stomach. It's got a smell to it. Kind of wild, kind of sweet."

With her skin going clammy, Caroline inched back. "Josie." The word came out in a cracked whisper as their eyes met again.

"When Daddy died, the knife came to me." She held it up so it glinted in the lamplight again. "The knife came to me."

Caroline stared at the glint of silver. Behind her the first fiery lights exploded in a black sky.

Chapter 30

THE PRETTY LITTLE GUN seemed like a joke now. Beside the long-bladed knife, it was more of an annoyance, something to be swatted away like a fly. But Caroline made no move toward it. All of her attention, and all of her fear, was focused on the slick gleam of silver.

"Josie, you can't protect Dwayne this way."

"You don't believe me." Josie nearly laughed. There was a part of her, the part she had no longer been able to control, that capered with glee. "Who would? No one even considered a woman—least of all our fine special agent. Look for someone who hates women, I told him. But he didn't understand. You and I know that no one can hate the way a woman can hate."

A jolt shook Caroline as the fireworks rocketed and boomed. "Why would you?"

"I have reasons. I have plenty of reasons." She moved closer until she was framed in the terrace doorway. Her eyes were as brilliant as the lights that studded the sky behind her. "I had to protect the family. I had to protect myself. Just as I will now. But it's different with you, Caroline. I won't enjoy it with you because I like you, I respect you. And I know how much it's going to hurt Tucker. Don't," she said as Caroline edged away. "I don't want to have to shoot you, but I will. No one will hear."

No, no one would hear. She could scream—just as Edda Lou had screamed—and no one would notice. The derringer was pointed at her throat. A tiny bullet, she thought. A small death.

"I don't want you to suffer," Josie told her. "Not like the others. You're not like the others."

Think, Caroline ordered herself. She had to think. The key to this was family, if she could only find a way to use it. "Tucker and Dwayne will suffer, Josie."

"I know. I'll make it up to them." Her eyes shifted for a moment as gold lights flashed, bloomed, and faded in the sky. "Isn't that a pretty sight? The Longstreets have had fireworks here at Sweetwater for more than a hundred years. That means something. I remember Daddy carrying me on his shoulders so I could get closer to the sky. I was his fire-cracker, he'd say. And Mama would just watch, and say nothing. She didn't want me, you know."

"Talk to me, Josie." How much longer could the fireworks go on? How much longer before Tucker or someone came to look for them? "Tell me, Josie, so I can understand why you had to do it."

"I can talk to you. There's time. It'll be easier if you see. Maybe easier for both of us." She took a long, deep breath. "Austin Hatinger was my father." Her lips twisted at the shock on Caroline's face. "That's right, that Bible-thumping, snake-mean bastard was my blood father. He raped my mother, and while he was raping her, he planted me inside her. She didn't want me, but when she found she was pregnant she had to go through with it."

"How can you be sure?"

"She was sure. I heard her talking to Della in the kitchen. Della knew. Only Della." Satisfied with the knife, Josie slipped the derringer into her pocket. "She hadn't told Daddy. I guess she was afraid to. And she would have wanted to protect him, and the family, and Sweetwater. So she had me, and she tolerated me, and she watched me to see how much like him I'd be."

"Josie."

"I was a grown woman when I found out. She lied to me all my life. My beautiful mother, that great lady, the woman I wanted to be like more than anything, was just a liar."

"She was only trying to keep you from being hurt."

"She hated me." The words ripped out of her as she slashed the air with the knife. "Every time she looked at me she'd see the way I was con-ceived. In the dirt, planted in the dirt while she cried for help. And wouldn't she have to ask herself how much was her own doing? Why did she go there? Did she really care so much about Austin and his pitiful wife?"

"You can't blame your mother, Josie."

"I can blame her for giving me a lie to live with. For looking at me out of the corner of her eye and thinking I was less than her, or any other woman. She said to Della, that day, that maybe I wasn't meant to be happy, to have a home of my own and a family because of my blood. My tainted blood."

She spat out the words while outside the sky rocked with color.

"I'd come back here after my second divorce, and she had that look in her eye. That look that blamed me for it. And she said to Della that maybe I wasn't meant to have a home and children. Maybe it was the Lord's way of punishing her for keeping the secret, for holding the lie inside her. She was feeling poorly, had been feeling poorly for some time. When she went out to her roses, I went, too. I wanted her to tell me face-to-face. We had a terrible argument, and I left her there, standing in the roses and crying. A little later Tucker went out and found her dead. So I guess I killed her."

"No. No, of course you didn't. It wasn't your fault or hers, Josie."

"That doesn't change anything. I had something growing inside me. It wasn't a child—the doctors had already told me I'd never have a child. But what was growing was real, and it was hot. It started with Arnette. She wanted to get her hooks into Dwayne, just like Sissy had. She thought she could use me, and I played along. I thought about it and thought about it. I'd spend whole nights lying in bed and thinking, wondering. Mama had kept a secret by giving life. I was going to keep one by taking it."

There was a roar from outside as rocket after rocket shot up in the grand finale.

"There had to be a reason, though. I wasn't an animal. It had to make sense. So I figured it would be those women who teased and strutted and lied to get men. I've had myself plenty of men," Josie said with a smile. "But I never lied to get them."

"Arnette—I thought she was your friend?"

"She was a slut." Josie shrugged her shoulders carelessly. "Not that she was my first choice. I thought about Susie. I'd always figured if Burke and I could get together . . . Well, anyway, Susie didn't fit. She never in her life looked at another man but Burke, so killing her wouldn't have been right. It had to be right," Josie murmured while iciness spread in Caroline's stomach. "So there was Arnette. It was so easy to get her a little drunk, drive out to Gooseneck Creek. I hit her with a rock, then I took off her clothes and tied her up. It was cold. Jesus, it was cold, but I waited until she came around. Then I pretended I was my father and she was my mother. And I did things to her until it wasn't cold anymore.

"It was better for a while," she said dreamily. "I felt so much better. Then it started growing in me again. So there was Francie. She was dangling for Tucker, I knew it. Then it was supposed to be Sissy, but I made a mistake there. But each time it was better. When they called in the FBI, I wanted to laugh and laugh. No one was going to look at me. Teddy even took me to the morgue so I could see Edda Lou. At first it was awful, but then I realized that I had done that. I had done it and nobody was ever going to know. It was my secret, just like Mama. And I wanted to do it again, again, while everybody was looking around. Darleen was so perfect, it was like it was meant."

"You were right there with Happy when they were looking for her."

"I was sorry Happy had to suffer. It seemed right that I comfort her some. Darleen isn't worth her crying over. Not one of them was worth a tear. But you are, Caro. If only you'd let it be. I was going to try to keep my promise to Dwayne and stop, since it seemed so important to him. But now I have to break that promise, at least this one last time."

"This time they'll know."

"Maybe. If they do, I'll take care of it. Always figured I'd have to end it one day, my own way." The last of the rockets went off like machine-gun fire. "I won't go to jail or to one of those places they put people who do things other people don't understand." She gestured with the gun. "Turn around now. I'll have to tie you up first. I promise I'll make it quick."

◆ ◆ ◆ ◆

*T*UCKER MOVED RESTLESSLY THROUGH the crowd as the colorful bombs burst overhead. He hadn't seen Caroline for the past half hour. Women. As if he didn't have enough on his mind with Dwayne and the FBI, she'd pick this time to wander off.

He shook his head at the offer of a beer, and continued to wend his way through the clutches of people.

"It's a right good display," Cousin Lulu said from her director's chair.

"Umm-hmm."

"How would you know? You've hardly looked at it."

To please her, he looked skyward and admired an umbrella of red, white, and blue lights. "Have you seen Caroline?"

"Lost your Yankee?" Lulu cackled and lit a sparkler.

"Looks that way." He raised his voice to be heard over the cheers of the crowd. "I haven't seen her since she finished playing awhile back."

"Plays right well." Lulu wrote her name in the air with the sparkler. "Guess she'll be going along soon to play for the crowned heads of Europe."

"Something like that." With his hands in his pockets, he scanned faces. "I don't see how you can find anybody out here in the dark."

"Ain't going to find her here anyway." Lulu pouted a moment when her sparkler fizzled out. She wanted to wait until things quieted down before she set off her pocketful of firecrackers. "I saw her heading for the house around twilight."

"Why would she—oh, probably wanted to put her violin away. But she should have been back." He turned to study the white ghost of the house in the distance. He'd always thought the best way to figure a woman was not to figure at all. "I'll go take a look."

"You'll miss the finale."

"I'll be back."

He started off at a lope, annoyed at having to hurry. For the life of him he couldn't figure out why she'd be holed up in the house. It nagged at him that maybe he'd pressured her into playing. She could be upset, or the whole business might have brought on one of those headaches. On an oath he quickened his pace and nearly ran over Dwayne.

"Jesus Christ, what're you doing sitting back here in the dark?"

"I don't know what to do." Dwayne kept his head pressed to his knees and rocked. "I have to clear my mind and figure out what to do."

"I said I was going to take care of it. Burns is just blowing hot air."

"I could say I did it," Dwayne mumbled. "That might be the best way for everyone."

"Goddammit." Tucker reached down to shake Dwayne's shoulder. "Don't start that shit on me now. We'll talk about it later when I've got time. I've got to go up and see if Caroline's in the house. Come on with me. It'll be better if you don't talk to anybody tonight."

"I told her I wouldn't." Dwayne dragged himself to his feet. "But something's got to be done, Tuck. Something's got to be done."

"Sure it does." Resigned, Tucker put his arm around Dwayne and took his weight. "We'll do it, too. I know all about it."

"You know?" Dwayne staggered to a halt that had Tucker cursing and pulling. "She said you didn't. When I said that we had to tell you, she said not to."

"Tell me what?"

"About the knife. Daddy's old buck. I saw it under the seat of her car. Christ, Tuck, how could she do it? How could she do all those things? What's going to happen to her now?"

Tucker felt his blood slow. He felt it slow and stop until it seemed to hum in his veins. "What the hell are you talking about?"

"Josie. Oh, Jesus, Josie." Dwayne began to weep as the weight of it pounded at him. "She killed them, Tuck. She killed them all. I don't know how I can live with turning my own sister over to the law."

Slowly, Tucker backed up, leaving Dwayne swaying. "You're out of your fucking mind."

"We have to do it. I know we have to. Chrissakes, she meant it to be Sissy."

"Shut up." With rage and fear blinding him, Tucker plowed his fist into Dwayne's face. "You're drunk, and stupid. If I hear you say another word, I'll—"

"Mr. Tucker." Eyes wide, Cy stood on the verge of the driveway. He'd heard, heard all that they said, but he didn't know what to believe.

"What the hell are you doing there?" Tucker demanded. "Why aren't you down watching the fireworks?"

"I—you said as I should keep close to her." Cy's insides were shaking with the kind of fear he hadn't known he could feel again. "She went on in, but she told me to stay outside. She said I shouldn't come upstairs."

"Caroline?" Tucker said blankly.

The blow had shocked Dwayne back to reality. As Cy's words sunk in, he grabbed Tucker by the shirt. "Josie. She took the knife with her. She took the knife and went into the house."

Tucker's breath came in pants. He wanted to fight, wanted to fight out the horror that was settling inside him. But even as he balled his fists, he saw the truth, in Dwayne's eyes. "Let go of me." With a strength born of fear he shoved Dwayne back to his knees. "Caroline's in the house."

He began to run, hurtling toward Sweetwater, chased by the roar of the crowd and the cold breath of terror.

♦ ♦ ♦

I WON'T MAKE IT EASY for you, Josie." She wasn't afraid of the gun, wouldn't let herself be afraid. But she had a deep primal fear of that sharp length of steel. "You know it has to stop. No matter what you feel, no matter what your mother did, you can't fix it by killing."

"I wanted to be like her, but people always said I was like my father. They were right." Her voice took on a curious, almost musical calm. "They didn't know how right—and they won't. It's my secret, Caroline. I'll kill you to protect it."

"I know. And after you do, Dwayne and Tucker will suffer for it. Dwayne because he'll know, and it'll eat him alive. Tucker because he has feelings for me. And because you love them, you'll suffer, too."

"There's no choice here. Now, turn around, Caroline. Turn around or it'll be so much worse."

With the last echoes of celebration ringing in her ears, she started to turn. She didn't dare close her eyes, didn't dare, but she offered one quick and fervent prayer. When her body was three-quarters turned from Josie, Caroline threw out a hand to smash the lamp to the floor. Blessing the dark, she tucked up her legs and rolled across the bed.

"It won't matter." Excitement sharpened Josie's voice. Now there was a hunt, and with a hunt there was hunger. "It'll only be easier for me now. I won't have to look at you, and I can think of you like the others."

Her feet whispered across the carpet as Caroline hunched beside the bed and strained to see. If she could only get to the door. If she could only get quickly and soundlessly to the door.

"I like the dark." Holding her breath, Caroline inched away from the bed, feeling her way with her fingers.

"I never minded hunting in the dark. Daddy used to say I had cat eyes. And I can hear your heart beat." Quick as a snake, she pounced on the spot where Caroline had crouched only seconds before.

Caroline bit her lip to hold back a scream. As she tasted blood she forced herself not to move. Her eyes were adjusting, and in the pale moonlight she could see Josie's silhouette, and the edge of the death she held in her hand. Only a turn of her head, and they would be face-to-face.

And she did turn it, slowly. The moonlight glinted in her eyes. Her lips curved. Caroline remembered how Austin had looked when he had loomed over her filled with murder and madness.

"It won't take long," Josie promised as she lifted the blade.

In a last plunge to cheat death, Caroline rolled away. The blade caught the skirt of her dress, pinning it to the floor. On a cry of terror, she ripped it free and stumbled to her feet. She raced toward the doorway, waiting to hear the whistle of steel through the air, the heat of the blade as it cut into her back.

The light in the hall flashed on, blindingly bright after the dark.

"Caroline!" Tucker pounded down the hall, grabbing her as she fell through the doorway. "You're all right? Tell me you're all right." He dragged her close, and holding her there, stared at his sister.

She had the knife in her hand, and in her eyes was a wildness that gripped him with horror. "Josie. In the name of God, Josie, what have you done?"

The wildness faded as her eyes filled. "I couldn't help it." As tears spilled onto her cheeks, she turned and ran to the terrace.

"Don't let her go. Tucker, you can't let her go."

He saw his brother hesitate at the top of the steps. "Take care of her," he said to Dwayne, and pushed Caroline toward him before he raced after Josie.

He called her name. Some of the revelers who were heading home stopped at the shouts and looked up, with much the same curiosity and expectation with which they'd watched the fireworks. Tucker sped along the terrace, dragging open doors, switching on lights. When he tugged on the doors that led into their parents' bedroom, he found them locked.

"Josie." After a few frantic yanks, he pounded on the door. "Josie, open up. I want you to let me in. You know I can break it down if I have to."

He laid his brow against the glass and tried to reason out what his mind simply couldn't grasp. His sister was inside. And his sister was mad.

He pounded again, cracking the glass and bloodying his fingers. "Open the goddamn door." He heard a sound behind him and whirled. When he saw Burke come toward him, he shook his head. "Get away. Get the hell away. She's my sister."

"Tuck, Cy didn't tell me what this is all about, but—"

"Just get the hell away!" On a scream of rage, Tucker threw his weight against the door. The tickle of breaking glass was lost under the blast of a single gunshot.

"No!" Tucker went down to his knees. She was lying on the bed their parents had shared. Blood was spreading onto the white satin spread. "Oh, Josie, no." Already grieving, he dragged himself up. Sitting on the bed, he gathered her into his arms and rocked.

♦ ♦ ♦ ♦

I'M GLAD YOU CAME to see me." Caroline poured coffee into two cups before she sat at her kitchen table across from Della. "I wanted to talk to you, but I thought it best to wait until after the funeral."

"The preacher said she was resting now." Della pressed her lips together hard, then lifted her cup. "I hope he's right. It's the living that suffer, Caroline. It's going to take some doing for Tucker and Dwayne to put this behind them. And the others, too. Happy and Junior, Arnette and Francie's folks."

"And you." Caroline reached out to take Della's hand. "I know you loved her."

"I did." Her voice was rough with the tears she blinked away. "Always will, no matter what she did. There was a sickness inside her. In the end she did the only thing she knew to cure it. If she'd have hurt you—" Her hand shook, then steadied. "I thank God she didn't. Tucker wouldn't have been able to get beyond it. I came here today to tell you that, and to say that I hope you won't turn away from the brother because of the sister."

"Tucker and I will settle things ourselves. Della, I feel you have a right to know. Josie told me about her mother, about how she was conceived."

Under Caroline's, Della's hand convulsed. "She knew?"

"Yes, she knew."

"But how—"

"She found out from her mother, inadvertently. I know it must have been hard on you, and on Mrs. Longstreet, holding on to that secret."

"We thought it best. She came home that day, after he hurt her. Her dress was torn and dirty, and her face was pale as spring water. And her eyes, her eyes, Caroline, were like a sleepwalker's, all dazed and dull. She went right on up and got in the tub. Kept changing the water and scrubbing and scrubbing till her skin was raw. I saw the bruises on her. I knew. I just knew. And because I knew where she'd gone, I knew who."

"You don't have to talk about it," Caroline said, but Della shook her head.

"I wanted to go over and take a whip to him myself, but I couldn't leave her. I held her while she sat in the water, and she cried and cried and cried. When she'd cried out, she said we weren't to tell Mr. Beau, nor anybody else. She was afraid the two of them would kill each other, and I expect she was right. There was nothing I could say to her that could get the idea out of her head that she was responsible. It was always Mr. Beau for her, Caroline. She was a pretty girl, and young, and she saw a bit of Austin now and again. But she never promised to marry him. That was an idea he got fixed in that hateful brain of his."

"He had no right to do what he did, Della. No one could think otherwise."

"She did." She sniffled and wiped a tear away with her knuckle. "Not that he had the right, but that somehow she'd pushed him to it. Then she found out she was carrying, and Mr. Beau had been up in Richmond the whole two weeks during her fertile time, so she had to figure Austin had gotten her pregnant. There was no question of telling anybody then. She didn't want the child hurt. She did her best to forget, but she worried. And when Josie would go off wild, she worried more. She had her mama's looks, Josie did, just like her brothers. But I guess, because we knew, we could see something of him in her."

So could she, Caroline thought, but said nothing.

"She wasn't to know. Not ever. But since she did, I wish she'd come to me so I could have told her how her mother tried to protect her." Della sighed and dabbed at her eyes. Then she went very still. "But she knew. Lord help us, she knew. Is that why she . . . Oh, my baby, my poor baby."

"Don't." Caroline cupped Della's hand between both of her own and leaned close to comfort. There was much that had been said in that shadowy bedroom that would remain there. In the dark. "She was ill, Della. That's all we know. They're all dead now—Josie, her parents, Austin. There's no one to blame. I think because of the living, because of the ones we love, the secret should be buried with them."

Struggling for control, Della nodded. "Maybe Josie'll rest easier that way."

"Maybe we all will."

♦ ♦ ♦ ♦

SHE'D HOPED HE WOULD come. Caroline had wanted to give him time, but it had been a week since Josie's funeral, and she'd hardly seen him. Never alone.

Innocence was doing its best to lick its wounds and go on. From Susie, Caroline had learned that Tucker had been to see the family members of each victim. What had been said behind those closed doors remained private, but she hoped it had brought a kind of healing.

The summer was passing. The delta had a short respite from the heat when the temperatures dropped to the eighties. It wouldn't last, but she'd learned to appreciate each moment.

After hooking the pup's bright red collar to his leash, she started down the lane. The flowers her grandmother had planted years before were thriving. It took only a little care and patience.

Useless tugged at his leash and she quickened her pace. Perhaps they would walk all the way down to Sweetwater. Perhaps it was time to try.

She turned at the end of her lane and saw Tucker's car almost instantly. It looked as snazzy and arrogant as it had the first time she'd seen it barreling toward her. The sight of it made her smile. A heart wasn't as easily healed as mangled metal, but it could be done. With care and patience.

With a cluck of her tongue she pulled Useless back onto the lawn. She knew where to find Tucker.

♦ ♦ ♦ ♦

HE WAS FOND OF water, of still, quiet water. He hadn't been sure he could sit here again. Coming back had been a kind of test. But the deep green shade and the dark, placid pond were working their magic. Contentment was still out of reach, but he'd gotten a grip on acceptance.

The dog raced out of the bush, barking, and plopped his forelegs on Tucker's knees.

"Hey there, boy, Hey, fella. You're getting some size on you, aren't you?"

"I believe you're trespassing," Caroline said as she moved into the clearing.

Tucker offered a halfhearted smile as he scratched the dog's ears. "Your grandmother let me come and sit here a spell from time to time."

"Well then." She sat on the log beside him. "I wouldn't want to break tradition." She watched the dog lick Tucker's hands and wrists. "He's missed you. So have I."

"I've been . . . hard to be around lately." He tossed a twig for the dog to chase. "Heat's let up," he said lamely.

"I noticed."

"I expect it'll be back before long."

She linked her hands in her lap. "I expect."

He stared at the water awhile longer, then went on staring at it when he spoke again. "Caroline, we haven't talked about that night."

"And we don't have to."

He shook his head as she reached for his hand, and stood to move away. "She was my sister." His voice was strained, and as he continued to study the water, Caroline saw how tired he looked. She wondered if she'd ever see that carefree grin again, and hoped.

"She was ill, Tucker."

"I'm trying to see that. The same as if she'd had cancer. I loved her, Caroline. I love her now, too. And it's hard, remembering her, and how full of life and spit she was. It's hard, remembering all those graves she's responsible for. But it's hardest, closing my eyes and seeing you running out of that room, and Josie just behind you, with a knife in her hand."

"I can't tell you it'll go away, not for either of us. But I've learned not to look back."

He bent down for a pebble and tossed it into the water. "I wasn't sure you'd want to see me."

"You should have been." She rose, as agitated as the pup who ran in circles with a twig in his mouth. "You started this between us, Tucker. You wouldn't let it alone. You wouldn't listen when I said I didn't want to be involved."

He threw another stone. "I guess that's true. I've been wondering if it wouldn't be best if I just let you go on your way, pick up where you were before I got messed up in your life."

She watched the pebble plop and shoot out its spreading ripples. Sometimes you accomplished more by stirring things up, she decided, than by letting them run smooth.

"Oh, that's fine. That's just like you, isn't it? Head for the door when things get complicated with a woman." She grabbed his arm and shoved him around to face her. "Well, I'm not like the others."

"I didn't mean—"

"I'll tell you what you mean," she tossed back, giving him a hard thump on the chest that had his mouth falling open in surprise. " 'It's been nice, Caro. See you around.' Well, forget it. You're not going to stroll in and change my life, then walk away, whistling. I'm in love with you, and I want to know what you're going to do about it."

"It's not that I—" He broke off. His eyes closed, as if on a pain, then he laid his hands on her shoulders, rested his brow against hers. "Oh, God, Caro."

"I want you to—"

"Shh. Just hush a minute. I need to hold you." He drew her closer, his grip tightening until she felt his muscles tremble. "I've needed to hold you so much these past few days. I was afraid you'd back away."

"You were wrong."

"I was going to try and be noble and let you go." He buried his face in her hair. "I'm not much good at being noble."

"Thank God for that." Smiling, she tilted her head back. "You haven't answered me."

"I was thinking more of kissing you."

"Nope." She put a hand on his chest to hold him off. "I want an answer. I said I loved you, and I want to know what you're going to do about it."

"Well . . ." His hands slid away from hers. He found the best thing to do with them was to jam them in his pockets. "I had it pretty well worked out before—before everything happened."

She shook her head. "There is no before. Try now."

"I guess I was thinking about you going on this next tour. You do want to go?"

"I want to go on this one. For myself."

"Yeah. I was thinking. It occurred to me that you might not object to company."

Her lips curved slowly. "I might not."

"I'd like to go with you, when I could. I can't leave for weeks at a time, with Cy to look after, and Sweetwater—especially since Dwayne's going to be up in that clinic for a while—but now and then."

"Here and there?"

"There you go. And I was thinking that when you weren't touring or playing somewhere, that you'd come back here and be with me."

She pursed her lips in consideration. "Define 'be with.' "

He let out a deep, shaky breath. It was hard to get it out, he discovered, when he'd spent most of his life being careful to hold it in. "I want you to marry me, have a family with me. Here. I guess I want that more than I've ever wanted anything in my life."

"You're looking a little pale, Tucker."

"I guess that goes with being scared to death. And that's a hell of a thing to say after a man's just proposed marriage to you."

"You're right. You're entitled to a simple yes or no."

"Hold on. There's nothing simple about it." Terrified, he grabbed her close again. "Just hold on and hear me out. I'm not saying we wouldn't have to work at things."

"There's one other thing you're not saying. One very important thing."

He opened his mouth and closed it. The steady patience of her gaze had him trying again. "I love you, Caroline. Jesus." He had to take a moment to be sure he had his balance. "I love you," he said again, and it was easier. In fact, it was just fine. "I've never said that to a woman. I don't expect you to believe me."

"I do believe you." She lifted her lips to his. "It means more that it cost you some effort to get it out."

"I s'pose it'll get easier."

"I s'pose it will. Why don't we go on back to the house so you can practice?"

"Sounds reasonable." He whistled for the pup as he slipped an arm around Caroline's waist. "This time you didn't answer me."

She laughed up at him. "Didn't I? How about a simple yes?"

"I'll take it." He scooped her up as they stepped into the sunlight. "Did I ever tell you about one of my great-great-aunts? Might've been three greats. Her given name was Amelia. That's a nice soft name, don't you think? Anyway, she ran off and eloped with one of the McNairs back in 1857."

"No, you didn't tell me." Caroline hooked an arm around his neck. "But I'm sure you will."

About the Author

NORA ROBERTS was the first writer to be inducted into the Romance Writers of America Hall of Fame. The number one *New York Times* bestselling author of such novels as *Public Secrets* and *Sweet Revenge*, she has become one of today's most successful and best-loved writers. Nora Roberts lives with her family in Maryland.